"Triumphant and full of hope . . . an unforgettable story."

—Robin Lee Hatcher, author of *Ribbon of Years*

"The hope in Bedford's writing beckons like the sun over the western mountains."

—Tim Sandlin, author of *Social Blunders*

"A beautiful story of faith and renewal . . . a must-read . . . a book by Deborah Bedford is always a joy."

—Carol Lampman, author of *A Window in Time*

"Deborah Bedford delivers a winner in this tender, heart-tugging tale of love and loss, endings and beginnings, and the miracle of second chances. Savor and enjoy!"

—Carole Gift Page, author of *Becoming a Woman of Passion*

"A poignant novel that is impossible to put down. Deborah Bedford holds up a mirror to the universal flaws in our faith and shows us how the grain of a mustard seed can triumph in the most dire situation . . . a touching tale of tragedy and reawakening."

—Carolyn Zane, author of *The Coltons*

"A wonderful book, rich in love and tears. If you love having your heart touched and you delight in surprise, A ROSE BY THE DOOR is for you."

—Gayle Roper, author of *Spring Rain*

"One of the best books I've read all year. Could not put it down!"

—Lori Copeland, author of *Glory* and coauthor of the Heavenly Daze series

A Rose by the Door

Deborah Bedford

WARNER BOOKS

An AOL Time Warner Company

This book is a work of fiction. Names, characters, places, and incidents are the product of the author's imagination or are used fictitiously. Any resemblance to actual events, locales, or persons, living or dead, is coincidental.

Published in association with the literary agency Alive Communications, Inc., 7680 Goddard Street #200, Colorado Springs, CO 80920.

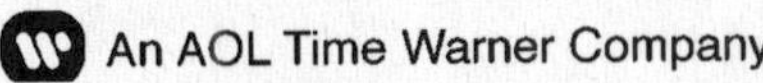

Printed in the United States of America

ISBN 0-7394-2118-2

Book design by Giorgetta Bell McRee
Cover design by Shasti O'Leary
Cover artwork by Franco Accornero

To all whose broadswords have become
marred and battered and tarnished in battle;

To those who would return to the shining,
simple faith of a child.

Acknowledgments

To Jack, my helpmate, thank you for your love, your opinions, and your willingness to cook supper. Without your encouragement, and that of our children, this project might never have even begun, much less been finished. I have brought you all along on this wild journey for the Lord, and I have watched, astounded, as each of you have obediently taken your seats and not grumbled too much during the ride. This makes my joy complete.

To Bill Jolliffe, thank you for your thorough down-homey tours of Oshkosh, the Ash Hollow area, the cemetery, the senior center, and the Garden County golf course. Here's hoping you find plenty of time to play through that course twice.

To Bill Patterson and Clara May McConkey, thank you for answering so many questions about Garden County.

To the coffee-drinkers at the Garden County Senior Center, I salute you!

To BettySue Allen, rose expert at McIntyre's Garden Center in Cheyenne, Wyoming, for keeping pioneer rose traditions alive and for letting me glimpse them.

To Julie Barker, Michael Barker, Carolyn Lampman Brubaker, and Richard Brubaker, dear friends and family, who were willing to share their stories. May the Father bless your own willingness to risk and love and believe.

To carpool moms Bobbi Wild, Eileen Thomsen, Charlene Zuckerman, Karen Hodges, Maria Miller Henderson, Deb Sanford, and Natalie Stewart. Thank you for chauffeuring my children to and from basketball tournaments, football games, play practices, dance classes, and the snowboard mountain while I was writing.

To Tim Sandlin, who has broadened all my horizons and has been like a brother to me.

Sherrie, Jonnie, and Barb—there are not words to tell you how blessed I have been by your wise counsel and by your prayers. You are a firm foundation sent by the Father, and I humbly offer thanks.

To Sherrie Lord, Pam Micca, and Pat Markell, intercessors who have kept the arms of prayer around this novel and around my family. May the Father who sees in secret reward you openly.

To Sandy Sandburg and Justice Court Judge George Kurinka. Sitting in the courtroom that day was almost as much fun as hanging out at Cowpasture Ballpark.

To Mike Atkins, senior pastor of the Jackson Hole Christian Center. Your one-mindedness, your thirst for God's Word and for the Father's Holy presence continues to be a wellspring for all who are privileged to learn from you and to worship beside you.

Finally, to Kathy Helmers, Agent 007 with a briefcase and a cell phone and so much more! Your insight, encouragement, and enthusiasm have been a mighty pillar to me. And to everyone at Warner who has caught the vision and given me this opportunity—Rolf Z., Jamie R., Leslie P., Preston C., Paul S. and Kathie J.—Paul says it best in 1 Corinthians 9:25: Run in such a way as to get the prize. Everyone who competes in the games goes into strict training. They do it to get a crown that will not last; but we do it to get a crown that will last forever.

May all our work rest soundly in the Father's hands.

"The shame of your youth and the sorrows of widowhood will be remembered no more, for your Creator will be your husband. The Lord Almighty is his name! He is your Redeemer, the Holy One of Israel, the God of all the earth. For the Lord has called you back from your grief—as though you were a young wife abandoned by her husband," says your God.
ISAIAH 54:4-6

But now the Lord says, "Do not weep any longer, for I will reward you. Your children will come back to you from the distant land of the enemy. There is hope for your future," says the Lord. "Your children will come again to their own land."
JEREMIAH 31:16-17

"Set up road signs; put up guideposts. Mark well the path by which you came."
JEREMIAH 31:21

A Rose by the Door

Chapter One

Beatrice Bartling jolted awake. Something banged on her front door, twice, three times, cutting through the stark silence of night. The sharp blows came again. A fourth time. A fifth, terse, hollow, insistent.

She hadn't any idea what time it was or what the emergency might be. "Just a minute," she croaked into the darkness. *Just a minute*, while, to no avail, she did her best to quell the pounding in her own heart.

Across the room, she could just make out the silhouette of her bureau, the shapes and shadows of the night reflected back to her in the mirror, rainbow shades of gray. The digital clock in the corner read 3:08 A.M.

Who could need her at this hour?

Why would someone come to the house in the middle of the night?

Fear made her move slowly. She folded back the covers, swung her feet to the floor, gathered her nightgown around her with one clutched hand.

"I'm coming."

She stumbled her way to the hall, flipped on a light in the bathroom, and donned her robe from the hook.

Her feet felt their way down the stairs; she made certain every step supported her before she put her full weight on it. When she reached the front foyer, she turned on the porch light and squinted through the peephole.

Parts of two people extended into her vision—an officer's hat, a beehive nest of someone's hair. "Who is it?" She didn't dare open the door before she heard an answer.

"Mrs. Bartling?"

"Who are you? What do you want?"

"Deputy Triplett from the Garden County Sheriff's Department. Can you open the door, please?"

She opened it partway, saw the whole of the sheriff's deputy and his cohort.

"Can we come inside?"

"What is this about?"

He glanced past her left ear, as if he expected someone else to be standing there. "Are you here alone, Mrs. Bartling?"

Bea kept her fingers wrapped around the edge of the doorknob, unwilling to let them enter. Even though she wondered whether or not she should tell them that she was alone, she nodded anyway. He showed her his badge and she read his name. Jay Triplett. He motioned to the woman who stood at his side. "This is Jane Rounsborg, from Garden County Social Services."

She knew Jane. They'd sat at the same table during the BPO Doe's meeting, a female version of the local Elk's Club, last month. The woman was several years her junior, with a tendency toward domed hairstyles and the profession of counseling those who couldn't afford mental-health services anywhere else. Beneath her tortoise-shell bifocals, Jane Rounsborg's skin was bare. She smelled faintly of Pond's Cold Cream.

"Is there someone you could call to come be with you?" Jane asked. "I'm afraid we have difficult news."

The officer's car waited beside the curb, its engine still running, its lights throbbing blue-red-blue-red against the leafy limbs of her neighbor's trees. From someplace far away she heard the broken static of a police radio.

"No." She removed her hand and stepped aside so the pair could enter at last. "There isn't anyone I can call."

Later Bea would remember how she'd led them to the stiff old armchair in the family room, how the deputy had gestured for her to sit there instead, how he'd waited for her to situate herself with Jane Rounsborg beside her so she'd have support as he delivered the news. He wore so much leather—his holster, his belt, his boots—that his body creaked when he knelt before her. Handcuffs jangled. She smelled the starch of his shirt, saw the sharp crease etching a line of shadow. His nose bore a smattering of freckles. All of this seemed real to her; the deputy's words did not.

"We've had a report from the coroner's office in Omaha, Mrs. Bartling. There was a motorcycle accident in the city yesterday morning."

Bea stared at him.

"A man named Nathan Roger Bartling was killed."

The only reality around her the buzz of the overhead light in the kitchen, the flashing red and blue through the gauze curtain in the front window.

"How did you find me?" she asked and she could see, the moment she said it, that he was startled by the unreasonable hope in her voice.

Had Nathan asked for her? Had he told someone where to find his mother?

"They ran a search of birth records, Mrs. Bartling. In this case, it's taken almost twenty-fours hours to notify the next of kin."

Her hopes plummeted. "I'm the next of kin."

"Yes."

The realization, the anguish, began somewhere deep inside her spirit and burgeoned within her, filling her until there was no room for anything else inside her—not breath, not even the beating of her own heart.

Numbly she counted backwards in her head. Yesterday morning. Where had she been and what had she been doing?

Heavenly Father. She remembered repeating it even twelve hours ago while she'd snipped wilted blossoms off her pioneer rosebush in the heat of the day. *When will you bring Nathan home?*

"I'm sorry, Mrs. Bartling. Apparently your son was traveling at a high rate of speed when the accident occurred. There wasn't another—"

Bea held out a hand to stop him. "No. Don't tell me about it. I can't bear it right now." She gripped the arms of the chair with both hands.

Yesterday morning. So long ago. If only Nathan had been home, this might not have happened. Perhaps she could have done something; perhaps she could have stopped it some way.

"Let me call someone for you." The social worker brought over a glass of water and a wrinkled hanky that she must have found on the writing desk in the corner. "Bea, I have sedatives. Would you like to take something?"

She shook her head at them.

"Isn't there a friend? A neighbor? A pastor? Someone?"

"No." She saw her own hands gripping the armchair as if they belonged to someone else, the knucklebones white knobs beneath the skin. She whispered the words to no one. "Nathan is never going to come *h-home*."

Jane stood and moved toward the door. She talked as if Bea wasn't even in the room with them anymore. "I'm going to find one of her neighbors. Surely there's someone who can sit with her until the sun rises. Or until we can contact someone in her family."

The officer laid his hat beside him on the floor. "I've heard she doesn't have family."

"I know her. She drives to the Antelope Valley Church over in Oshkosh. Call her pastor, Jay."

He creaked again as he rose to his feet and Bea could smell the leather of him. A pistol dangled in the tooled holster at his side. He had kind, sad eyes. "I'm so sorry, Mrs. Bartling. Jane and I won't leave until somebody else comes."

Most visitors arrived on Bea's front stoop during the time of early summer gardens, when children were kept busy catching katydids and lightning bugs, when fathers fired up outdoor grills and lawnmowers whirred from faraway yards, when whole neighborhoods smelled of supper and new-cut lawn.

A stream of cars pulled up to her curb and parked there for long moments, the drivers and passengers trying to decide whether they should intrude at someone's private home.

But intrude they eventually did, spilling out onto the carefully trimmed grass, moving closer toward the house, *oohing* and *aahing* over the profusion of yellow roses that grew en masse on the sunny side of the porch.

"We were just passing through town," they would explain when Bea met them, smiling her welcome, at the door. "The curator at the museum told us about your place."

Bea would point to the blossoms lining her walk and proceed to tell stories that they'd already heard once at the museum. How a pioneer woman had brought the roses with her along the Oregon Trail. How she had grown the bush from a cutting. How she'd kept the cutting alive poked in half of a raw potato, wrapped in burlap on cold nights, while the wagons jolted across the moving, shaggy red grass and the swells of unbroken prairie. She told how the wagon had broken down near Ash Creek and how they'd decided to not go along further, but to stay.

"Did they build a house right here?" someone would always ask.

"In this very spot. A sod house made of thick mud and fine grass."

"This is right where she planted the roses?"

"She planted them right here."

"Can we pick one?"

"No. Because if everybody did, then they'd be gone." Then, because she couldn't stand for them to be dejected by her answer. "If you'd like to take a cutting with you, I'd be happy to pass one of those along. Long ago, these roses grew in some places where grass couldn't grow. In places they couldn't find the ruts or the trails anymore, some people followed the roses instead. Just one sucker is all you'll need—one wood stem with a bud. Keep it in water and, I promise you, it will root when you get home."

More often than not, after the tourists had seen what they'd come to see, Bea would bring out a tray of warm cookies and hurry along to brew up a pot of tea. "Don't rush off." She'd set the teapot and a tray of cups in the shade beneath her maroon-striped awning. "Stay a while longer. I'll tell you more about the area's history. There's so much."

But those who came were just traveling through with other places to go, other attractions to see, and nobody spent too much time there or wanted to linger. They would make their excuses, Bea would wave them off, and she'd be alone again. Every time it happened, folks in the little town of Ash Hollow, Nebraska, thought it sad. Because everyone from miles around knew the history of Beatrice Bartling's roses. And everyone knew the history of her family as well.

For each person she hurried to greet on her doorstep, she longed to greet someone different instead. Everyone she welcomed she looked past, to the next and the next and the next. Each face that peered through the screen, she searched and found no resemblance to the child who had run away from home years before.

With every visitor who appeared on her lawn, she yearned to greet, not a stranger, but a son.

And though the townspeople knew of her sadness, they did not know of the hours that she spent on her knees beside her bed, her head bent in supplication, her heart uplifted to God.

Dear Father. Please, please let Nathan return to me.

Long ago, as she'd watched her children departing for school each morning, bounding up the steps on the Garden County school bus with their backpacks wagging, she'd never thought that Nathan would be the one to forsake her. Nathan, with his shining green eyes and his small manly fingers curled around her own, who'd once gazed up at her and asked, "Mama, if the sky is the floor of heaven, then wouldn't we hear God walking around?"

The years had passed and still she'd stood each morning with her fingers threaded through the Venetian blinds and her nose almost pressed to the glass, watching the bus go, even after she'd realized they wouldn't turn to wave at her anymore before they embarked on the bus. It wouldn't do for their friends to see them looking back on their way to school as if they had qualms about leaving home. But she'd stood at the window anyway, knowing if one of them glanced back to find her, he'd be forlorn not to see her there.

"Enjoy your children while they're this young," she'd say to frazzled mothers of toddlers when she overtook them in the aisle at the Oshkosh Superette. "The time goes by so fast."

The time goes by so fast. Until one day no more time can be had at any price.

From the other room, Bea could hear Jane Rounsborg whispering on the phone. Deputy Triplett retrieved his cap from the floor and ushered in the neighbors. From somewhere in another world, the telephone rang. The room overflowed with people. Voices murmured like the sound of gentle water, undistinguishable, indistinct. Nancy Law from across the street placed tea beside her on the table, the china cup set firmly in the center of the pretty shell-shaped saucer. "Can you lift this without spilling?" Nancy asked. "If you can, it will make you feel better."

Bea tried and, despite her hand shaking, found herself able to slowly sip the hot brew. It did help. The fragrance tickled her nose and seemed to open her, at last, to breathing. Their eyes met over the rim of the cup.

"Poor Nathan. We always thought he had so much going for him, until he left home. We're going to get you through this, Bea."

Jane Rounsborg came to Bea's chair and bent low beside it. "Your pastor called. He's on his way, but it's going to be fifteen minutes or so. He's driving over from Oshkosh."

The tea jostled precariously as Bea set the cup and saucer on the end table beside her. She squeezed Jane's hand in silent, sad gratitude. "Thank you."

"Is there anyone else I should call? If you've got an address book, I could go through the pages and find the numbers."

This would be the perfect time to phone Ray. The perfect time to phone Nathan's father and tell him to come home, that their son had died.

Nancy suggested it aloud. "Nathan's father?"

Bea sat very, very still for a long while before she shook her head. She wouldn't know where to find Ray, even if she tried. Her chin lowered against her chest in despair. Why invite someone who had deliberately chosen not to share his son's life to come share in his death instead?

"No. No, I don't think so."

Ray left a long time ago. He didn't care to see his son while Nathan was alive. Why should he care now?

"Are there other relatives? Or someone I should call at your job?"

"I have aunts over in Potter. Or my boss at work." Bea wrapped her arms around herself, below her bosom. "But it's the middle of the night." She needed time herself to absorb this. She needed time to work her way through the numb, awful fog of acceptance. "Don't call anybody else yet. I'm just not ready." She squeezed her arms tighter around her own ribs. "Please."

Outside, the dark shroud of night sky had begun to lift, replaced by the lilac tinge of early dawn. Another sharp rap on the door, then another. Finally Bea heard the squeak of hinges and, amidst all the other talking, Pastor Sissel's soothing baritone. "I got here as fast as I could. How is she holding up?"

"Like most people do when they first find out. She hasn't taken it all in yet."

"This is a shock. Such a shock."

Someone, she didn't notice who, led George Sissel to her side. She struggled to push herself up out of the armchair, but he stopped her. Instead he knelt and clasped both of her hands in his own, her sadness reflected in his face.

"Why, Bea, this is a nasty turn of events, isn't it?"

Bea felt tears pooling in her eyes for the first time. She mustn't let herself cry. For in her soul there waited to spring up an eternity of tears, from a fathomless depth of sorrow. She fought for control even as she spoke. "This isn't what I expected to happen, Pastor George." She removed her hand from his and gripped the hanky beside her just in case. The tears slipped down her cheeks anyway, no matter how hard she tried to keep them at bay.

"Bea," he said. "I know that the Father must be feeling your pain."

She squared her jaw and pursed her lips in reply. Words would no longer come. Tears flooded. They streamed down over her mouth and dripped from her chin. Pastor George gathered her in his arms and held her close against him as she wept, rocking her, sometimes her weight bearing toward his, other times his body leaning into hers. She felt nothing, no other sense, except for the vast desperate *goneness* of her son. She might as well have been a heavy stone of loss entrapped beneath a single thin layer of flesh.

"I can't do this." She cried the words into the warm tweed wool of his jacket.

"You must, Bea. You must know that the Lord will lead you through."

He repeated it over and over again until, after a good length of time, Deputy Triplett stepped forward, his hat in his hands again, to make his good-byes. Perhaps he thought since the pastor had come he needed to say something especially kind before he took his leave. "I'm so sorry," he told her once more. His voice was soft, almost a sigh. "It's terrible, what's happened. I know how you must feel."

On the outside, Bea could only shoot him a sad smile. On the inside, she screamed, *You've never lost a child. There isn't any way to describe this pain, or to imagine it. You don't know how I feel.*

Indeed, no one could. No one, not even Pastor George Sissel, knew the immeasurable, awful circumstances that had brought her to this place. All she'd ever asked was that Nathan return home again. All she'd ever sought was for her boy to accept what had happened to them. To perhaps give her a second chance. To love her in spite of the choices she'd made, the ones that had torn their lives apart five long years ago.

How many times had she'd watched Nathan return home in her dreams, taking his place around the table again, with his knobby knees bumping the underside of the wood, jostling everyone's milk and his Oreo cookies all in a stack on his napkin? He had always been so long-legged and handsome. Maybe he would even say, "We all make mistakes, Mom. Even though you did what you did, I still love you."

The Bible said, "Ask and it will be given to you; seek and you will find."

How many years had she begged the Father for this? How many nights, on her knees at her bedside, had she sought resolution?

She supposed the Bible must have been written with somebody else in mind besides Beatrice Bartling.

God, if you ever really listened to me, how could you ignore the cries of my heart?

Now that the pastor had come, Bea's neighbors and other friends began to depart.

"I'll be back over with a casserole in a while."

"If you need someone to sleep over tonight, I'll come."

"Don't you worry about watering the roses today, Bea. Cory can walk over and do that."

"Thank you," she told them all again, as she managed to heft herself up out of Ray's old chair.

With most, she accepted their offers of assistance with a careful, sad smile. But when Geneva proposed to send her grandson over to water the roses, Bea solemnly shook her head and nixed the idea.

"It will do me good to have something to do out in the yard."

Those flowers were the only living things that had ever flourished under her tending. Grief or no grief, she wasn't about to let anyone else take care of her roses.

Chapter Two

Potted plants in pleated foil wrappers and rainbow-sprays of flowers edged the chancel at Holechek Funeral Home. Jo Nell Roberts, longtime organist for the Antelope Valley Christian Fellowship, adjusted the fat hymnal to what seemed her liking on the music stand. Bea watched as she flexed her wrists with great drama, sought out a bass pedal with her foot, and began to play "Leaning On The Everlasting Arms." As the music began, Bea kept her jaw raised, her back straight as a grave stone against the pew, her hands cupped with care—left hand over the right—in her lap. At her side lay her crumpled hanky and three yellow blossoms, snipped from her rosebush only this morning. Already the blossoms were beginning to wilt.

Bea knew the seats in the little memorial chapel would fill to capacity behind her squared shoulders. After news of Nathan's death circulated, the townspeople of Ash Hollow had poured out their support and love. Casseroles and deli trays crammed her refrigerator. Cakes, cookies, and plates of sticky buns vied for counter space in her kitchen. Sympathy cards, with all their kindhearted sorrow and their prudent jotted notes, overflowed the mail basket beside the television. Any odd hour of the day or evening the bell would ring again, heralding the arrival of another floral arrangement, another tray of goodies, another coworker from Nebraska Public Power District stopping over to offer human comfort and a hug.

No matter everyone's efforts, the anguish in Bea's soul could not be assuaged. *How could you let this happen, Lord? What have I done, that you could let Nathan perish?*

When Jo Nell had quietly requested a list of songs to play at Nathan's service, the inconsolable pain broke open and, like gall, flooded Bea's heart. Every aspect of this funeral—the message, the memories, the music—trounced her. Every rite, meant to salve families' spirits and bring about healing, served only to reveal another layer of wounds instead.

As the service began, George Sissel, dressed in his green, billowing chasuble, took the lectern and glanced just once, but long and intently, at Bea. He opened his black leather-bound Bible, found his place in his notes, and began to speak.

"We are gathered today to celebrate the life of Nathan Roger Bartling. Many of us knew him when he was a young boy. We have not seen him during the past five years. But, still, he was a person who was once loved deeply here."

The pastor continued on with the particulars of Nathan's life, those undisputable facts that could be found on county records in any courthouse about anyone. "Nathan Bartling was born on May 27, 1978, at the Garden County Hospital in Oshkosh, Nebraska. He died July 8, 2001, in Omaha, Nebraska."

At the mention of Garden County Hospital Bea

thought not of death but of the swaddled, snug bundle the doctor had handed her, the white knit cap her baby had worn those first few days, the navy-blue eyes that gazed up at her for the first time as if in her face lay the explanation to every mystery.

"I'd like to tell personal stories about Nathan at his funeral," George had said with great heed last night when he'd come to Bea for another visit. "Can you tell me some of your memories of your son?"

"No." She'd shaken her head emphatically at him. "I can't do it. Don't ask me. It hurts too much."

But he hadn't relented. "For this to be done right, you're going to have to think past the times when you haven't known him. You have to go back. You owe yourself that much."

"I can't."

"I want you to try. You'll be glad you did, later."

From the pulpit now, he began to recount the tales that he had at last been able to coax from her. How Nathan loved the speech team and played baseball and ran track at Lewellen Rural High School. How he took great pride, during his junior year, when his team broke a school record and took District and State in the 440 Relay.

Others in the audience stood to volunteer their remembrances. Chuck Fairbanks, one of Nathan's baseball coaches, remembered how he'd been nicknamed "The Grape" after an incident on the school bus traveling to a tournament in Oshkosh. Frank Lubing, owner of Oshkosh Sporting Goods, told how the boy tagged along with Frank's dad whenever the men went goose hunting. "I let him put his own goose call on layaway at the store. He brought me fistfuls of pennies and nickels until he had his account paid off." He had a special knack with that goose call, said Lester Smith, who'd been news director at the local AM station for seventeen years. "One night he climbed on the roof to practice his goose call and, I'll swan, someone called the radio station to say that a whole flock had landed on the north side of town."

Bea's eyes did not rest on the pedestal at the center of the altar. She did not allow herself to glance at the mahogany coffin that, when gently prodded by mortuary staff, she'd chosen to keep closed for the length of the public service.

If she didn't look at it, perhaps she could deny her son was there.

As everyone spoke, Bea reached for the little wilted bouquet beside her and clutched it. She didn't know which was more horrific—hearing aloud the accounts that she'd shared last night with George or hearing the ones from others that she'd never known. She suddenly loathed all of these tales about Nathan's childhood. Recounting them made it seem as if Nathan's life had ended ten years ago instead of only last week. And each story proffered only bare inklings, only hints, of the vast treasure that had been lost to her.

Pictures began to eddy in her mind.

Nathan's lashes against his baby cheeks while he slept.

Nathan's arms and legs wrapped around hers like tongs when she held him.

Nathan's chubby feet discovering mud puddles for the first time.

Bea glanced at her hands. She hadn't realized she'd pricked herself on the rose thorns. She stared, the spot of blood growing. Her heart brimmed with fresh anger, bitterness, disbelief. Nothing remained for her now except emptiness—the slow, cold regret of knowing she would never have the chance to put right the matter that had sundered her child's life from her own.

The music began anew. One by one guests began to file out of pews and up the aisle to pay their last respects to the closed hardwood casket. The faint, sweet scent of carnations filled the room.

After they'd taken silent pause before Nathan's coffin, everyone trooped past Bea, grasping her hand and clasping it tightly, tendering empty condolences.

"We're so sorry."

"He was a good boy."

"There wasn't anything you could have done, Bea."

Outside, a sleek black limousine awaited her. She would load, Nathan would be loaded, and together they would lead a procession to the cemetery plot. For the past four days she had dreaded this ending—the parade through town, the gathering beneath the tent, the gaping dark hole in the ground that the carpets of turf and the folding chairs and the cascades of flowers could never really hide.

After the crowd had dissipated, after she had gone, someone nameless would begin the purposeful shoveling of earth, the spadefuls of brown Nebraska dirt thudding against the coffin, the smattering of sand and pebbles tumbling down the sides of slick wood into the chasm below.

Bea had chosen to have a closed-casket ceremony because she wanted to keep her memory of Nathan hidden next to her heart forever. It was a private sight. Those last, longing gazes at Nathan's face belonged to her and her alone. She hadn't shared them with anyone except her pastor, who had insisted he be present when she attended the family viewing.

She had leaned on George at the entrance to the Holechek Funeral Home, trusting him, gripping his shirt sleeve as they stepped past a well-placed floor lamp, a sofa designed to keep the family viewing area from seeming sterile.

"I'll hold you up," George had told her. "I won't let you take a step without me."

She'd whispered, as if the thought evoked childlike wonder, "I'm going to see my boy. I'm going to see him for the first time in five years."

He'd touched her hand where it grasped his sleeve. "Yes, you are."

The casket she'd purchased had been the nicest one she could afford for her son, with a pressed-doeskin interior and soft folds of taupe satin. From across the room, looking at him laying there, he could have been sleeping. If she watched long enough, she could almost imagine she saw breath. Bea had stepped toward him, apprehension lodging in her throat.

When she'd looked down at him, his appearance had surprised her. How could there be such quiet and peace in Nathan's face when he'd been the source of so much turmoil in her life?

It made her almost angry with him, seeing him appear so serene. Only the skin of his brow was scraped, in one place crosshatched with little cuts.

How could you do this? she had wanted to scream. *How could you leave me with all these scars, and you with only a few scratches on your face?*

George had stood behind her, gripping both her shoulders. When she spoke, her voice had come as an unfamiliar whimper, one she didn't recognize in her own ears, faint and strange.

"He looks so grown up, doesn't he?"

"He does, Bea." A pat on her right shoulder, reminding her that George was still there.

"He's filled out some. He was so gangly when he left home."

"Most boys fill out when they hit twenty."

If George hadn't been there, she would have fallen. She realized he bore the full brunt of her weight. Clasped together, they stared down at the body.

The same familiar nose, so like his father's. The fringe of brown bangs, like dusty straw against his forehead. The cowlick beside his right temple, still pronounced although some stranger at the mortuary had attempted to tame it. She whispered, "He just looks like . . . N-Nathan."

"He was a handsome boy, your son."

"Yes."

She had known she mustn't cry. If she began, she wouldn't stop. So great was her grief, her soul couldn't contain it. She'd felt as if she was made of thin, brittle glass, ready to shatter.

Oh, my baby! My baby.

No matter how big he'd grown, her arms ached to hold him.

Just once more, Lord. Please, God, that's all I've ever prayed for. To hold him once more.

Now, with the service ended, she laid her hand against his wooden coffin, her fingers longing even for the remembrance of the ripple-smooth grain of the wood. Oh, that she might have been tracing Nathan's warm, living brow instead.

I loved you so much, son. I loved you.

Anyone she'd ever loved had left her.

When she'd given Jo Nell a music list, she'd chosen only one song for Nathan, one she remembered him humming while he'd still been in overalls, before he'd ever even known the words.

"What a fellowship. What a joy divine . . ."

When he'd been little, she had hummed the notes every time she'd gotten in the car and driven somewhere. She'd once been pumping gas with the car door open when she'd heard him humming from the car seat in the back; he was only a toddler, holding his own beside her and almost getting the tune.

"Ling-ling ling-ling."

"Lee-eaning, lee-eaning, leaning on the everlasting arms."

Nathan, fat little legs dangling high above her face as she held him, the two of them laughing and nuzzling noses. "Sing me the 'Ling-Ling' song, Mama," he'd asked her in his little baby voice, giggling.

Bea laid her three wilted roses among the latticework of carnations already covering the casket.

I've leaned on your arms for a long time, Father. Why is it that this time, when it mattered most, your arms let Nathan go?

Chapter Three

Dozens of small details remained to be resolved in Nathan's death. Blessed details, because they shielded Bea—kept her mind from the dreadful stirrings of anger and loss and sorrow she knew waited for her whenever she searched her own soul.

Several of her aunts had driven in from Potter, and although they had booked a double room at the Gander Inn Motel, they needed to be looked after.

The morning after the funeral Bea drove them through the state historical park. All the while they chatted and tried gently to distract her over the Soddy homes and the early Nebraska homesteads, Bea thought, *How can any of this be real? How can I be here and Nathan not be coming home?*

Her employer at Nebraska Public Power District insisted that she take a leave of absence to sort out her affairs. Once the aunts had left, she kept herself busy by washing and sorting mountains of Pyrex casserole dishes. She spread out her pretty floral stationery, took pen in hand, and set about acknowledging the condolence cards that she'd fingered and sorted and reread, and the memorial fund donations made in Nathan's name to the Antelope Valley Sunday School Fund. All the while she worked, she wanted to declaim, *I don't thank you, God. I don't thank you for letting this happen to us.*

She met with the president of Nebraska State Bank and pored over funeral bills and tax papers. Nathan's death certificate waited for her signature atop a mountain of other legal documents.

Before she ordered Nathan's headstone, Bea struggled to decide how the small granite gravestone should read. "Beloved son," she had scribbled, her emotions numb, on a crumpled page of the notepad she kept handy by the phone. "Nathan Roger Bartling."

Every time she stared at the words, she denied herself the opportunity to count what they represented—the gangly boy who ate too fast and turned goose calls into music and broke into a purposeful, retainered smile whenever she'd be bent on scolding him. Such heartbreak. So many mistakes and so much love. "Beloved son."

It's my fault. I'm the one who made the choice that sent him away.

Day-to-day life continued around her. The Prime Timers at the senior center held their weekly luncheon with a special program entitled "How Herbal Remedies Can Change Your Life." The Monday night golf tournament at the nine-hole Oshkosh Country Club, where participants had to bring their own steaks if they wanted to eat and had to tote in their own iced-down coolers if they intended to imbibe, continued this week as planned. The Ash Hollow Planning Commission spent the entire July meeting debating the future of Pete Staley's swine operation, which he proposed to bulldoze so he could construct an RV campground and travel park instead.

Just before noon one day, still thinking about the headstone, Bea drove her decade-old Chevrolet Monte Carlo to Ash Hollow Cemetery. She parked on the gravel road and walked out across the grassy knolls, shaded her eyes and gazed toward the bluffs hewn deep into the rock by the slow-moving Platte River.

She'd bought this cemetery plot too quickly last year, in a huff because Geneva had read in the paper where city people from Denver were opting in droves to be buried there, a rural setting beside a river within driving distance that cost only sixty dollars a plot. Even now, just two days after they'd buried Nathan, no evidence remained of the striped yellow tent and the rows of chairs and the little pine pulpit where George Sissel had stood. Only a neatly edged oblong of fresh-turned Nebraska dirt and three easel flower arrangements that had begun to slightly lose their color.

When she'd bought the plot, she hadn't thought about needing it. She'd only bought it to save against time.

In the low draw beside the river, cottonwoods raised leafy broad limbs like supplicating hands lifting toward the sky. It was all very peaceful and solitary, with only the sough of the wind and birdsong for company. As soon as the headstone arrived, this spot would be marked: "Nathan Roger Bartling. Born May 27, 1978. Died July 8, 2001. Beloved son."

Beloved son.

Off in the distance, a golf cart topped the narrow brow of hill and jostled toward her. The gardener. He stopped once and rummaged through his equipment and Bea could hear the heavy buzz of a motorized garden trimmer as he lopped off weeds around a little fence. Soon the fellow climbed back in, came bouncing along. "Halloooo." He gave her a wave.

He wore unfashionable green army pants and a decrepit sweater with holes unraveling in each elbow. He cut the engine, disembarked, and brandished the trimmer again, going after wayward bluestem grass on the stone footpath three plots over. "Nice day," he said over his shoulder.

Bea didn't know what to say. She supposed, for some people, it was a nice day. But it wasn't for her. Not a nice month or a nice year or a nice life. She didn't answer him exactly. Instead she announced, "This is my son here," as if she was introducing them, as if Nathan was standing beside her peering over her left arm instead of laying beneath freshly dug earth.

The man propped his power trimmer against a monument, pushed both hands in his pockets, and jangled what sounded like a mixture of keys and lawnmower bolts and pennies. He whistled once and surveyed the blue, sun-drenched sky above them. "Well," he shrugged, "I'm mighty sorry to hear that."

"I'm not really in the mood to talk."

"The funeral a couple of days back. Must've been for you."

"Yes. I mean no. Not me. My son."

"Funerals are always for the people still living."

She thought about that. "I suppose so."

"Everybody you meet in this place has some story to tell. Folks just up and die, no rhyme or reason to it. It's always sad, no matter when folks go." He nodded his head toward the Platte River before he stooped down on all fours and surveyed the buffalo grass from ground level as if to make sure each blade was even. He pulled out a small pair of clippers and snipped one or two places. Then he rocked back on his heels, satisfied. "Still, if you have to be dead, this is a fine place to be."

She didn't answer. She stared at the clean-cut edges of Nathan's grave, wondering if this man had made them. "Sometimes people die too soon," she said at last. "They die before they get a chance to—" Just those few words threatened to be her undoing. She couldn't finish.

He filled in for her. "—tell you what they're thinking?"

She met his eyes, wondering how he could know, if he had heard all the talk around town. "Yes. Something like that."

"You looking for forgiveness, you won't find it in a cemetery." He made a broad gesture toward the butte where Bea could see the chimney tops of her little town. "You find it out there." The squat skyline of Ash Hollow rose against the vast Nebraska prairie, with its steeple of St. Elizabeth's and the sign that read "Goose Hunting Capital. Museum. Antiques. Grass Greens Golf Course. Free Swimming."

Bea surveyed Ash Hollow in the distance, thinking he couldn't possibly be right. "There isn't anything out there for me."

The gardener pulled out a trowel. He began to dig a thistle that had just started to grow between two stepping-stones. "You know, some roses would be pretty growing here. I'm so busy taking care of stones and fences and weeds, never have time to think about a rose. You know how to grow a rose?"

Bea's chin jerked up in surprise. "Who did you say you were?" She peered at him from beneath narrowed brows. "You been around here long?"

He pitched the thistle into a growing pile of cuttings and debris. "Couple of months is all." He reached out a wrinkled kidskin garden glove to shake her hand. "Name's Goodsell. Carrington Goodsell. Folks who know me call me Care."

"You been listening to talk around town?"

He glanced up at the azure sky, the wisps of cloud, as if he expected some answer. "Nope. Get's a soul in trouble, listening to talk. That's why I got me a job out here. These folk—" He pointed to the plots that surrounded him. "—don't say much."

He'd overstepped his bounds with her and she thought it best to let him know it. "You ought not be suggesting how to decorate people's graves. When they bring Nathan's headstone in, I'll decide what to do about the flowers."

"Is that your boy's name? Nathan?"

"Yes." She knelt to the earth and took a fistful of it, crushed it tight inside her fingers as if she was trying to hold on to something. She hadn't yet begun to touch her grief. It terrified her, knowing that the monstrous, detestable thing laid in wait inside her—that it would somehow have to be taken out and looked at, maybe even tomorrow, maybe even today.

All around her she smelled and saw living things. The sweet, poignant fragrance of grass. The orange ladybug that waddled across her knuckle. The bee that hovered over a thistle blossom and then was gone.

Care Goodsell stooped beside her. He scrubbed his sweaty forehead with the top of his gardener's glove, leaving his bangs sticking straight up in wet prickles. He yanked off his glove and stuck out one grimy thumbnail so the ladybug could continue its journey, crawling from her hand onto his.

"When I make my rounds, I'll give special attention to this grave, ma'am. I can promise you that."

A child's garden verse ran through her head. *Ladybug, ladybug, fly away home. Your house is on fire and your children are gone.*

Bea stood and dusted off the dirt against her legs with three decisive slaps. Having this man offer to tend Nathan's grave gave her no consolation.

"It makes no difference to me, Mr. Goodsell. Suit yourself."

As the days that passed turned into a week, and a week turned into two weeks, the townsfolk of Ash Hollow did not abandon her. They knew well how to take care of their own.

Tom Hodges, her employer at Nebraska Public Power, stopped by to tell her to take whatever time she needed before coming back to work. The Lisco Presbyterians, the Episcopalians from St. George, the Lutherans from St. Mark's, the Oshkosh Wesleyans, the Methodists, the bereavement committee from the Garden County Church of Christ, and the Catholics from St. Elizabeth's all appeared at Bea's door, stopping by to visit or to bring a copy of *The Garden County News* with the obituary or a paper sack of fresh tomatoes from Sterbin's Produce Stand down the road.

All the while her visitors sat with her and did their best to ease her trouble, Bea couldn't help but feel envious of her neighbors going about their routine evening chores and puttering in their yards. Charlie Law across the street bringing out a bucket and sponge to soap down his car, stopping long enough to pick up a tennis ball and toss it for his dog. Next door, Fiona Kepler spading dandelions. Someone hammering a deck down the street.

"I know it's awful." Geneva, who had stopped in one evening to bring two jars of her best plum jelly, followed Bea's eyes to Charlie and his dog. "I've heard there isn't anything to do that makes it any better, either. Josephine told me that after her Great-Uncle Orley died. She said you just have to fight your way through."

Although Bea felt closer to Geneva than so many of the others, she had learned long ago to speak with quiet reserve around her friend. Geneva repeated everything. She was considered the best source of information in the entire county, ranked higher than both *The Garden County News* and the local radio station.

"Thank you for not lying to me."

Geneva stood from the sofa and gave Bea a determined hug. "I wish you would let Cory come over and water the roses. It would be one less thing for you to worry about right now."

"The roses take my mind off things."

"Everybody hates to see you hurting like this. We're all looking for things we can do to help."

"You brought me plum jelly."

"We *all* thought Nathan would come home, Bea. *All* of us. Harry Wickstrom told me that his daughter Susan used to moon around after school and say, 'Nathan Bartling is the nicest boy in the whole class.' And Vince Wiley down at Otter Creek Marina told me he accidentally gave Nathan a dollar's worth of extra change once when he came in to buy a carton of earthworms. He said Nathan got clear to the car before he came back and said, 'I counted this, Mr. Wiley, and you gave me too much change.' "

"Geneva. Please. I can't bear hearing any more stories like this."

"You raised a good son, Bea. I don't care what anybody else says. I don't ever want you to doubt that."

Bea didn't know where it came from at that precise moment, but she took a small burst of satisfaction in petty anger. "You know what Lillie Curfman said to me this morning? She said it was a good thing Nathan hadn't come home before he died. She said I should consider it a blessing that I hadn't had the chance to see him in a long time. As if that should make it *easier*."

"Oh, Lillie Curfman wouldn't know the curved end of a spoon," Geneva humphed. She slung the handle of her purse over her forearm and draped her cotton-knit sweater, absolutely needless in the warm Nebraska evening, over the crook of her elbow. She reached up for a parting hug. "You call me if you need anything, okay?"

"I promise. I'll call."

"I mean it, Bea. Are you going to be okay? I don't have to leave if you don't want me to."

Bea turned on the porch light. "I'll be fine." She stood behind the screen and watched Geneva's retreating figure cross the wedge of artificial light that splayed over the grass.

Seconds later, the car engine revved to life and the vehicle backed down the driveway, stopped, turned, changed gears. Then it was gone, tires crackling against loose gravel along Pattison Drive, leaving an empty memory of a woman's hand waving in a flicker of glass.

Bea turned away, determined to make it once more through her go-to-bed rituals without breaking down. Charlie Law had rinsed his car, wiped down his whitewall tires, and gone inside. Fiona had left a little pile of weeds beside her curb, probably to be picked up in the morning. Down the street the hammering had stopped.

The nighttime and all of its emptiness loomed large and impossible before her.

Dark. So much dark. After supper before bedtime proved to be the loneliest time of all. Someone she'd known once had called it the harsh of the night. She didn't think she could stand nine hours of it again.

Bea opened the refrigerator door and surveyed the dozen or so casseroles stacked there. She was already growing tired of this mourning food. Where were the steaks, the lacy edges of fresh lettuce, the crunchy nuts and carrots? She lifted one corner of foil, then another. Finally she settled on none of the above and selected two eggs instead.

She dug a small skillet out of the cabinet, pleasing herself slightly with the racket she made rattling through her vast assortment of pans. In no time the eggs were bubbling and hissing in the skillet. But as she stared at the yolks and whites in the pan, desolation and longing overcame her, exploding like the splattering eggs from somewhere deep within her chest. Her eyes began to sting; the pan and its contents began to shimmer.

For days Bea had fought to hold back her tears. But she could not hold them back any longer. Sorrow engulfed her.

She laid the spatula aside.

Bea hadn't any idea where anyone had moved her boxes of Kleenex and she didn't care. Tears fell into the pan on the stove and sizzled. They ran down her jaw and soaked the collar of her old, frayed shirt. They streamed down her face and plopped from her chin.

I'm not crying because I'm lonely. Salty drops rolled the

length of her nose and dangled there, waiting to drip. *I'm not.*

Beatrice Bartling had been living with loneliness for a long time.

When other people lost someone they loved, they faced the task of cleaning out bureau drawers, going through letters they hadn't seen, sorting through hair-brushes and silly mementos and shoes with lopsided worn soles and underwear.

Bea didn't have even that much to look forward to.

Other people spoke of a comfortable easy chair in a corner, a faint scent on a favorite shirt, something they could take from a hook in the closet and smell.

It had been so long since Nathan had been present in this house, nothing remained for Bea to cling to.

No smell.

No presence.

No hope.

In the skillet before her, the eggs burned brown around the edges. She dropped her head into one hand and sobbed. "I c-can't do this. I can't," she bawled through swollen lips, wet from her tears of grieving. "I can't."

She had been living without Nathan for a long time. But now, because Nathan had died, her hope had died, too.

"It isn't f-fair. My *baby*."

The eggs had gone to stiff rubber in the pan. Bea couldn't have choked them down anyway, not even in the beginning, not even before they'd fried for ten minutes too long.

She would never know what wild thing Nathan had done for his twenty-first birthday. She would never know whether he preferred furniture arranged in angles or pushed flat against the walls. She wouldn't know if he still slam-dunked the basketball when he got mad or if he ate too many Ramen noodles or if he'd made the gun cabinet he'd designed in high school shop. She wouldn't know if he'd died still wanting to be a teacher.

She would never know if he'd wanted to forgive her.

Helplessness engulfed her. Then anger—like a battlement cast in the fortressed stone of all she'd asked for, all she'd been certain God would give her, all she had expected and had been denied—rose up and took possession of her.

She worshiped a God who had let her son die.

She worshiped a God who had shut a door on her lifelong prayer.

"N-nathan." Bea said his name once and thumped the kitchen counter hard with both fists. She thumped it again. And again. And again. She cried for a long time. Then, as suddenly as they'd started, her tears tapered off.

Lord, you took away the one dream I've clung to ever since Ray left and this family fell apart.

She flipped off the stove burner in a fit of practicality and discarded the ruined eggs into the trash.

Lord, you took away the only thing I've wanted since the day Nathan set foot out that door.

She found the Kleenex, ripped a tissue from the box, and wiped her eyes hard with it.

I trusted you.

Bea yanked a second tissue from the box and blew her nose with stubborn determination. She turned on the faucet and ran a dishcloth beneath the cold issue of water, rung it out with both hands, and used it to mop her face.

Chapter Four

"Mama, I'm hungry." The little girl craned her chin over the top of the seat. "Can we get something to eat?"

"No, we can't." The truth be known, Gemma didn't have enough money left to buy them lunch. And it terrified her to think of stopping. The Corolla had developed a clank about twenty miles back and as long as she could keep the old car running she figured she'd be better off just to nurse the thing along. If she turned the engine off, she had her doubts whether it would ever start again.

"You have to be quiet, Paisley. I'm concentrating on the driving."

"Are we there yet?"

She ignored the question and asked one of her own. "Is your seat belt on?"

"You answer mine first."

"You can't lean forward like that and have your seat belt on."

"I'm wearing an invisible seat belt. One that's magic."

Gemma glanced in the rearview mirror. "Put it on, Paisley Rose. Now."

There hadn't been anything magic about their lives in years, not since Grandma Hardeman had said she couldn't stay around with a baby. Not since Paisley's father had written to say he wouldn't stick around to raise his kid. Not since after the accident when Gemma had come back to the little trailer to find her clothes, her small collection of books, and Paisley's huge collection of Barbies all set out in a trash heap on the withered grass.

Absently, Gemma fingered the simple gold wedding band on her left hand.

Paisley made a tumbling dive over into the front and landed halfway in the dusty seat beside her mother. With her came her baby blanket, frayed and faded, the quilted black-and-white Holsteins on the fabric vanishing amidst tatters. "I wanna sit in front with you, Mama."

Hair streamed across Gemma's face, riding on hot blasts of air from the open window. She tucked it behind her ear so she could see the green highway sign they were passing. "Oshkosh twelve miles. Ash Hollow seventeen." Then another more rustic billboard. "Goose Hunting Capital. Museum. Antiques. Grass Greens Golf Course. Free Swimming. Exit 43."

With all the speed she could marshal out of the Corolla, Gemma still had plenty of time to read both signs twice. She checked the gas gauge. A little under a quarter of a tank. "We're almost there, honey bananas. That sign says 'Ash Hollow seventeen miles.'" She bent forward over the wheel, gripped it tighter with both hands as if by sheer force of will she could speed them along. "I wish he had told me more about where to stop."

The only thing he had ever told her was that anybody

who needed to find the place could ask around town about the roses. He'd said if folks had a mind to search her out, it would be as easy as finding any landmark, once they got to the right town.

"Will I see her roses, Mama?"

"Sure you will. And if everything he said was right, they'll be the prettiest things you ever laid eyes on. All yellow. Like little suns."

"I'm hungry."

This discussion of roses softened Gemma's heart. "Let's see what we can do, okay?" She signaled and took the next exit. They turned into a Kwik Stop parking lot and Gemma got out. With knees on the buckled blacktop and the engine still running, she ran her fingers beneath the floor mat, searching for stray coins. Good. A quarter and three pennies. She climbed back inside and slipped her fingers as far as they'd reach between the seat cushions. When she'd finished, she'd rummaged up sixty-eight cents. "Come on, Paisley Rose. We'll go buy you a candy bar."

When they stepped inside, they saw a gleaming cooler with rows of canned soda and bottled juice transfused in light. Paisley started toward the beverages but Gemma tugged her back. She whispered, "You want something to drink, go find the water fountain. We don't have that much to spend."

On the candy aisle, it took a long five minutes to narrow Paisley's choices to a fistful of Lemonheads and one Hershey Bar. "We've got to hurry," Gemma prompted her. "We're using up gas out there, keeping the car running."

The little girl stood beside the colorful bins, her face filled with desperation. "But I'm thirsty, Mama."

Gemma sighed and glanced around to find the water

fountain. "You can get a drink, but hurry up." She took her daughter by the hand and led her into the innards of the storeroom. Between mop buckets and a pile of stacked boxes stood two glistening stainless steel water fountains—one tall, and the other child-sized. "You need help?"

"I can do it myself." Paisley pushed the button with her thumb and a gusher of water hit her square in the nose. She pursed her lips into a kiss and began to drink.

While she waited, Gemma found the cash register and stood in line to make her purchases. Beside the register, fanning out with wayward abandon from the wire rack, stood the day's issue of *The Garden County News*. Of course! Why hadn't she thought of checking the newspaper before?

Gemma twisted her jean skirt farther down over her thighs and helped herself to a copy. She unfolded the front page and thumbed her way past the movie listings, letters to the editor, and a blazing Superette ad that announced "Gatorade. Two six-packs for $5." At last she found what she'd been looking for, buried deep on page nine. The Society and Garden section. Her eyes raced down each column, searching for anything that might give her a clue. No pictures were printed, only the confetti of headlines about parties, places, names: *Armour Donates Seedlings*. *Prime Timers Offer Program on Herbal Remedies*. *Golf Tournament Supports Library Auxiliary*.

Nothing sounded familiar. She'd have to read all the stories, she supposed. Gemma had just scanned the first column when the fellow in front of her, after adding two packages of beef jerky to his purchase of gas and three donuts, signed his credit slip and stepped aside.

"You gonna buy that paper?" the clerk asked.

Gemma started, guilty as a thief who'd gotten caught.

"Well, no, I—" She flipped back to the front page and found the purchase price. Fifty cents. "No, I am not."

"You read it, you buy it. Can't you see the sign?"

Gemma jabbed the newspaper back into the rack. Page corners poked out at every imaginable angle. "A Hershey Bar and four Lemonheads, please."

She laid Paisley's candy on the counter. The clerk scowled at the register keys while he rang up the meager items she and Paisley had chosen. "That'll be seventy cents."

She'd added wrong. "I don't have that much. I'll have to put something back."

Disgruntled, he pointed to a jar where customers discarded their spare pennies. "How much you need? Take it out of there."

He wore a nametag that read "Gary." Gemma fished every bit of change out of her pocket and handed it to him, then added two pennies from the jar. "Thank you." Then, in hopes she could entice him into being a friend, she clasped the little sack he handed her in both hands and didn't move. "Do you know people around here?"

"Yeah. Everybody stops in this place at one time or another."

"I'm looking for a lady who grows roses. She's got a famous rosebush. An old one that got carried along the Oregon Trail."

Gary thought for a moment and then shook his head. "Lots of folks grow roses around here. Nobody famous that I know of." He made a point to glance past her left shoulder, an obvious reminder that she wasn't the only customer waiting in line. "Never heard of anything like that."

Here came Paisley with her face dripping water and

her shirt so wet that Gemma could've wrung water from it. "I drank as much as I could, Mama."

When they got to the car, they found the donut fellow munching on a glazed and staring at the white smoke billowing from the rusted Corolla tailpipe. "Your car ain't gonna make it much further, young lady. That's the smoke of a cracked engine block if I've ever seen it. How many miles you got on her?"

"Too many."

"I could've told you that."

"I guess I'll have it looked at," she lied. She didn't even have money for another tank of gas, much less a repair bill.

"Looks mighty bad." He pitched the last half of his donut into the trash. "Hope you're not trying to get much further."

Gemma stared after the donut, her stomach churning with hunger, thinking that if only he'd offered it to her and hadn't thrown it away, she would gladly have eaten it.

"I'm not." Paisley climbed into the front seat and flapped the hem of her T-shirt in the air, trying to dry it. Gemma buckled the seat belt around Paisley's damp little stomach, knowing that to fasten a child's seat belt herself was sometimes the only surefire method to get it done. She dusted off her hands in a measured show of determination to the man who told her that her car wouldn't go, to the four-and-a-half-year-old girl whose belly had been rumbling for miles. "I've almost gotten us to where we're going."

The Corolla gave out fourteen miles up the road. The engine made one last valiant sputter, the warning lights blinked on, and the wheels ground to a gravelly halt on the shoulder.

"Oh, great." Gemma whacked the steering wheel with one open palm. "What do we do now?"

"What's wrong?" Paisley asked, her mouth wreathed with melted chocolate. "Why did the car stop?"

Gemma tried the key, pumped the pedal. The engine gave a dead click and didn't turn over. "It's sick." She set the parking brake and shoved open the driver-side door against the warm wind. "You stay right where you are. I'm going to check this out, okay?"

Traffic rocketed past on the highway, flattening the endless grass and plastering Gemma's shirt against her frame with every passing squall of hot air. She tugged her skirt down again and struggled to find the latch behind the ancient rusted grill. When she lifted the hood, an acrid burning odor rose from the engine. Gemma stared down at the innards of the car. "Three more miles," she said aloud to the tangled, filthy jumble. "You only needed to get us three more miles."

She heard another vehicle pull to the shoulder in front of them. When she raised her head, a trucker had guided his rig off the road. He jumped down out of the cab, touched the brim of his ball cap without actually lifting it, and talked to her without coming too close. "You know what's wrong?"

"No." She shook her head from behind the hood.

"Want me to have a look?"

"Don't know as it'll do much good. But, yeah. It'd be great if you looked at it."

With her permission, he sauntered over to check it out and gaped down at the oil-covered belts and hoses. He jiggled one hose and shook his head. "We can try the jumper cables, but I don't think that'll do it. This isn't going to be any quick fix."

She wiped greasy hands on the denim of her skirt. "That's what I was afraid of."

He slammed the hood shut for her. "Just dropped off my load and I'm headed east. Is there someplace I can drop you? You two look like you could use help."

"Ash Hollow."

"What's in Ash Hollow? You on your way home or something?"

"No. Just need to get to a gas station. Some place I can use the phone."

He gestured with his arm. "Well, hop in."

She bounded around her old Toyota to open the door for Paisley, then popped the trunk and hauled out their flimsy pink suitcase. She saw him smiling at the bag, its childish caricature of a doll, its jolly words: "Happiness Is A Visit To Grandma's." That suitcase held everything she and Paisley owned, not including the clothes on their backs and the two dusty jackets she'd retrieved from the backseat and now carried over the crook of one arm. Gemma pitched the suitcase into the truck first. Next, she pitched in the coats and shoved Paisley up onto the seat. Last, she grabbed hold of the handrail and hoisted herself up, too.

The engine clattered beneath them. The air brakes released with a huge hiss. Their rescuer drove ten feet and shifted, drove ten feet more, shifted again, drove and shifted, using the colossal gearshift that jutted clear from the truck floor to the height of his hand. The world smelled of diesel. Beside Gemma's knees, a CB radio squawked.

He gestured back over his right shoulder. "Little one's

welcome to sit up on the sleeper if she wants. Kids enjoy that, sitting up there and dangling their legs down."

"She'll stay in my lap. Thank you."

Paisley clung like a possum to Gemma's neck.

"You two going to grandma's?" He took a toothpick from the ashtray and wiggled it into the space between his two front teeth.

She didn't answer. *We haven't had much luck with grandmas. We have yet to find one who wants us anywhere around.*

He let them off at the Sandhill Texaco. "Sure I can't drop you somewhere else?" he insisted. "Hate just leaving you off in the middle of nowhere like this. You could make your phone call and I could take you on further."

"No. That's all right. Thanks." Gemma did her best to make her voice commanding. She grabbed the two coats, clambered backwards from the cab, seized the pink bag from the floor, and held up her arms so Paisley could climb down. With one curt nod, she dismissed him, her stance widespread by the unleaded gas pump, her feet planted in false certainty. As he drove off, she gave him a wave good-bye.

Heat and gasoline fumes rose, skimming the black tarmac in waves. The pay phone hung in a cubicle against the curb, bordered by a little patch of mowed green lawn. She laid the suitcase sideways on the grass and thumped it right on the word "Grandma."

"Sit here, kiddo. It'll take me a minute, finding what I need to find."

A thin Ash Hollow directory dangled inside its metal casing below the telephone. She lifted it and thumbed through the dog-eared pages until she found the *B*s and ran her index finger down the inventory of names. Bark and Bounce Dog Grooming. Barneses, about eight of them. Bartlett. Bartley.

And then, she found two Bartlings.

Staring down at that name in the phone book made her heart pummel. Which could it be? Adam J. or the other listing with nothing more than initials?

Gemma figured she wanted the one with initials. Everybody knew that a woman living alone used her initials in a phone book. She jotted down both addresses just in case—117 West Pattison Drive and 103 Fairview Street.

She walked over and poked her head inside the service garage. Broken carburetors lay end to end. In one corner the skeleton of a Ford Fairlane stood without its headlights or drive train. A stout boy wearing a dirty jumpsuit appeared from behind a stack of tires. "You need something?" He mopped his hands with an oily rag that he'd yanked from his back pocket.

He seemed a most unlikely person, it seemed a most unlikely place, to ask about flowers. But Gemma didn't have much choice. "I'm looking for a lady who grows roses at her house. She's got an old rosebush."

"Oh, sure. Everybody knows her. You interested in seeing it?"

Gemma nodded, unable to speak.

"Stop by the museum first." He pointed. "Two blocks down that way. They've got a whole printed page of facts that they hand out to tourists before they head over to the house. That'll save you from having to ask too many questions."

She trained her eyes on his face to keep herself from springing up and down. They had found her! A lump of bittersweet hope wedged itself deep within Gemma's chest. "Do you know where she lives?"

He jammed the rag back into his rear pocket. "Everybody does. You can walk it from here. She's three blocks over, on Pattison." He chewed his gum lazily, making it snap.

Gemma whispered the words, stared down at her own grimy hands. "Tell me how to find this place."

"You mean you aren't gonna stop by the museum first?"

"I just want to go to the house, if you don't mind telling me the way."

"Museum makes it easy with that printed map and directions. Don't expect *her* to answer any questions for you today. Mrs. Bartling used to come out on the stoop with pitchers of lemonade and cookies whenever anybody stopped by, she loved talking about those flowers so much. But not now. Now, I doubt she'll even come to the door."

Gemma clasped both hands behind her hipbones and said nothing.

"Take Avenue C two blocks to the traffic signal. Turn right on West Third. First left you come to after you cross the railroad tracks is Pattison. Roses are on the left, four or five houses down."

By the time they found the Bartling place, it was late afternoon.

Gemma gathered Paisley against her and left the sidewalk, approaching the house through a grove of ancient cedar trees in the side yard where she couldn't be seen.

The notched red-brick chimney towered over the porch; a slight entryway constructed of the same brick with one round windowpane faced the street. Each gutter and gable had been painted maroon to match the striped awnings that hung over each window like a scalloped petticoat. A tin watering can sat on the bottom step, a circle rusted on the brick because it had been there so long.

Gemma's heart had gone leaden in her chest. Now that she'd finally arrived, she was afraid to knock on the door. Faded pink blinds had been snapped shut, shrouding each window as if the occupant wanted to disconnect herself from the world.

The place seemed pleasant enough. Gemma didn't know why anyone would want to run away from a home that appeared so cozy.

A jumble of yellow roses lined the brick sidewalk. A webbing of them swayed along a trellis that divided the expanse of bluegrass from the porch. Paisley scrambled down and pointed. "Are those the roses, Mama? Is that them?"

"Yes, honey bananas," she whispered. "That must be them."

For the first time in an hour, Gemma noticed the chocolate smudges on her daughter's chin. She considered using the watering can on the steps, but she couldn't be sure how long the water had been standing. Instead she licked a finger and did her best to spit-polish the chocolate off. Paisley scrunched up her cheeks. "Don't, Mama."

"You're filthy." But cleaning was a lost cause and Gemma knew it. She smoothed her own hair. They were two bedraggled waifs, exhausted and road worn and alone as they mounted the brick steps to the little covered entrance. Gemma rapped on the front door and waited.

It didn't take too long. The door opened, singing on its hinges, and out wafted the stale smell of last night's supper.

"I'm sorry." The woman spoke from the darkness behind the screen and her voice sounded flat, wary. "I'm not showing these flowers. If you'll stop by the museum, someone will give you information there." She started to shut the door.

"We aren't here to see your roses," Gemma said. "We came looking for you."

"Looking for me?" the woman repeated, and she seemed to be squinting so she could have a better look through the screen. "Why?"

Gemma moved no closer, but stayed where she was at the edge of the brick steps. "Mrs. Bartling? Are you Mrs. Bartling?"

"I don't know what you want." The woman kept both hands on the jamb, ready to slam the door. "Whatever this is, I'm not interested."

"I'm Gemma." She stepped forward then, quietly and with solemn purpose, her child's spindly arms adhering around her leg. She extended her hand into nothingness. "I was just coming to meet you," she said. "I'm Nathan's wife."

Chapter Five

"Mama? Is this her?" The little girl's question rang out, a clear bell across the front yard, pure and guileless and true. "Is she the one?"

Bea stared into the dark, wide eyes of a little girl. The child's cheeks were grubby with what looked like an entire boxed array of chocolate candy. The sticky gunk had oozed between the little girl's fingers, had coated strands of her curly dust-brown hair, and had stained a spot the shape of Minnesota on a baby blanket so loved and worn that it might fall to tatters as she stood there on the porch.

Beside the child, holding her hand, stood a young woman with ragged teenager hair, chopped short at the nape of her neck with long, unruly strands around her face. She wore a blue-jean skirt smeared with oily handprints, so short that it swung with her hips every time the girl nervously shifted her weight from one foot to the other. Her rumpled blouse, the color of dishwater, looked like it had been worn for days.

"Hush, you." As if the young woman knew exactly what drew Bea's attention, she tugged down her skirt and tried to scrub some of the chocolate off the little girl's cheeks.

She smeared it even worse than it had been before.

"You have to be quiet, Paisley Rose. We're concentrating on meeting each other." That handled, she straightened again, her expression containing an unfathomable mixture of awe and dread. "Mrs. Bartling, I—"

Bea took one step toward the door, as if to banish these strangers from her territory. "What did you say?"

The girl retreated backwards, down one step. It appeared she took a deep draught of air for courage. "Are you Nathan's mother?"

"Yes, I am."

The girl's whisper came soft, disbelieving. Her green eyes pooled with emotion. "We've found you then," she breathed.

"I must have heard you wrong. I thought you said—"

"I did say it."

"—that you were Nathan's wife."

"I did."

At the young woman's words, anger and uncertainty began to gnaw inside Bea, wretched, hollow. Even though Nathan had been gone from home so long, he never would have done something like this without her, would he?

He wouldn't have gotten married.

No, Lord. I can't. You can't do this to me, too.

The three of them stood riveted to the spot, not one of them giving an inch, not one of them willing to take this conversation forward even one more word.

There isn't even anywhere for us to start with this, Bea thought. *I don't even know what to ask. There isn't anything I know that would prove it. Or disprove it.*

"Mama, I've got to go potty."

The young mother frowned down at the chocolate-covered child. "I guess you should have gone at the Kwik Stop."

Paisley's legs crossed and she wore such an expression of desperation that, in spite of this new anguish, even Bea could not deny the necessity of allowing her inside.

The girl issued a deep, apologetic sigh and spoke in a tone of someone intruding. "Do you mind if we use your rest room?"

"What did you say your name is? Gemma?"

Gemma nodded.

"Where have you come from?"

"Omaha."

Bea glanced out suspiciously toward her front curb. There wasn't a vehicle in sight.

"The car broke down a few miles back. Somebody gave us a ride."

For the first time, Bea noticed the dilapidated pink suitcase, skinned along the corners, frayed plastic jutting from its underbelly. "Happiness Is A Visit To Grandma's."

"Mama, I've got to go."

Bea stepped back from the screen and let them inside for a moment, pointing the way and then following them through the house as if this was the height of imposition. She watched the girl named Gemma traipse down the long hallway lined with yellowed portraits hanging at odd spaces along the wall, smiling with inward satisfaction because the girl walked through Nathan's childhood home without showing any sign of recognition. They passed the bedroom with the two oak beds that Ray had made, designed to set one atop the other as bunks if space became a consideration; the shelf with its collection of rocks and blunted map pencils, scratched metal Tonka trucks lugged home from some garage sale over on Third Street, and the ball in its plastic case that read "Nathan 'The Grape' Bartling. #14. First All-Star Homerun 6-28-91 -vs- Bucktail"; the red-and-white banner tacked on the wall that proclaimed "Go Huskers!" But just when Bea had satisfied herself that the girl had made the entire trek without once noticing any of Nathan's belongings or pictures, the young woman stopped, her breath only a wisp, and reached up to touch a photograph.

Tears welled in the young woman's eyes. "How old was he in this?"

"I don't remember." A hard-hearted tactic, Bea knew, but she didn't feel comfortable giving anything else away.

Paisley came banging out of the bathroom with her pants hanging open. "Is that Nathan, Mama? When he was a little boy?"

Gemma stooped and started buttoning Paisley's pants. For a moment, neither the mother nor her child could take their gazes from the portrait. Nathan in his striped Izod shirt with his hair brushed in a sweep across his forehead, his brown eyes bright, his gap-toothed grin as wide as a Nebraska mile.

"Did you flush?"

"No." Paisley shook her head.

"You go right back in there and flush."

Paisley's little bottom gave an endearing waggle when she turned to go back. After a minute, from inside the bathroom, they heard the flip of the handle, water rushing.

"That little girl—?" Bea's inflection left an open blank. She didn't dare try to fill in that blank herself.

Gemma helped her. "You want to know if she's Nathan's?"

Bea nodded.

"Well, she isn't." The girl in the short skirt nudged the toe of one worn sneaker against the other and gazed down at them as if she was afraid to gaze anywhere else. "I already had her when I met him."

Oh. That kind of girl.

For one disorienting moment, Bea didn't know whether to feel keen disappointment or relief. There was nothing about this young woman—nothing—that could bind them together in any way.

"I'm so sorry," Gemma whispered. "So many times I've wished that she was his."

After Paisley slammed her way out of the bathroom, this particular subject could no longer be discussed. A lull fell. They stood silent, uneasy with being alone, just staring at Nathan's picture, side by side, shoulder to shoulder.

I've just seen my son laid into his grave. I'm struggling every minute not to break down or fall apart. Please, please don't expect me to ask you to stay.

Gemma turned to Bea and waited, her eyes fixed on the open button at the neck of Bea's blouse, at the hollow of Bea's throat that worked as she swallowed.

Since Nathan's died, you are the only thing we have left. Please, please don't ask us to go.

The silence between them grew and grew until it became an unbearable thing.

When they finally spoke, they spoke all at once.

"Don't think—"

"This isn't—"

"We've left our things on the porch," Gemma said. "We'd better go."

"Yes," Bea said. "Yes. You go."

"We shouldn't have come," Gemma said. "We've bothered you." Gemma seized Paisley's hand and started up the hallway. Their sneakered footsteps made sad little squeaks on the polished oak floor. Bea's Naturalizers made a decisive *tap tap tap* as she accompanied them to hold open the screen door.

The two visitors, mother and child, stepped back out into the daylight, back out to where this whole thing had begun, where their little suitcase and the wad of faded jackets laid waiting.

"Mama?" Paisley gripped her mother's hand as if she gripped onto a knot at the end of a rope. She clung for dear life. Her voice sank into a whisper, but not so low that Bea couldn't hear her. "Aren't we going to stay?"

"No, honey bananas. I don't think we are."

"Do you think if we go, we could have that little-boy picture?"

"Sh-hhh. Paisley, you have to be quiet. No picture. We haven't any place to put something like that."

Bea's hand stayed the door. She felt a vague need to apologize for something, to make this girl understand that she had absolutely nothing left to give them—that Nathan's life had been so far removed from her own that she hadn't any way to ferret out the truth of Gemma's claims. She struggled for a long moment to find the words. "I'm sorry. I'm afraid I haven't talked to my son in a very long time."

Even though a four-and-a-half-year-old could be much too heavy to carry, Gemma lifted Paisley and perched her on the ridge of her pelvis. Paisley stuck a finger in her mouth and sleepily laid her forehead against her mama's jaw. "That's okay." Gemma hefted their tiny suitcase and those coats with her free hand.

She stepped off the porch, barely able to manage the load, and started down the walk.

"Wait."

Gemma turned from where she stood and waited.

"When you asked how old he was, I lied. I know how old he was. He had turned six just a few months before."

"Pardon?"

"In that picture. He was six. I kept him back from kindergarten that first year because I couldn't let him go yet. I wanted him to be safe."

Gemma let Paisley slip down and stand by herself, braced against her knee. "He looked cute without any teeth. I'm glad we got to see your picture."

In all the stories of Nathan that had been circulating during these past days—the sad remembrances, the funny yarns—this one was the first story that Bea Bartling had shared with anyone herself. "He put his tooth under his pillow but he kept climbing out of bed. No matter how I chastised him, he wouldn't go to sleep. Finally, I asked him. 'Nathan, are you afraid of the tooth fairy?' He said, 'I'm not afraid, Mama, but the tooth fairy's somebody I just don't know.' "

Gemma hefted the suitcase a little higher. "I know you don't know us, Mrs. Bartling."

"Ended up with his tooth in a bowl on the table. That's the only way I could get him asleep. He lost his first tooth and he was afraid of her coming, because she was a stranger."

"I'm sorry you're afraid of us." Gemma gave one careful, sad smile. "If I'd had my way, we wouldn't have been strangers."

Bea came out on the porch behind them and took one wary step down. "Can I ask you one thing?"

"Yes."

"Why did you really come here?"

A pause. "To find you."

"Why?"

The girl seemed to choose her words with great care. "He always said that, if anything ever happened to him, we ought to come find you."

"He told you that?"

The words emerged quickly and quietly, as if she could not keep herself from saying them. "Of course, when you say those things to people, you never actually think they might happen."

"No, you don't."

A breeze worried the maple leaves in the tree at the corner of the yard. Bea heard the whistle of mallards overhead as they flew toward the little pond where the children fished for perch at Goose Leg Park.

"He told us how to find the roses, really. He said all we had to do was ask anybody about it, that everybody in town knew how to find this place once we told them what we were looking for. So that's what we did."

"Anybody could come into this town and find me." Bea pronounced these words with great emphasis, as if she could measure this girl's mettle by her reaction to this one, forceful word. "Anybody."

Gemma said, "He told us how the roses smelled in summertime. Like sweet tea. How he used to sneak the petals when you weren't there to get after him and squeeze them, just for the smell."

Bea's backbone went rigid as a hoe handle. Without realizing what she was doing, she pressed her hand against her stomach. Nathan had done just what the girl said. She'd caught him squeezing rose petals once and had sent him straight to his room.

An astonished silence hummed between them.

Bea felt the first warning signals burst forth inside her belly. *I don't care what you know about him. I can't accept it. I just don't have the fortitude to allow you into my life. Not now. Not this way.*

It got so quiet they could almost hear the maple leaves growing on the tree.

Bea grasped for the first subject that seemed to have reason. "Where are your people?" she asked. "You got family back in Omaha?"

"Sure I do," Gemma lied. "I've got plenty of family."

Perhaps she was being cruel, not inviting this girl to stay. But Bea had herself to think of. Her own survival was at stake these days. She had her own grief to bear.

While she mourned her son's death, she did not have the courage to confront her son's life as well.

Lord, not now. I just can't do this now.

How easy it would be for some desperate person to take advantage of her at this time. Someone who'd read an obituary and decided to come into her life, to use her tragedy for some personal gain.

"I'm sorry." Her words came so soft that the girl standing on her front walk leaned forward a bit as if she couldn't hear, as if she had to try doubly hard to understand it. "I cannot manage my own sorrow and welcome strangers in this house all at the same time. I'm sure you understand."

"Yes," Gemma said, showing no emotion on her face. "We understand. We do."

Chapter Six

The only family Gemma had left in this world was Grandma Hardeman, and Grandma Hardeman hadn't let Gemma cross her threshold since the day she'd been seventeen years old and had started showing with the baby.

Gemma had walked home from school that day, dumped her books on the seat of the porch swing, jangling the chains, while Doreen Hardeman barely moved the swing with her toes and sat viciously shelling peas.

"I've got to take the money for my graduation gown tomorrow, Grandma. Do you mind if I walk down to Mosher's again and see if they need help stocking shelves?"

"Sounds like a fool idea to me, Gemma Lee. Sure don't see no sense earning money for a graduation gown you aren't going to wear."

"Of course I'm going to wear it. Everybody has to wear one when they walk across the stage."

Those hands, hulling peas, breaking off the tapered ends, peeling strings until the shells popped open. Peas plunking against the sides of the bowl—a hollow, helpless sound that Gemma would never forget.

"You heard what I said. Don't pretend you didn't understand it."

"The principal said I could graduate with my class, Grandma. They've already decided."

"Turn sideways, child."

When Gemma hesitated, Grandma Hardeman picked up the flyswatter beside her. She waved it in the air as if she planned to whack something with it.

"Did you hear me? I said turn sideways."

Gemma turned sideways.

"No grandchild of mine is going to walk across a stage looking like that. Strutting around like a barnyard goose, growing fatter by the minute. Everybody in town already knows what happened with that Jimmy Forrester boy. Everybody in town already knows you're PeeGee."

"Grandma."

Doreen gave a curt nod toward Gemma's midsection. "That baby in your belly ain't never gonna amount to anything. Nothing that starts its life out in sin ever does."

That had been Grandma Hardeman's opinion then. Her opinion had not changed since. Not since she had forbidden Gemma to attend the high school graduation ceremony. Not since she had forbidden Gemma to set foot anyplace in town where anyone might see her protruding belly. Not since she had finally waved Gemma off, telling her she had to make her own way, that there wasn't any way she, Doreen Hardeman, was getting coerced into raising another kid.

"I paid my dues the first time around with your mother. Then I paid my dues double the second time around with you. I'm an old woman and there's no way in flip I'm going to get stuck again. You get rid of that sin baby some way, you'll be welcome to come back here."

"I'll take care of her, Grandma. You won't have to do anything. I promise."

"Yeah," the old woman stated with sarcasm. "I've heard that story plenty of times before."

"I'm sorry I did what I did with Jimmy, Grandma. But you're getting two things mixed up. If you don't run away from some bad choice you make, then I think something good can come instead."

Gemma hadn't given up hope even after she'd gotten a job waitressing. Even after she'd sublet a room in an old, dilapidated house with three other girls. Even after the first time she'd held her own tiny, slippery daughter in tremulous arms. *If only Grandma would look at her. I wish she could see what I see.*

But Doreen Hardeman had never come to see the baby.

Now they'd been turned away from Mrs. Bartling's house, too. Fear edged its way into Gemma's spirit. They had nothing to eat for their next meal. They didn't know a soul in this strange town and nightfall was fast approaching.

Gemma and Paisley walked toward downtown Ash Hollow without talking, green acorns crunching every few steps beneath their feet, the suitcase and the jackets bumping against Gemma's left knee. The sun was beginning to sink behind the grasslands, turning the sky the soft, gray color of a kitten. Overhead in the trees, katydids had begun to hum.

Paisley kicked an acorn. It bounced onto the grass. "Why didn't we stay there, Mama?"

"Because she didn't ask us."

"Why didn't she ask us?"

"Because she doesn't know who we are."

"Oh." That brought on a long measure of silence. Then, "Are we going home now, Mama?"

Gemma shook her head. "Where's that, Paisley Rose? Where are you thinking that we've got a home?"

"It was a home. Where we lived with Nathan. I liked my bed."

Gemma tousled her hair. "It wasn't a bed at all, little girl. It was a breakfast table in a camper with the benches folded down."

"I liked it when you made spaghetti and we had candles. I liked it when Nathan put a sock on his hand and came up over the table like a puppet. I liked it when Nathan cooked supper and tucked me in."

"Yeah." Gemma backhanded her eyes. "I liked it, too."

The mention of supper filled Gemma with new despair. She had no idea where she could scrounge up their next meal. She had no idea where they would sleep tonight.

All the miles they'd driven, all the times they'd slept at roadside parks or the car had acted like it was about to blow up, the only thing she'd aimed for was that one moment—climbing the steps to Mrs. Bartling's house, knocking on the door, saying, "My name is Gemma and I've come to meet you. I'm Nathan's wife."

You should have come home a long time ago, Nathan.

Gemma felt cold panic start somewhere between her shoulder blades and trickle down her spine. Fear swamped her. *Where are we going to sleep? My daughter has no food.*

They walked on a little further before she was able to

keep her voice even enough to say, "We can't go back to that place in Omaha. Not anymore."

"Why not?"

"Nathan had that place because of working at the meat plant. Now that he's gone, somebody else gets to live there. Somebody else who works at the meat plant."

"Somebody else gets to sleep in my bed?"

It wasn't a bed. Only a table with two benches folded down. "Yeah, some other little girl."

The only two places in town she knew how to find were the gas station and the museum. "You tired?" Paisley's legs were short and they'd walked a long way.

Paisley nodded.

"We're almost to the museum. You want to stop?"

"What's at a museum?"

A mosquito buzzed Gemma's ear but, because she had too many other worries, she didn't bother to swat it away. "Things to look at. A place to rest."

Paisley kicked another acorn. "Yeah, let's go there."

The museum, when they found it, was built of large sandstone blocks, whitewashed and gleaming, with a steep, pitched roof and weathered shingles overlaying one another like scales on a wide-mouth bass. The sign on the front door read "Free to the public. Summer Hours: 9 A.M. to 8 P.M. Winter Hours: By appointment only."

They entered and were met with the pungent, magic smell of old, cherished things. No one greeted them at the reception desk.

"Hello?" Gemma stood on tiptoe and lifted her chin, trying to spot the museum proprietor. "Anybody here?"

No one answered.

Gemma and Paisley waited for five minutes or so. When still nobody came, they took it upon themselves to amble into the cavernous exhibit room filled with spotlights and mannequins and a labyrinth of glass cases. Once inside, they found any number of amazing items on display. A pair of wire-rimmed spectacles and a pocket watch and a business log belonging to a man named Cy Frates who had founded the Ash Hollow bank. A headless mannequin wearing a lace wedding dress. A pair of salt and pepper shakers shaped like someone's false teeth, the salt pot constituting the upper jaw, the pepper pot constituting the lower.

"Would you want that on your table?" Gemma asked in a hushed voice.

"It looks like it would bite."

They perused two ancient fire trucks, a wing from a biplane with a placard that read, "First known crop duster in Nebraska," and three volumes of black leather-bound ledgers, hand lettered with a fountain pen and an inkpot, of cash receipts from the Lewellen Country Store. They discovered a collection of wicker doll buggies, a primitive operating table, and a shelf of apothecary jars—some still labeled—containing moldy black stains.

Since they'd arrived in the museum, their conversations had continued in barely audible whispers. A certain reverence seemed in order. Here, lost among old-fashioned belongings and treasures, Gemma's panic ebbed. It became possible to forget their plight for a while, to forget how far they had come and how desperate they were and how Mrs. Bartling had turned them away.

"What's that?" Paisley asked softly.

"It's a row-crop plow, drawn by horses. And that's an X-ray machine."

The second mannequin they happened past wore a

brown velvet shirtwaist and a traveling skirt. Someone had set a wicker valise alongside to give the impression of a person just arrived on a train. For the time being, this seemed as good a place as any to stow their suitcase. Gemma piled the jackets and their own luggage next to the valise—a modern, plastic, pink bag flanking the historic wicker one. Ah. It felt wonderful not to be carrying things.

They found themselves in the middle of a reconstructed kitchen with a cast-iron meat grinder and spice tins in a row. A brass plaque on the wall read "The Willa Cather rooms." A washtub hung from its handle beside a nickel-plated stove. Paisley whispered, "We're in somebody's house."

"I can see that."

But they weren't in the house where Gemma had dreamed of being welcomed. They weren't in the house where Gemma had thought they might, in some form or fashion, find a new home.

"Oh, Mama. Come look." Paisley had found the parlor. In the middle stood a table set with embroidered linen napkins and china plates, each of them scalloped around the edges like a seashell. Curlicues of silver adorned each fork, knife, and spoon. Everything lay polished and clean, as if someone had just arranged the table to her satisfaction and supper was nearly ready to come out of the oven.

After being so soundly turned away from the Bartling household, it seemed strange to stand in the midst of such a welcoming room. Gemma placed a fist beneath her breast, touching the big lump of emptiness that welled inside her. She sighed and dropped her fist. "It's pretty, isn't it?"

"I wish we lived in a house like this. Mama, her house is like this."

"Who?"

But Gemma already knew. Mrs. Bartling's house.

"She's got dishes, and fancy forks and glasses that ring when you thump your fingers on them."

"Paisley. You don't know that. You didn't see them."

"But I can *think* about them."

"No sense talking about things that don't matter."

"She had a candle that smelled like oranges and a glass bottle of lotion and a box of matches."

"Why were you worrying about her matches? You know you mustn't touch matches."

"I didn't touch them, Mama. I just *looked.* The same as we're doing here."

From somewhere in the distance, Gemma heard the jangle of keys. She glanced up. "It must be nearly closing time. We'd better leave." *But where will we go?*

"I don't want to leave. I like it here."

"We'll come back another day."

"Please, Mama."

"No."

Gemma took Paisley by the hand and pulled her along, starting out the way they'd come, weaving to and fro among the display cases, past the traveling suit and the luggage, where she gathered their belongings.

"Mama, I'm hungry."

"Me, too."

"Are we going to eat?"

She finally had to say it, finally had to admit her failure—she didn't have the means to care for them any longer. "I don't think so." Gemma had seen a coffee shop down the street. Perhaps they'd let her sweep up tonight or wash dishes in exchange for a meal. "We don't have any money left. I spent the rest at the Kwik Stop."

Paisley was quiet for two minutes, probably thinking about no supper. "Mama, I'm scared."

Those three, simple, anxious words magnified Gemma's desolation tenfold. *Everything I've done up until now, I've done to protect my child.* It all came down to this. She had let her daughter down again. *Paisley doesn't feel protected when she says "I'm scared."*

Gemma heard sharp footsteps, the closing of a door. The lights had been dimmed in the front room by the desk, but the spotlights still glowed.

"I wish Nathan was here, Mama."

"Sometimes I think he is. Sometimes I think he still looks at us, that he's gone somewhere but he can still see us here."

"Do you think, if he sees us, that he's happy or sad?"

Gemma thought about that. "Both. I think he's both."

They'd gotten to the front of the museum, but the reception desk was still empty. Gemma glanced around and couldn't find a soul. "I don't know why no one is ever at this desk."

"Mama, it's dark in here."

"Well, it is. I don't know what's—" She stopped. She glanced around them as the truth began to dawn. "Wait." Gemma ran to the door and tried the handle. It rattled, but didn't open. "*Wait.*"

"Mama?"

"Hey." She rattled the door again. "Don't leave. We're in here."

Paisley had trailed toward her, her head of disheveled curls appearing out of nowhere at Gemma's side. Together they peered out the window. Together they banged on the glass.

"Hey! We're locked in. Let us out!"

No one came. Outside, the one strong floodlight illuminated a yard sign that read, "Garden County Pioneer Museum." The street was empty, the parking lot bare.

There would be no supper for Paisley, no finding anyone to help. The police would be summoned and they'd be arrested for breaking and entering. Only they hadn't broken in. They'd been here, not trying to hide from anyone at all.

Gemma trudged back to the desk, Paisley in tow, wondering if they might set off alarms. She almost wished they would. Then somebody could come and find them. Gemma held her breath, waiting for something to happen, for lights to start flashing or cameras to blink on or for the loud trill of a security system to announce their presence. But no sound shattered the stillness, not noises or beeps or buzzers.

"Looks like we're going to be here a while," Gemma said, falling back into a whisper.

"Mama? Why are we whispering? Nobody can hear us."

"You're right." Gemma straightened her shoulders somewhat and raised her voice, with just a hint of reassurance in her smile. "No one can hear us at all."

"Can we go back now? To see those rooms?"

Gemma considered before she answered. "I don't think so. We ought to sit right here where we won't cause any trouble." Or where, if someone walked past on the sidewalk outside, they could pound on the glass and make themselves known.

Side by side they sat on the floor and bunched their knees beneath their chins. Side by side they waited on a hard wooden floor until their leg bones ached and their bottoms went numb. They clasped their shins, laced their fingers, and rocked back and forth, back and forth. After a while, Paisley gave up. She leaned her head against her mother's thigh and yawned.

"You getting sleepy?"

A wordless nod bunched Gemma's skirt.

Gemma did her best to think ahead. Perhaps if she rummaged through the drawers in the reception desk, she might find something to help them. Maybe a package of saltines. A candy bar. A key. But it seemed slightly dishonest, rummaging through somebody else's things, and she didn't want to set a shameless example. She didn't want Paisley to be disappointed, most of all, in case she found nothing there.

She would search the desk after Paisley fell asleep.

"I'll tell you what. I don't guess it would hurt any if we had a look at those rooms again."

"Really?"

"Let's do."

Gemma gathered Paisley against her, heart to heart, their arms intertwined, the little girl's legs locked in a vise around the brim of her mother's hips, the dead weight of her tired body twice as heavy to carry.

This time, as Gemma lugged her daughter through the odd assortment of antiques, the museum didn't feel magical anymore. She set Paisley down in the parlor beside the table that had been laid out to perfection and fingered one of the forks.

We've found a safe, warm place for tonight. Just for tonight.

Tomorrow would take care of itself when it came.

The only room they hadn't viewed was the bedroom. Gemma bent around the corner and peeked in. A scrolled wrought-iron bed with both a headboard and a footboard, swathed in a crocheted coverlet and set dead center in the room; a chair made of black cowhide and a jumble of antelope horn; white lace curtains covering an imaginary window; a rusty milk can in the corner holding a clump of Nebraska grama grass, Indian tobacco, and cattails.

"Oh, Mama," Paisley breathed. "Let's pretend this is our house and we live here. Can we?"

Gemma didn't hesitate for more than a moment. "Yes, let's pretend."

They untied their shoes, pushed them off with their toes, and climbed on the bed.

Looks could be deceiving. The bed wasn't as squashy as they'd hoped. What Gemma had expected to be a soft mattress with hay ticking was really only a wooden platform with thick linens spread over it to make it appear cozy.

But the pillows were real, and if Paisley curled herself tight and tucked her knees against her belly, she could just fit her socks and feet beneath the two jackets that Gemma arranged over her.

"Are you going to stay warm enough, little one?"

Paisley nodded into the monogrammed pillowcase, her eyes already half closed.

Gemma stretched out beside her daughter and they snuggled, their bodies nesting against each other like two ladles.

She whispered, "I love you, Paisley."

"I love you, too," Paisley whispered back.

Gemma lay against her daughter in the room where they shouldn't be, trying not to hear their stomachs growl, trying not to give in to the wave of emptiness that terrified her more than anything thus far. Then, half because it was true, and half because it made her feel lonely to think of Paisley falling off to sleep yet, she said, “Your toes are sticking out again. Here. Let me get them underneath the coats.”

She folded the hem and sleeves of her jacket around Paisley’s little wrinkled socks.

Paisley smiled and whispered against the pillow. “This is just like Nathan used to do, Mama. This is just how he always tucked me in.”

Chapter Seven

Paisley and Gemma awakened the next morning to the not-so-hushed conversation of someone else exploring the Garden County Pioneer Museum.

"Would you look at this china, Ardis? It's wonderful."

"Such a shame no one uses pretty things like this anymore, isn't it? Got a whole cabinet full, but I never get it out. Can't bear using something that doesn't go in the dishwasher."

"Oh, but it sets a lovely table, doesn't it? And it brings back such lovely memories. Oh, my—"

Gemma rolled to one side, nuzzling her jaw deep into the old feather pillow. She opened one eye. Two women gawked at her through the open doorway.

"There's someone asleep in here," one of them shushed.

The other gave an awful hoot. "They're defacing the Cather exhibit!"

With languid slowness, Gemma rolled onto her back, doddering on the edge of a night's luxurious sound sleep. Her arm curled tightly over her daughter. She reveled in the little girl's breathing, heavy and even and moist against her left shoulder.

"Heaven's to Betsy, Ardis. We've got to do something about this."

It took Gemma a good minute or so to acknowledge the implication of the two terrified museum patrons in the doorway. She came fully awake. "Wait."

"Mrs. Perkins!" The women fled into the annals of the glass display cases and fire trucks and mannequins, each of them bellowing in a very unladylike way. "Mrs. Perkins, there's someone *sleeping* in Willa Cather's bed!"

Gemma sat up, swung her feet to the floor. "Don't. Please wait."

She had meant to stay alert last night, wide awake, so she could protect Paisley. When she'd gone back to search the desk drawers after Paisley had drifted off to sleep, she had found nothing useful, only heaps of papers and crumpled files, one gold earring, and a tube of Chap Stick half melted away. Against one wall, she had discovered a nook with cabinets and cups and a miniature refrigerator. The refrigerator hadn't even been turned on. The cabinets were empty except for several foil packets of coffee, filters, and one tall jar of powdered creamer.

Gemma had shaken some of the creamer from the jar and mixed it with warm water from the faucet. Then she'd carried it back to Paisley and awakened her, coaxing her gently to drink the concoction so her stomach wouldn't be empty. Even as Gemma had fallen off to sleep later, unable to ward off her own exhaustion, she'd vowed to wake up early, to have them both well hidden before anyone discovered them.

In their roaming among the displays last night, she and Paisley had encountered a menagerie of ancient pendulum clocks. Not one of them had worked. She'd depended on noises outside to awaken her. She sat on the bed now and heard them, the sounds of Ash Hollow already come to life—traffic whooshing past on First Street, dogs yapping, a garbage truck making the rounds.

Paisley sat up, too, scrubbing her sleepy eyes and whimpering as a mad ruckus began somewhere near the reception area of the museum. They heard hollering and loud chattering. "Call *The Garden County News*, Ardis. They'll want to get our picture." From the reception desk, Gemma made out the sound of automatic dial on speakerphone, the clatter of a telephone receiver being dropped to the floor.

"Jay. Mabel Perkins here. Someone's broken in . . . How should I know if anything's been stolen? I haven't gotten the chance to look around . . . No. No, I haven't noticed anything vandalized . . . No. There aren't any signs of forced entry. Not that I can see . . . Will you stop asking questions and get over here, Jay? They could be armed and dangerous. They're *still here*."

Within seconds, the wail of a siren split the morning melody of Ash Hollow. In the reception area of the museum, all went deathly quiet, a sure sign they'd decided to avoid confrontation until the law arrived. Gemma's hands shook as she folded the jackets neatly and stowed them atop the suitcase. They'd been caught. There wasn't any way out of this mess now. She neatened the bed, although they'd both slept so hard that the linens hadn't even gotten overly mussed. The siren grew louder and then slid downscale to a loud, frightening halt somewhere outside. She adjusted her filthy skirt, which had twisted halfway around her legs, then hunkered forward and tried to finger comb a rat's-nest tangle out of Paisley's hair before the arresting officer arrived.

This is exactly how Sheriff's Deputy Jay Triplett

found them when he jumped through the door of the parlor, his hat slung with low menace over his eyes, his pistol drawn. He swaggered in with his face registering annoyance, towering a good eighteen inches over Gemma, his shoulders as broad as the badlands in the crisp, pocketed shirt he wore. His uniform lent him the appearance of brute authority. A nightstick dangled at his side. His name badge and county insignia and an array of medals dazzled even in the muted light. Paisley clung to her mama's leg in mute fear.

Deputy Triplett took one long look at Gemma, surveying her from the top of her snarled hair to the tips of her toes. Up to down, then down to up again. "Well, good morning," he drawled, his words a careful measure of dispassion. "You got people out there riled up, you know that?"

Just one nod, just one slight upward tilt of Gemma's nose. "I know that."

"You also know that you are trespassing. You know that you are breaking the law."

Gemma didn't say anything to that. She just stood, her eyes meeting his condemning gaze head on.

"Well." He straightened his back somewhat and took a deep breath that paunched out the buckle on his belt. He drummed his fingers on the handle of the pistol as if he didn't quite know what to do with them, then jutted his jaw in the direction of the silverware. "You come in here to steal something? There's a lot of stuff in this place worth plenty of money."

"We aren't criminals—" Gemma eyed his name badge. "—Deputy Triplett."

"You want to tell me how you and your little girl here got into the museum last night?"

Because she had been preparing for this, Gemma

found the presence of mind to match his slow, measured words. She met his gaze defiantly, eye to eye. "Put your gun away. Please. You're frightening my daughter."

His eyes wrinkled at the corners as if he had to try hard to keep his eyebrows narrowed. He smacked his mouth, evidence that he saw her and her small daughter as a great aggravation, and holstered his pistol. "I'll tell you what," he suggested. "You answer my questions, I'll put away my gun." He took one step toward her, approaching her the same way he'd approach a cornered badger—as if she might suddenly snarl and leap at him.

"We're in here because we got locked in."

"You sure about that?"

"Ask that lady out front. She wasn't at the desk last night. Nobody saw us come in. We went into the exhibit room to look at things for a while. It got to be closing time. Nobody even knew we were here."

"That seems a mighty lame excuse for breaking and entering."

"All those old clocks back there, and not a one of them tells what time it is."

He hooked his huge fingers inside his heavy, black leather belt and all the cases and leather snap pockets that hung there rasped with the movement. "Ma'am, you and your kid have got to come with me. I've got to take you up front there and fill out about five hundred duplicate forms."

With chin raised and eyes fixed straight ahead, Gemma marched through the ornate parlor with Paisley straggling along, one hand still on her mama's leg. "We played pretend after we got locked in," Paisley told the officer. "We pretended we didn't have anywhere else to go to sleep."

Out of the mouths of babes. Gemma glanced back

and surveyed the officer's broad expanse of medals and badges and ammunition cases. She thought she saw his expression soften but she couldn't be sure.

When they arrived at the welcome desk, the smell of scorched coffee stung Gemma's nose. Another pot was being brewed on the Bunn Burner against the wall, the stream of brown liquid trickling merrily into the round carafe below. Beside that, making these morning refreshments seem even more heartbreaking, stood the tall jar of Carnation Coffee-mate she had used for Paisley's makeshift milk the night before. Beside that sat a red plate of homemade sticky buns.

Warm cinnamon oozed in rivulets down the sides of the coiled, baked dough. Pecans had been sprinkled with hearty abandon amidst gooey glaze. The pastries smelled like heaven—yeasty like bread and sweet enough to send Gemma's stomach into tumults. She heard Paisley's belly give a deep rumble. Without stopping to think about being under arrest, Gemma reached her fingers to take a sticky bun.

Mabel Perkins swatted furiously at her. "Don't touch those."

Gemma jerked her hand back.

"Jay, you've got to get these . . . these *felons* out of the building. They ought to be handcuffed. If nothing else, they have disturbed the displays."

But Deputy Triplett wasn't listening to Mabel Perkins. Gemma noticed he'd begun watching her face instead, as if he wanted to gauge her reaction to something. His eyes conveyed deep kindness, concern. "Can you tell me something? Have you two eaten any time recently?"

She shook her head, furious at herself because she couldn't keep tears from welling in her eyes. "No," she said, her voice gone soft and yearning and sad. "We haven't."

Gemma watched the deputy turn back to the gathering of local biddies, all of them obviously awaiting some severe verdict from him. "I don't think these two girls need to be arrested, Mabel. I think they need to find somewhere they can take a warm bath and eat a square meal."

"Oh, this is ridiculous. They were sleeping in the Cather rooms. Surely you're going to write them up or something."

"Yes, I'm going to write them up. I'm assuming you're going to insist on pressing charges."

"Of course I'm going to press charges. Someone around here needs to protect Garden County property."

"Well," he said. "Let's hurry and do this then. Let's fill out the papers so they can be on their way."

Ardis chimed in, obviously incensed. "Jay. You can't just write them up and let them go."

"I'm not going to let them go, Mrs. Jacobs. I'm going to release them into someone's care." He raised his eyebrows pointedly at Mabel again. "Someone in Ash Hollow who might be kind enough to let them eat a few sticky buns."

Mabel Perkins let out one long, disgruntled sigh. "Oh, all right. But I made those buns myself." She checked her wristwatch. "They were supposed to be for the tour group we have coming through in half an hour."

Gemma watched, stone-faced again, while the deputy found two heavy chairs and aligned them along the wall. He thumped the seat of the nearest one with his big hand so Paisley would know it was acceptable to climb up and sit down. He handed her a napkin with three sticky buns on it and turned to Gemma. "You want coffee?"

She shook her head.

"Buns?"

She nodded and her throat went so tight she thought she might cry again.

The deputy didn't talk for a while after that. He let them each take time to eat. When they'd almost finished, he rose, his knees cracking, his nightstick swaying. "I'll be right back."

Gemma sat staring at Mabel Perkins and Ardis Jacobs and the other nameless biddy. The three of them sat staring unabashedly right back at her. Now that Deputy Triplett had gone outside, they did not utter a word. Gemma wished for the officer to return. The uniformed man, who only minutes ago had seemed an enemy, now seemed a protector instead. If she jumped right now, or made some sudden movement, she got the feeling all three of these little ladies would jump, too.

"Here we go." The deputy stomped back in the door, whistling, with a clipboard, a stack of carbon papers, and a pen in hand. "Just had to go out to the patrol car and get these."

Now that he'd returned, it seemed the three ladies had plenty more to say. "You should call Social Services, Jay. They'll send Jane Rounsborg. She always takes care of the difficult cases."

"No, silly. Jane only takes care of the county cases. These—" Ardis gestured toward them. "—are not from Garden County."

"Remember when the town council wanted to establish that shelter? Well, this is the reason. So people won't come to sleep in our *museum*."

"As soon as you know it, homeless people will be moving into the library, too."

"Oh, they've already moved into the library. You know Dave Morris? He lives at the library. He wears that fedora and pedals his bicycle against traffic and pays all his overdue fines with two dollar bills."

"That's different. He has a house. He just doesn't like to go home to it."

"The only thing he's got to complain about is that Alva yells when he goes home. She gets mad because he doesn't ride on the right side of the road."

The deputy laid his hat on the floor beside him and poised pen over paper. He smelled like leather. His hair had a furrow in it from where his cap had been, and Gemma sensed that, for the first time in a long while, she had found a friend.

"You up to answering questions for this report?"

She nodded, her mouth full, and pulled Paisley across the chair into her lap.

"Good." His stiff leathers creaked and all the little compartments on his belt waggled when he sat in the chair beside her. He waited, pen in hand. "Name?"

She gave him her maiden one, not wanting to burden Mrs. Bartling any more than she already had. "Gemma Franklin."

"Do you live in Ash Hollow, Gemma?"

"No." She propped her chin atop Paisley's head, willing her eyes to remain dry. "We don't."

"What's your address?"

She shook her head. "We don't have one."

"No?"

"We had a place, my husband and I. But he died and I—" She broke off.

He glanced at her left hand, at the simple gold band she still wore. "You lost the place?"

Gemma nodded.

"You on your way somewhere?"

"My car broke down on the highway."

He bit the end of the pen. "That your Toyota Corolla we found out there yesterday?"

She nodded again.

"Well, that answers a few questions, too," he said, sounding relieved. "We ran a check and knew that car was registered to a woman. And we found a Barbie on the floor in the back. We were wondering if you were okay."

Her eyes leveled on his. "I'm fine."

"Lots of folks do that here, you know. This place was on the Oregon Trail. Wagons lost wheels. Oxen died. Roses bloomed. And folks just stayed. Else we wouldn't have a town named Ash Hollow at all."

"Makes for a nice story."

"So, you looking for work here or something? Or are you planning to move on?"

She and Paisley were by themselves, on their own, and the time had come for Gemma to accept that. She leaned back in the chair and inhaled deeply. "Back in Omaha, I was a waitress. The only thing I could think of, maybe I could find work at that place down the street. Maybe I could wash dishes and earn a place to live, or some food, until we get back on our feet."

He poked his pen back inside his pocket. "I tell you what I'm going to do about you. I'm going to call George Sissel over at Antelope Valley Church."

Gemma hugged Paisley closer. "You're going to call a preacher? What for?"

"George Sissel isn't just any preacher. He's . . . well, he's . . . *George*."

Mabel Perkins jumped in again. "You can't expect George to let these vagrants move in."

"I'm not talking about him taking them in to his house, Mabel. I was thinking maybe the church could do a little something."

"George won't let them move into the fellowship hall, either. They might steal something. I'll bet they've got over three thousand dollars worth of canned goods and clothes stacked in boxes over there. You know. That huge end-of-school food drive they have every year."

It seemed as if the deputy hadn't heard a word of it. He donned his wire-rimmed aviator sunglasses as if he didn't want to see Mabel Perkins anymore and lifted the telephone receiver, stopping with his finger poised to dial.

"And just who was that food drive for, Mabel? Tell me that."

Mabel raised her chin. "Homeless people."

He smiled again, satisfied. "You can't very well steal something if it's already been given to you as a gift."

Chapter Eight

Bea sat in Ray's old, lumpy La-Z-Boy recliner, her quilted robe gathered around her breastbone with one determined fist, her feet propped up, the afghan spread over her legs, and glared across the room at the ancient Sneed family Bible.

The mammoth black-bound book lay closed and dusty on the oval coffee table beside the July issue of *Good Housekeeping* and the current edition of the *TV Guide*. Its embossed leather cover laid split and broken on the larboard side, its pages dog eared, its cowhide worn to a smooth sheen by four generations of her family's hands. Almost halfway through, a black satin bookmark parted the worn leaves, the gold edges gone, marking some long-forgotten psalm.

Lately, Bea had found it difficult even to muster enough energy to dress for the day. There she sat, the pad of her thumb against her lips, staring at the Bible she'd read through, cover to cover, many times in many years. How well she knew what it said.

Pray unceasingly . . . Ask and it shall be given . . . Seek and ye shall find . . . Knock and the door shall be opened.

Bea shed the afghan and set the recliner aright. She picked up the Bible and opened it to the first page. The births, deaths, and marriages of her mother's family, starting with the marriage of her great-grandmother Margaret Louise Sneed, had all been documented here, first in her great-grandmother's painstaking hand, then her mother's hand, and then in her own. Different handwritings and different shades of faded ink. Covenants made. Babies born. Families united.

Families torn asunder.

Here, in her own judicious handwriting, Bea had declared with guileless joy the bright beginnings of her life with Ray—the date of her wedding, the date of her son's arrival. Here she'd filled in Nathan's birthday, never guessing the time would come when she'd be expected to fill in the date of Nathan's death as well.

How complicated Bea's own entries in the Bible had become. How did one document a divorce within these solemn pages? How did one record the loss of a child? How did one record the day-to-day decisions that made up a life, a history? The trivial details that made life both grand and heartbreaking? The only spaces provided here were meant for names, places, dates, marriages, deaths. But so much else happened in between.

Bea closed the Bible with a resounding thwack and set it on the table. She propped her forehead on her fingertips.

Nothing good ever came out of that Bible for me. A lot of warm feelings and hope, maybe, but when it mattered most, none of those parables or messages or love poems ever applied to my life.

Outside she could hear children shrieking and talking. She gave one resigned sigh, stood again, and sauntered down the hallway to find clothes. She opened the closet door and stared indifferently at the row of skirts and trousers, caring little what she chose to wear.

The ranks of garments disappeared as she stared at them and for one haunting moment she saw instead the yearning, uplifted faces of one small girl and one young woman halting in her dark hallway, eyes riveted to a kindergarten picture hanging on the wall.

How old was he in this?

Is that Nathan, Mama? When he was a little boy?

Heaviness engulfed Bea, a darkness of mourning that settled over her shoulders like a weighty cloak. She felt unable to lift or move or breathe.

If Nathan had married that girl, then that girl had something of Nathan's that Bea would never have.

His last five years.

Nathan would have carried things too heavy for Gemma and reached things that were too high. Gemma would have listened to his goofy, off-pitch songs while he showered and watched him make sideways faces against his jaw while he shaved and chastised him for gulping milk out of the carton while his Adam's apple bobbed criminally up and down. Gemma's toothbrush would have stood handle to handle with Nathan's toothbrush. If he'd ever been angry or happy or concerned about something, Gemma would have known.

At that moment the telephone rang from the nightstand across the room. The shrill bell made Bea's heart stop. Ever since she'd been startled out of sleep with the dire news of Nathan's death, any ringing of the telephone and any knocking on the door had the power to terrify her. When it rang now, Bea gave herself a list of careful instructions. *Cross the room. Carry the phone back to the closet. Draw a deep breath, and answer.* She leaned hard against the closet wall. "Hello?"

"Hello, Bea? This is Geneva. What are you doing?"

There. See. No reason to panic. Only Geneva. She tucked the receiver inside the crook of her shoulder and willed her pounding pulse to slow down. Meticulously, she began to slide hangers along the rod. "I'm trying to pick out something to wear."

"How are you?"

"Okay. I mean, better. I suppose."

"Glad to hear it. Bea, I'm really glad." A pause, now that quick pleasantries were taken care of. Geneva's phone calls always began this way. "You up for the latest news? You aren't going to believe what I just heard."

"Well, I—"

As Geneva was wont to do, she didn't give Bea much of an opportunity to respond. Instead, she plunged right in, eager to expound before anyone else got the chance to scoop her.

"A group of hoodlums broke in over at the pioneer museum."

"No. Oh, goodness, Geneva." What dainty morsels rumors were. "Those things *never* happen here." Bea knew everybody in town, including Geneva, expected her to be engrossed in daily Ash Hollow happenings. She should *try* to sound interested.

But, today, trying took too much effort.

Bea sorted through the hangers once more. Two-thirds of the outfits here, just as in every other closet in Garden County, had come from the factory outlet store in Oshkosh, the home of Cabela's catalog returns. Bea settled on a pair of navy knit pants from Cabela's, so worn that they would have been better off going into the ragbag. She pulled them off the hanger and said nothing.

"Ardis Jacobs told me about it. She was there going

through the exhibits. Nobody knows if they stole anything yet. You know what it's like in that place. All those square feet and they're still looking for space to display Francis Clupney's Korean War memorabilia and Jason Stone's guitar collection. It could take years to figure out if anything's missing."

"Geneva, I'm sorry. I'm just not up to gossip right now. There's too much else going on in my head."

Humph, she could almost hear Geneva say. This wouldn't sit too well with her friend. And she was right. Geneva waited several long moments before replying. "I know it's got to be difficult. But you can't close out the world, Bea."

"I know I can't."

"But you are."

Bea decided on a plaid shirt from Cabela's, the cotton rubbed as thin as gauze at the elbows. She took it off the hanger and sat down hard on the dirty clothes hamper between a pile of folded blankets and her jumble of rubber-soled walking shoes. "I'm trying not to."

Silence again from Geneva on the other end of the phone—the potent, blame-filled sort that, in its wordlessness, says "Oh no, you aren't!" Bea sighed, determined to ask some sort of question just to prove Geneva wrong. "What happened to those people? Did they get arrested?"

Geneva forged ahead then, sounding thrilled to be back on track. "You won't believe this when I tell you. Jay Triplett wrote up a formal complaint because Mabel Perkins insisted on protecting county property. But, in the middle of all that, he made Mabel Perkins feed them her famous sticky buns. Ardis said they ate like animals, growling and shoving food into their mouths like they hadn't seen any for weeks."

"My heavens. Those things *never* happen here."

"Ardis thought they ought to all be toted down to the county jail, but Jay called George Sissel instead. Pastor came right over, met them, and invited them to move in for a few days."

"To the church?"

"No! To his house."

"Oh, goodness." In spite of herself, Bea decided this *was* turning into an interesting story. First the museum and now Pastor George. If George was involved, perhaps she ought to step outside of herself and find a way to help. "How many are staying over at Sissel's? I've got casseroles in the deep freeze and I'll never eat them all. I could certainly donate a few to the cause."

At that question Geneva paused. "You know, I'm not sure how many."

"You do, too, Geneva. I can tell by your voice. Six? Ten? What?"

While she waited for Geneva's answer, Bea balanced the receiver beneath one ear and began to tug the pants on, working first on one leg and then the other. She lifted her rear end off the laundry hamper and maneuvered them all the way on. She could tell by the waistband of the pants that she'd lost pounds. All those casseroles to eat, and she still couldn't force herself to choke down much of a meal.

The hollow within her wasn't something that could be filled with food.

"How many?" Bea asked again.

Geneva's voice sounded rather cagey when she spoke up this time. "Actually, I may have exaggerated. A little."

"Geneva. Tell me."

"Well, actually . . . I only know of two."

"*Two?*"

"And one is a small girl. A very small girl."

Bea's heart gamboled forward double time. Apprehension sluiced through her. *It couldn't be. No.*

"Two." Bea began to fasten the mother-of-pearl buttons on her shirt. Her hands shook violently and she couldn't work the buttons through the buttonholes. She asked the question carefully, making it sound like an afterthought. "What does she look like?"

"Who?"

"The very small girl."

Nathan would have lugged in bags of groceries for Gemma whenever she went to the store. Gemma would have smoothed out the pillow every morning that bore the indentation of Nathan's head. Gemma would have held his athletic socks up, heel to heel, to make certain they matched before she bundled them both together. Gemma would have brought him an aspirin and a Pepsi in bed whenever he got the flu.

"How should I know what she looks like? I haven't seen her. I've only heard about her. That's the way gossip is."

For some vague reason Bea felt protective. "Maybe you ought to learn from that, Geneva. Maybe you ought not to talk about folks until you've seen them with your own eyes." She shoved her foot into a shoe and wiggled it sideways until her heel went in, her heart wavering dangerously between anger and mistrust. Where before she had struggled to sound interested, she now fought for nonchalance. She asked Geneva with forced looseness, "Who are those two? Where have they come from? Do you know?"

"Well, listen to you asking questions now, Bea. I didn't think you cared about any of this."

"Did you hear a name? Any name?"

She heard Geneva rummaging around in her own cabinets, running water, finishing her own chores. "Not sure. Gemma. Gemma somebody. That's all I remember of a name."

"Gemma?"

"Yes, I think that's it."

"Did you happen to hear? Are they from Omaha?"

"I didn't hear where they come from."

Their coats would have hung side by side, Gemma's and Nathan's, on two hooks beside the door. The magazines Nathan best liked to read when he got stuck for a while in the bathroom—*Reader's Digest* and *Sports Illustrated*—would have driven Gemma crazy, splayed out in a jumble on the bathroom floor. The top drawer in his dresser would have been an untidy muddle of treasures he'd found—a pinecone, a cord switch, a pack of gum.

Too much had come upon Bea too quickly. Her emotions turned off. She did not *feel*, anymore than someone feels after receiving a grave cut. She felt tired and battered, as if someone had kicked her. Tired and battered and numb.

"Bea, don't you need to go lay down or something? You're sounding strange over the phone."

"I'm fine, Geneva." Bea struggled to bring the careful steadiness back into her voice. "I'm sitting right here on my laundry hamper putting on my shoes."

"Well, at least you're wearing shoes. That's a start. You're getting better by my book."

"I've worn shoes every day since Nathan died, Geneva. That doesn't have anything to do with it."

"I need to let you go, Bea. But I almost forgot to tell you the rest. Alva Torrington hired her on. Gave her a job so she can survive."

"Who? Who did Alva hire on?"

"That girl you ask so much about."

"Oh."

"She's waitressing over at The Cramalot Inn. She told Alva and Pastor George both that she'd only be around long enough to earn money to fix her car."

"They won't be here long, then."

"No. They won't. You know, you *could* call George Sissel and see if they need casseroles. That sounds like a nice thing to do."

"Talk to you later, Geneva."

"Bea. Good-bye."

For a long time after Bea hung up the phone, she sat staring into the deep annals of her closet. She could just make out her own reflection, distorted by the convex of the metal shoehorn hanging beside her—huge nose and lips, tiny forehead, pinpoint eyes.

She bent over and tied one shoestring into a perfect bow.

She tied the second shoestring the exact same way.

Chapter Nine

Sunday morning services at Antelope Valley Christian Fellowship in Oshkosh began promptly at 10:10 A.M.

Look it up in the Garden County Yellow Pages and the service officially began on the hour, at ten. Look it up in the Religion Section of *The Garden County News* and the listing there read exactly the same thing. But local folks all understood, no matter what any printed schedule told them, that Ash Hollow ran on High Prairie grassland time, and that meant things didn't get going good until fifteen minutes after everybody showed up.

If Bea attended church today for any reason at all, she attended out of pride.

It wouldn't do for her regular seat—fifth pew back, three spaces in—to remain conspicuously empty. It wouldn't do for the upstanding Christian folks in this town to notice she was absent. So she attended this morning's Sunday service with her chin up, her hat tilted at a spry angle, wearing her cheeriest summer dress and her bravest smile. She sat thumbing through the church bulletin, her eyes veering neither to the right nor to the left, while the sanctuary filled with noise around her and Jo Nell's heavy-handed organ music wafted to the rafters.

It was George Sissel himself who stopped beside her, laid a reassuring arm across her shoulders.

"Bea. Hello."

She stole a glance up at him, valiant smile pasted on, traitor tears glimmering. "Good morning, Pastor George."

"I'm glad you came today," he said, his gentle eyes peering deep into her soul. His entire demeanor seemed to say, "I know how hard it must be to sit here, to wear a hat with a flower, a lacy dress, a smile."

"I couldn't not be here today, Pastor George. Folks wouldn't forgive me if I didn't come."

"Oh, Bea. We would have understood if you weren't. You be careful with yourself. You let yourself heal."

"Do you think—" She bit her bottom lip. She'd been about to say, "Do you think I will ever heal, George?" Only she couldn't.

He sat down beside her for a moment while the organ music crescendoed, Jo Nell's obvious signal that she thought the pastor ought to be out of the congregation, behind the altar, preparing to conduct the service. "You know how God does things sometimes. When you give him free rein to be in charge, sometimes things get messy."

"Well, things sure are messy right now."

Once George had spoken with her, others began to speak to her, too. They came around the pew and hugged her, patted her shoulders or kissed her on the cheek—onslaughts of empathy shared without words.

Everyone around her greeted her or waved or smiled her way.

"It was such a nice funeral for Nathan. I hadn't gotten a chance to tell you yet."

"How are you faring? Better after this time?"

"Have you eaten Jan Blackwell's crumb cake she brought over? She's decided to enter it in the Garden County Fair."

At Bea's recommendation, Holechek Funeral Home had donated several dozen potted plants from Nathan's memorial service to the Garden County Senior Center. The ones that the senior center hadn't found room for had made their way to the church altar committee instead.

"Altar plants in memory of Nathan Roger Bartling," the bulletin read.

Bea stared at her son's name in print, at the words written there, hating them for what they said. She glanced up when the call to worship began and her breath caught. Across the aisle, she saw someone else staring at the bulletin, too.

Someone else who could be staring at Nathan's printed name.

Someone else with a red nose and a clenched jaw, battling tears.

George Sissel motioned with his arms. "Please stand for Hymn 307." Jo Nell pounded out the beginning strains of "Standing On The Promises."

There could be no mistaking that girl, even with her unruly hair tamed just a bit, even with her hands folded in her lap and her face washed, wearing a print dress that Bea recognized as borrowed from Loren Sissel. Even with her little girl burrowed up like a frightened puppy at her side. Bea peered out at both of them, her chest constricting, from beneath the safe haven of her hat brim.

Around her they sang, “Staaanding, staaanding, standing on the promises of God my Savior.”

A strangling sense of subjugation rose like bile in her throat. Familiar. Helpless. How easy it would be for some young woman to take advantage of a lonely old woman—to have read a random obituary in a paper and decided to redesign her life to fit.

Friends had delivered at least a dozen copies of Nathan’s obituary in *The Garden County News* to the house, the page either folded or snipped out or circled to mark the spot. She’d read the article over and over again, perusing the words from beginning to end before she tucked the story away in her old maple magazine rack, wanting to know if anything printed there would be enough to have given Nathan’s intimate past away.

> BARTLING—Nathan Roger . . . Born to Ray and Beatrice Bartling . . . fond of the Masonic Lodge pancake breakfasts on July Fourth . . . worked two summers at Garden County Country Club, another summer making milkshakes at Campbell Drug . . . a respected boy in his school, considerate, smart enough not to have to study to make *B*s and so he made *B*s . . . taken into custody once for shooting off firecrackers underneath a trashcan behind the church . . . won the carp-fishing contest at Otter Creek Marina when he was ten . . . known around town for his authentic goose call . . . a tragic loss to the community even though he hadn’t finished Lewellen Rural High School and had left town five years before.

Although some of these stories came close, nothing published here explained someone recognizing Nathan's kindergarten picture. Nothing explained someone knowing about Nathan getting his backside walloped for squeezing rose petals.

Small details to hinge a lifetime of hopes on.

Small details to risk trust on, when you'd spent the past twenty years trusting folks and fate and Jesus, all three of which had let you down.

The song in the little sanctuary rose to the roof beams. "Staaanding, staaanding, standing on the promises of God."

Nancy Law nudged Bea with an elbow. "Who is that girl down there? You ever seen her before?"

Bea swallowed. Hard. She stood in the middle of a church with her hymnal propped open in her palms, as good a reason as any she could think of to avoid telling a falsehood.

She did it anyway. "I don't know. Must be a visitor."

"You don't have any ideas about her, do you? You don't know who she is?"

"No." The lie didn't sit well with Bea's stomach.

"I'm thinking that must be the people the Sissels took in."

"Must be. Have you heard her name, Nancy? Is it something familiar?" *Is it Bartling, like mine?*

"Nothing familiar. Nobody knows anything about her. Can't believe Loren Sissel would allow a stranger in her house like that."

Bea pressed the backs of her knees hard against the seat. "Loren's the preacher's wife, Nancy. I think preacher's wives have to do things like that all the time. It's the 'angels unawares' Scripture."

"Oh, that one."

"'Do not forget to entertain strangers, for by so doing some people have entertained angels unaware.'"

The hymn ended and they all sat down. *She isn't a stranger to me. She came to my door and told me her name. She said she'd been married to my boy.*

And still I didn't take her in.

As luck would have it, George chose that moment to deliver the first of a long list of announcements. He spoke to his congregation about the worshipers who had gotten ticketed last week for parking on the grass. He made an urgent plea for people with extra cereal boxes and carpet squares to donate them immediately to the VBS committee. He led everyone in a prayer for Saul, a missionary in Guatemala, while Bea closed her eyes and bowed her head, the words running through her mind not the words being spoken from the pulpit at all. Her own spirit taunted her with words instead.

Is it not to deal thy bread to the hungry, and that thou bring the poor that are cast out to thy house? when thou seest the naked, that thou cover him; and that thou hide not thyself from thine own flesh?

Words she'd memorized long ago from the ancient black Sneed family Bible that jeered at her from the coffee table at home.

Listen to George's prayer, Beatrice. Don't let your mind wander like this. Your own mind will do nothing but get you into trouble.

Bea had always come to her prayers with an expectant heart, a childlike faith that counted on miracles. That had been the only way she'd ever known to approach her God. She picked up her church Bible from her lap, the thin modern one she'd purchased at the bookstore after she'd gotten tired of lugging the big one around. She held the book unopened, its weight overflowing her hand.

When she'd been young, she'd prayed for the right husband. When she'd met Ray, she'd sought the Lord's will while they were dating, when they'd gotten engaged, and after they'd gotten married. While she'd carried her child in her womb, feeling him kick with butterfly movements beneath her ribs, she had prayed, "This child is yours, Father. Keep him safe and healthy. Keep him for your purpose."

After Nathan had left, her knees had gone numb and raw from hours spent beside her bed. She remained loyal and expectant, her head bent in supplication, her soul uplifted to heaven. Sometimes her prayers had gone too profound for words. She'd simply gathered up all her yearning and held it there, throbbing and broken, for God to see.

Every time she remembered now how hard she'd prayed for Nathan's return, the memory carried her to yet another deeper rank of grief.

First her husband. Then her sons. Then her God.

A heavenly Father who had turned deaf ears to her prayer.

That girl isn't my own flesh and blood. I don't even know if she's telling me the truth.

Ray had once said that he believed people had a right to go in any direction they thought was right. They'd been on a trip to Arizona, standing where captured heat radiated into the cool morning from the sand, watching the sunrise from the east over the desert.

"Look at that, Beatrice!" Ray said, wrapping an arm around her shoulder and drawing her close. "Would you look at that!"

"Where?" She scanned the horizon, not understanding what he wanted her to see.

"There." He pointed. Across the morning desert came a Union Pacific freight train, sleek and straight on its track, cattle cars glinting like a length of silver yarn in the rising sun, threading closer. "See."

Bea could see a hobo riding high atop one of the cars, his head thrown back, sitting straddle-legged, going wherever the Union Pacific would take him. "He's got the right idea, I think."

Bea laughed sharply, uncomfortably. "I didn't know we really had hoboes anymore. I thought they were only on television and in stories."

"Oh, we still have them, all right." They waited the short while it took for the train to trundle past them. It passed so close, Bea thought Ray might lift his hand and wave at the man, only he didn't. "I feel so strange watching a man like that pass by," Ray said. "Like he's reminded me how freedom feels. I had forgotten."

"Freedom?"

"Just to follow the rails. To go any direction the train takes you. That fellow doesn't have a care in the world. Look at him. He knows what it's like to really live. Maybe we'd all get by better if we'd be willing to do that."

She couldn't keep silent. "You don't know a thing, Ray. Maybe he really wants a couple of kids. Maybe he wants a wife who gets up early to cook breakfast."

"It doesn't matter." When Ray glanced down at her, he still held that faraway expression in his eyes. "He doesn't get that." He pulled her tighter against him and kissed her hard on the lips. "Those things are all mine."

Bea forced herself to concentrate on the words echoing over the sound system. From the pulpit, the pastor happened to be reading a Scripture that felt every bit as derisive as the one playing through Bea's head. "I tell you the truth, if you have faith and do not doubt, not only can you do what was done to the fig tree, but also you can say to this mountain, 'Go, throw yourself into the sea,' and it will be done. If you believe, you will receive whatever you ask for in prayer."

Words. All of it is just words.

So many layers of hope . . . destroyed.

So much joy and anticipation . . . shattered.

I shouldn't have come to this place. I shouldn't be sitting here, with a Bible in my lap and my eyes closed, acting like I believe.

Bea opened her eyes and stared out the church window at the nothing sky.

The prayer ended and, horror of horrors, George Sissel gave everybody several minutes to leave their seats, shake hands, and greet visitors they might have overlooked the first time around. Bea felt the presence of the girl and her daughter as keenly as if some mystical, irrevocable bond tied her to them. She turned to her right, to her left, desperate to exchange pleasantries with anyone else who might be near and willing to jabber. But, like the parting of the Red Sea, folks moved away from her. Those two, the young woman and the waiflike child, stood conspicuously alone in the midst of a hugging, welcoming crowd. If she turned around, *oh, my*, she and Bea would be staring straight up each other's noses with nobody else standing in between.

Bea's throat worked, practicing words. But she couldn't think of anything to say. Not here. Not now. Not when exchanging pleasantries and welcoming two people to a worship service seemed ridiculous because she hadn't welcomed them into her house two days before. She stood there aching, clutching her hands together, yearning, not knowing what she was yearning for.

The knot of church women clustered around, talking about the state of the melons at the Oshkosh Superette and the rain due to move through on Tuesday and the Idaho truck that had jackknifed on the highway yesterday noon, halting traffic for two hours while people parked their cars and picked up packages of frozen Tater Tots.

What would it take to find out if that girl was telling the truth? What would it take to find out if she'd been married to Nathan?

Bea took a deep breath and let her shoulders sag. She felt like a drained vessel without a single droplet left to draw on for sustenance.

Don't make it be me. Somebody else go over there. Somebody else shake her hand and welcome her and tell her you're glad she's visiting.

But everybody else stayed well away.

Bea stood rooted to the spot, as unable to move as a hackberry tree would be to sprout legs and walk across the floor.

Pastor George stepped from behind the podium. "If the kids would come forward now, we have a special program for them this morning." He extended his arms to the children, robe sleeves billowing. "We've got a special week coming up and this is to give you all a taste. Come learn about Jesus. And bring your friends. I hear we've got prizes for those who bring the most friends. Really *good* prizes. Not to give anything away, but I do have one clue to give you." He glanced back and forth conspiratorially, as if doing something he shouldn't, then leaned forward and announced in a loud stage whisper, "Roller blades."

A cheer went up from several little boys behind her. My, but vacation Bible school was becoming almost as commercial as Christmas. Bea allowed herself a little scowl.

Before she could let the annoyance sink too deep, the children in the sanctuary began to stream forward, a goodly number of them, all the way from Ryan Staley, the gangly sixth-grader with the braces who had already had three visits from the middle school basketball coach, to Vera Champlin, two, who had to be led by hand while she gathered her dress in a fist and sucked on the hem of her ruffled petticoat.

In the chancel there appeared a makeshift cardboard throne and a pharaoh with blackened eyebrows wearing a gold brocade bedspread. "Everybody crowd on up here," George motioned, making sure everyone who'd like had responded. They climbed up the steps, encircling the altar, sitting on their knees or cross-legged, their chins craned, their eyes wide. Some sat two abreast. Little ones nestled into the laps of big ones while others scooted sideways and patted the carpet, making room for their friends. All were enthralled, amazed by the props and the funny actor dressed up as Pharaoh and the summons to come forward.

Not until Pastor George issued his second invitation did Bea notice the little girl who remained huddled against her mother's ribcage, clinging for dear life, burying her face in the folds of a borrowed print dress.

Bea could read their gestures from across the aisle—the mother urging her child to go, the little girl shaking her head, burrowing deeper. At the front of the sanctuary, music began. Five teenagers lined up behind the pharaoh, donning sunglasses and black hats. They snapped their fingers in rhythm and spread their arms wide, performing clumsy hand motions to the song.

"Come learn God's stories, come learn the Bible true, come hear all about Jesus, come find out how much He loves you . . ."

The little girl lifted her head.

"Come learn God's stories, come learn the Bible true . . ."

In fascination, she let go of her mother, moved forward on the pew, her eyes on the performers, her spindly legs dangling.

"Come hear all about Jesus . . ."

The little girl clung to the pew in front of her with all ten fingers, her pixie nose resting right there.

"Come find out how much He loves you."

Pastor George took to his pulpit again. In his hand, he held a sack full of clothespins. Pharaoh stood from his throne at the end of the song and began to recount the story of his life in Egypt. "Moses came to me in my palace and demanded, 'Let my people go!' Can you say that?"

Without much prompting at all, the children on the chancel joined in. "Let my people go!"

One clear voice ringing from the pew across the aisle: "Let my people go!"

Pharaoh stooped low and crossed one arm over the other knee to talk to the children on eye level. "God promised to take care of his people. And God always keeps his promises. When Pharaoh wouldn't do as Moses asked, God sent plagues to Egypt."

The Bible suddenly seemed a huge weight in Bea's hands.

God did things like that for the Israelites. But He never did anything like that for me.

The more stories Pharaoh told in front of the church, the more rapt that one little girl became. Her feet touched the floor. With eyes glued to him, she meandered into the aisle. "God showed everyone that He cares for His people," the actor said as the little girl stood listening with her eyes wide. And suddenly it wasn't the young woman who tore at Bea's conscience anymore, it was the innocent little girl, standing alone in a strange place, hearing a message of God's love.

"One of the plagues God sent to protect His people from Pharaoh was a swarm of locusts." Pastor George began digging in the sack and handing out clothespins. "These are the locusts. Now, you each get a turn to come up here and clip your locusts onto Pharaoh."

"No! No!" Pharaoh shielded his face with his hands. The group of giggling children overran him, clipping clothespins onto his robe, his hair, his belt, his backside.

She's just a little girl. Seeking protection and love any place she can find it. But she won't find it with me. Not here in Ash Hollow.

Bea should have brought her handkerchief. She had been crazy to leave it at home. She clutched her hands in her lap.

Nathan used to go to vacation Bible school. He would come home laughing with fists full of papers and his heart full of songs.

The air around her seemed suddenly as thick and unbreathable as water. Try as she might, Bea couldn't force it into her lungs.

I turned them away from my door, Lord. I turned them away for good reason.

The sanctuary walls closed in around her. She needed

out. She needed to breathe, to pull moving, fresh air into lungs ready to explode from a ballast of unhappiness.

In her desperation, Bea didn't care who was watching. She didn't care what anyone thought anymore. She fumbled with her Bible and hooked the handle of her purse over one arm. She kept her hat brim low, her head down, as she lurched through a row of knees and feet, everybody moving in every direction to avoid getting stepped on.

She kept her head down as she stumbled up the aisle, away from the sound of children at an altar, away from the view of a seeking child. She opened the heavy front door of the church and slipped out, leaning on it when it shut and latched behind her. Like someone who had almost drowned, she took great gulps of summer air into her lungs and raised her face to the sun.

Chapter Ten

The Cramalot Inn stood on Main Street directly across from Barn Butte Electric, its broad glass window front glinting gold in the afternoon sun. From the shop on its right, the one beauty salon in town, came the tuneful swarming sound of blow-dryers in action. On the opposite side, the door to Cedar Vu Hardware stood propped open with a bin of dollar-sale items all in an untidy heap.

Bea stopped on the sidewalk and rummaged through the bin—the drawer pulls and sun-tea jars, light bulbs and galvanized elbow joints. She dawdled on purpose, unable to escape the troubling memory of a child captivated by a Bible story played out on a stage. Unable to escape the awful recollection of the young mother alone in a place where no one should have to be that way.

She picked up a turkey baster and squeezed it. Hmmmm. Guess she didn't need another one. Already had three. She tossed it back into the jumble. Try as she might, she could not delay this any longer. She gripped her pocketbook with both hands and squared her shoulders, terrified.

What if she isn't who she says she is and I've let myself be drawn in?

In a huge blaze across the front window of Cramalot Inn, someone had lettered with yellow tempera paint: "Welcome Oregon Trail Visitors. Home Of The Famous Roses." One enormous rose had been painted on the glass, looking more like a gigantic scribble than anything else.

The heavy door creaked when Bea opened it, and a tiny bell jangled to announce her arrival. The smell of fish and stale grease greeted her as she stepped into the dimness. She paused a moment so her eyes could adjust. Beside the cash register sat a display of Ash Hollow T-shirts and a rack of brochures advertising everything from Cabela's factory outlet store to the Crescent Lake Wildlife Refuge. A jukebox in the corner played an old country song she used to know but couldn't remember anymore.

Every table sported yellow plastic chairs and red-checkered plastic tablecloths. At each place a plastic vase held plastic flowers. Small plastic American flags, left over from July Fourth almost two weeks before, waved jauntily beside plastic squeeze bottles of mustard and ketchup. Each booth boasted a shiny undersized jukebox against the wall—the sort that keep children busy turning knobs, punching buttons, flipping placards, and reading song titles the entire length of a meal.

When Bea walked in, several customers at the counter regarded her without removing their elbows from beside their plates. Charlene Grover, a buxom hostess Bea had known since Ray's softball days, ambled the length of the counter and drawled, "Nice to see you, Bea. What can I do for you?"

"Thought I'd come over for lunch."

"You picked a good day. We got pot roast."

Bea trained her eyes on the row of cake stands where cherry and cream pies winked an invitation. "That sounds real nice."

"You meeting anybody? Or are you by yourself?"

"I'm by myself."

Charlene grabbed a plastic menu from beside the cash register and started toward a table near the kitchen. But Bea had already seen the girl carrying a platter of Tater Tots to a customer on the other side of the room. "I'd rather sit over there, Charlene." She gestured toward the Tater Tot table. "I'd like a booth by the window."

"Alva T. would want me to put you here, Bea. You need somebody who'll take care of you. That waitress is new."

"I want that booth, Charlene. Please."

The hostess smacked her gum and shrugged. "Well, suit yourself."

She made an about-face and led Bea the other way, her wide girth squeezing between the chairs. When they got there, Charlene slid the menu across the appointed tabletop like she was dealing a playing card. She set down a glass of water so hard in front of Bea that it splashed. As Bea sidled into the seat, the hostess laid out one thin napkin and a knife, fork, and spoon with military precision. "Don't say I didn't warn you."

Bea opened the menu and glanced at the list of luncheon specials. Meat loaf. Corned beef and cabbage. And the Tuesday Catch-of-the-Day—baked halibut and green beans with corn bread and a peach half on the side.

"Can I bring you anything else?" The girl's familiar

voice serving the table behind Bea sent anticipation coursing up Bea's spine.

"Nope. Guess that'll do me. You tell the cook I don't like my corn bread so dry. He's got to do something about that tomorrow." The girl was waiting on Walt Snell, a dry-waller from Ogallala who often came to Ash Hollow working on a job. Whenever Geneva saw Walt coming up the street, she'd say, "That man could say 'Merry Christmas' in a tone that would make you want to punch him." Everybody knew he grumbled about everything.

"I'll say something to the cook if you'd like."

"I'd like."

"Here's your check then." A ripping sound directly behind Bea's head. "Come back to see us soon."

The items on the menu swam together in Bea's vision. She lowered her menu and peered over the top of it like a prowler peering over a fence top as the girl walked away.

Her heart hammered in her chest. Again there could be no mistaking this young woman, the one she'd seen across the aisle at church yesterday, her denim skirt now laundered and pressed, the red Cramalot Inn apron big enough to swallow her.

"Hey, honey." Walt Snell gave a little whistle and, with no warning at all, the girl—who had been retreating—spun in the direction of her customers again. Bea hoisted the menu just in time to hide.

"Yes?"

Bea heard quick measured steps coming, a worried question. "Is something wrong?"

"I had the meat loaf lunch," Walt announced in a belligerent voice loud enough for the whole place to overhear. "The price was listed as $4.99 on the menu. This bill says $7.49. It's wrong."

A moment of silence passed in which, Bea assumed, the girl made mental calculations. Her voice had gotten a little shakier when she explained, "It's my first day working. Sorry for the mistake. Here. Let me fix it." The sound of a ballpoint pen scratching out and scrawling. "There. How's that?"

"We'll see. You stand right here while I double-check your math. I don't want to have to flag you down again."

"Yes, sir."

Bea couldn't stand it. She had to peek over her right shoulder, over the plastic booth seat that came to her neck, to see what was happening. The girl stood beside her patron, her head hanging in humility, while Walt Snell held his own mechanical pencil in hand and calculated beneath his breath. Anger choked Bea. The protective feeling surprised her. She wanted to jump out of the booth and swat Walt Snell with her pocketbook for being so unkind.

"It adds up right this time. You'd best learn your prices, girl. No one wants a problem like this when they come out to eat."

"Yes, sir. I'll learn things, sir. I will."

Bea faced forward again. After Walt left no tip and clomped out the door, Charlene Grover called out, "Don't you mind him, Gemma. He'd complain if you hung him with a new rope."

Even so, when the girl finally appeared at Bea's tableside, she was already flustered. The crests of her ears had gone red. She tried to hold her pen at the ready, but shaking fingers gave her away. She didn't glance up from her green order pad. "Have you decided what you'd like, ma'am?"

"No. No, I haven't."

"The pot roast is good today," the girl said. "The meat loaf and halibut look pretty good, too. And we're having a special on Tater Tots for the whole week. Truck jackknifed on the highway and we ended up with extra Tater Tots."

"I'm not—" Bea looked up.

The girl looked down. "Oh." She sent out a startled cry and went as white as the napkin on the table.

Bea sat absolutely still, not a nerve flinching.

Two beats passed, maybe three, before the girl lowered her eyes to her order pad and said, "You don't know what you'd like, I can come back in a few minutes."

"Miss," someone called from another table. "Can we get ketchup over here?"

"I'll just—" The girl backed away from Bea as if afraid to turn away. "Let me get that ketchup."

Bea sat perfectly still after the girl had left, her stomach clenching and unclenching with its enormous load of regret and fear. When the girl returned at last, uneasiness exuded between them. For long moments, the girl's gaze went everywhere except for Bea's face. No questions this time, no careful smiles. She took a dozen weighted, wordless seconds before she said, "Hello, Mrs. Bartling."

"Hello."

"How are you today?"

"Not real good," Bea answered. "Not real good at all."

The girl picked up the fork, laid it down again, didn't take her eyes from it for a long time. She bent over and checked the peppershaker, screwing the lid off and on. She tried to do the same with the saltshaker but salt spilled out and with her fumbling, anxious hands, she couldn't make the lid scrape back on again. She gave up on that, grabbed a wet rag from her apron pocket and scrubbed hard, sending salt granules flying everywhere. With each of these motions—with the determined slant of her head and the rigid sweep of her arm—came the subtle, strong message. She wanted nothing from Bea Bartling.

Bea had just finished dusting salt off her lap when the girl finally stopped messing with objects on the table and looked her in the eye. "Guess I'd feel the same way if I didn't know if somebody was telling me the truth or not."

"You would."

It wasn't the time for Bea to say she'd been wrong or that she might have done things differently if she'd known they didn't have a place to stay. It wasn't the time to say "I'm sorry," because she wasn't. It wasn't the time to say, "If only I had a way to know you are who you say you are."

And so she didn't. "The halibut," Bea said instead.

"Huh?"

"Put me down for the halibut. The Tuesday Catch-of-the-Day."

"Oh, I'm sorry." The girl colored and fumbled for her pad. "I got myself all shook up because you're here. You know how people say 'halibut' instead of cussing? 'I'm going to do something just for the halibut?' That's what I thought you were doing."

"Well, no. I'm just trying to order lunch."

"Sorry." The girl flushed even deeper. "You want something to drink with that?"

"Iced tea."

"For dressing, we've got Ranch, Thousand Island, Bleu Cheese, and French."

"French."

"Okay." The girl scribbled it all down and brushed a strand of hair from her face. From somewhere in the kitchen came a clattering of plates, a dinging of a bell, and someone hollering, "Order up!"

The girl glanced over her shoulder. "That's mine. I've got to get it."

When she walked off, Bea studied her, the sway in her slender hips, the way she held her neck rigid with pride, the camber at the small of her back where the big apron knot gathered her shirt. Emotions eddied inside Bea. Guilt. Longing. Dread. Hope. What had she come here searching for? Evidence of this girl's duplicity? If she had, then perhaps she would leave disappointed. The girl's cool behavior, her forced detachment, did more to attest to the soundness of her claims than anything else Bea had seen.

A salad appeared before her, the pale chunks of lettuce and shreds of carrot slathered in French dressing, delivered by the girl's quivering hand.

After setting the plate, the girl stood back. She crossed her arms over her chest as if she was protecting herself from something. At last she said, "I know he never told you about me."

The salad sat uneaten.

"No, he didn't."

"I know you two didn't ever talk. Not for as long as I knew him."

Bea used her knife and fork to mix lettuce and grated carrot with the same zeal as if she were flinging weeds in her garden. Outside the window, a truck from Jake Jab's American Furniture Warehouse rattled past, rattling the window, its load of mattresses and box springs jostling against each other in unison. The dreadful joke ran through Bea's head unbidden. *Why don't the customers bend over at American Furniture Warehouse? Because Jake Jabs.*

A little boy slalomed along on his razor scooter, his leg paddling in long strokes, a perfect rhythm with the cracks in the sidewalk. Across the street in the town square, Joe Metzger stretched high with a long-handled pair of shears and chopped wayward boughs off the old box elder tree.

Someone hollered from another table. "Hey, hon, can we get a coffee over here?"

The girl pretended not to notice. Instead she asked, very quietly, "Why did he leave home?"

"He didn't tell you that?"

"No."

A woman at the booth right beside them joined in with the other customers. "What's a body got to do to get coffee in this place?"

Charlene Grover came from behind the counter, her tray loaded with hamburgers and Tater Tots. "Gemma. You need to get those coffees."

With one sad glance backward, the girl uncrossed her arms and hurried to get the pot. Then, taking her time, she freshened everybody's coffee around the room. Alva T. stopped by Bea's table to say hello. "I see you've met my new waitress. What do you think? She's going to court in a few days, did you know? It's the strangest thing, her getting arrested. Maybe I'll go, too, so she'll have someone to support her."

The bell dinged in the kitchen again. "Order up!" A Tuesday Catch-of-the-Day slid into view beneath the warming lamps. The girl carried Bea's lunch over, balancing it against the crook of her elbow. Bea didn't touch her food. She spread her fingers wide and pushed the rim of the plate away before she laid ten fingers decisively on the tablecloth. "Your name's Gemma." It was a statement, not a question.

"It is."

"Pretty name."

Gemma stuck her hands in the pocket of her Cramalot Inn apron. "It's common, I guess. Lots of people have it."

"Not too many."

The girl's expression got all soft and sad, like she could see something far away. "My daddy named me that." She picked up the salad plate and laid it aside. "Said he'd read it in a book once, that it reminded him of buried pirate's treasure. You know. Like precious gems."

Beside the cash register, the telephone rang. Alva answered it and then bellowed into the kitchen, "Harvey, you mind making a pot roast lunch to go?"

Bea said, "Saw your little girl at church yesterday."

Gemma tucked a strand of hair behind her ear again and gave a brittle laugh. "They've been real nice to us over there, taking us in the way they did. George and Ellen Sissel are nice. I don't know where we'd be without them."

"When you came to my door, you didn't tell me you were stranded. You didn't tell me you had no place to go and your car had broken down. You said you had family. You said you were headed back to them."

"No, Mrs. Bartling." Gemma shook her head. "I said I had family. The rest of it's what *you* said."

Bea had the grace to hang her head. "It's just . . . so hard." She raised her eyes, though, after a moment. "Everybody in town's talking about you two, you know."

"They are?"

"Well, maybe not everybody. But I have a friend

named Geneva who is. She talks about everybody. We don't have many strangers that come through here and stay more than an hour or so."

Gemma said, "Sure made it hard, seeing Nathan's name printed out on a church bulletin like that."

Nathan's name.

The subject presented itself almost before Bea was ready to speak of it. This one baffling detail had been haunting her for days. The words to the awful question popped out before she had the chance to stop them. "If you were married to my boy, how come you didn't take his name? How come you been going around town telling everybody your name is Franklin instead?"

Gemma's chin dropped to her chest. She stood motionless for an eternity before she raised her face. "I figured that would shake things up too much, me coming to Ash Hollow, telling everybody I was a Bartling. I figured that wasn't anybody's business but ours."

Bea's thumb made tiny polished circles on her teaspoon.

"Besides," Gemma said with false confidence, "never changed my name on that old Toyota. Franklin's what the deputy pulled up when they found the car on the highway."

Bea thought about the girl's answer. And thought some more. Finally she pulled in a deep breath and began to stir her tea. She stared into the glass a long time before raising her eyes. "I've read Nathan's obituary in the paper over and over again, checking to see if something there gives those stories of yours away. Nothing does. No way for you to have known those things, except if he had told you."

Gemma spoke in a hushed way that hid neither her confidence nor her hurt. "I know there isn't any way for you to figure out if we're telling the truth or not. We talked about that before." Her eyes started roving the room again, not settling on anything, not even the customers waiting with frowns at other tables. She snapped up Bea's butter bowl to tote it someplace else. "Best get back to work if I want to keep this job past the first day."

Bea grabbed her wrist with a firm hand. Pats of butter, still wrapped in their white wax-paper squares, went sailing out of the bowl onto the table. Their gazes met. "Isn't anything in that paper that would have told you how I used to get mad at Nathan whenever he squeezed petals off my roses."

Gemma wrenched her hand away, grabbed the rag from her pocket again, and began scrubbing the red and white plastic hard enough to rub a hole in it. "You look for ways to prove we're not who we say we are, Mrs. Bartling, and you'll probably find them. You look for ways to prove we knew Nathan, and you'll probably find those, too."

"Isn't this what you wanted? For me to try to figure it out? For me to acknowledge that you could be who you say you are? Isn't that why you came to my door in the first place?"

"No."

Bea pressed her elbows to the tabletop, linked her fingers together, and gave it to Gemma sad and straight. "If you knew Nathan, you knew him better than I did. You knew him better because you knew him last. That's what I've been thinking."

"Maybe so. But that isn't the same as knowing somebody in his own place."

The halibut lunch sat untouched before her. Bea linked her hands tighter together, desperate to hold on to something. She shook her head, her voice a mere whisper. "Neither one of us had all of what we wanted of him, I guess."

"No. We sure didn't."

Bea unlinked her hands and felt like she was letting go of everything that protected her. She swallowed, trying to speak the words. But, for a long time, they just wouldn't come. She forced herself to utter them anyway. "I know you two are all settled in over at Sissel's. But I hoped you might want to stay at my house for a few days. I know you won't be here long. But at least until you get your car fixed . . ."

"You'd want us?" The rag in the girl's hand lay motionless on the table. The girl lifted her face to Bea's. Her plaintive expression made Bea's throat constrict with doubt.

Even so, Bea couldn't turn back now.

"I keep thinking about how maybe you're Nathan's family now." She stared at her splayed fingers, her pulse clamoring. "Yes. I believe I would like you to come."

The rag began to move on the table again, first in little circles, then in larger and larger sweeps. "Paisley's doing vacation Bible school this week. She likes it real well, too. Then she goes home to Loren Sissel's before I get off. Sometimes she takes a nap, but I can't promise it. That's getting to be a struggle."

Bea said, "I could do that schedule, too."

"You could?"

"Yes." Bea picked up her fork, cut a bite of the fish. "So, are you going to be at my place for supper?"

"Yes. Please. I—I'd really like that."

"Call Loren Sissel and let her know, would you? So she's not worried about fixing you anything."

"I will. I get off here at five."

"I'll be along about five to get you."

Gemma made one more round of coffee with everybody, splashing it haphazardly into cups. She turned in another order to the kitchen before she returned to Bea's side. She twisted the plain gold wedding band around and around on her left ring finger. "Nathan told me once there was nothing better than waking up in a place to make you feel like you owned it. He said that's why he loved to go camping up at Lake McConaughy so much. He said it makes you feel like you belong, seeing a place as it wakes up, as the fog lifts off the lake and the mallard drakes glide on glass water before the dew burns away and the day gets hot. Morning is fragile, he always said. Makes you belong to something in a way that someone who hasn't slept over never would."

"Nathan said that?"

"I always thought some day he would take me there. That one day he would show me the place he was talking about."

"Why did you come here, really? Are you just looking for a place to belong?"

"I belonged to Nathan." Gemma began picking up butter pats that had fallen, dropping them one by one into the little white bowl. "Nathan's all I ever needed."

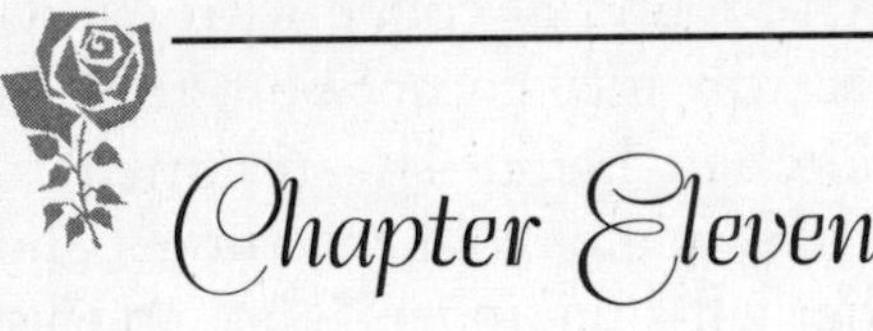

Chapter Eleven

When the ten-year-old white Monte Carlo turned in at 117 Pattison Drive, the rosebush beside the Bartling's front stoop stood laden with yellow blossoms. Lacy and hearty, as cheerful as the sun and as fragrant as perfume, the wind stirred the flowers delicately as though it tested them, and every so often a petal coasted to the ground.

"This suitcase." Gemma elevated herself on her knees and tried to reach into the backseat to grab it. She couldn't quite get hold of it. "I feel like I've carried that thing halfway across the country." When she glanced sideways, she realized Mrs. Bartling was eyeing the hem of her skirt, seeing how it sidled up high against her thighs. Gemma tugged it down as far as it would go.

"I've got the suitcase." With solemn fortitude, Nathan's mother set the emergency brake, opened the driver door, and extended stiff legs to the pavement. Leading with both feet, it took another moment for her to work her way out from behind the steering wheel. She opened the rear door and gripped the handle of the dilapidated pink suitcase. "Happiness Is A Visit To Grandma's."

"Don't you have any other skirts besides that one?"

Mrs. Bartling pulled out the little bag and set it hard on the pavement. "That one looks to be about three sizes too small."

"Sure, I do," Gemma lied. *She doesn't like the way I look. She doesn't like the clothes I wear. Even though she's letting us stay, she doesn't think somebody like me is good enough for her son.* "I just didn't bring any more with me, that's all. At home I've got plenty of them."

But there was no home. There were no other skirts. Only a small assortment of necessities in the suitcase and a hope that had begun dying its slow death.

"Well, no sense standing out here where all the neighbors can see you. Let's get you inside. Let's get the two of you settled."

"Thank you."

It had been a long time since anyone had invited Gemma to *get settled.* She climbed out of the Monte Carlo and stretched, her wrists jutted high and her fingers folded, breathing in the pungent, sweet incense of fresh-mown lawns and water sprinklers, of car wax and roses, of someone grilling on a back porch. From down the street came the steady singsong of a swing set, chains creaking in distant cadence to the rhythm of some child's swinging.

Here they were.

Nathan's home.

Gemma stood beside the grass, eyes closed, arms upstretched as if she were reaching for him, expecting to find traces of her dead husband here. She had thought she would feel closer to Nathan the minute she climbed out of the car. But she didn't. If anything, she felt vague disappointment. This place should have brought her closer to him and, instead, he felt further, further away.

Forget about it, Gemma. He's gone. There isn't anyplace

you can go, anybody you can see, who's going to bring Nathan back again.

She dropped her arms, opened her eyes. Paisley tumbled out of the car behind her, toting a plastic grocery sack looped around one arm. In it she carried three pictures she'd drawn with crayons on construction paper in vacation Bible school, two packs of Juicy Fruit chewing gum that George Sissel had given her, a yo-yo, a bouncy ball, and a painted flowerpot that read "Jesus Christ, The Same Yesterday, Today, and Forever" in which Gemma knew her daughter anxiously awaited the sprouting of some sort of bean.

"Watch out. Don't drop your pot," Gemma warned Paisley. "It'll break. I don't want you getting dirt all over Mrs. Bartling's floor."

"I won't." Paisley skipped toward the house, confident, innocent. "I'll be careful."

In the driveway next door a man tinkered with his truck, encircled by Kendall motor-oil cans and funnels and wrenches. He slid beneath the pickup with a rumbling scrape of his creeper, emitted a few grunts, then slapped his hands together in satisfaction as the ping of oil hit the aluminum pan.

A woman came trekking up the street, round as an airship and wholesomely happy. "Oh, Bea," she shouted and waved broadly at all three of them where they stood together at the front fender of the car. "I've been worrying about you. How are you doing, anyway?"

"I'm okay, Lucinda. Fair to middling." Mrs. Bartling handed Gemma the suitcase. "Got out and went to church Sunday."

"Good to see you getting company." Lucinda inclined her head pointedly at Gemma. "Company always helps."

The oil-changing neighbor propelled the creeper out

from under his truck. "When are you going to start showing folks those roses of yours again, Bea?" He polished his crescent wrench on the sleeve of his greasy coveralls. Then he, too, gave a keen nod toward Paisley and Gemma. "Sure don't seem right without you puttering and pruning," as he slid back under, the exhaust pipe and the transmission muffling his words, "in the dirt next door."

Mrs. Bartling shook her finger at him. "That's my business, Corwin Kepler, not yours." But, as if the neighbor's comments had made Mrs. Bartling suddenly self-conscious about her flowers, her steps broke their cadence. She stared disconsolately at the jumble of leaves and browning blossoms. Just as quickly, the woman raised her chin and marched with great purpose up the front brick steps. "Oh, never mind those roses." She held open the screen and shooed Gemma and Paisley through like a brood of chicks. "Come on in. Come on in. No sense standing out here all day and letting everybody ogle you."

Mrs. Bartling led the way up the hall again, past the row of familiar photographs, past the bathroom, past the child's room with its two single oak beds, rock collection, and baseball pennant. Paisley stopped short, making Gemma pull up behind her. "Don't we get to stay in Nathan's room?"

Mrs. Bartling seemed not to hear Paisley's question. She opened the door to a different bedroom and turned on a bedside lamp. Even though their hostess must have aired this room out for them, the room still smelled faintly of mildew and sachet. "You'll both stay in here."

A formidable wooden headboard stood against the far wall. In the window Gemma saw the grill and knobs of an ancient air conditioner. An assortment of perfume atomizers stood in a row on the pink linen-covered dressing table and an array of clean, fresh towels sat folded and stacked on the bed. Gemma set the suitcase on the white luggage rack with linen ribbons that stood open and waiting in one corner.

Paisley stood in the center of the room and asked the same question Mrs. Bartling had pretended not to hear the first time.

"Why don't we get to stay in Nathan's old room? Nathan said if we ever came to visit, I could stay there. He said I could play with his Tonka trucks."

Even though Mrs. Bartling's answer was quiet and calm, her face had blanched to the color of parchment. "But now Nathan is gone. That makes everything very different," she said. "You mustn't touch anything. No one is allowed to sleep in his room. No one has slept in his bed since he last slept there himself."

Mrs. Bartling left them alone to unpack. One by one, Gemma opened each drawer on the dresser and found it empty except for the fragrant, floral papers lining the bottom. She placed Paisley's few pair of underwear and shorts in one drawer and situated her meager supply of T-shirts, panties, and socks in another.

"Where do you want to put your crafts from vacation Bible school?" she asked her daughter. "There are six more empty drawers here."

Paisley hugged the bag and the little flowerpot against her chest. "I don't want to put them anywhere," she said. "I want to keep them with me."

"Are you sure? I'm worried about you spilling dirt. You need to find a window for that plant."

Paisley shook her head.

Gemma gave up and moved to other things. On the counter in the bathroom she positioned their two toothbrushes and their small, wrinkled tube of Crest beside the sink. She aligned a pot of lip gloss, a hairbrush, and a stick of Mennen Teen-Spirit deodorant on one side of the tile counter.

It had taken precious little time for them to move in.

Gemma took Paisley's hand and led her to the family room. "Sit down," Mrs. Bartling said as she bustled around the house. "Make yourself comfortable. Do whatever you'd like."

They sat down together, side by side, in the plump, old, tweedy recliner, two girls—a big one and a little one clutching a paper bag and a flowerpot—staring at the taupe wallpaper with little sprigs of green. Over the years, the paper must have faded. Two diamond shapes stood out in relief where, long ago, something must have hung.

Gemma's breath caught. Two mahogany wooden carvings had hung in that spot once, two silhouettes of gazelles leaping a fence. Nathan's father had yanked them off their hooks and taken them with him when he left.

Nathan had told her about that.

Gemma stared at her feet.

Beside her on the floor sat a wooden sewing box and in the box, beside the miscellany of threads and scissors and the pincushion shaped like a tomato and filled with sawdust, sat a tiny bird's nest with one glimmering Christmas icicle woven in among the twigs and hair.

Nathan had told her about that.

Gemma drew one pained, shallow breath and gaped at the nest. "He found this in a tree outside. He told me about it."

Mrs. Bartling grabbed the sewing box, cradled it against her chest as if to protect it. "This nest is no business of yours."

But Gemma couldn't stop. "Nathan found it in July," she said. "He left it alone in the hackberry bush for three months after that, wanting to make sure no bird was going to lay a clutch or return to it before he took it away. Even after he brought it inside, he worried."

"Don't pretend you belong here," Mrs. Bartling said, "just by knowing about a nest."

"Nathan was always tenderhearted about things like that. Worrying about a bird."

The question stood in stark silence between Gemma and Mrs. Bartling: *Why would a boy who could be tender-hearted toward a sparrow run away from his mother?*

Suddenly, everywhere Gemma looked, she saw things that seemed familiar to her. The hole in the linoleum by the door. The simple chandelier that hung from a chain over the table. The tapestry on the wall of The Last Supper.

Nathan had told her about all of these things.

"The day he died," Gemma said, "we had hamburgers for lunch. He built one so thick with tomato and lettuce and pickles that he couldn't get his mouth around the bun. Then he told me he wanted to take Paisley fishing just the way his dad had always taken him. And he kissed me good-bye—"

Mrs. Bartling set the sewing box down with a thump and a rainbow of thread spools rolled out across the floor. "Stop it. Oh, please, stop it. I want to hear these things. I really do. That's why I invited you here." She buried her face in her bony fingers. "But it's too soon. It hurts too much today to hear what Nathan did, or said, or how he acted."

Gemma stood abruptly from the chair, making it rock to and fro with Paisley still in it, realizing she'd crossed some forbidden, invisible boundary. When she spoke now she went cautiously, the way a dog would go, nosing her way into unsafe territory. "I feel as if—" Gemma scanned the room, the hole in the linoleum, the tapestry, the faded diamonds on the wallpaper. "—as if I already know this place."

"Don't try to make me accept you," Mrs. Bartling told her. "Don't think you can be family because you were married to my son."

Gemma stood in the room like an animal, caught in truth, trapped.

"I wasn't trying," she lied. "I wasn't pretending." Then, much softer. "I wasn't pretending I belonged here. I really wasn't."

Mrs. Bartling turned away toward the kitchen and stared at the floor beyond her left foot, as if she couldn't bear meeting their faces while she answered the question that hung unspoken between them. "I'm the reason, you know. I'm the reason he left and never came home."

Outside the window, evening was beginning to fall. A single car drove along Pattison, sending up a muted hiss of tires along the pavement. In the meadow behind the house, Gemma could make out the round shapes of cows as they grazed a close-cropped summer pasture.

She could think of nothing to reply.

Paisley was the one to break the oppressive quiet between them. "Can you put this in your window?" She rose from the recliner and with one little hand held up her flowerpot to Mrs. Bartling. "It has to be in the sun so it can grow."

"No, honey bananas." Gemma tried to stop her. "This isn't the time—"

Mrs. Bartling took the flowerpot from the little girl with some relief, as if she was thankful for the diversion it gave. "It's all right," she said to Gemma. She went and set the pot on the windowsill beside the sink. "We'll keep it here. That way, one of us will remember to water it. Outdoor plants get plenty of attention around here, but sometimes the indoor ones get slighted."

But Paisley wasn't finished. She began rummaging in her sack. She pulled out one of her construction-paper drawings and held it high so Mrs. Bartling could see.

"Can you hang this on the refrigerator?"

"Oh, my," Mrs. Bartling gushed. "What a nice picture! Who is this?"

"I drew a picture of us. See?" The little girl pointed to each face as she named them off. "Here's Mama and me and Nathan."

"No, Paisley Rose." Again, Gemma tried to stop her daughter. "No pictures right now. Because seeing those makes us so sad."

As most four-and-a-half-year-olds are prone to do, Paisley didn't listen. She kept right on talking, holding the drawing high and letting it dangle in midair. "I made Nathan's hair sticking up all over his head like it did when he let me brush it."

From where she stood across the room, Gemma could make out the drawing, a child's rendering of the happy family they'd once been—three wobbly stick figures standing side by side with massive heads and grinning, plain faces, their arms outflung toward one another, their clothes outlined around straddled, spindly legs.

Paisley said, "Nathan said we should be in some sort of contest because we looked like we belonged together."

Gemma flinched at her daughter's words, a direct contradiction to the censure Mrs. Bartling had already issued.

Don't tell me what he did, what he said, how he acted . . .

But to Gemma's surprise, what Mrs. Bartling would not accept from her, she accepted from Paisley instead.

The woman smiled with great sadness and tousled the little girl's hair. "From looking at your picture, I can see how he'd say something like that."

Paisley smiled, satisfied.

Mrs. Bartling reached for the proffered drawing. She turned the picture right side up and peered down at it, her eyes gone soft and grave. "Is this what Nathan looked like when he was with you? He looks very happy."

Only Gemma noticed the careful, bitter edge to her voice. Only Gemma knew what else Mrs. Bartling must have been thinking.

If he hadn't been this happy with you, maybe he would have come home to me.

Mrs. Bartling opened a cabinet, pulled out a wheel of Scotch tape, and tore off little pieces. "Here. Stick these on each corner of your picture. I'll let you put it up, okay?"

"Okay."

With pride, Paisley hung her drawing, smoothing it out across the width of the refrigerator door with two slender little hands. For the rest of the day, every time Gemma happened to glance at Mrs. Bartling, she noticed how the woman's eyes paused often on the child's drawing, on the big smiles, the outstretched arms.

Chapter Twelve

Bea had a certain unsettled feeling about going to bed with guests in her home. Like a faultless hostess, she had fed them supper, folded back their mint-green sheets and blankets, plumped their lopsided pillows, even offered them a snack of Geneva's homemade banana bread and glasses of milk before bed.

She had turned off the window air conditioner in the family room, opened all the windows, and started the attic fan, drawing the balmy, fresh night air into the house like tendrils of warm breath. She made certain her two guests had everything they needed before she yawned purposefully and excused herself to don her nightgown, robe, and slippers. She pulled her squiggly gray hair back with a stretchy headband, splashed water on her skin, brushed her teeth and smeared Pond's Cold Cream all over her face. Then she climbed into bed, leaned her head against her own plumped pillows, pulled her own covers up to her ribs, and listened for them.

Even though the lamp had been turned out downstairs, she could still hear sounds she wasn't accustomed to—whispers and mouselike movements and the rustling of bed linen. She couldn't hear their words from this far away, but she could certainly guess at what they might be saying.

"Scoot over a little, would you?"

"Can I have that other pillow?"

"This is a comfortable bed."

"And a comfortable house."

"What do you suppose she did that made Nathan leave and never want to come back?"

Bea stared at the ceiling, her chest hollow, her temples aching, as tears squeezed out of the sides of her eyes and dripped down the sides of her face.

It's my fault.

Nathan had told them about the bird's nest. Nathan had been happy with them. Nathan had talked about visiting and staying in his old room.

There's a child's drawing of my son hanging downstairs on my icebox, a picture of grasping hands and smiles in a row.

All the things a mother should have rejoiced in, only she hadn't been allowed to rejoice, because she had never known.

"Lord," Bea whispered into the darkness. The simple name, the plaintive cry, came almost unintentionally. "Lord."

No answer came.

Only silence. Breathtaking silence.

As long as Bea had been sequestered here in this house, alone and hurting since Nathan's death, she had been able to close out the presence of her heavenly Father in her own heart. The dry, dusty distance had claimed her, had whispered its awful lie to her and made her believe it—a song sung, a story ended, a dark dirge of separation that repeated itself in broken litany over and over again.

Didn't you pray and ask God to bring your son home safely?

God forsook me when He let Nathan die.

Doesn't George Sissel say God loves you no matter what is happening around you? That you shouldn't doubt He is there?

If He cared about me, He would have listened to my prayer.

You're the one that pulled away. You're the one who is shutting God out of your life.

I didn't seek Him in sorrow yesterday so why should I seek Him today? The further away I've let myself become, the further away He is. Once far away, there can be no going back.

Five years it had been, and she couldn't remember how it felt not to be alone. She couldn't remember how it had felt to have a husband laying beside her in this bed, drawing her close beneath the covers, keeping her toes warm after they'd turned down the heat in the house.

Then, even though she vowed she couldn't remember, *wouldn't* remember, the memory came. The front yard on moving-in day. Ray sneaking up behind her and crooking his arm around her shoulders.

"Beatrice?"

She turned toward her husband, circled her arms around his waist, and pressed her face into the worn cotton of the old khaki shirt. She could feel his ribs and bones and hear the beating of his heart. His arms came around her and they simply stood there in the grass, very close, for anybody who drove by to see.

"Don't know why you keep wearing this old shirt." She straightened the collar of it for him as she spoke. "I bought you that new one for Christmas."

"You know why."

"You're stubborn as a goat, Ray. And you aren't even old enough to be an old goat yet."

She'd had his new shirt monogrammed, thinking to make the gift something special. RTB. Raymond Theophilus Bartling.

"If I wear that shirt in public," he told her, "somebody's bound to ask me what the T stands for."

"Stubborn as a goat. Won't wear a perfectly good shirt."

"How about you? Out here working on these roses before the furniture's even been loaded into the house."

Ray's recliner, handed down from his father's house, still waited beside the front steps. Two rickety lamps, donated by Bea's Great Uncle Halden, sat looking ridiculous in the middle of the sidewalk. A coat rack stood in the grass, propped against the side of the house. They'd been lucky just to get the two lumpy mattresses and box springs inside before their friends with the truck went home to supper.

She studied his face, searching for that faraway expression that came sometimes, the expression she'd noticed the day he'd seen the hobo on the train. It always frightened her when the expression came. It whispered of discontent, and she didn't understand why.

"We're going to be happy here, don't you think, Ray?"

He turned from her. "Happy?" He stared at the front façade of the house as if the house would give him his answer. "How could we not be happy in a house where pioneer roses have been growing for a hundred and fifty years?"

Downstairs, the whispering and nestling sounds had stopped. Bea sat up in bed, sipped from the water glass she kept on her nightstand, used a Kleenex to dab at her eyes. She pitched it into the wastepaper basket and reached to turn off her own lamp.

Her hand faltered on the light switch.

Bea did not want to turn out the light.

A terrible longing welled up within her, so compelling and strong that she could not escape its power. Her eyes felt gritty and hot, her chest gone tight with yearning.

I'm so tired of having nothing to hope for.

She turned back the covers and knelt at the side of her bed. For a long while, she stared at the stitching on her comforter without lowering her head.

Downstairs, she knew a mother and child lay together in one place. She pictured them, their arms entangled, their dreams intertwined, their breath moist and soft against one another's skin.

"Lord. Please," Bea pleaded, never even closing her eyes. "Please."

How long had it been since anyone had embraced her with assurances? The way a father embraces a child in his arms?

She couldn't remember.

Like the child she pictured downstairs, she yearned for someone to hold her in safety while she slept.

"All rise," the bailiff pronounced. "Garden County Justice Court is now in session. The Honorable Judge Solomon Leroy Veeder presiding."

The spectators, defendants, and plaintiffs all stood as Solomon Veeder entered the courtroom.

"You may be seated."

They all sat down again.

Already Gemma's hindquarters had gone numb. She

scrunched first to one side and then to the other. The seat didn't get any softer, no matter what she tried.

Alva Torrington leaned over from the bench behind her. "Hope you don't mind that I showed up in court. You're my employee. It's in my best interest to support my employees in times of strain."

"Thank you."

"Judge Veeder's known for being fair. You answer his questions straight and you won't have any cause for worry."

It didn't matter what Alva said; Gemma worried anyway. She couldn't help worrying when the judge glowered down from his perch and asked, "How come we got so many spectators sitting out there? What's everybody in Garden County so interested in this afternoon?" She couldn't help her heart pounding when the judge handed down a decision in favor of Ralph Coney, who had been brought to court by Lana Simms for not fixing the dent on her ATV. She couldn't help her pulse racing when the judge explained to Mavis Atkinson three times why she should not have cashed the rent check with "paid in full" written on the memo line. "It's called a conditional offer, Mavis. You cash the check, you agree to the condition. It's the law. I can't change the law."

Most of all, Gemma felt her stomach wrench when Judge Veeder said, "Next case. State of Nebraska, Plaintiff, versus Gemma Franklin, Defendant. Everyone involved step forward to take the oath, please."

Mabel Perkins and several of her associates stormed toward the front of the courtroom. Gemma stood on shaky legs.

"Go get 'em, girl." Alva gave her arm a little squeeze.

"I think I know what sort of person you are. And Solomon will see it, too."

Judge Veeder waited until they'd all arrived at their places before he said, "Everybody involved in this case raise your right hand."

The ladies standing with Mabel Perkins began to twitter.

"Your *right* hand," Judge Veeder repeated to Gemma, who quickly dropped her left hand and raised her right one instead. "Don't look so terrified, Miss Franklin," he said, smiling kindly. "It happens all the time. Someone raises a left hand instead of a right one. Sometimes I raise my left one, too, just to confuse everybody."

He raised his left hand now, making everyone in the courtroom laugh, and repeated the oath so fast that Gemma almost didn't know what she was answering to.

"Do you solemnly swear the testimony you're about to give will be nothing but the truth, so help you God?"

"I do," Gemma whispered.

"I do," Mabel Perkins announced with fortitude.

Judge Veeder didn't start the proceedings just yet. He glanced around the courtroom. "Hmmm-mm. I see the hardened coffee drinkers from Alva T's place lined up along the back row. You all here to offer moral support?"

Alva answered before the rest of them got the chance. "We are, your honor."

"Good for you." Judge Veeder pursed his lips as if he was impressed before he turned back to the matter at hand. He slid his bifocals the length of his nose and peered down at the Garden County Sheriff's Department Supplementary Report in front of him. "Miss Franklin, you are charged with criminal entry. How do you plead?"

"Not guilty, sir," Gemma whispered.

The judge took a deep breath and chuffed out his cheeks at her. "Miss Franklin. This session is being taped. Besides, I am an old man with corncobs stuck in my ears. You cannot communicate with nods or whispers. You have to speak up. Now, again, how do you plead?"

Gemma took one step toward the microphone. She lifted her chin toward Judge Veeder. He sat glaring down at her in his menacing black robe with his hair standing up in gray tufts all over his head like a dandelion gone to seed. Behind his right shoulder stood the flag of the United States of America. Behind his left shoulder stood the Nebraska State Flag, bearing a silver and gold reproduction of the state seal centered on a field of dark blue.

"I plead *not guilty*, sir," she said, louder.

"Much better."

He tamped the report against his judge's bench and turned toward the plaintiffs. He scanned Jay Triplett's report and repeated aloud some of the high points. At approximately 0830 hours . . . reference a subject found sleeping in bed . . . proprietor believed a burglary could be in progress . . . subject admitted to spending night in museum . . . museum displays unharmed but subject to minor disarray.

"Mabel. It is my understanding that you are pressing these charges because there was damage done in the museum. Is that correct?"

"Yes, Your Honor." Mabel Perkins puffed up like a guinea hen.

"Will you describe the type of damage done?"

"Both emotional and physical damage, your honor. My patrons were distraught. My morning was disrupted. A tour group we'd been expecting for two weeks had to go without refreshments because these vagrants ate my sticky buns."

Deputy Jay Triplett stepped forward. "They ate the food on my recommendation, Your Honor. This woman and her child were hungry."

Judge Veeder leaned farther out over his bench. "Triplett, with all due respect, you are speaking out of turn here. I am questioning Mabel Perkins."

"Yes, Your Honor." He stepped backwards. "I'm sorry, sir."

"I want you to focus on only physical damage, Mabel. Provable damage. Do you have pictures of any physical damage to the museum, Mabel? You do understand that yours is the burden of proof here, don't you?"

"Well, no. I—" Mabel's shoulders slumped a bit. "I didn't take pictures."

"Did you have anyone come in and give you an estimate for repairs? Do you have some sort of receipt with a dollar amount?"

"No, I—" Mabel stared at the floor. "I conducted the repairs myself, Your Honor."

"And what sort of repairs did you do?"

"I . . . Well, I put silverware back where they had rearranged it, Judge Veeder. And I made up the bed."

The judge inclined his head vaguely in the direction of Gemma. "Are you from Nebraska, young lady?"

"I am, sir. I grew up in Omaha."

"Then you are well aware that our great state motto is 'Equality Before The Law.' Will you tell me why you are pleading not guilty when all of us agree that you spent the night in the Garden County Museum?"

If Gemma was afraid now, her words and her widespread stance no longer showed it. She gripped the table in front of her and spoke into the microphone at a plucky volume. "I am pleading not guilty to a criminal entry charge, Your Honor. As you'll read in the report, my daughter and I were locked in the museum by mistake. We never intended to break into the building." Her mouth stayed open for another beat. Gemma had a great many other things she'd intended to say. She thought better of it, though, and clamped her mouth shut.

"You haven't done this again? You've found a place to live? You have gainful employment?"

"I do. I have witnesses to that, your honor. That's why the coffee drinkers are here."

Judge Veeder grinned at the back row of spectators again. "Ah, so that explains the crowd in my courtroom."

He interlaced his fingers behind his head and leaned back in his tall leather chair to ponder. He swiveled the chair to the left in the direction of the Nebraska State Flag. He swiveled it to the right in the direction of the Stars and Stripes. At last the chair came to rest dead center again as he directed Jay Triplett to come forward. "Help me out here, son. It's finally your turn. Tell me about the way you handled this case. Tell me why you didn't cuff this woman and cart her in to jail."

Gemma clutched the table again, not from fear this time, but from a sense she had of being drawn forward by something beyond herself. No matter how imposing Jay Triplett looked in his uniform, she couldn't help liking him.

"The physical damage was minimal, Your Honor. It was the same sort of disarray that would occur in a house because somebody lived there. They'd been locked in for hours. And I could see by the way she made sure that her daughter ate first that she had the child's interest in mind above her own."

"Very good. Thank you, Triplett. You've helped a great deal." With one more sweep of the judge's hand, Jay Triplett was dismissed. "I always appreciate it when our officers keep a level head about the law. Now, on to a ruling." He glanced at his clerk, who was madly tip-tapping the keys on her computer keyboard. "Are you getting all of this?"

"I am, Judge Veeder. Keep talking."

"Pay close attention."

"I am, Judge Veeder."

"I hereby reduce the charge from criminal entry to loitering."

Mabel Perkins came up and out of her seat before his decision had a chance to register in anybody else's brain. "You can't do that, Solomon. That means we'll have another hearing."

Judge Veeder pushed himself up out of his huge leather chair with two robust, berobed arms. "Who's running the show here, Mabel? Is it you? Or is it me? You sit down or I'm going to charge you with contempt of court."

Mabel sat down.

He nodded at her. "Thank you."

"I'm sorry, Your Honor."

"We will not have another hearing. There's no reason to delay this process any further. I've read the report and I've heard the testimony. Therefore I find the defendant guilty of the charge of loitering in violation of statute 6-3-302. Gemma Franklin, approach the bench." He adjusted his eyeglasses again as she came before him.

"Yes, sir?"

"I have in my hand two Community Service Assignment Sheets, one for residents of Garden County, one for nonresidents of Garden County. Which of these forms applies to you?"

Gemma stared at a spot of mud beside her left shoe. Of all the questions Judge Solomon Leroy Veeder had asked her today, this was the first one she wasn't able to answer. "I don't believe I am a county resident, sir. I will only be a resident here until my Toyota Corolla is repaired."

The judge's voice could be either as gentle as goose down or as demanding as an impatient king's. He growled at her and snapped his fingers, "Now we're talking about repairs again. What sort of repairs? Do you have a chip in the windshield? Need an oil change? What?"

"I am paying for a rebuilt engine, sir."

"Well, that answers that." He handed her the paperwork specifically meant for county residents. "Gemma Franklin, I sentence you to fifty-four hours of community service. If you fail to appear at any agreed upon time, if you are not cooperative, or if you are in any way not completely participating, the agency has the option to release you from the program and not to accept further work from you. Your failure to comply with this order may result in the issuance of a bench warrant for your arrest or the loss of the hours you have already worked and a doubling of hours required. No credit is given for partial hours."

Gemma stood stock-still. It had all happened so fast. She didn't know what to say.

"You will serve your community service . . ." He began leafing through a different chart, apparently a listing of local agencies that needed volunteers. Abruptly, he dropped the listing in his lap and gave a broad, fixed grin. "Gemma Franklin, you will serve under Mabel Perkins, director, at the Garden County Museum. The museum is located on the corner of—"

Mabel Perkins leapt from her seat and interrupted the judge one more time. "She knows where the museum is, Solomon. She *slept* there!"

"Mabel, stop your cheeseparing. Can't you see I'm handing down a sentence from up here?"

"You can't sentence that girl to do volunteer work for me!"

"I can. The museum is listed right here and I'm the Justice Court Judge." He held up the paper and poked it with one crooked finger. "Here you are. Page two. 'Needs minors or adults. Uses volunteers frequently. Monday through Friday and weekends in summer months until eight P.M. Type of work available: clipping newspapers, typing, cleaning exhibits, clerical, tour guide, cleaning, snow shoveling, painting, etc.' Looking at her, I'd say she ought to be above average at performing any of these tasks."

"You're making me carry out her sentence; that's what you're doing."

Judge Solomon Leroy Veeder ignored Mabel Perkins and kept the procedures in his courtroom moving right along. "You are dismissed. Next case, please. State of Nebraska, Plaintiff, versus Ronald J. Hanrion, Defendant. Everyone involved in this case come forward and take the oath."

George Sissel had the astounding job of pastoring Antelope Valley Christian Fellowship, which meant a great many things more than some folks seemed to think it did. Andy Cleeland was always calling him on sermon-preparation day to see if he wouldn't rather go bass fishing with the new fish-finder in his boat on Lake Mac. Corwin Kepler came by the office at least once a week in his new truck, to rev the engine in the church parking lot so George could hear it purr. And Pearl Glazener brought him a box of watercolors one afternoon because she felt it was God's will for her to teach him to paint.

It was Jim Royal who finally came forth and voiced what George knew everybody in every congregation all over the country was thinking. "Sure would be nice having a job like yours, where you only have to work on Sundays. Heck, George, you just stand up there talking about whatever comes to mind, lead the benediction, go home to a good dinner, then you got the rest of the week to go fishing. Sure would be nice."

Pastoring the flock in Ash Hollow took a good deal more time and energy than most people knew. George's job description included everything from repairing the pinball machine in the youth room to the all-night vigil he kept, trying to identify one particular beaver that insisted on gnawing ash saplings paid for and planted by the Ladies Auxiliary.

It was he who received the first call when the ancient furnace conked out in the basement. It was he who received the first call when the church's yearly budget floundered. It was he who received the first call when the choir director came down with the measles and somebody else was needed to take over.

Often, in the wee hours of the morning, he would counsel those who faced tragedy. He would remind husbands and wives that they needed to have faith in God as much as they needed to have faith in one another. He would pray fervently for Ash Hollow citizens with depression and doubts. All this, while occasionally he also had the opportunity to water the periwinkles beside the rear sanctuary door and take out the trash from the church kitchen and administer bandages to scraped knees.

This is how it came to be that, on this morning of vacation Bible school when Paisley Franklin was dragged in by the activity director from a rousing game of Duck-Duck-Goose in the church parking lot with a bloody scrape on her shin and a runny nose, the child was handed off to the pastor himself for prompt doctoring.

"Come on in here, young lady." He took her by the hand and led her into the church secretary's office. "I've got a first-aid kit I use whenever anything like this happens."

No answer, only a sniff to tell him she was listening.

"Let's set you up here." He perched her on the edge of a counter where Sheila kept the fax machine and collated copies. "Now. What first?" He dug around in the bag and came up with a bottle of hydrogen peroxide. "How about this?"

"Will it hurt?" a pitiful little voice asked him.

"Don't think so. It makes bubbles instead. You can sit and watch it killing all the germs."

That earned a little smile. "Can not."

"You just watch." He uncapped the bottle and dribbled a little on her bloody knee. "Ah!" He clutched at his neck. "I'm dying. I'm a germ and I'm dying. Help me. Help me!"

"That is the most ridiculous thing I've ever seen," Paisley said matter-of-factly, swinging her legs, her heels kicking the counter.

"Okay. How about this? How about I get you a Band-Aid?"

This time she nodded.

"Big or little? Big ones always make it look like you've hurt yourself more."

He stepped aside to reach for the box of bandages. He heard the little gasp, the sharp intake of breath the moment he moved out of the way.

"What is it, Paisley? What's wrong?"

She pointed to the bulletin board across the room where Sheila kept photographs posted of church members.

"Do you know," the little girl asked as she puffed out her chest and lifted her gaze dramatically to the ceiling, "that she is Nathan's mama?"

George felt his breath catch in his chest. "How do you know about Nathan? Did she tell you about him?" If Bea Bartling was telling these strangers about her son, then perhaps she was beginning to heal.

But the little girl shook her head this time. "We already knew about Nathan when we came here. Nathan lived with us. He married us."

"You *knew* him?"

The tiny curls bobbed up and down as the little girl nodded harder. "Yep. He *loved* me."

"He did?"

"Yep. And he loved my mama, too."

"Oh, dearest." George applied the Band-Aid with great zeal, then picked Paisley up and swung her around, the hope for his friend Bea Bartling catching someplace deep in his belly. He loved that odd, quirky feeling he got when he discovered that God might be working. He wanted to sing out to his heavenly Father who was Master over all things, including the happenings in Ash Hollow, Nebraska. "Good for Bea. Oh, good for Bea."

Because he didn't know how to explain it so a little

girl could understand it, George did what he always did when caught in a bind.

He quoted Scripture.

"'All things work together for the good of those who love the Lord.'"

"What?"

"'All things—'"

"I know what you're saying," she interrupted him. "You're saying stuff from the Bible. I just don't know why you're saying that."

"Romans 8:28. It's such a good Scripture to fall back on, no matter what happens. Does Mrs. Bartling know who you are?"

For the third time, Paisley Franklin nodded. Only this time, the child's gesture wasn't quite so certain. "She knows. But she won't let me play with anything in Nathan's room. Whenever she thinks about us, it only makes her sad."

Chapter Thirteen

This morning began for Bea like all the others. Not for one moment could she forget that, although she was lonely, she wasn't alone. She measured ground coffee into the filter and slid it into its place. She poured a carafe of water into her coffeemaker and flipped it on. She dribbled the small amount of water left in the decanter into Paisley's little pot with the bean. She listened for sounds of her guests awakening as she stood staring out the window.

How many mornings had she stood at this window, praying for the safe return of her son. *Lord, keep Nathan safe. Lord, please bring my son home.*

"Good morning," Gemma murmured, poking her head around the door as the coffee pot began to gurgle and spurt steam. Right behind her came Paisley, tousle-headed from the bed, face still slack and rosy from sleep. The little girl climbed up into a kitchen chair, the shredded blanket with the Herefords bunched against her chest, her eyes only halfway open.

Three of them together in one small area, moving around each other with fearful, polite care, leaving huge spaces between one another as they went about their routine. Bea stood at the stove with her back to the room, her robe cinched tight around her middle, her elbows jutting at a protective angle while she scrambled eggs.

"Would you like me to pour you some coffee?" Gemma asked in a timid voice. "I think it's ready."

"No need. I'll get it myself. You'll be doing enough coffee pouring at the Cramalot Inn."

"Well." A long pause while Bea knew Gemma was waiting behind her, only she didn't know what for. "Can I pour some for me?"

"Oh, yes. Yes, of course. Sorry." Bea pulled out a bowl and began scraping eggs out of the pan. "No need to even ask. Help yourself. Pretend you live here."

"Is there a cup you'd like me to use?"

"Mugs are right there. Second cabinet to the left."

"Thank you."

"Sugar's in the canister over here. Milk's in the refrigerator. Spoon's in the drawer right below you."

"Thank you."

After they ate breakfast, there were showers to take, more spaces to be shared, more wary, courteous assurances given.

"Are you going to need the bathroom?"

"For a little while. Do you mind if I shower before I go to the museum?"

"Yes. Fine. I'll take a tub bath."

"Well, I can wait, if you'd rather shower. I don't have to do it now."

"Go ahead."

"I'll be fast. I won't use too much hot water."

"Use as much as you'd like. There's plenty. You want me to drive you over to the museum?"

"No. That's okay. It isn't too far. I'll walk over."

"Do you want me to pick you up at the Cramalot after you're done? Don't mind driving you, Gemma, if you'd like."

"You've done so much already, letting us stay here. I don't want you to worry about chauffeuring us around."

"You're sure?"

"Yes."

"If that's what you want . . ."

"I don't want to overstay our welcome, Mrs. Bartling. As soon as I get the money to fix the car, we'll be on our way. Until then, I'll figure out a way to get around town without imposing on you."

"If you ever need me—"

"We won't." Gemma jumped in quickly, as if she thought she needed to reassure their hostess. "I'll make sure of it."

How long will it take to fix their car? Bea wondered. *How long will it take before they decide to move along? Now that I've taken them in, how long will I have to learn something of Nathan's history?*

Bea held up Paisley's pot from the windowsill. "Your plant's growing. Something's breaking out of the soil."

"Can I see?" Paisley stood on her tiptoes and peered over the edge. In the flowerpot, a new living thing had broken through the crust of dirt. A fat curl of green bowed beneath the weight of a bean, still two-thirds buried, once hard and brown, now succulent and yellow, splitting into two halves. "It's growing!"

"By next week, it'll be sticking straight up. You just wait and see."

While Bea returned the flowerpot to the windowsill, Paisley clambered up into her mother's lap and snuggled close. "Mama," she said very quietly. "There's a show we're doing at vacation Bible school today. Can you come?"

Gemma brushed her daughter's hair back out of her eyes with one hopeless sweep of fingers. "What time?" she asked, the apology already thick in her voice.

"At lunch. There's pizza and everything. And then we're going to sing."

"I can't get away, honey bananas. I've got to spend an hour or so serving my time at the museum. After that I'm due at The Cramalot Inn for lunch. That's when my new job is the busiest of all."

"Can't you just ask? Maybe they would let you."

"It doesn't work that way, Paisley Rose. When you grow up, you can't just ask for things the way you do when you're a kid. People don't take it right."

Disappointment flooded the little girl's face. "You're working all the time again, Mama, just like you used to."

Gemma took that pixie, sad face and held it between two cupped hands. "I'm sorry, little one. You know there's nothing I can do. The judge said I have to work at the museum. And you know I've got to make enough money to get us back home."

"But we don't—" Bea turned back at that moment and saw Gemma shushing Paisley. She didn't know what it meant.

"You'll just have to sing in the show by yourself, honey bananas. You sing real pretty, and Mama will be real proud."

Bea spritzed glass cleaner on the windowpane over the sink and rubbed it hard with a paper towel, buffing off spots. She stepped to the left, peered through the glass with the sun at a different angle, checking to make sure she hadn't missed any more smudges. Her heart pummeled in her chest.

I've taken them in, she said to no one. *I'm feeding them and giving them a place to stay and trying to open my heart. Surely they can't expect any more from me than that.*

Bea stepped to the right, surveyed the window again, found three spots she'd missed. Glass cleaner ran down the pane.

Why should I be faithful, if I serve a God who isn't?

She started scrubbing. Hard. Harder than she ever knew she could scrub.

I could offer to go to the show. I could offer to stand in the audience and applaud her. I could.

Bea stepped back, eyed her work critically, and pronounced it acceptable. She tossed the damp paper towel into the trash and stared at it for a long time before she shut the pantry door.

But I'm not the one she wants. She wants to be with her mother. Or Nathan. But of course it's too late for that.

Piece by piece, Bea began to dismantle the cookstove, letting the old, rattling stove parts stand in for everything broken and rattling inside of her. She dismembered each burner, yanking the prongs from the electrical elements. She pried up each drip pan, screwing up her chin in distaste when she saw the grease and charred drippings below. She squirted cleaner on a rag and went after the mess, the heel of her hand bearing the brunt of her anger.

What were these two girls doing, hanging around in her kitchen? They had places to go. "You'd better get on in there and take your shower," Bea chided Gemma, her voice sounding harsh. "Won't have any money to pay for that car if Alva fires you because you're late for work."

"Oh." Like a frightened animal, Gemma skittered halfway across the kitchen, coffee sloshing out of the mug she still carried. "You're right. I'd better go." She hurried off down the hall.

All that, though, and Paisley didn't move. Bea sensed rather than saw the four-year-old still sitting in the kitchen chair, still waiting for something, behind her.

You are a tired, worn-out old woman who's never amounted to a thing in anybody's life. Why would you think you could change that now?

Bea projected her chin in Paisley's direction. "You, too. What are you still waiting there for? Don't think I'm driving you to church if you miss your ride. Doesn't your mother have to help you get dressed? Sissels aren't going to wait around for you if you aren't ready."

Of course I can't do it, she said to no one but herself. *There's no reason for me to go to any show.*

Bea cast one furtive glace sideways in time to see Paisley slide out of her chair. The little girl only looked back once. She padded with bare toes across the floor, never saying another word.

It seemed like everywhere Gemma went today, people were busy washing windows. First, there was Mrs. Bartling washing windows in her kitchen. Then Mabel Perkins assigned Gemma an hour of window washing out in the yard at the Garden County Museum. "Here's your bucket of vinegar water." Mabel plopped it down so hard in the grass that it splashed all over Gemma's feet. "Here's a pile of newspapers. Wad these up and use them to polish after you've scrubbed off all the spots. Screens come off like this. See here?" Mabel wheeled around and caught her staring at the stack of papers like she'd never seen newsprint before. "You do know how to wash windows, don't you? Don't tell me Judge Solomon

Veeder assigned me fifty-four hours with somebody who doesn't wash windows."

"I know how." Everybody knew how to wash a window. It's just that Gemma had never done it. There hadn't been any need to see out, not in a trailer with only two tiny windows, some five inches square. Not with a view of a littered empty lot and a row of Dumpsters and the hulking, remote back passage of the meat packing plant. Gemma didn't even know that screens could come off.

She picked up the rag and smeared the smelly solution across the first windowpane of the eight that lined the southern side of the museum. She wadded a page of newspaper, an old editorial from *The Garden County News*, and used it to burnish the glass.

"No. Not that way." Mabel took her arm and scrubbed for her. "You've got to rub hard in a circle or it won't do any good at all. And don't miss the corners. If you do, I'm going to make you go back and do them all again."

An hour and eight gleaming windows later, Gemma carried the bucket and a sack of used newspapers back inside, her shoulders aching, her nose scorched red from the sun. She squinted her eyes, unable to adjust to the cool, dim light inside the building. The bucket clattered as she set it on the floor. Her vision began to clear and she saw Mabel and an elderly man she didn't recognize setting up a barrel in one corner of the exhibit room. "You finished out there?" Mabel twisted the barrel to her liking and situated a square of plywood on the top. "I'm planning on working you another hour. You got the time?"

"I do."

"This is Orvin Kornruff. I've got to run to the bank

but, while I'm gone, Orvin's going to start setting up our new reenactment exhibit. Thought since you were here to help, it would be an excellent time to do this."

"I'll help."

"Good."

Mabel had no more disappeared out the door before Mr. Kornruff spread out a checkerboard on top of the barrel table and began arranging checkers on the black squares. "Red or black, Miss Franklin?"

"What?"

"Red or black? Which checkers would you like to play with?"

"I can't play games," she told him. "I have to work."

"Nonsense. I'm in charge now, young lady. I'll get this exhibit arranged in record time before Mabel gets back. I saw how hard you were working out there. And I know you've got an eight-hour day ahead of you at the Cram-alot. Besides, just look at this as a part of the exhibit. We're going to add more to this display of the Lewellen Country Store. A whole group of fellows from the senior center in Oshkosh have volunteered to come over here and dress in old timey clothes and play checkers whenever a tour bus comes through. I want you to sit down and play me a game now."

"But I've never played checkers before."

"I'll teach you. Come on."

"But maybe that means my work time today won't count toward my sentence. What if the judge finds out?"

"Oh, Veeder wouldn't care, even if he *did* know. I've lived around this town long enough to know people's history. I've been around this place long enough to know people's secrets. Veeder isn't nearly as tough to satisfy as Mabel Perkins."

Gemma pulled up a stool and banged her knees

against the metal rim of the barrel. Mr. Kornruff turned the board so she'd be playing with the red checkers and he'd be playing with the black. He began to explain to her the basics of checker playing. Black always starts . . . move diagonally . . . men can only go forward and never go back. The object is to capture your opponent's men by jumping them . . . a checker that makes it all the way is crowned a king . . . a king can move backward or forward.

Try as she might, Gemma couldn't concentrate on the instructions Orvin Kornruff was giving her. She could only replay his boasting in her mind. *I've lived around this town long enough to know people's history. I've been around this place long enough to know people's secrets.*

"Your turn. I've made my move, Gemma. Now you have to decide what you want to do."

She pushed one checker forward with one finger.

"No, you weren't listening to me, young lady. You can't move that way. It has to be *diagonally*. Onto another black square."

Embarrassed, she moved her red checker sideways to the black square. "I was listening to you. I was just thinking about something else."

Ever since she'd moved into the house on Pattison Drive, the house with the roses, Gemma couldn't stop thinking about Nathan's defection from his mother. She couldn't stop thinking about why he would have left a home he loved—a mother who cared about him—and never share the reason with his wife.

For the past three years, she had grown closer to Nathan than any other living person. She'd mentioned this to him with great care so many times after they'd first gotten married. "Nathan, you've told me so much about your home. So, why don't you ever take me there? Why don't you ever call and talk to your mother?"

"We'll go there someday, Gemma. I promise you that. My mother will want to meet you. But not now. I can't handle that yet."

"What is it, Nathan? Why can't you tell me about this? Why can't you open up to me and let me help you?"

"Leave this alone, Gemma. There isn't anything you can do to help. I've get everything I want now, right here, with you and Paisley Rose. That's the only thing I want you to concern yourself about."

What could have happened that tore the two of you apart, Nathan? What could have been so shameful that you wouldn't have shared it with me?

The time had come for Gemma to move again. This time, she moved the checker forward toward Mr. Kornruff's oncoming man. "How's that?"

"Much better," he told her, grinning. "You'll make a checker player yet."

"I've got a long while to go."

"You'll get there. You learn how to play checkers as fast as you learned to wash those windows out there, you'll be beating me in no time."

Gemma lowered her eyes to the board and didn't raise them as she pushed a second checker onto a second black square. "You mind if I ask you something?"

"What is it?" He pushed another checker forward, too.

"You said you know things. About people's history. About people's secrets."

"Yes."

Gemma pushed a third checker out into the center of

the board. "Do you know anything about Mrs. Bartling? The lady we're staying with?"

"Bea Bartling?"

"Yes."

"Of course I do. I've known Bea a good long time."

"How long is a good long time?"

"Since before Ray walked out of his job building houses for Homestead Construction. That must have been twenty-four years ago or so."

"He just walked out?"

"Yep. Left them pregnant with no insurance, him doing such a fool thing as that. After their son was born, it took them a good three years to pay off the bill over at Garden County Hospital."

"That was when Nathan was born?" she asked.

He nodded. "Yep. Sure was."

"So . . ." Gemma's pulse was pounding so hard, she thought the man across the checkerboard from her might be able to hear it. "Can I ask you something else?"

"Sure. Fire away."

She positioned another checker then lifted pleading eyes to him. "Can you tell me why Nathan left home when he did? I'd really like to know."

"Hm-mmm." Orvin Kornruff studied the game. He clutched his fingers over his mouth, squeezed his whiskery chin, and stared at the black and red squares on the board for an inordinately long time. At last he picked up one of his men and began jumping Gemma's red checkers. One. Two. Three. "You want to know why Nathan left. Now, there's a hundred-dollar question for you." He removed the checkers he'd jumped and stacked them in an organized stack beside his left elbow. "Bea Bartling has been as tight lipped as a soldier whenever anybody's asked her about that. If somebody in Ash Hollow knows the answer, I sure don't know who it is."

"Oh, well." Gemma shrugged her shoulders, resigning herself to losing this game. She didn't want Mr. Kornruff to sense her sharp disappointment. *I'll find out the answer some way. Even if nobody else in Ash Hollow knows, I'm the one who knew Nathan.* "Guess it doesn't matter anyway. I just thought it couldn't hurt to ask."

Bea wandered from room to room in her home, closing the windows, turning on each separate air conditioner unit, making ready for the heat for the day.

She paused in the doorway of Nathan's silent, empty room.

The same sensation came over Bea every time she stood in this place. The intense longing to step inside. The awful fear of going there, of facing her deprivation, of admitting to herself that her son would not return.

Bea couldn't stop herself. She took one step into the room she had kept ready for her son's homecoming all these many months and years. She had pictured it so many times. How Nathan would come to the door, how she would take his hand and lead him here.

"See, Nathan," she had planned to tell him. "I always knew you would come back home. I kept everything ready."

Every child who has ever needed me has been let down.

The last time she had attended a vacation Bible school program, Nathan had been eleven.

"Look, Mama," Nathan said as he dragged a dark-headed little boy toward her through the crowd. "I made a new friend. This is Jacob."

"Hello, Jacob," she said, not paying much attention. "It's nice to meet you."

Very solemnly, Jacob extended his hand to hers. "Hi."

She shook his proffered hand. "You must not be from around here."

"They just moved here," Nathan interrupted. "He's two year's younger than me, but he's really nice. Can he come over and play sometime? He likes to play baseball. Do you think we might be able to play on the same team?"

"I don't know." Bea narrowed her brows and released Jacob's hand. She didn't know the answers to so many questions at once. She felt backed into a corner. "We'll see."

"Can Jacob come to our house today?"

"No. Not today. You've spent enough time with him here. We have errands to run this afternoon."

"Can Jacob come tomorrow? It's Saturday. Dad will be home."

"I don't know about tomorrow. We might want to do something for a family day."

"Jacob could be a part of our family. Couldn't you?" Like a traitor, Nathan turned to the small, dark-headed boy beside him and involved him in this uncomfortable conspiracy. "Jacob could come, too."

Jacob answered very quietly. "I could probably do it."

"I don't know, Nathan," Bea said, her voice thin, taunt. "Jacob has his own family. We'll have to wait until tomorrow and see."

Even now, the memory of that day—the humility and the desperation of the things that followed—felt huge in her, holding her to the spot so she couldn't move.

I was afraid of Jacob. I didn't want to let him in even then. And I didn't understand why.

All of a sudden, Bea couldn't get out of Nathan's

room fast enough. She stepped out into the hallway, heard the buzzing of the air conditioners cooling the house from every room.

That's how I lived my life with Ray, with Nathan, with all of them. Always afraid, when I should have been secure. Always secure, when I should have been afraid.

Oh, God. Oh, God. Look where it's gotten me now.

Without turning back, she closed the bedroom door behind her.

As Gemma walked from the museum to work that morning, she could see Alva Torrington clear down at the other side of Main Street, going after the front window of The Cramalot Inn with a razor knife, scraping off the rose.

"What is she doing out there?" Gemma asked Charlene as she signed in on her time card and started tying on her apron.

"Oh, there's no telling. You don't know Alva as well as I do. She's always coming up with something."

As if she'd heard them talking about her, here came Alva, marching in through the door with such ardor that the tinkling bell almost fell off its bracket. She pushed the razor knife inside her apron belt in much the same gesture as she would holster a weapon, tramped to the back storeroom, and came back brandishing a paint can and a wooden-handled brush. She set both of those items on the counter in front of her two waitresses. "Who wants to help me paint?"

Gemma lifted her hands to show that, when it came to paintbrushes, she was helpless. "I'm still learning to wait tables."

"Okay." Alva hefted the can and waddled across the room under its weight. Brown paint sloshed around inside. "Charlene, that means you. You come do this, would you?"

Charlene flipped her hair over her shoulder. "I already painted that rose out there, Alva. I don't know why you weren't satisfied with that."

"I've decided I want you to paint a giant meat loaf instead."

"I don't think that can be done."

"Why not?"

"It's like playing Pictionary. You start out thinking something's easy to draw, then you get into it and realize there aren't any identifying details that'll make it look right. If I try to paint a meat loaf, it won't be anything except a big, brown rectangle."

"Well, I want you to come up with something. Don't want to be advertising famous roses around here anymore. It's misleading."

Gemma removed a fresh coconut crème pie from its domed pedestal and began to cut the pastry into precise, ordered triangles. "How so?" She didn't look up.

"Those roses used to be something joyous. Now they're just something sad. Bea Bartling isn't coming out in her yard to show them to tourists now that Nathan's gone."

Gemma didn't flinch at the sound of her husband's name. She kept right on at what she was doing, paring deep into the crust with the knife, making eight perfect pieces.

When she was finished, she put the pie under its dome and ran the knife under a stream of hot tap water, watching the whipped cream melt away.

I've got no business falling apart every time somebody talks about Nathan, she lectured herself. *This is Nathan's home. He's going to be talked about every place I go.*

Alva spoke up proudly, oblivious to Gemma's silence. "I've decided to run a contest. Gemma, you can cover extra tables while Charlene's out creating us a masterpiece, can't you? I know it's busy in here, but if she doesn't start now, we won't get it finished before we close."

Charlene started stacking coffee cups one on top of the other. "What kind of a contest?"

"You get out there and start painting and you'll find out about it soon enough."

Gemma started cutting the cherry pie. "I can cover the tables."

For the rest of the afternoon, Charlene worked outside. Each time Gemma glanced up and saw her face through the broad front glass, she seemed more and more engrossed with her artwork. Gemma watched as her friend began to make little flourishes with the brush, adding detail to one side of the picture, stepping back to see if it worked. Twice she came in to mix paints and add different colors. Gemma grinned as Charlene added gray in tiny curls to imitate warm fragrance rising. At last, a good hour after she'd gone outside to get started, here came Charlene back in again, looking pleased with herself, a swath of brown paint across her nose, her eyes sparkling. "Just wait until you go out there and see it, Gemma. I didn't think I could do it, but I did!"

"You aren't finished, Charlene, so don't even think about getting cleaned up yet." Alva set the small stepladder out so it looked like an aluminum A standing beside the cash register. "I got words for you to write out there, too."

"Words? What words, Alva?"

"Got myself two waitresses to keep busy these days and I'm aiming to increase business."

The lunch rush waned, but Gemma kept busy. She took orders, delivered full platters and poured over four carafes of fresh, hot coffee, glancing up every so often to watch the mysterious words appear backwards beyond the glass.

!FAOLTAEM SSELMOTTOB EHT FO EMOH

When Charlene finally finished, Gemma held up the weight of her apron, the coins jangling in her pockets. "You're getting all my tips today, aren't you?" Charlene asked. "Alva never thinks about things like that when she asks me to do projects."

"I'll share with you. Don't worry."

"You know what that contest is? If somebody comes in here and eats two pounds of meat loaf without stopping, he gets it for free. If somebody doesn't eat the whole thing, it costs twenty bucks. She's even put up a sign down at Sandhill Texaco so she'll get people coming into town from off the highway."

"What if we don't want people coming in off the highway?" Gemma asked, not once stopping to think that she had just come in off the highway a week ago herself.

Her question was lost in the chugging of the old Dodge truck that pulled up and sat running, blue smoke issuing in dirty puffs from the muffler, a good two feet away from the curb. The green-and-white mountains on the license plate meant Colorado. The driver finally cut the engine and swaggered into the Cramalot, standing in the open front door a minute or two too long, like he wanted to be certain the place was good enough for him before he shut the door and came on in.

Gemma got a sick feeling from the very start.

One of the things she could tell he saw when he looked around to see if he liked the place was her. When his murky green eyes rested on her, his mouth took on the approving shape of someone saying the word *prune*.

Dread coursed through her.

Gemma didn't know how to put off someone's advances any longer. It had been too long. And, oh, goodness, not nearly long enough.

She kept right on doing what she was doing, stacking clean glasses from the dishwasher tray onto a shelf beside the pop machine, sorting them according to size—tiny, narrow ones for the juice; medium, fat ones for the milk; taller ones for the folks who ordered Pepsi or Alva's hand-squeezed lemonade.

"What's a fellow got to do to get a table around here?"

Gemma glanced around for Charlene, but the other waitress was nowhere in sight. She tugged her skirt down, stuck a menu beneath her arm, grabbed a glass of water and directed him to a table as far away from the kitchen as possible. She set the water down in front of him, making sure when she did so that her wedding ring was in plain view. "I'll be back in a minute to see what you want."

"Hey, hon," he said, catching her arm just as she turned away. "They got you on the menu? You're what I'd really like."

The ceiling wobbled. Of all the battles Gemma had fought these past days—the night Nathan never returned home and she had to telephone the police from a pay phone to find out he was dead, the morning Joe Stedman set their belongings in the yard behind the meat-packing plant and said he needed her out of the trailer since Nathan wasn't there to work anymore, the day Mrs. Bartling turned them away and they'd spent the night on the old bed at the museum—this simple, small one turned out to be the most brutal.

There isn't anybody in this world who's going to protect me. I am alone. Totally alone. I could die, too, and there'd be no one anywhere who cares what happens to me. And no one to raise Paisley.

"If my husband were here," she said to him, "he would punch your lights out."

"Well . . ." The fellow made a big show of looking around the room for her husband. "I sure don't see him standing around. You got me shaking in my boots, honey."

She poised her green order pad in the air, willing her hands to remain steady and her gaze to remain level on his. "You want to order something for lunch or not?"

He leaned back in his chair, still appraising her. "I'll have that meat loaf special. The whole two pounds of it. I'm aiming to show y'all what I can do and get the whole thing for free."

Gemma didn't take the time to write his order. She scurried away from him, scribbled the ticket at the counter, and hung it on the stainless steel wheel beside the grill. She didn't return until she had no other choice but to deliver his dinner roll.

"I'm on a deadline, you know," he announced to her as he picked up the pat of margarine and peeled off the paper. "But I could push it back maybe an hour or two. What time you get off from this place? I could take you out."

"Mister, please. Just leave me alone."

"After this, I got to drive this truck all the way over to North Carolina. You ever been to North Carolina?"

"No. Never been any place but Nebraska."

"In North Carolina, they've got real pretty little hills.

Hems you in, all those hills. Gives you something to hold on to. All covered with trees that turn about a hundred different colors when the weather gets cold."

"Don't want to see any trees. I like it here where you can see the sky."

"Could always use the company of a pretty little thing like you."

The sudden, awful possibility presented itself, enticing and easy, terrifying her.

I could go. I could walk out of here and never look back and leave all this pain behind me. Somebody else could raise Paisley. Somebody else could grieve over Nathan. Somebody else could struggle to make ends meet and find a place to live and keep that old junk-heap of a Toyota running.

I could run away from all this and nobody would even know where I'd gone.

Gemma shoved her hands inside her apron pockets and found all those coins jangling around inside, a quarter here, two dimes there—the very thing she depended on to save her. "Don't you even talk that way," she said to Mr. Meat Loaf Special, sounding frantic. "Don't you even mention me leaving like that."

She saw him stretch out his legs even longer and figured he must have crossed his boot tops under the table. "You know, I got you all figured out." He folded his beefy arms over his chest. "Only one reason such a beautiful woman with a wedding ring would be acting so uptight. He's gone off and left you here alone, hasn't he? Some good husband you've got."

Something heavy slammed into the pit of Gemma's stomach. "That's not true," she lied. "You hush up. Just hush up."

"I'd be willing to bet you've probably got a kid stashed away somewhere around, too. Aren't I right?"

Oh, if he only knew how right he is.

"What's your name, Pretty Little Miss Nebraska?"

"The name's Charlene." Charlene sidled up next to both of them and plopped a plate crammed with meat loaf in front of him. "Your order's been ready for five minutes. Two pounds just like you ordered. If you can eat all this meat loaf, mister, then I'll eat my shoes."

Charlene waited his table until he left with two-thirds of his lunch uneaten and had to pay the twenty dollars. She waited all the other tables, too, while Gemma stayed in the kitchen, sopping up her tears with a stained tea towel, trying to regain her composure. "I'm so sorry. I'm so s-sorry," she wailed every time Alva or Charlene passed her in the aisle.

"That's okay, honey. That's okay."

Charlene finally stopped to speak to her when the rush had tapered off and the din in the kitchen had settled to a dull clanking of the big industrial dishwasher. "Alva's taking you back to Bartling's in a few minutes so you can get yourself together."

"I'm so sorry."

Charlene gave her a tight, sisterly hug. "You don't have to apologize anymore, Gemma. We've all noticed that ring on your finger. And every single one of us has been scared to death to ask."

Chapter Fourteen

Paisley Franklin stood where she'd been placed for the vacation Bible school singing program, in the center on the front row so everyone could see her, squeezed in between Sam Wyatt—who had wiggled his right front tooth so much that it made his gums bleed—and Amy Huff, a short seven-year-old who had been bragging ever since Monday because her mama was in charge of refreshments and she got to help.

Paisley's heart pounded. She loved to sing. She loved this song.

The music began. She sidled over as close as she could to Amy; Sam's loose tooth was sick. She lifted her chin and put on her special sunglasses. She gave a big smile just the way her teacher had told her to and began to sing a song about Jesus.

The pizza outside had already disappeared from its mountain of boxes—so fast that Paisley wouldn't have gotten a piece except for Ryan Staley, the sixth grader who towered over her, who'd asked, "Here? Want one?" and before she could answer had handed her a sliver of pepperoni pizza. The sanctuary at Antelope Valley

Christian Fellowship was filled up with parents and acquaintances and someone had lined extra chairs in the aisles. A group of fathers with video cameras stood just inside the double door, focusing elaborate equipment on the front of the church, red lights blinking, lens covers dangling like Oreos from strings.

"Come learn God's stories, come learn the Bible true . . ."

No matter how many parents filled the sanctuary, Paisley kept scanning the room, looking for one more.

"Come hear all about Jesus, come find out how much He loves you!"

She kept thinking that maybe Mama had decided to come anyway. She kept thinking that maybe that lady at work had said, "Doesn't matter how busy we are today. This is important. Go on and hear your daughter sing."

But as Paisley sang and searched with her eyes up one row and down another, down one row and up another, her heart began to sink.

Mama hadn't come. She never should have hoped.

Paisley forced herself to keep singing anyway, her smile pasted on her face even though she didn't feel like smiling at all.

After the song ended, Pastor Sissel asked the children to sit quietly on the floor so the teachers could give out special, individual awards. Everybody got an award as their parents and friends stood up and rooted for them. Sam Wyatt got *Most Likely To Lose A Tooth*. Jake Rucker got *Mr. Capture The Flag*. Hilary Hern got *The Purple Heart Award* for falling down and breaking her new eyeglasses. And Paisley Franklin got *The Littlest Songbird Award* for being the most likely to sing loud during the performance.

When Paisley's name was called, the audience applauded politely. But nobody stood up to cheer and clap loud. Nobody videotaped. Nobody took a picture.

If Nathan had been here, Paisley thought, *he would have cheered for me*.

Pastor Sissel stepped up to the microphone and adjusted it to his liking. "Now we come to a serious part of the program. These children have spent all week learning about how much God cares for us. They've learned how God sent His only son Jesus to save us from our sins, if we'll only invite Him into our lives."

Paisley started to pick up the new crayon drawings she'd laid on the floor beside her. Only she didn't. Something stopped her hand.

"We thank you for letting us share the blessing of your children this week. And now, I can go no further this afternoon without offering the gift of Jesus Christ to you." Piano music began to play softly. "All you need to do is invite the Lord into your heart at this moment. I'm here to greet you at His altar, to pray with you. If you don't want to step forward, you can ask the Lord into your heart right where you're sitting."

Paisley glanced around at people putting away their cameras and fidgeting with the hymnals and picking up their belongings in the pews. A gentle whisper of certainty sang through into her spirit. With one gentle touch, one gentle rousing from the depths of her heart, Paisley knew the truth. *Wait!* she wanted to tell the grownups. *Wait and don't leave before you've heard what Jesus can do!*

Paisley couldn't breathe. She couldn't move. She felt something strange and wonderful inside herself. Something warm and true. As if a daddy was holding her in his arms and loving on her.

Pastor Sissel isn't just talking to the grownups. He's talking to me, too.

"Did you know," Pastor Sissel asked as he continued the altar call, "that the Lord delights in your singing? Did you know that no one can praise Him exactly the way you can praise Him?"

Jesus?

Why would Jesus call her? Paisley wondered. She was almost the littlest one of the bunch. She didn't even have a mama in the audience. He ought to be talking to Ryan Staley, who had been nice enough to give out pieces of pizza. Or Amy Huff, who could really use Jesus helping her not to brag. Amy and Ryan were bigger. They could do something.

Why would you want me, Jesus?

"Jesus is calling you," Pastor Sissel said, "because God loves you more than you can ever understand. Jesus died for you on the cross. If he could have only saved one person and that person was you, He would have done exactly as He did when He did it. From the beginning of Genesis to the end of Revelation, God is crying, 'I will buy you and carry you out and set you free. Where are you? Call my name, beloved, and be with me.'"

Paisley had heard all week that it was easy, that all you had to do was say a prayer either out loud or in your head—whatever you were in the mood to do. Jesus could hear it all. Just like He could hear her singing.

Pastor Sissel had said Jesus liked her singing!

When you prayed, you told Jesus that you needed Him more than anything in the world, that you wouldn't be happy unless He was living inside you. Then you asked Him to bring all of Himself and move into your heart and live with you all of the time. And when you asked, He would come! A new daddy and a best friend, just as easy as all that.

When Nathan had been in their family, he had made her feel like she had a daddy. But Paisley knew the truth. No matter how much Nathan had loved her, she had never had a real daddy before.

Jesus, I want you. I want you. Would you like to come in?

But Paisley didn't need to ask that question. Because she already knew His answer.

Laughing, she stood up and stepped forward with happiness, into the arms of Pastor Sissel.

Chapter Fifteen

Three times during Gemma's ride back to the Bartling's in Alva T.'s ancient Chrysler New Yorker, the glove compartment door crashed open and smacked Gemma across the knees.

Each time, Gemma slammed the door shut and rubbed her bare shins. "Ouch."

"Sorry about that." Alva didn't miss a beat. She checked her vermilion-coated lips in the rearview mirror, making a little kiss at herself. "You just have to slam it real hard so the thing won't open again. Hy and I decided not to fix it because it's too sentimental."

"What's sentimental about getting your knees smashed when you least expect it?" Gemma fiddled with the latch, trying to make certain the box wouldn't spring open again.

Alva's red lips spread across her face in a grin as broad as a melon slice. "That's how he asked me to marry him. He put the ring in the glove compartment. Drove us clear to Oshkosh to a movie on a little farm-to-market back road, hitting every bump he could along the way. By the time we got there, I was so carsick I was ready to climb out the window. He pulled up into the parking lot, turned off the key while I kept yelling at him about the way he was driving. Then smack, the minute the engine died, the glove compartment whacked open, hit my legs, and there was that little square velvet box."

Gemma didn't say a word to that. She stared out the window, at the wild tangle of sunflowers and goldenrod just beginning to bloom along the side of the road.

"How about you?" Gemma sensed rather than saw Alva glancing across the front car seat at her, glancing at the simple strand of gold that encircled her left ring finger. She asked a question they all must have been gossiping about over at the Cramalot. "How did your man ask you to marry him?"

Gemma didn't turn her face away from the window. She took one long, deep breath and sighed it back out again. "I don't want to talk about that, Alva."

"Oh."

Alva T. had obviously learned long ago how to cover up uncomfortable situations. She didn't wait very long before she turned on the radio and began to hum, tapping her vermilion fingernails against the steering wheel in rhythm to *Daytripper* by the Beatles. She peered over the top of her tortoise-shell sunglasses and squinted into the sun.

They drove another block before Gemma finally turned to her employer with regret shining in her eyes. "I'm sorry you had to bring me home. I'm sorry I wasn't any good waiting tables today."

"I get mad about it, I'd have to remember you probably made up for it, waiting all Charlene Grover's tables this afternoon while she painted my window."

"That doesn't make up for it at all."

"You've got to get thick skin, waiting on some of these customers. Particularly the flirty ones. Some of them can really get to you."

"I've worked in a restaurant before, Alva. I know how it is."

Alva didn't signal when she made the last turn onto Pattison Drive. She didn't slow down, either. "Listen, honey," she said. "You have a man who left you, it isn't anything to be ashamed of."

"He didn't leave me. He died."

"Oh."

They'd pulled up in front of the house now, but Alva started the whole routine all over again. Radio up even louder. Humming the tune. Tapping her nails on the steering wheel with little annoying clicks.

Gemma fumbled to find the door handle.

"It's up there." Alva nodded. "Reach forward."

Gemma reached forward and still couldn't find the handle.

Alva moved the gearshift to P for Park and scooted over to do it for her. "You'll get back on track at the Cramalot, honey. I'll bet it's rough, but you just get some rest and pull yourself together." The door opened. "You aren't going to be any good to me if you don't stop blubbering around the pop machine and using all my Sysco napkins to blow your nose."

"Oh, Alva, I'm so sorry."

"I've got to get back before the boys from the Senior Center come in for their coffee. Would you stop apologizing?" Alva shook her head. "I'm trying to make you laugh is all. See you in the morning." She moved the gearshift back to D for Drive and the Chrysler nudged forward almost before Gemma had the chance to climb out.

Bea knew something was wrong with Gemma the minute she saw her jump from Alva T.'s car. She stood in the window watching for a moment as the young woman tramped slowly up the walk, her head hanging. When she arrived at the door, Bea saw Gemma hesitate, as if she didn't know whether to reach for the handle and come on in like she belonged there or to knock and wait like a houseguest.

Gemma compromised, knocking lightly on the door, then opening it and sticking her head inside just in case no one came. "You don't have to knock." Bea unfolded the afghan and draped it over Paisley, who had mercifully drifted off to sleep for a rare nap on the sofa.

For one brilliant moment, Bea kept looking down, softened by the child's innocence, her hand poised in mid-air, aching to brush the curls from Paisley's sweaty little face. Wonder tinged her heart.

What would it be like if she could pretend this girl was really Nathan's child? His daughter? Her own granddaughter?

Would it feel any stranger than this already felt?

"Didn't know if I could just walk in, or what."

"You're home early."

Gemma touched the little, worn leather purse slung over her shoulder, glancing around the room as if she was looking for some comfortable place to hang it. Apparently she didn't find it because she kept it on her shoulder. "I got good tips today so I can afford to go to the laundromat. Came home early so I could do our laundry."

Bea knew Alva Torrington too well for that. Gemma was lying. "You sure you didn't get fired or something? Alva never lets people off early."

The Flintstones played on the TV across the room. The volume had been turned low so as not to disturb the sleeping child. "I didn't get fired," Gemma said. "Don't worry. I'll still make wages there. I'll be able to pay for my car repairs."

"You think all I ever worry about is your car." Bea

scowled at her. "That car will get fixed in its own good time, and you know it."

Surprise registered in Gemma's eyes. For a good two beats, maybe three, she looked as if she wasn't certain what she should say. Finally she gestured toward her daughter, bringing the conversation back to more comfortable ground.

"Thank you for covering her, Mrs. Bartling," she whispered. She stepped forward and laid her hand against the little concave of Paisley's back, covered by the afghan, a gesture not so different from the one Bea had caught herself yearning to make before. "She likes to be covered when she sleeps."

On the television, Fred told Barney that they ought to tell Wilma and Betty they had to work late when they were going bowling instead. Canned laughter swelled. Bea took one step toward Gemma and the child, her hands in knotted fists at her side, her frown softening. "You don't have to go to a laundromat to wash your clothes. You can do that here."

"I don't want to impose, Mrs. Bartling. You've been kind enough already, giving us a place to stay."

"Kind? No, I haven't been kind." Is that what Gemma Franklin thought? Of all things, Bea knew she owed it to this young woman to be truthful. "I've only done what I thought I was expected to do."

Gemma squared her jaw. She gave a slight, downcast nod of acceptance. "I see."

"You go get your clothes. I've got a project going out in the utility room, too. This is as good a time as any to show you how to start the washer."

While Bea waited for Gemma, she fumbled through one of her cabinets for a tower of little terra-cotta pots.

"What are those for?" Gemma asked when she returned, a bundle of dirty clothes balanced beneath her chin.

"Utility room is in the garage. Come with me." Bea held the pots together high above her head so they wouldn't topple. Gemma followed her to the laundry room and dumped the little pile of clothes onto the work table, crudely covered with cracked linoleum. She watched while Bea dismantled the tower of pots and set them beside one another, all in a row. With a shiny quarter-cup measuring scoop, she dipped into a half-filled bag of potting soil and meted out some into each pot. She lifted a mason jar from the shelf. In it, leaves and stems floated in water like a cut flower bouquet, their wooden canes submerged, buds tightly furled, rootlets breaking through in new, tender sprouts. "Detergent's in the cabinet above the washer. There." Bea pointed.

"Are those roses?" Gemma asked.

"Yes."

"You're starting new ones?"

"They've already started. I have to harden them off."

"What?"

"Harden them off. Put them in soil. Transplant them in dirt and then wean them from water. So they can put down roots where the ground is dry and bloom."

"What do you do with them?" Gemma reached high overhead for the laundry soap and hauled it down. "Give them to people?"

"No. I never give them away anymore."

Gemma began to fiddle with knobs on the washer. "Is this how to turn it on?"

"No. Turn it. Then push it in. You have to load the clothes first, anyway."

Gemma turned a pair of shorts right side out. Then she began to strew Paisley-sized socks and shirts into the tub. Bea noticed, as she watched, how shabby and meager the little assortment.

"You go right back inside and bring out the rest of your things," Bea insisted. "I know you're trying to be careful, but there's no sense you doing all this work and not getting all your clothes clean."

Bea saw Gemma's hands pause over a pair of her own tea-colored briefs. She saw Gemma's ears redden. "This is . . . I-I mean . . ." She clutched the frayed cotton underwear and stared at the knobs of the washing machine. "This is all I brought." Her chin fell. So did the tenor of her voice. "This is all we have."

"It is?"

Gemma clenched her eyes in embarrassment, and nodded. "Yes."

Bea didn't know what to say. She didn't know what to do. Had Nathan lived this way? What's worse, had he let his family live this way?

"You don't have any other skirts, do you?"

Gemma shook her head. "No, I don't." She began to throw everything else from the workbench into the washer, piece by piece, as fast as she could, as if she wanted Bea to stop taking stock of her belongings. "We were getting by just fine, Mrs. Bartling." In went two more pairs of underwear, a frayed nightgown, a shirt. "It's just that he wanted to start to Creighton so bad. He'd worked a road crew in the summer and the meat plant in the winter, trying to save up enough. They let him go to nights in the meat plant and gave us a place to live after he started classes. We had to sacrifice whenever tuition came due."

"Nathan was going to the university?"

Gemma nodded without glancing over, her ears still crimson. She turned the knob and water began gushing over the clothes. Her palms rested on the side of the pulsating machine. "He wanted to be a teacher."

Bea reached for a flowerpot and stared without seeing it. "A teacher." She poured a fistful of potting soil into her palm and squeezed it, letting it siphon through her fingers, back to the pot.

She took one tiny sprig of sprouting rosewood and bud and thrust it upright into the prepared soil. With great care, she pressed the peat and dirt around it, careful to seat the rose deeply. She gave it a heavy watering and aligned it inside the box beside several others. Then she turned to Gemma. "I'm hardening these off for Nathan. Someone suggested they'd look real pretty, growing—" She hesitated. She couldn't bring herself to say it yet. *On his grave.* Bea made a large sweeping gesture with her hand in the direction of the broad countryside out the window. "Out there."

When Gemma didn't chorus her approval, Bea touched her shoulder. But Gemma shook her head, never looking up. Inside the washing machine, iridescent bubbles set forth in swirls among the floating clothes. Gemma swabbed tears with the back of one hand and turned her face away. "I did something *awful* today." The words burst forth from her like the sorrowful, weak chirp of a sparrow. "I'm so *ashamed.*"

"What is it?"

Gemma slammed the lid of the washer with a great clang and tried to back away. "No. Don't."

Bea wouldn't let her. "Gemma, what happened?"

"A man in the restaurant today told me I was p-pretty," she sobbed. "He wanted to know if I'd ever seen North Carolina."

Bea's palm still rested on the girl's shoulder. The awkward moment came when she couldn't decide whether to pull her hand away or draw Gemma close. She did neither. "You *are* pretty," Bea said, at a loss.

"I don't want anybody but Nathan to think I'm pretty. Not anybody but Nathan."

"Gemma—"

"I d-didn't know what to do." Gemma's words interspersed with deep, broken gasps of air. "He kept calling me *h-honey*."

"Oh, Gemma."

"And for a minute, w-when he asked, I wanted to go."

"Oh, my."

"I'm so *ashamed*."

Comprehension burgeoned in Bea's chest. A sudden, amazing awareness struck her, stole her breath away. *I'm not the only one who's hurting. I'm not the only one*. Hard and cold and stunning, it slammed into her breast. *I thought I was. I thought I was the only one who hurt this much.*

"Gemma." Her words came so soft that she doubted if the girl even heard her. "I'm sorry."

Perhaps it happened because Gemma had been forced to be the strong one so long, never breaking down, standing staunch for her daughter. Perhaps it happened because Gemma had never given herself the chance to cling to someone and cry out like a child. Perhaps it happened only because Mrs. Bartling smelled like talcum powder and outdoor flowers and earth—a motherly smell. But Gemma turned to Bea at that moment, releasing her hold on the washer and the soap.

"They d-didn't even tell us when he died," she managed. It seemed to Bea that every protection this young woman had built around herself was crumbling. Her lips quavered as she spoke. "We'd moved twice since he changed his address on his driver's license and they didn't know." Gemma pressed her hand tightly against her mouth, and then gasped the rest of the words against it. "I w-waited for him—"

"Oh, Gemma."

Bea didn't think twice. She gathered this young, broken woman fiercely against her, breastbone to breastbone, feeling the deep throbbing of each sob. "I'm so sorry. Oh, I'm so sorry. None of us knew. None of us knew, Gemma, or we would have called you."

"I miss him so much."

Bea clutched her with the desperation of a mourner. The girl's hair was wet with tears as Bea stroked it. "There now. There there now."

I'm not the only one who hurts. I never was.

Gemma sobbed for a long time, her body erupting in little chirrups of sound, her lungs filling and then shuddering to emptiness, her small, bony body wracked with regret. "Why didn't he tell anybody *why?*" Hers were the cries of two hearts, two spirits, two lonely women—one young, one older—who had thought that loving would be easier, that the mistakes they'd made wouldn't fall so hard.

All that night, Bea couldn't sleep. She lay for hours in the darkness, determined not to pray, remembering the feel of another human being clinging to her, needing her, burrowing against her shoulder.

For the first time she allowed herself to feel anger at her son.

I know I was wrong, Nathan, but you were wrong, too!

How could you have let something you held against me bring so much pain to so many people?

A glimmer of light downstairs made Bea start. Someone had gotten out of bed downstairs. She rolled over and checked the digital clock on the nightstand beside her. Four in the morning.

Bea sat up and listened. Who could be up at this hour? She heard footsteps, feathery and cautious, in the hallway below. "Hello?" she called in a whisper.

Nobody answered.

Bea threw back the covers and drew her arms into the sleeves of her robe. She belted the heavy terrycloth as she began to tiptoe down the stairs, one at a time. She made it all the way down, from the top step to the bottom one, before the floor squeaked beneath her weight. She hesitated.

The light came from Nathan's room.

Bea crept across the hardwood floor and peeked in.

There, with bare feet poking out from beneath the hem of a raggedy nylon pink gown fresh out of the laundry, with her hair in an untidy heap and her toenails still imbedded with yesterday's dirt, stood Paisley.

The little girl stood with her nose propped against the lowest wooden shelf, clutching the varnished wood with her fingertips, pulling herself just high enough on her toes to see all of Nathan's old toys aligned on the shelf.

Paisley lifted her fingers as if to touch one of the Tonka trucks. Then she stopped. She must have decided to abide by the rules because she didn't touch. She pulled her hand back. She stared in awe, the same way she might have pressed her nose up against a glimmering toy store window.

Oh, Nathan.

When the question came, it came from someplace deep inside of Bea—the place that used to cry out for help without even thinking, without weighing the possibility of loss, without counting the cost of not being heard.

What would you have me to do with your family?

Bea waited an inordinately long time, afraid to even breathe for fear she'd frighten the little girl. But at last she exhaled gently and poked her head around the doorjamb.

"Paisley?" she asked in a soft, timid whisper.

"Yeah?"

"What are you doing up in the middle of the night?"

"I had a bad dream. I woke up."

"Don't you think you ought to get back in bed?"

"No."

"You'll be tired tomorrow, if you don't." Bea came around the doorjamb and stepped inside.

Paisley let go of the shelf with one hand and pointed toward the yellowed baseball in the round shiny case. "What's this?"

"It's a baseball."

"I know that. But it's got things written on it. I can't read yet. But it says *Nathan*. See? N-A-T-H-A-N. He taught me how to spell it. How come it has Nathan's name written on it with pen?"

I wanted them here so I could find out about Nathan. How could it be that I end up telling them things about him instead?

"He hit this ball in a game once. They gave it to him for a prize and he kept it a long time."

"Will you read the other words to me? I want to know what they say."

"Okay." Bea lifted the special case from its place. And what happened next made her breath catch in her lungs. Two little arms wrapped around her legs. Two little eyes closed as the child squeezed tight and laid her head against Bea's waist.

Bea stared down at the top of Paisley's head. Her chest tightened with expectancy and a strange joy. "You're hugging me?"

Paisley nodded.

For a good minute, maybe two, Bea stood stock still

with surprise, staring down, not knowing if she should move, her heart pounding. What did you do when somebody hugged you like this? How long did you wait before you stirred or pulled away? Bea decided not to move at all. She closed her own eyes and waited in wonder.

"I love you, Mrs. Bartling," the child whispered steadily. She kept squeezing tight.

Merciful heavens, but that got Bea all choked up. It had been years since she'd experienced a child's hug. Years since she'd remembered how a hug could make a person feel needed. Wanted. Cared for and loved. She struggled to speak for a moment, but couldn't do it. She sat down hard on the side of the single bed, a lump in her throat the size of Scotts Bluff.

She patted the blue coverlet beside her to mark the spot. "Come sit up here. Come hop on the bed."

Paisley released her hold and climbed up. But she didn't stop there. She clambered into Bea's lap, the crown of her little head leaning against Bea's cheek.

Bea clasped her tightly, willing her old bones to support them both, willing the unwanted tremble in her hands to go away. How long had it been? How long had it been since she'd held a child this way?

For a moment, she allowed her nose to fall forward against Paisley's little face, drinking in the sweet, sweaty pungence of little girl, rocking as if they were in a chair, taking strength from the small and perfect body drooping against her arms.

She turned the ball sideways and held the words under the spill of the lamplight, reading them carefully, one by one, even though she could recite them by heart.

"Nathan 'The Grape' Bartling. #14." As Bea read the ball, Paisley craned her chin so she could see. "First All-Star Home Run 6-28-91 -vs- Bucktail."

"He hit a home run?"

Bea nodded, her cheek against Paisley's cheek. "That was the first of many."

"Where does it say 'The Grape?' "

Bea pointed. "Right here."

"Why does it say that?"

"Because," Bea said, "for awhile that was Nathan's nickname."

"How come?"

"You really want to hear this story?" It seemed that everywhere they went together, every question asked, everything they began together, evoked yet another memory of Nathan. Bea traced the outline of the frayed red ball stitching with one finger.

"Yeah. I do."

Bea rumpled the soft curls on Paisley's head. "They were headed to a baseball game over in Oshkosh and the school bus passed through road construction. Someone threw a grape out of the bus window. It thumped one of the construction workers in the head."

"Did it hurt him?"

"Well, it was just a grape, pretty harmless, but I guess the road workers decided they had to be tough. They couldn't have motorists or school kids or baseball teams throwing things out of windows at members of the Dembergh Construction Crew. So they radioed to the other end of the roadwork, had a flagman stop the bus and climb on board."

"He got on the school bus?"

"Yes." Bea made her voice sound like a gruff man. " 'Somebody tell me who threw that grape,' this fellow yelled at the whole team. Nobody said a word. Nobody told. Not until Nathan stood up and said, 'I did it. I threw the grape.' "

"Did they arrest him?"

"No. Because he confessed they let the bus go through and the team made it in time to warm up for the game. Everybody called him Grape all summer long after that. Every time he'd come up to hit, they'd holler, 'Just a little poke, Grape!' 'Blast it out of the park, Grape!' 'Belt it, Grape!' "

"If I would have known that, I would have called him Grape all the time, too." Paisley raised her gaze to grin at Bea. "Read me a story, Grape. Please push me on the swing, Grape."

Bea couldn't resist a smile. From somewhere deep inside herself, she felt something uncommon. Something like magic. Something she was almost afraid to acknowledge. A hint of happiness. "He would have laughed. He would have thought it was the funniest thing, you calling him that."

For the first time, Bea looked down and noticed Paisley's hands. They lay in the little girl's lap, palms upturned and open, fingers curled as if the child expected something. Her tired, tiny body swayed against Bea's like prairie grass in slight breeze.

"You want to hold this ball?"

Bea couldn't keep her eyes from Paisley's tiny bent fingers, barely opening, barely closing, as if she could already feel Nathan's baseball sitting there. Paisley didn't answer aloud. She just bit her bottom lip and nodded.

"Here. Don't miss this." Their heads bent together again and Bea rolled the ball over to the other side. "See this green scrape. You can feel it. That's where Nathan hit it with the bat. Smacked it right out of the park."

And with that, Bea placed Nathan's baseball inside the chalice of the little girl's hands.

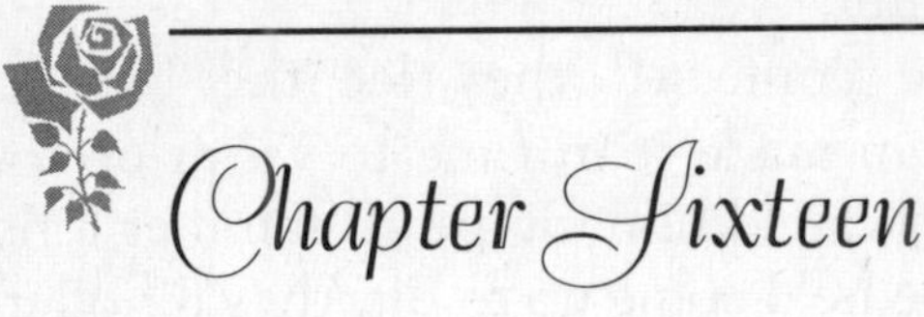

Chapter Sixteen

"Alva T.?" Gemma asked the next afternoon while she polished the silver lids of two-dozen saltshakers. "Do you mind if I ask you a question?"

Alva punched a button on the cash register and the cash drawer came sliding out. It bopped her in the midsection before she could catch it with her hands. "What?"

"I thought since you've been running the restaurant for awhile, you might have heard people talking about something."

"Talking about what?"

"About—" Gemma stopped. She had been about to say "About why Nathan left home." She struggled to make the question sound a little less personal. "About Nathan Bartling. About why he left home."

Alva pulled a pile of bills out of the drawer and began to count. "Now, why would you be interested in a thing like that?"

"I . . ." Gemma didn't know what she should say. If Mrs. Bartling hadn't acknowledged her to anyone as being Nathan's wife, it seemed wrong for Gemma to announce it to Alva now. "I just wondered, I guess."

"Does Bea Bartling talk to you much about her family?"

Gemma shrugged, being deliberately vague. "Some."

"Humph." Alva set the cash tray down on the counter with a clatter. "You think it's your business, digging for gossip about somebody who took you in when you needed a place to stay?"

"I'm not digging for gossip, Alva T."

"Oh, really. That's sure what it seems like to me." Alva unlocked a plastic moneybag with a tiny key and made ready to fill it. "Never could figure why they tell you to lock these bags," she said. "Never could understand why the bank goes through all the trouble of locking a bag that somebody could pick up and run with."

"I wasn't digging for gossip," Gemma insisted again. "I was thinking if I knew something about it, I could help." This was a close to the truth as she could come. If she discovered the answer, maybe she could say something that would help Mrs. Bartling heal. It seemed like a last gift, a last token of devotion she could offer Nathan.

Alva pitched the moneybag into the back room. "If Bea Bartling is talking to you about anything at all, she's telling you more than she's told anybody else in town. Nobody understands what happened with Nathan. He was three weeks away from graduating. Then one day he was gone. Bea has never talked about it."

"Never?"

"No. But we've all heard rumors."

"Rumors of what?"

"There's folks that tell all sorts of stories. That he struck out for what she did the only way he knew how."

"Fow what she did? What? What did she do?"

"Get back to work, Gemma. If I started telling you stories, I'd be no better off than the rest of them."

Resigned, Gemma turned back to her task and began

aligning the shakers along a brown, plastic tray, defeat pounding hard against her ribs.

Maybe I have no right. But, if I did, there might be something I could say to her, something I could say about Nathan that would make things better. For Nathan's sake.

The telephone rang. Charlene's voice called from the kitchen, "Gemma! Phone's for you!"

When she went to answer it, she could hear the loud whirr of an air-powered impact wrench in the background. "Gemma Franklin?" a man's voice bellowed over the racket.

"Yes?" she hollered back.

"This is Bill at Sandhill Texaco. Wanted to let you know we found a rebuilt engine for your Toyota this morning."

"You did?"

"We're trucking it in from Sumner. Found an old one sitting on a shelf at Butch's Repair over there. Can you imagine that?"

"You did?"

"Of course, I don't know how long it's going to take us to get the thing in. We haven't gotten the old one out yet, and some of those bolts couldn't be tighter if they'd been welded on."

"What do you think?" Gemma talked loud so he could hear her over the noise. "Do you have an estimate? Any idea how long it will take?"

"That engine weighs over five hundred pounds. We'll have to wench it up with something and drop it down in. I'd say it's going to be a good three weeks at best," he told her. "I'd say that's a pretty good guess."

Three weeks.

"Thank you," she told him.

"I can't believe we found that engine," Bill told her. "All that, and it wasn't even very far away."

Three weeks seemed like no time at all.

Three weeks seemed like an eternity.

"Alva?" Gemma asked on her way out. "If you've got extra work to do around this place and Charlene doesn't mind, I could sure use the hours. I'm going to need to pay off my car pretty soon."

"I don't mind, honey," Charlene called out. "I don't need extra hours these days. You got emergencies. I'm just sailing along."

As Gemma walked home from work late that afternoon, everything around her seemed to whisper "Three weeks . . . Three weeks . . . Three weeks." The words rustled from the lawn grass beneath her feet and the leaves in the trees overhead and the green acorns that skittered along the walk when she kicked them. "Three weeks . . . Three weeks."

When she got to the house, Mrs. Bartling's car wasn't in the driveway. She opened the door without knocking. During the past few weeks, she'd gotten used to doing that. "Hello? Is anybody home?" Nothing.

She walked the length of the hallway and found no one in any of the rooms. Of course Mrs. Bartling must have driven them somewhere. She went to the bottom of the stairs and called, "Mrs. Bartling?" And then, "Paisley?" Nothing.

Gemma found herself standing outside Nathan's room. The door was closed. She opened it an inch. Two inches. "Hello? Anybody in there?"

She rested her fingers against the doorknob as lightly as an alighting butterfly. For one moment, she considered the possibility of going inside. She considered the possibility of handling all that was left of Nathan in this place, of touching his belongings, and nobody else would ever have to know. It was tempting. Cruelly tempting. She pushed the door open a little more.

Why shouldn't Mrs. Bartling share this part of him with me? Why should she keep it to herself?

A car pulled into the driveway. A car door slammed. Guilt-ridden, Gemma flung Nathan's door shut and yanked her hand away. She heard Paisley laughing and Mrs. Bartling's quiet, gentle reply. She strode into the family room to meet them. "Hi," she said, sounding breathless in her own ears, as if she'd just run away from something.

"Hi," Mrs. Bartling said back.

In their arms, the homecomers carried wrinkled shopping bags from Wal-Mart. Mrs. Bartling set a shoebox on the floor before she began to rifle through their sacks. Sales tags littered the floor.

Gemma stood there and stared at it all. "What's this?"

Mrs. Bartling shrugged as if these items had no significance whatsoever. "They were having a sale over in Oshkosh."

"You took Paisley to Oshkosh?"

"Of course I did. I couldn't very well go without her, could I? It's a good thing she was there to try on, or else I would have bought her play clothes at least two sizes too big."

"You bought things for *Paisley?*"

Gemma stared at the sacks and the little piles of clothing that were growing by the second. Shame and disparagement stirred in her. What had she been thinking at the Cramalot when she'd thought she could find out about Nathan and help Mrs. Bartling? While here came Mrs. Bartling, doling out benefaction? The last time anyone had bought a gift for Paisley had been when Nathan bought her a fourth-birthday present. A

Jewel Girl Barbie. The very same Barbie that Gemma had forgotten to fish out of the Corolla's backseat when Mr. Sissel had driven her to chain up the Toyota and tow it in to the Texaco.

"I got things for both of you. Just look at these." Mrs. Bartling stooped to the floor, her hand supporting her backside as she did, and wrestled a pair of strappy brown sandals from the tissue paper in the shoebox. These were small enough for Bea to lift in one hand. "This was the splurge. They were $12.99, but they were so *cute*. I couldn't resist."

Paisley must have sensed that something was wrong. "Don't you like my new sandals, Mama?"

"Oh, sweetie. Oh, they're very nice." For as far back as Gemma could remember, with the exception of Nathan, no one had ever wanted them around. Not Grandma Hardeman. Not the aunts and uncles she'd lived with after her mother had left them and her father had been killed in a freak accident with a construction crane. She sat down hard on the old recliner, feeling dismal. "I'll count up what I've made so far at the Cramalot, Mrs. Bartling. I can pay you for these things."

"Oh, *no*, Gemma." Mrs. Bartling wrapped the little shoes in tissue again and began to work her swollen feet out of her own cracked leather Naturalizers. "That isn't what I had in mind. I just picked out a few necessities to help—"

Humiliation roiled in Gemma's belly. She knew the reason behind this. Mrs. Bartling had watched her load their laundry into the washer yesterday. She had finally seen all that they didn't have. "I don't want you to give us things. You've already given us enough."

Mrs. Bartling straightened with surprise and held up a tiny pink bathing suit with a fish on the front. "This isn't charity, Gemma." She spread the bathing suit out on the coffee table. "At least, not in the way you expect." Her hands, gnarled and weathered after so many hours in the garden, began to smooth wrinkles from the little garment. "I wanted to make things better. I wanted to make the hurt better. That's all."

Paisley began to dig in the shoebox. She pulled out one new sandal and began to struggle with the leather buckle.

Three weeks. I don't even have a suitcase large enough to carry these things away when we leave in three weeks. "Nothing's going to make the hurt better. You know that. You're his mother. Nathan's *gone*."

"Look, I bought you this," Mrs. Bartling said, still making an effort. She pulled a gauzy teal skirt from the bag and laid it across her arm. "This one is very feminine. And it's longer than the other one. I thought you'd—"

When Mrs. Bartling displayed the skirt, it confirmed every one of Gemma's suspicions. "You're embarrassed by us, aren't you?" she asked. "You don't like my clothes." Gemma saw straight through these gifts to the meager, horrible truth. Gemma was mortified by the skirt that would reach below her knees, by the little package of underwear for Paisley she could see still in the bag. "You don't like my life. I'm certainly not the kind of girl you would have wanted your son to marry."

"Gemma, please—"

"Mama," Paisley said. "Don't get mad at Mrs. Bartling. It was fun. We got new toothbrushes and soap and she got you a different bra."

"How do you know what size bra I wear?" Gemma asked.

"Well, I looked."

"I did finish high school, you know," Gemma told

her. "I got pregnant and my grandma wouldn't let me go through graduation but they mailed me my diploma anyway. She didn't want me anymore because she didn't want—" Gemma's hands fluttered somewhere in the direction of Paisley so she wouldn't have to say it aloud. "Nobody ever wanted us. Except for Nathan. But if he hadn't wanted me, maybe he would have come home to you. I know you feel that way, Mrs. Bartling. I see it every time you look at me."

Mrs. Bartling spread the pretty skirt across her lap and stared down at it. As she sat, it dangled all the way to her ankles. All Gemma could see was the cowlick shaped like a whirligig in the top of Mrs. Bartling's gray hair.

"I want to be grateful, don't you see? I *ought* to be grateful. But I can't be. Don't you see?"

At last, when Mrs. Bartling spoke, she spoke to the pretty skirt in her lap, to her swollen ankles, to the sales tags in a jumble on the carpet. "I see," she said, her voice becoming soft with weary sorrow. "You're right, you know. I think those things. Yes, Nathan might have come home if not for you. Or he might not have. But there isn't any way for either of us to know that, is there? We have to sort this out as best we know how."

As Bea often did when she felt unduly troubled, she plodded out into her front yard the next morning, struggled with the faucet, turned on the hose and stood alone in the late morning heat. She squinted into the sun, taking sudden, surprising pleasure in the water splattering amidst the dirt and the moldering petals beside her feet.

No matter what else changes in my life, this never does.

The woman who had watered these roses a hundred years before hadn't had the luxury of a garden hose. Instead, she would have lovingly tended these flowers with what was left of the dishwater or a few drops left over from someone's weekly bath. Bea didn't stop watering the old bushes until she made certain all the roots got a soaking clear through.

She traipsed around to the potter's cart in the side yard where she kept gardening scissors, pruning shears, bags of oak-leaf mulch, and tin buckets for carrying things. She came back with a little trowel and, on her hands and knees, began to turn dirt with the spade, digging and dumping, until she'd cultivated a new batch of bone meal and potash deep into the soil. Petals showered down around her ears, their fleeting fragrance impossible to capture or keep.

So many times during the past years, she'd found it easy to forget herself here, to cast away the outside world. To pretend she was a pioneer woman from an earlier time, coddling roses brought as a tiny cutting along the Oregon Trail—the only beautiful reminder of home that could be toted along among provisions on a wagon.

But not today.

We don't wear the right clothes. We don't act the right way. We don't say the right things.

If Nathan hadn't wanted us, he might have come home to you. You think that. I see it in your eyes every time you look at us.

Bea had left her gardening gloves behind. She began digging anyway, finding gentle solace in the repetitive motion of the trowel, the fresh breeze that ruffled her hair, the dirt clods biting into her knees, the jumble of leaves and thorns, the rich carol of a lone fat robin, *cheer-up cheerily*, as it sang from its perch in the tall cedar beside the house.

"Oh, Lord," she whispered aloud to the dirt. "I'm trying so hard to let it go. But no matter how hard I try, I'm blaming people. And they see it. They *see* it."

For even as she had heard Gemma's accusations against her and realized they were true, she had heard the echo of another time, another voice.

"You said you would be different if we came someplace different," she said to Ray. "You said you'd try to be happy." She didn't know how to fight what was going on inside her husband. She didn't know how to fight the discontent she saw in his life. In their front yard beside the roses, she stood on tiptoe, laid her head in the valley between his shoulder blades, wanting to heal him with her touch.

He backed away. "Don't."

Tears came to her eyes. "Is it me, Ray? Am I doing something wrong? Am I not being a good wife? A good mother?"

"A good wife? Sure you're a good wife. The problem is I'm a lousy husband. That's what you're thinking every time you look at me. I see it in your eyes."

"I'm not thinking that."

Oh, I am. I am. But I don't want to be.

"You're thinking if I didn't lose my jobs, our lives could be different. You're thinking if I said the right things to the right people, I could get raises instead of bad reviews and lousy cost-of-living increases."

"Ray, I just want to help."

"There's all sorts of helping that doesn't help."

"You weren't watching what you were doing the other day, Ray. If you had been, that lumber never would have fallen. You were standing on the roof with your head thrown back, yearning for some distant place. Like that hobo on the train."

"Maybe I'd like to be that hobo. Bea, you don't realize it, but you do this."

When had she silently begun to disapprove of her husband? She knew she mustn't feel this way. It wasn't fair to Ray. It seemed odd, how other people knew what you felt about them before you ever admitted it to yourself. She could be content. She was content. She loved puttering with the roses. She loved when Ray came in from the hardware store and set his little brown sacks of nails on the kitchen counter, each one creased and folded into a roll at the top. She didn't mind scrimping on groceries when he'd lost another job. She loved listening to the boys giggle in the bedroom and then the soft rustlings of them giving in and drifting off to sleep. She loved creeping in and finding Jacob in Nathan's room, blond hair on the pillow in the bed on the right, brown hair on the pillow in the bed on the left, both of their mouths wide open.

"I want you to try and see something, Ray," she had said to Ray that day. "I want you to see that life is here. It's where you are. It isn't somewhere else that you have to go looking for it."

I'm content. If I'm not, I can change that. I can.

But Bea hadn't been able to change. Not in time to save her marriage.

That girl sees more of myself than I do. If I'm ashamed of her, I can change that. I can.

Bea disentangled herself from the rose limbs and rocked back onto her heels. She sighed deeply before she brandished the pruning shears and rummaged through the leaves in search of blossoms withered on the stems. She found one and snipped it off. It fell in the dirt beside her knees.

She stared at it.

Just then, George Sissel's Ford Taurus pulled up in front of the house. It ran up over the curb and plunked down again in the street. "Hello, Bea." Pastor George climbed out of the driver's side, slammed the door with a satisfied thwack, and strode purposefully up the walk. "Up to your elbows in the rose patch. That's a good sign, isn't it?"

"Well, yes. I suppose it is."

Bea set aside all her gardening paraphernalia and George stretched out a hand. "Need help up?"

"I've got dirt all over. You don't want to touch me." She managed to upright herself without assistance. She brushed loose grass and mulch and dirt from her behind. "You came to check on me?"

"Actually, I stopped over to bring this to Paisley." He held out a small black Bible. "Is she inside?"

"She's playing with a neighbor down the street."

"Some special things have happened to her lately, Bea. Did she tell you? She's invited the Lord into her life."

The little spade lay on the ground beside where she'd been sitting. For lack of nothing better to do, Bea touched it with her toe, sending the wooden handle up and down again. She watched it seesaw up and down. From a great distance somewhere out across the plains came the piercing call of a sandhill crane, *garooo-a, garooo-a.* "I see." This news, coupled with the events of yesterday, left Bea staring at her pastor with a millstone of heaviness in her chest. "That's impossible, isn't it? She's much too young."

For a moment, Bea felt almost envious of Paisley. How she longed for the freshness, the joy. How she longed for the beginning, those times when her body and her heart and her very *life* vibrated with the possibility of the Lord.

Why on earth would I begrudge a child her budding faith?

"I don't think it's impossible at all, Bea. That isn't what the Bible says."

Because my own old faith has been battered and tarnished, that's why. Because I don't think God listened to me or loved me, not even when it all began.

"Bea." He stared down for a moment, his eyes riveted on the scuffed toes of his wingtip shoes. When he lifted his gaze, he spoke the words to her with new, firm determination. "I don't know what you're feeling right now. I cannot comprehend it. But the emptiness in your eyes frightens me."

"What of it?" she asked. "I'm trying to make that emptiness go away. It will some day. That's what everyone says. In three to five years, I'll be better. Every time I go through one more birthday, one more Christmas, one more Thanksgiving, I'll be getting closer."

"There's something I want you to think of, Bea, whenever your spirits are low."

"I'll be thinking about it often, then, I suppose."

He reached over and touched her arm. "There's one thing I've learned about human nature over the years. It's simple, and important. You often never know about the people whose lives you change."

"What are you talking about, George?"

"In this world, it's easy to recognize the mistakes you see in someone's life and to blame yourself for them. But you never see the mistakes someone *might* have made if not for your touch. You never realize that people are still going on because of what you may have said to them or because of what you may have shown them. Just by being who you are."

"I'm an old woman. My chance for changing people's lives was over a long time ago."

"I hear the conversations at funerals, Bea. They all say the same thing. 'I could have phoned him, but I didn't.' 'I could have visited her, but I didn't.' 'I could have told this child I cared about him, but I didn't.' Missed chances."

"Is that what I'm doing?" she asked him. "Seeing only the missed chances?"

Pastor George closed his eyes and nodded. "I think so."

"The chance I missed, though," she said, "was with my own son."

He nodded again.

She seemed to have forgotten the dirt embedded in her nails, the state of her grimy hands. She ran her fingers through her hair. "Do you know who they are, George? That girl was married to Nathan."

"Yes. I know who they are. Paisley let me in on the secret."

"They were with him a little over a month ago. They were *with* Nathan."

"Yes."

"And when she came here, she recognized things because Nathan told her so much about his home."

"I imagine that's been difficult."

Bea bit her bottom lip and nodded. Yes. *Yes. This had been difficult.*

The sun had risen higher, bathing Bea's bare arms with golden, warm light. From where she stood, she could see heat shimmering against the prairie grass along the far hills and the long fronds of the golden willow that Ray had planted ten or more years ago drooping toward the ground.

George reached out to take Bea's hand and, when he did, his smile held great sadness, great gentleness. "Don't underestimate the way God works, Bea. You may think you've brought them in to teach you something about Nathan. When, perhaps, the Father has brought them in to teach you something about yourself."

Chapter Seventeen

Alva T.'s meat loaf special brought more notoriety to Ash Hollow than anyone could have ever imagined. A reporter from *The Denver Post* stopped in one afternoon for a piece of coconut crème pie and ended up interviewing Alva about her meat loaf instead. Two days later, a photographer appeared with his padded camera case and plastic bags filled with film canisters and a Rolleiflex camera with a detachable flash.

He took pictures of Alva in front of the window glass pointing at Charlene's huge painting of a meat loaf. He took pictures of Alva in the kitchen instructing Harvey how to slice carrots. He took pictures of Alva stretched out along the serving counter with her frizzy hair propped next to a crystal display that housed two-thirds of an apple pie. He took pictures of Alva leaning on one elbow over the hood of her Chrysler New Yorker.

That particular shot was the one that appeared on the cover of *Empire* magazine, distributed to everyone in the *Post*'s multistate circulation area—a full-color depiction of Alva Torrington in her red apron, strings untied and dangling down toward the hubcaps, every wrinkle on her face shadowed as she grinned, with a two-pound plate of meat loaf sitting on the hood.

Not three days after the *Empire* article hit the stands, out-of-town business had picked up noticeably at the Cramalot. Business picked up noticeably at The Garden County Museum, too. So much, in fact, that Orvin Kornruff decided he had better convince Mabel Perkins to let Lon Johnson and his checker-playing buddies appear in the country-store exhibit every afternoon and every other morning.

"Ah," Gemma said to them one day, leaning against the front door of the museum in exhaustion after she'd closed it behind her. "Alva T. and her meat loaf have turned this town into a zoo."

"Come on over here, Gemma," Orvin gestured. "Lon, get out of her way. Make room for my favorite checker opponent."

Gemma quit leaning and walked over to the checkerboard. She tugged on her skirt, the short one she wore now solely from pride. "That's just because you beat me all the time."

"Well." He shrugged. "Everybody has to have a favorite pastime or two."

"You can't play checkers right now," Mabel told Gemma. "We've got another group set up for a tour in five minutes. It wouldn't be historically correct for a woman to be playing checkers in the 1890s. Back in those days, women never played games with men."

"Oh," Orvin winked broadly at his collection of pals. "I don't know about that, Mabel Perkins. I don't know about that at all."

When the door opened again, they all turned, expecting the next tour. Mrs. Bartling entered instead. "Gemma?" she asked, her eyes resting for a moment too long upon Gemma's shabby, old skirt. "I was just on my way back to the house. Thought you might need a ride over."

"I can't get away just yet," Gemma said, tilting her chin, raising a challenge. *I'm fine in my own clothes, thank you very much.* "There's a tour coming in. I'll walk home."

"You sure? I could wait for you."

"There isn't any need for you to wait on me."

"Are you sure, Gemma?" Orvin stood from the table and headed toward the gun display. "She might enjoy waiting around and seeing how we bring this country store to life. She might enjoy the part where I pick up this gun from the display and tell them how my grandfather in Garden County owned one like it."

He held up the shotgun for a short moment and surveyed it.

"Nothing like this Old Model 97 for shooting geese."

He pulled the trigger.

Of course, a gun in a museum would not have a bullet in it. Of course. But some hint of gunpowder must have remained in the chamber. Some hint, while the barrel had long ago gotten clogged with dirt.

The gun exploded in Orvin's hand.

Metal shards ricocheted off the ceiling and imbedded in the walls. He dropped the gun and grabbed his fingers, hollering from both surprise and pain. For a long moment, he hid it between his legs and they couldn't see the blood.

"I've got a first-aid kit," Mabel screeched. "I just have to find it."

"You want us to call an ambulance, Orvin?" Lon Johnson asked.

"Goodness, no. I'll drive myself over to the hospital.

It's just a little cut. I'm sure they'll stitch me up and send me on my way."

"You don't know that," Gemma said. "You haven't looked at it yet."

"I'll look soon enough."

Mabel had arrived back with the first-aid kit and, very slowly, Orvin held his hand out for everyone to see. Even Orvin flinched when he took stock of the blood oozing between his fingers.

Mabel put her hand to her chin and looked like she might faint.

Lon Johnson groaned. "Orvin, that's some wound, all right."

Gemma felt bile rise and fought to swallow it down.

Mrs. Bartling opened the first-aid kit and laid out the supplies she needed. She was the only one who remained calm as she unraveled a roll of gauze. "They're not going to stitch you up without cleaning it out first," she noted in a level voice. "It will be a little more involved than that. I'll drive you to the hospital, Orvin, once we get this done."

"Should I call the ambulance?" Lon asked again.

But Mrs. Bartling didn't seem to hear his question. She squeezed disinfectant onto the man's lacerated fingers. She began to gingerly wind the gauze around his hand. And, as if she needed to talk her way through some trauma as she worked, Mrs. Bartling began to tell them a story. "I've had some experience with this, you know. That boy's hand looked just about this bad the day I wrapped it up and sent him off with the sheriff. Tried to wrestle away his knife from him and it stabbed him in the hand instead. So much blood. It was hard to stay cool headed."

"Bea?" Orvin asked, obviously forgetting his own hand. "When was that? What are you talking about?"

"That boy was fighting mad because Ray had left. Fighting mad because another person had disappeared from his life."

Orvin wiggled his fingers. Lon asked, "Bea, how much of that gauze are you going to put on?"

Mrs. Bartling began to swathe strips of gauze around the man's wrist. Gemma touched the woman's arm, compassion surging from some unknown place within her. "Did Nathan do that? Did Nathan pull a knife on you?"

"Nathan? Oh, my heavens, no. It wasn't Nathan. Nathan would never do a thing like that."

So much love . . . lost. So many hopes . . . come to nothing.

"Bea," Lon said. "I'm going to call the hospital and say that Orvin's coming in. What should I tell them?"

"Tell them we're bringing him over right now," she said. "Tell them he may still have metal in his hand. Tell them it's pretty bad."

Bea had not dreamed, when she'd asked, *Nathan, what would you have me to do with your family*, that anything would answer her. Yet in some miraculous way, all during the time Orvin Kornruff was healing, it seemed that something did.

Bea was organizing her sewing box one afternoon when, all of a sudden, she developed a sudden craving for an orange Dreamsicle, the very kind she'd loved in third grade and probably hadn't eaten for forty years. Not five minutes later, as she arranged thread spools in a row, Bea heard the calliope music of an ice cream truck approaching the house.

Paisley appeared, her eyes wide. "What's that?"

"It's strange, is what it is. That old ice cream truck hasn't come down this street for three years. He knows there aren't any kids on Pattison."

"What's an ice cream truck?"

"You don't know?"

Paisley shook her head.

"Well, it's a man who drives around looking for little kids who want Popsicles. He plays music so you'll come out and chase him."

"Does he *give* them *away?*"

"No. You have to dig around as fast as you can and find quarters. Then you have to—" Bea straddled her hands and came to her feet. "What are we doing sitting here talking about this? I'll show you! Let's go catch him."

Bea scrabbled in her purse for loose coins and away they went, slamming the screen and bounding across the yard, Paisley skipping and shrieking, Beatrice laughing and coming as fast as she could, doing her best to keep up.

He must have looked in his rearview mirror and seen them running because, just as they'd decided they'd missed him, the ice cream truck made an illegal u-turn in the middle of Pattison, its music twice as loud and distorted now that the speaker was coming toward them. The ice cream man crooked his elbow out over the door, where he was driving from a steering wheel on the right-hand side. "What'll it be, ladies?"

Bea looked at Paisley. Paisley shrugged. Bea was still gasping so hard from running that she could barely speak. "We'll have . . . two . . . orange Dreamsicles . . . please."

The ice creams were so cold that Bea and Paisley

could hardly peel off the paper. They situated themselves on the brick steps, their knees lined up like peas in a pod, with Dreamsicle on each of their noses, their teeth and their heads aching from eating the cold things too fast.

Not two days later, Bea was busy dusting the photo frames in the hallway when she suddenly got the urge to add some color. *This hallway is so drab and dark. I'll bet these walls haven't been painted in twenty years. Oh, I believe a nice peach would do.*

At that moment, Paisley appeared with a coloring book and a green-and-yellow box of crayons. "I'm in the mood to color," Paisley announced. "If I do this picture on this side, will you color the picture on the other side?"

"I don't know, Paisley. I'm dusting these frames and I've never seen so many cobwebs in my life."

"Yes," Paisley said, "but this box of crayons has *peach*."

That's all it took. Bea put away her dusting rag and sprawled out on the family room floor with a coloring book instead. What followed was a discussion of every page in the book, what things Paisley best liked to color (flowers, monkeys, and houses), what things Bea best liked to color (ladies in beautiful dresses, kittens, and birthday gifts with ribbons), and how to find the nicest page where the two of them could be satisfied to share. For the longest time, after they decided, the only sounds were the scrub of crayons scribbling paper or someone saying, "I like the way you did that" or "Are you finished yet with the green?"

They watched the bean in the pot grow daily—one strong, slender stem arcing up out of the loam to stand on its own, the kidney-shaped pod splitting into halves to reveal tiny leaves.

One evening Bea couldn't resist peeking in at the goings-on for bedtime—the final sleek rinses of bathwater leaving Paisley's skin little-girl pink, the smell of Ivory soap, the towel gathered in folds beneath her tiny chin. As Paisley tugged on her pajama legs and began to jump on the bed, Gemma waylaid her and cuddled her close, floppy arms and legs akimbo, mother and child nuzzling down into the pillows, their noses together.

While resting an elbow on the bookshelf, Bea smiled softly. She had not missed this in her own life. Tussling before bed had always been a favorite thing for boys. The sight of these two brought the same yearning to Bea as it brought to every mother who has cherished her children, every mother whose children are growing up or gone.

Ah! I remember when we used to do such things. Those nights, neverending and wonderful. When did they end? I don't remember when we stopped.

With a stab of melancholy Bea realized that, as long as these two remained at her house, she could take part in this vignette every night. She could be available for stuffing wayward limbs into pajamas and sponging down a bathtub ring and turning back the bed linens and scrubbing behind ears.

Gemma spread the blanket up to Paisley's chin, handed her the blanket with the cows, and tucked the edges tightly around her like a cocoon. Just as Bea thought she should go, Paisley wriggled free, sat up, and rumpled the covers. "Mama, I wanted Mrs. Bartling to put me to bed."

Bea's elbow came off the shelf in surprise. Gemma's

gaze met hers across the dimly lit room. "She wants you to do this," Gemma said.

"Me?" Bea felt like an intruder in her own house even though her lungs tightened with expectation. Paisley raised her arms. Bea glanced again at Gemma, scratched the nape of her neck, and gave a pained, little laugh, feeling clumsy, graceless, out of place.

"Go ahead," Gemma encouraged her. "It's okay."

Bea sat on the side of the bed, knowing full well what to expect—another one of those unfettered hugs, another one of those quiet whispers the child so willingly bestowed. "I love you, Mrs. Bartling."

I love you, too.

Well, isn't that what one said at a time like this?

Bea didn't dare say such a thing. "Get down under the covers now. Your mama already had you tucked in."

"But I don't want to be tucked in yet. I want to pray."

"You do?"

"Yep. I want to talk to Him." Paisley tumbled down off the side of the mattress and knelt beside Bea on the floor. "Because He likes it." She aligned all ten of her fingers to the tip of her nose, bowed her head, closed her eyes. She waited for a good while before she opened her eyes and turned her head sideways, trying to see what Bea was doing.

"Aren't you going to pray?"

"Well, I—"

"We can either do it out loud or to ourselves. Which do you want?"

"I don't know—" Bea's chest tightened with regret. "It's been a long time since I prayed with anybody else."

I've been saying it all to myself. God certainly hasn't been listening.

If Nathan wouldn't forgive me, I don't see how God ever would.

"I'll do it," Paisley volunteered. Before Bea had gotten her forehead halfway down, the little girl had begun.

"Dear Lord, hi. We're here and we love you. We think about you and hope you're doing good. God, take care of my mama, would you? She's been worried about so many things. Help her to ask you to take care of her because she's always taking care of herself. Take care of Mrs. Bartling, because she is scared. Tell Nathan that we love him and that we found each other. I think that would make him real glad. And now that we found each other, help us find our home. Thank you for Jesus. Thank you that you sent Him and He could come for His home in my heart. Amen."

"Amen," Bea whispered beside the child, her spirits subdued, as if they'd been trounced over and over again in some desperate battle.

Why did children always make prayer seem so easy? Didn't Paisley understand that Nathan was gone? Didn't Paisley understand that God gave you what you wanted only as long as it suited His purposes—as long as it fit into some part of His master plan?

"You get yourself into this bed." Bea gave the formal order as Paisley clambered up onto the mattress again and delved with joy beneath the covers.

Children made faith seem so easy. They prayed for whatever they wanted.

You weren't supposed to pray for what you wanted, were you? You were supposed to pray for what God wanted.

Not my will, Lord, but thy will be done.

Selective listening, they called it. Perfected by children, dogs, and God.

Is it your will, God, that people make so many mistakes by themselves? That people don't love each other? That people die?

As the days passed, Gemma tucked away her tip money into Mrs. Bartling's small wooden cedar box. She collected quarters, nickels, dimes, and a heap of crumpled, faded dollar bills. When she received her first paycheck from The Cramalot Inn after two weeks, she cashed it with Alva and put that aside in the cedar box, too.

"How much?" Paisley asked one evening as they both scrambled up on the bed with the little box and Gemma unfastened the clasp.

Gemma dumped its contents on the bedspread and made stacks of nickels, dimes, and quarters. She leafed through the dollar bills.

"Do we have enough? Can we do it, Mama?"

"Hm-mmm-m." Gemma rearranged piles of quarters and counted them again, just to make sure. "Twelve . . . Thirteen . . . Fourteen." She rolled over and grinned at her daughter. "Well, yes. Yes, I think we can."

Paisley jumped up and immediately began to dance around. "We can! We can!"

"Sh-hhhh. If Mrs. Bartling hears you, then it won't be any surprise at all."

Gemma counted out several bills and thrust them into her purse. The rest of the money she scooped back into the tiny cedar chest. Oh, she couldn't help herself! She was every bit as excited as Paisley. "We'd better go and help with supper."

Oh, please, oh, please, oh, please. Gemma's heart hurt just from wishing. *Please let her accept this from us.*

They'd only gotten halfway through their meal before a horn sounded outside. Mrs. Bartling raised her head. "Who on earth could that be?"

"It's Alva T. honking her horn," Gemma announced, folding her napkin on the table and scooting back her chair.

"What's Alva doing here at this time of night? She ought not be making that racket. The neighbors will complain."

The subject in question appeared at the door without twenty seconds lapsing. She pounded on the screen with a fist. "Okay, you three. Hurry up! Me and Charlene can't stay out here all night waiting."

"Waiting for what?" Mrs. Bartling asked.

Paisley burst forth with the answer as if it were a breath she'd been holding. "A surprise. We're taking you to—"

"Hush up, Paisley Rose. It isn't time to tell."

"Where are you taking me?"

Charlene burst through herself since no one had seen fit to let Alva in. "Hurry up, Gemma. The line's gonna be too long if we don't get there soon."

Mrs. Bartling sat at the supper table with her eyebrow cocked, her elbows propped at an unladylike angle. "I'm not going to go anywhere with you four. It's dangerous." But when she said it, she was laughing.

"Leave the dishes." Gemma picked up her own dirty plate and dumped it in the sink. "We'll do them when we get home."

Paisley tore off at a dead run, slamming the screen, yelling, "Hurry up, Mama! I get to sit by Mrs. Bartling."

"Do you have your walking shoes?" Gemma asked Mrs. Bartling.

"I do. I wear my walking shoes all the time."

Gemma turned Mrs. Bartling toward the front door and gave her a little nudge. "I promise you can trust us."

One beat passed between them. Then two. Mrs. Bartling must have been taken by surprise at that promise because she was slow to reply. "Can I?"

Funny how one question, one reply, can have so many implications, Gemma thought. "Yes, you can," she answered.

Gemma followed Mrs. Bartling out, closing the front screen squarely. She tried the knob to make sure she'd locked the door. When she skipped down the steps, Alva T. and Charlene had already climbed in the front seat of the New Yorker, while Paisley scrooched all over Mrs. Bartling's lap in the back. "Sit on the seat beside her, Paisley. You can't sit on top on her. You're too big."

Charlene leaned over the seat and handed out sticks of Juicy Fruit gum all around. "You have to close your eyes, Bea," she instructed. "We aren't going to drive anywhere until you aren't looking."

"Oh, heavens," Mrs. Bartling said as she covered her face with her hands. "Okay. I'm not looking."

The radio was already blaring when Alva started the car. "Bluer than blue, life without you . . ."

"Can you turn it down, Alva? We can't hear a thing back here." Gemma buckled her seat belt.

"Can you guess where we're going?" Paisley's little hand rested against Mrs. Bartling's covered face, her tiny splayed fingers warm and moist.

"I have no idea."

"If you think about it, you'll know."

Mrs. Bartling's answer was muffled behind her hands. "Well, no. I can't imagine. I can't guess at all."

The car made a right turn, then a left. After that, they traveled straight a long way before Alva signaled and steered the Chrysler left again, into a parking lot. The tires bumped over rocks and jostled into potholes. By then Mrs. Bartling must have heard the carousel music and seen the lights and heard the engines of carnival rides revving, because she yanked down her hands and stared out the front window. "I can't believe it," she gasped. "You've brought me to the fair."

In front of them, the rides on the midway soared and spun, and half the people from Garden County rode them, screaming and laughing, waving baseball caps in the air. Flags swayed and snapped in the high breeze. Red, yellow, and green tubes of light whirled and glimmered as the last of the sun reached into the horizon behind the western High Plains.

Alva turned off the car.

"You've brought me to the fair," Mrs. Bartling said again as she aligned her two palms flat against one another and propped her fingers against her lips.

Gemma touched the woman's knee and felt a pang of terror. "Is it okay that we've done this?" she asked. "I mean, are you glad that we came?"

"Why . . . Oh, goodness. I never thought about the fair. It's been so long."

Paisley snuggled beneath the crook of Mrs. Bartling's arm and peered up at her with big hazel eyes. She wriggled closer still. "Will you ride the merry-go-round with me? Pleeease?"

The expression on the woman's face told Gemma that Mrs. Bartling found herself quite at a loss. "You want *me?*"

Paisley's curls bobbed up and down when she nodded.

Mrs. Bartling touched the little girl's nose. Old and young, their foreheads inclined together. When Mrs. Bartling answered, she sounded as if this one invitation meant everything to her. "Of course I'll ride the merry-go-round with you. Only you make sure I'll get a horse that goes up and down. Don't like the boring ones that just sit still."

"I'll make sure!"

"And we have to visit the exhibit hall. I've got to see the ribbon on Jan Blackwell's crumb cake."

"That's it, then. Let's go."

The mixed, sweet stench of cotton candy and Sloppy Joes and popcorn met them as they climbed out of Alva's New Yorker. While they waited in line at the red-and-white striped ticket booth and the others fished in their pockets for change, Gemma laid her hand on Mrs. Bartling's shoulder. "I'm treating tonight."

"You don't have to do that. I've got plenty of money."

"Paisley and I counted, to make sure we could do this. We wanted this to be special."

Mrs. Bartling acquiesced. "Only if you want to."

"We do."

They bought long curls of tickets for the rides and headed toward the exhibit hall. Once they'd gotten inside the crowded Quonset hut, they marched down the rows of displays with purposeful determination, eager to see every beribboned item before they hurried out to make themselves dizzy and slightly sick on the rides.

"Look at that," Alva noted, pointing toward an arrangement of blue flag and larkspur and poppies that cascaded from a child's shoe. "I could do something like this on all the tables in The Cramalot. Oh, wouldn't that be unusual?"

"Seems to me," Charlene surmised as she started off in the direction of the Boy Scout gun-safety posters in search of one that had been submitted by her nephew, "that folks in a restaurant might take exception to having someone's shoes on the table."

Mrs. Bartling found Jan Blackwell's crumb cake, which had one tiny piece cut from the left-hand corner for the judges, and a grand-prize rosette fastened to its tray. Gemma and Paisley laughed aloud at one photograph of a mule in the sunset and another of a baby who was sitting in the mud. They carefully inspected a display of hand-tooled leather belts and a village built out of Legos. Mrs. Bartling admired a floor-length satin skirt that had been awarded a blue ribbon for construction. "My, this is beautifully made." She fingered the tiny stitches on the seams. "Oh, how I'd love to have a place to wear something fancy. I get so tired of wearing sweatshirts." She read the tag. "Laura Stell made this! When I see her at the Superette, I'll have to say something."

In the animal pavilion, they saw bunnies and sheep and bulls with names like Elvis Parsley and Baa-Baa Walters. They made their way to the front of the pavilion only to be sidetracked by a crowd of rowdy parents cheering their children in the diaper derby. Six babies at various stages of undress had been freed on the racecourse—some sitting up and crying, others going backwards—while dads gestured wildly with toys and bottles and lollipops from the finish line, trying to make their babies crawl.

"Look at that baby with all the curly blond hair." In the excitement of the moment, Mrs. Bartling slipped her arm around Gemma's shoulders. "He looks so much like Nathan used to. He's so fat. And those two little bottom teeth!"

Such a curious feeling, being embraced for no reason but happiness, to Gemma who hadn't had much practice being embraced at all. She found herself afraid to breathe. She found herself afraid to turn or speak. She stood stock-still, her heart clattering against her ribs, while Mrs. Bartling enjoyed the memory and seemed not to notice that anything out of the ordinary had happened.

"That's what Nathan looked like?"

"Oh, I've got pictures I could show you. Wearing those tiny overalls and those scuffed white baby shoes. I still have those shoes somewhere."

A spark of hope burgeoned in Gemma's spirit. She opened the flap of her little purse and dug around for her wallet.

"I have this picture of him right here, too, if you'd want to see it."

Mrs. Bartling's hand slipped from Gemma's shoulder. "You have a picture of him? A recent one?"

Gemma dug around some more and finally came up with her billfold. "It's the only one I have of us together. Somebody at the courthouse took it on our wedding day."

"You've got a picture?" Bea repeated herself.

"You know how it is when there's just two of you? You get plenty of pictures of each other alone because there's never anybody else around to take pictures of you side by side. I mean, we had Paisley, but we were afraid she'd hold the camera upside down or something. We only have this one—"

"Why didn't you show me before?"

"I guess I didn't want to. It felt like I'd be using it to prove something." Gemma opened her wallet and thumbed through an assortment of cards—an Omaha Public Library card, a discount card for groceries, a Sears credit card. "Here." She drew the little photo out of her billfold with a hesitant motion, a gesture that showed it cost her dearly to bring this to light and hand it over.

"Oh, I can't see close things without my glasses." Mrs. Bartling scrabbled in her purse, too, and pulled out a pair of bifocals that Gemma rarely saw her use. She slipped the frames over her ears and squinted keenly at the tiny picture.

Gemma's hand shook as she held the photograph under the harsh pavilion lights.

Mrs. Bartling seemed to take in every detail of the wedding photo. The chiseled sign beside them that read "Douglas County Courthouse." The patches of crusted snow on the grass because they'd posed for the camera outdoors in February. The Honorable Judge R. C. Riley standing with them, beaming with pride because he had joined them in holy matrimony.

Gemma had dreamed of a pretty wedding in a little church somewhere, with a white dress and a cake, and ribbons tied in puffy white bows along the aisle. Nathan had told her they couldn't afford anything so extravagant. They'd waited on the hard wooden bench outside Riley's office for well over three hours while the judge finished up a bad-check court case downstairs. By the time the judge had flown in—the sleeves of his black robe flapping like a crow in huge, winglike sweeps—to marry them, Paisley had been overwrought, a one-year-old slumping all over the seat and whining from having to wait so long.

Gemma had worn a green street dress two sizes too big. Nathan had borrowed a sports jacket from the night supervisor at Omaha Corn-Fed Packing Company and had worn it with his jeans.

They'd stopped by the supermarket on the way and

Nathan had bought her one yellow rose to carry, in clear, crackly paper.

A civil ceremony, Gemma imagined Mrs. Bartling thinking.

"It wasn't a fancy wedding," she hurried to explain, feeling her color rise. "We went to the jewelry counter at Sears and bought my ring one morning. Then we drove to the courthouse and got the license. Easy as that."

Gemma waited, but Mrs. Bartling didn't say she could tell it wasn't fancy, just by looking at them in the picture. Maybe the starkness of it didn't matter to her. Maybe Mrs. Bartling wasn't appalled by the plainness of the ceremony.

When Mrs. Bartling raised her face to Gemma's, though, Gemma understood the woman's true answer. She hadn't come to the place where she could look at any sort of ceremony and think it mattered. She sought out only the features of her son's face, only the solemn expression in his eyes, the new lines of maturity at his brow, the square determination of his jaw.

Mrs. Bartling seemed unable to speak.

"I'm sorry," Gemma whispered. "I shouldn't have gotten it out now."

Mrs. Bartling folded her bifocals away. She struggled for words. "That boy hadn't changed as much as I'd thought. He still looked like Nathan."

Gemma opened her billfold again and filed the photograph away with care. Mrs. Bartling wiped her eyes with the back of her hand. "We don't ride that merry-go-round soon, they'll have all the horses put out to pasture."

"They don't pasture merry-go-round horses, silly-silly." Paisley grabbed Mrs. Bartling around the loins.

"They leave them standing in a circle all night because they aren't alive."

The diaper derby ended and a grand prize—a medallion on a red-white-and-blue striped ribbon—was awarded with much pomp and circumstance to the winner. Mrs. Bartling gestured to Charlene and Alva. "You two ready for the midway?" She gripped Paisley's hand. "Come on, little girl. You lead the way."

They rode every ride they could possibly stomach. The Zipper turned them upside down. The Matterhorn raced them backwards. Pharaoh's Fury, a favorite with the teenagers because it gave them reason to sit eight abreast and wrap their arms around members of the opposite gender, swung them back and forth so high that they felt like they'd left their innards behind. Mrs. Bartling bought them cherry slushees at the concession stand, which left Paisley with a cherry-colored moustache as broad as a clown's mouth that, try as she might, Gemma could not get off with spit and a napkin. At the merry-go-round, Charlene, Alva, and Gemma stood in a cluster and waved furiously every time Mrs. Bartling or Paisley passed by.

On a roller coaster so small Gemma could barely get her knees in, Deputy Jay Triplett, dressed in his full uniform, waved from the next car up. "Having fun?"

"Yes." Gemma waved back.

On the Spinnaker, which Gemma, Mrs. Bartling, and Paisley rode alone after Charlene and Alva complained of vertigo, Gemma and Mrs. Bartling had a slight disagreement over who might be heaviest and therefore ought to ride on the outside. Mrs. Bartling won. "Or lost," she announced, "whichever way seems best to look at it." She settled herself on the outside, Gemma sat in the middle, and Paisley came last. When the engine on the metal whirly-gig began to hum and, spider-like, the cars began to spin clockwise across the ground, Paisley giggled in glee. Without stopping to think about it, they all three clasped hands in Gemma's lap.

"Hold on!" Mrs. Bartling shouted.

The amusement ride picked up speed, and their hair started flying straight behind them. Paisley shrieked with joy. The entire time they twirled, they clung to one another for dear life, laughing. When the ride ended, they staggered off, Paisley grinning, Gemma losing her step from dizziness, announcing, "I should have taken a Dramamine," and Mrs. Bartling shaking her disheveled hair, saying, "Oh, my, I haven't done such an unladylike thing in years!"

"And now," Gemma grabbed onto a railing and steadied herself, "for the grand finale."

"What could be a grand finale to that?" Mrs. Bartling spread her hands wide as if to say anything better was impossible.

"Come with us." Paisley took Mrs. Bartling's hand and led her toward the colorful strip of arcade, each striped-canvas awning glowing gold from harsh light-bulbs beneath it. Big teddy bears and lime-green alien dolls dangled from their multicolored bowties, their plump bodies swinging whenever anyone jostled the tent. "Ever'body love da dog race!" the barkers sang out as Gemma and Paisley and Mrs. Bartling strolled past the booths. "Ever'body play da dog race." "Get your ring-toss prize. Only three dollars for three rings!" "Knock over the jugs and win a bear." "Goldfish here. Hey, ma'am, you wanna win a goldfish for that little one to take home?"

"No, thanks. Not now," Gemma answered. "We've got something else in mind."

They stopped in front of the shooting gallery. "Here we go." Gemma fished three dollars out of her purse and plunked the bills on the counter.

"Shoot out the star. That's all you gotta do," the fellow in the tent instructed. He slapped a paper target in front of their noses, five inches square, and indicated a small red star in the center. "If there's any red showing when you're done shooting, then you don't win a prize." He gestured toward the ranks of monstrous teddy bears peering down from above him.

"Well." Gemma crooked her elbow on the counter. "I guess you'd better have at it, Mrs. Bartling."

"What do you mean, 'have at it'?"

"You know what I mean."

Paisley bounced up and down beside Mrs. Bartling's hipbone. "Will you win me a prize? Will you? Pleeease?"

The dollars had long since disappeared from the counter. The man clipped the target on a pulley and ran it clear to the back of the booth.

Mrs. Bartling stepped forward and lifted the butt of the automatic air gun from its stand. She ran a hand along one side of its wooden stock. "What did Nathan tell you?"

"That you're the best crack shot at the Garden County Fair."

"He said that?"

"He did."

Mrs. Bartling's eyes gleamed with a sudden, unnatural brightness. "He might have been wrong, you know. You might have just wasted three dollars."

"I doubt he was wrong."

Mrs. Bartling lifted the BB gun and squinted through its sights. The barrel wavered an inch to one side, an inch to the other. "I don't . . . know." When she spoke, her cheek touched metal. She straightened, lowered the weapon to arm's length and tested its weight with both hands.

"Come on, Beatrice." A man with a baseball cap that read "Cleeland Boat Supply" stepped up beside her and eyed the gun. "None of us are getting any younger, waiting in this line. Either shoot or let somebody else take a turn. We all got grandkids bugging us for prizes."

Gemma saw Mrs. Bartling's face when it registered slight surprise. She doubted anyone had ever mistaken Paisley for Mrs. Bartling's grandkid. Dread deluged Gemma. She waited for the awful response she was certain would follow.

Mrs. Bartling would say, "I'm not her grandma."

But that response never came. Mrs. Bartling hoisted the air gun back to its stand and propped her hands on her hips.

"You hold your horses, Andy Cleeland. It's my turn to shoot and, if I want to take my time at it, that's my business. I am inspecting my firearm. You have to be careful. You never know when one of these things might explode in your hands or something."

"It would be nice if you could shoot sometime before midnight, Bea Bartling."

"I've got advice for you, Andy. If you're trying to win your poor grandchildren a prize, maybe you ought to try the goldfish pond. You'll never be able to hit this target."

Mrs. Bartling turned back and took hold of the BB gun again. She raised it to shoulder level and aimed the barrel at the target. "Here goes nothing."

She squeezed the trigger. *Pop. Pop. Pop-pop-pop.* BBs flew. Twelve times the pellets ripped through the paper target, clean in the center, forming one gigantic hole.

"There." Mrs. Bartling grinned down at Paisley. "Let's see how we did."

The target moved toward them on the pulley. As it came close, Andy Cleeland laughed behind her. "See that, Bea? You shot *too* good. Got it so clean in the center that you left all the red spikes of the star." He pushed up beside her. "Why don't you let somebody show you how this is done?"

"Hey." Gemma had already started fishing in her purse again. She plopped another three dollars on the counter. "Not so fast. I think she gets another try."

Mrs. Bartling picked the money up and handed it back to Gemma. "I'll pay. No sense you throwing your good money away on some gray-headed old woman who doesn't even know how to win her granddaughter prizes anymore." She plunked a five dollar bill on the counter. "Now, mister. Why don't you line me up another target."

Down the pulley the new target flew. Alva and Charlene shoved their way up through the sparse crowd, clapping and hooting to cheer her on. Mrs. Bartling sighted down the length of the barrel. She squeezed the trigger. *Pop-pop-pop. Pop-pop. Pop.* She took it slower this time, making certain she widened her aim on the target. She didn't say a word when she'd finished the twelve shots and returned the air gun to its stand.

The target zoomed forward.

Andy Cleeland leaned over her shoulder to inspect it.

"We have a winner!" the barker bellowed loud enough that everyone in the arcade could hear him. "Congratulations, young lady." He winked down at Paisley. From beneath the counter he pulled a tiny plastic bear that wouldn't have cost more than thirty cents at a dime store. "Enjoy your prize!"

"No," Mrs. Bartling said. "This won't do. We're going to trade this in on something bigger."

"You have to play again and win if you want to trade up."

She pointed high over their heads at the massive brown bear with the huge lavender bow that dangled above them. "How many times do I have to win to get that?"

"Six more times."

"Okay, then." Mrs. Bartling tossed out a twenty. "Winning this little girl a bear is worth a whole lot more than that. I've got something to prove to everybody here. Six more targets. Set them up."

Paisley stopped jumping up and down. The little girl stood frozen in place, her dark eyes as big around as walnuts. She waited in somber silence while Mrs. Bartling lifted the pellet gun, shot, and won. She shot and won again. And again.

The crowd around the shooting gallery grew quieter each time a target came up the pulley. Even Andy Cleeland yielded and in the end gave her slight applause. By the time the gentleman in the tent employed a huge metal hook and hauled down the enormous teddy bear with the lavender bowtie, Alva Torrington had rounded up at least a dozen Cramalot coffee customers to watch.

Deputy Jay Triplett, who had also stopped to see, kept shaking his head and saying, "We ought to sign you up for the sheriff's department, Mrs. Bartling."

Charlene Grover's Boy Scout nephew had appeared with a roving band of his closest friends. "Wow, Aunt Charlene," he announced. "I never knew grandmas could shoot like that!"

"Well, now you've seen it. They can."

When Mrs. Bartling handed Paisley the bear, the

monstrous stuffed animal seemed almost bigger than the little girl.

"It's the best teddy bear in the whole fair!" Paisley squealed. The little girl's arms clasped both the stuffed animal and Mrs. Bartling's neck all at the same time without restraint. Her small lips—moist and smelling faintly of cherry slushee—briefly pressed Mrs. Bartling's mouth full on.

"Thank you."

"No," Mrs. Bartling said, "Thank *you*, Paisley. You've reminded me how much fun it is to come to the fair."

Gemma revealed a pink cloud of cotton candy she'd been hiding behind her back. "If I had a candle, I would have used it. But I got scared that cotton candy might catch fire."

"Oh, my goodness."

"Happy birthday."

Mrs. Bartling took the cotton candy and shook her head despairingly at all of them. "How did you know it's my birthday today?" she asked in a soft voice filled with gentle pleasure. "Did Nathan tell you that, too?"

Gemma hugged her and grinned. "It wasn't Nathan this time. It was that old Bible on the coffee table. I was looking through it one morning and found the date written there." Gemma lifted her hands like a choir director, counted to three, and began singing "The Birthday Song." Everyone around joined in.

"Happy birthday to you! Happy birthday to you!"

Andy Cleeland and his grandchildren hummed along.

Five other people in line at the shooting gallery, who didn't know Mrs. Bartling from Adam, sang because everyone else was singing.

Jay Triplett took off his cap and lifted it to the sky with his words.

Gemma sang in a low, contented hum.

Alva's coffee customers chimed in with their gruff, eager voices.

Charlene's nephew and his friends sang, too, only they added words that little boys always add: "You live in a zoo! You look like a monkey! And you smell like one, too!"

And, oh, little Paisley, with her arms wrapped around the neck of the magnificent bear! She sang like a chirping sparrow, the notes she knew so well ringing sharp and clear.

Chapter Eighteen

By the second week of August, the endless grass on the far hills beyond the cemetery had begun to cure in the sun, the color and smell of strong weeds and heavy harvests.

For lack of rain, the dust on the little cemetery road had gotten so thick that it rose in billows, tingling nostrils, coating cars as they drove up and down each neatly trimmed, rocky lane. Wreaths that had been placed beside headstones on Memorial Day had long since faded and the bright sunflowers along the way, dancing with the breeze every time a vehicle passed, gave the impression that these loved ones rested in a living, golden place.

"It's time," Bea had said to Gemma without any warning this morning. "It's time for me to take you to see Nathan's grave."

Gemma sat beside Bea in the Chevrolet, her fingers plaited in the lap of her skirt, her eyes watching out the window, searching. Paisley occupied her normal place, sitting forward in the back with the huge teddy bear beside her, hands clutching the bench seat, her chin propped squarely between her mama and Bea.

Bea, who'd taken a much more authoritative role in Paisley's life since they'd chased the ice cream man and ridden the merry-go-round and shot targets like Buffalo Bill, glanced over her shoulder at the little girl. "Your seat belt isn't on, young lady. You can't sit forward like that and still have your seat belt on."

"But we're almost there. I want to see."

The car crested a small hill and, about the time Paisley got her seat belt buckled, Bea directed them to a cemetery plot off to the left, manicured and tidy, a narrow ridge of dirt no longer freshly turned, but bare compared to the others around it. She navigated the car alongside and parked out of the way of the road.

"Well." That's all she said, while Gemma hung out her open window and they all three peered at the tiny parcel of earth.

Well.

Bea turned the key to Off with one hand. The engine died. "They've gotten the headstone up. It must have come sometime this week."

Gemma didn't move. Bea could see the delicate stretch of the young woman's jaw, arched away from her, as Gemma looked intently out the window at the meadow grass and sky.

"If you look real far over that way—" Bea's gesture spanned the breadth of the town, her voice gone soft with reverence. "—you can see the steeple of St. Elizabeth's. See that street there? Follow it with your eyes and you'll see Pattison Drive. Back that direction is the highway, the exit signs, the tourist billboards that point travelers to Ash Hollow."

"It's pretty up here."

"Bought this for myself, you know. I thought it was a

nice plot. Nathan would have liked it because you can see the river."

"I'm scared," Gemma said. "I'm scared to get out of the car."

Bea reached across the front seat and took the girl's hand. "I'm scared, too, bringing you here. It's sad for me every time I come."

She could feel Gemma's pulse throbbing through their clasped fingers. The gold of Gemma's wedding band grew warm where the precious metal touched Bea's skin. Bea gazed down at it.

"I'm glad you haven't taken it off."

Gemma's eyes followed Bea's to her ring. "I don't know when I will. I can't imagine the day."

"You stay here in the car just as long as you need to." Bea released Gemma's hand and patted her on the knee. Then she reached forward and unlatched her door. "Paisley, do you want to help me plant roses?"

Paisley bounced up and down in the backseat. "Yep! Yep!"

The Chevy chassis bounced, too.

When Bea looked back, Gemma was still fingering her wedding band. "Nathan was the only person who ever loved me," Gemma said. "Nathan was the only person who was ever kind."

No, Bea wanted to say. She was beginning to see it more, in the stubborn way he'd stayed away from home so long, in the stark way he had married Gemma, in the selfish way he'd entered Paisley and Gemma's lives and had withheld them from those who might have cared for them the most.

I loved my boy. But Nathan was like everybody else. He was human. Nathan wasn't always kind.

"I've got to get my garden tools out," she said instead. "Can you pop the trunk, Gemma?"

"I'll get those, Mrs. Bartling. That box is too heavy for you to be lifting." Gemma climbed out, hurried around, and beat Bea to the trunk. She handed Bea the box with tiny pots and sprouting roses in it. "You carry this one. It doesn't weigh nearly as much."

They walked shoulder to shoulder across the brittle stubble, grasshoppers hurtling against their ankles, toward the place where tender blades of buffalo grass had begun to spike through the dark, loamy soil. Paisley had bounded ahead and they found her kneeling, scrutinizing the simple granite monument.

"Look. I can read this. Just like on the baseball." Little-girl fingers traced the engraved letters as she named them. "N-A-T-H-A-N."

"Nathan Roger Bartling," Gemma read with longing in her voice. "Beloved son."

The hot wind had unleashed Bea's hair from behind her ears. She tried to pin it back, to no avail. "Didn't know what else to write. Could only think of 'beloved son.' That's all." She set down the pots and yanked up a thistle from the ground, careful to uproot the full length of the weed from the spiny cluster of leaves all the way to the deep taproot. "If I had known about you, maybe I would have added something different."

Gemma crouched and splayed her hands against the dirt, as if she could touch Nathan by touching this raw, broken earth where his body lay. "If you had known about me, you could have written 'beloved husband.' And for Paisley, 'beloved father.' "

A platoon of Canadian geese drifted past on the river, following the glassy current with accidental grace. Their dark necks and black beaks made them look like heavy, black question marks bobbing along downstream. As Bea, Gemma, and Paisley watched, something startled the geese. The flock rose from the watercourse with a great flapping of wings and boisterous honking, taking to the air. Their slender bodies lifted and dropped with each stroke of flight. No sooner had they ascended than they circled back over a distant hayfield, dipping lower, seeking a safe place to land.

Paisley asked as she watched the birds descend. "Do you think Nathan's in heaven?"

"Oh, sweetie," Bea hurried to say. "Of course I—"

Her words caught. What right did she have to give a pat answer? What right to rely on religion when it seemed that the truth and the life she had once believed in had gone?

"Nathan did it the way you did, Paisley. He asked Jesus—"

Jesus.

The name she'd once spoken in trust and joy now seemed improper and tarnished for lack of use.

Jesus.

The name she'd once called in mystery and beauty and glory, now empty as dry dust, as far from sustaining her as her son's crumbling bones beneath the dirt.

I speak it because it's what Paisley wants to believe. I speak it because, at one time or another, it's what everybody wants to believe.

Jesus.

Bea felt sullied. Unworthy. Removed. How many times had she easily spoken to others about the love and faithfulness of Jesus Christ? How many times, in her trust, had she talked like she knew all the answers?

Well, she certainly wasn't such an expert on the subject now.

Bea had no choice but to finish the statement she'd so randomly begun. "He's in heaven because he asked Jesus to take over his life. When he was a little boy. Like you."

Before either of them could stop her, Paisley sprawled atop the wale of brown Nebraska soil, her feet in the direction of Nathan's feet, her head in the direction of Nathan's head. Her eyes followed the fleecy shapes in the clouds—dragons, faces of princesses, pirate ships—as they rolled by. "I wish I could see what Nathan sees in heaven," she breathed.

"Paisley." Gemma, affronted, took her child by the arm. "You mustn't lay on somebody's grave. It's disrespectful."

"Nathan isn't here, Mama. He's in heaven because he asked Jesus into his heart."

"Nobody knows if those things are true or not, Paisley. It makes people feel better, saying it. Especially when they know somebody who's dead."

"Mama," the child's plaintive little voice began. "It must be true. It says so in the Bible."

"The Bible is a good book. Some stories in there I believe. Others, I don't. Jesus was a good man. A prophet who lived a wild dramatic life. He might have performed a few miracles. But I don't see how it could go any farther than that."

From somewhere inside of Bea, somewhere beyond her own spirit, somewhere beyond her doubt, words filled her, touched her, forced their way out.

"You can't believe the in-between, Gemma. So many people try to fit it there, but it won't fit. Jesus was either who He said He was or He was a crackpot."

Lord, how can I say something like this when I'm the very one who feels like you've forsaken me?

Bea felt suddenly disoriented, breathless. Oh, heavens, they'd come here to plant roses, hadn't they? Where had she put the roses? "Let's get to planting, Paisley. Come over here and tell me which will be yours."

She didn't want to talk right now. She only wanted to dig. She didn't want anything to stop this clamoring in her heart. This *hope*.

Father? Are you who you say you are? Are you who I've said you are? Do you speak? Do you listen?

"How many are we going to plant? A whole bunch?"

"Three will be plenty. We want to make sure the bushes have room to grow over the years."

"Like the one in your front yard?"

"Yes."

They'd almost finished digging holes beside Nathan's monument when they heard a clatter—the sounds of metal banging and hackberry limbs jostling and an axle squeaking—as the cemetery gardener came whistling with his wheelbarrow over the furrow of the hill.

"Mr. Goodsell." Bea saluted him with a gloved hand. "My, but you have more modes of transportation than an emperor. Last time I saw you, you were driving a golf cart."

"A golf cart isn't as handy for carrying around brambles. I drive that when I do the weeding and the hedge trimming. I have a Dodge pickup, too, to use whenever I get out on the highway. A pickup does much better there than the golf cart or this wheelbarrow, either one."

He veered his little garden cart along past them until he noticed the pots of roses. "Harison's Yellow? Is that what those are? Pioneer roses, right here at Ash Hollow Cemetery?"

"That's what they are."

"Ah." He whistled under his breath. "You *do* know how to grow a rose." He propped the wheelbarrow on its two peg legs and readjusted his load of brambles. Bea noticed him watching Gemma as Gemma clutched the trowel, her knuckles gone white as coriander as she stabbed dirt clods away in chunks. He inclined his jaw at her, unable to pass without giving advice. "You want to dig that hole twice the size as a lazy person would dig it. Twice as wide as you think it should be. Twice as deep."

"I'm not finished yet." Gemma opened her grip and shut it, stretching her fingers as she held her palms up to him. "It'll be the right size for a rose when I'm done."

Mr. Goodsell poked one hand inside the oversized pocket of his ragged green army pants and pulled out his leather work gloves. He pitched them down, where they lay in Gemma's lap, crumpled and rotund, their fingers cupped and intimate, still in the shape of his hands. "I don't need these for awhile. You use them. You're getting blisters."

"This is my family, Mr. Goodsell." Bea heaved herself up from the ground and introduced them. "My daughter-in-law, Gemma. And Paisley, her girl."

The gardener touched the unruly bangs of his hair with his thumb and his forefinger, as if he had a hat brim to tip for them, only he didn't.

"Care Goodsell. Nice to meet you."

"Nice to meet you, too."

With bare hands, he removed the rake and the pile of hackberry limbs from the wheelbarrow. He thumped the inside of the empty wheelbarrow with satisfaction. "Who wants a ride? Mrs. Bartling?" He made a ceremonial bow before her. "Can I take you for a spin?"

"Heavens, no, Mr. Goodsell. I'm an old woman. I'd be tied up in knots if you bounced me along in that thing."

"I need a passenger." He winked at Gemma. "You want to give it a try? How about it?"

Gemma laughed. "I guess I'd better not have a ride, Mr. Goodsell. I've got roses to plant."

All this time, Bea could see him pretending not to notice Paisley sidling up next to him, her hands clasped behind her back in restrained eagerness. "Ah-ha!" He finally looked down and made a quick, surprised jump, as if he hadn't expected anyone to be standing so close beside his leg. "What's this? You mean I've found somebody who's brave enough to go?"

"Can I bring my bear?"

"Is he too heavy for me to lift?"

"No. He's soft and light."

"Well, you'd better go get him, then."

Paisley retrieved the gigantic bear and climbed in. Care Goodsell showed her how to hang on, each hand clutching the rim of the wheelbarrow beside each little hipbone. Off they clattered along the stone footpath, with Paisley's laughter rising like a steeple bell. Bea and Gemma watched them go.

After they'd seen them off, Bea and Gemma dug their holes twice as big as a lazy person would dig them. They dug them twice as wide, twice as deep. They worked fistfuls of humus and compost into each trench, knowing it was properly mixed when the planting beds smelled rich and cool.

Bea had brought everything necessary to feed the roses—decomposed leaves, well-rotted cow manure, and Osmocote Granular. As they added each ingredient, Bea began to speak.

"Once these roots establish themselves, they'll find what they need to survive. These roses have pioneer spirit. Just like the folks who came out west."

If God is who He says He is, He knows I'm struggling from lack of faith.

"A gardener will tell you to do this in June. But anyone who knows these roses will tell you they'll transplant whenever the spirit strikes."

If God is who He says He is, He knows I blame Him for not listening.

"These roses won't go deep at first. They'll want to stay the same depth they've been in their pots. But water and nutrients will draw their roots down."

If God is who He says He is, He knows I think that He's forsaken me.

If He's there, He knows.

They'd set their roses aright and had begun to pack earth firm around them when Gemma asked, "Would you tell me about Nathan's funeral, Mrs. Bartling?" Bea peeked across to see Gemma's face downcast, her hands flattening the dirt. She hadn't made any move to suggest that this subject held any higher importance than the hot summer weather or the exorbitant price of gas. "You've never told me anything about that day."

Bea's hands halted in the dirt. Then, with her thumb, she began to make circles in the dirt, watching ants skittering away, not wanting Gemma to know she'd glanced up, that she thought this question was anything different. "Guess I figured there wasn't anything to tell."

"Was it a good service? Would Nathan have liked it?"

Circles, circles in the dirt. Then Bea placed her weight hard on the heels of her hands. Her shoulders slumped, and she shook her head.

"I don't know if it was good or not. I don't know if it was right."

Gemma nudged a grasshopper away. "What do you mean?"

"All I could think to do at the service came from years before. Little-boy songs. Little-boy remembrances."

Bea noticed that the dirt in front of Gemma was already flat. But the young woman kept pressing. Pressing. "Little-boy things are good. He would have liked that."

"I didn't know how to say who Nathan was *becoming*. I couldn't share how my boy had grown to be a man." Bea began to smooth the earth with a small rake, leaving runnels in the dust beside her. "I wish—" Even though she stopped speaking mid-sentence, it seemed she'd completed her thought aloud. *I wish we could have done it together*.

Gemma's eyes locked on hers, a myriad of unspoken possibilities passing between them, hard-wrought, precious. *If things could have been different. If Nathan had brought me home. If I had only known you.*

Bea filled the tin watering can from the spigot beside the stone footpath, conveying it back to douse the fledgling roses. Together they listened to the agreeable noise of moisture soaking into the soil, the sound of something deep and thirsty being satisfied.

Gemma sat back on her heels and shaded her eyes from the sun. Bea saw her keeping a careful watch on Care Goodsell and Paisley in the distance as they trundled along the footpath in the wheelbarrow.

She's a good mother, Bea thought. *I like how she looks after her child.*

Gemma began to remove the unwieldy gloves that Mr. Goodsell had lent her, tugging off one roomy canvas finger after another. "There's a question I've been wanting to ask you," Gemma stated, lowering her voice. She didn't speak again until she shed the index finger, the ring finger, the pinky. And then, "Would you tell me why Nathan left home? I can't stop myself wanting to know. In all the times we talked about it, he never would say."

Lord, Bea thought *I will never be able to escape my own unfaithfulness. My unfaithfulness to you. My unfaithfulness to a child.*

Bea felt like she was tottering, balancing, struggling to break free of something that threatened to topple her over an edge. She yanked the bobby pins from behind her ears and stabbed them back in place again, impaling her scalp. *She's asking me questions I never wanted to answer.*

"Only Nathan could know why he acted the way he did," she lied. "Don't ask me to second-guess Nathan's reasons."

Gemma picked a handful of native grass from the ground and began to shred blades of it, separating each one into green, pulpy strings. "You said you were the reason. You said it was your fault."

Because I was weak, Gemma. Because I didn't fight. Because I wasn't reliable.

"Don't. Please. If Nathan didn't answer it for you, then don't make me answer it, either. Let dead things be dead. Please. It isn't your life. It's ours."

Blessedly, here came the wheelbarrow over the knoll of the hill again, with Care Goodsell at the helm, directing the little cart around headstones and brilliant clumps of flowers. Paisley waved.

The unanswered question stood between them. *It isn't your life. It's ours.* Bea did not wave to Paisley. Neither did Gemma.

Mr. Goodsell made a great show of dumping the little girl out right at their feet. She hugged his knees and he hugged her back. But the whole time he was hugging, Care Goodsell was looking into Bea's eyes. He was looking into her eyes and it seemed to Bea like he was looking into her heart as well.

"Something not good's going on around here," he said. "Something not good at all."

"How are we doing with these roses?" Gemma handed him his gloves. "We did everything you said."

The gardener pulled on his gloves and loaded his hackberry branches into the wheelbarrow all in one big bundle. He balanced the old garden rake counter-clockwise atop the load, its rusted prongs zinging like a harp.

"While Paisley and I were going along, we happened to have a little talk about things. Thought you might be interested in what we figured out. We figured out that faith is like a rose."

"What?"

"Faith is like a rose."

Bea stooped low and began gathering her planting supplies. Watering tin. Spades and trowels. Empty pots. "I know what faith is like," she said to him. "Everybody who's been to Sunday school knows what faith is. Have you ever been to Sunday school, Mr. Goodsell?"

He grinned and showed his teeth as if she'd said something funny. "No."

"Well, then, there you have it. Maybe you ought not to be talking about something you don't know."

"On the rose, you've got the roots, the leaves, and the blossoms. Healthy roots make healthy leaves and blossoms. Faith isn't about doing the right thing or being moral. Faith is relying on God's own roots inside you. Faith is knowing that what's underground has the potential to make a lovely bloom."

"Maybe," Bea said. "Maybe I can see that."

"Leaves so green a person thinks they never did see such color. Petals so soft and yellow they remind you of a sunrise. That's evidence of where the roots are. Those petals are a person who's trustworthy. Those leaves are a person you can rely on. You find a person full of faith, and that makes you realize God is faithful. You find that God is faithful, and that's how you are filled with faith. It's a reflection, like light on a lake. One mirrors the other."

"Who are you?" she asked. "Who are you that you would know about roses and faith, too?"

Mr. Goodsell didn't answer. He started off down the path, the prongs on his rake still zinging, while the lone wheel sang a trio of notes that blended with his off-key whistling.

"Any more advice on planting, Mr. Goodsell?" Bea called after him, all of a sudden aching to see him go. "Anything else I've forgotten that I need to know?"

The gardener parked his cart for the second time and shaded his eyes. "You sure you planted with humus?" he bellowed back. "With compost?"

Bea nodded, laboring up onto tiptoe in her ancient Naturalizers, as if she could raise her voice by raising herself on her toes. "I'm sure. We've done that!"

He shouted and waved. "That's good. A rose likes to be fed." The last of his voice blended with the wind and his whistling and the arpeggios of the squeaking cart as he pushed it forward.

Chapter Nineteen

Things were different for Gemma and Bea after they spent the day together at the cemetery.

All that talk about faith, and Gemma noticed Mrs. Bartling seemed distracted, quiet, given to staring out the window at the azure sky for long, silent intervals, with a melancholy in her eyes that seemed—in its way—magnified and more profound than in those first days after Gemma and Paisley arrived.

I never should have asked her why Nathan left home. I never should have tried to find out.

Four silent days together, and Mrs. Bartling announced one morning that, next Monday, she would return to her job at Nebraska Public Power. A victory of sorts. But one that seemed solemn, cheerless.

Alva T. had given Gemma the day off because she hadn't had a chance to arrange childcare. As Mrs. Bartling left for the day, Gemma and Paisley sat sedately on the sofa, their hands curved in their laps, still wearing their shabby pajamas. For a moment, as she headed for the door, she paused, turned back as if she might smile, as if she might say "I'll miss you." But she didn't.

She looked from one of them to the other with a pensive sadness on her face.

We remind you, don't we? I see it in your eyes sometimes when you think I'm not looking. You see us and remember what you did to make Nathan go away.

Why did Nathan go away? What did you do?

"You'll be okay here by yourselves?" Mrs. Bartling asked somberly from the front door. "You know how to turn on the air conditioner if you need to?"

"I know how. I've seen you do it."

"If the toilet makes the sound that scares Paisley, you just have to jiggle the handle."

"I know how to do that, too."

And then, she left.

Mrs. Bartling had been gone only an hour when the telephone rang. Gemma climbed up from the floor, where she'd been helping Paisley with a hundred-piece basket-of-bunnies puzzle, to answer. "Hello? Bartling residence."

"I'm looking for Gemma Franklin. You know her?" asked a rough-tempered male voice.

Gemma gripped the telephone receiver with both hands, her pulse quickening. "I *am* her."

"This is Joe Sampson. Mechanic over at Sandhill Texaco. You got a minute to talk?"

"I do."

"Got a buggy here that's ready for you to pick up. This old '83 Toyota Corolla."

"It's ready?"

"There's folks in this town who'd say you're crazy, putting all this money into a rebuilt engine. Before you did this, you should've gone over to Cornerstone Motors in Scottsbluff to see what they could find for you."

"I don't want a different old car, Mr. Sampson. I'm satisfied with the one I've got."

"Well, since you're so satisfied with it, when are you picking it up? It's taking up too much room in my garage."

Gemma opened the drawer beneath the phone and pulled out the notepad Bea always kept handy. She dug beneath the phone book, searching for a pencil that had lead. "I was given an estimate of nine hundred dollars. Can you tell me if that's what it's going to cost?"

"You want the total? Uh. Just a minute here. Let me find it." From over the phone line, Gemma heard him rustling through papers. "Let's see. Rebuilt engine. Add labor. Add the sales tax." He made a series of frightening grunts as he tallied up the total. "Yep, that's right. Here we are. Young lady, I hope you're sitting down. This isn't pretty. You're looking at nine hundred sixty-six dollars and thirty-two cents."

Gemma wasn't sitting down. She stood with her backbone straight as a fencepost and scribbled the number on the pad. She stared at it. She drew a circle around it. Then she drew another circle. And another.

Five weeks ago, that amount of money would have seemed like enough to make a downpayment on Memorial Stadium where the Cornhuskers played.

Five weeks, in which Alva Torrington had been paying Gemma a fair wage. Five weeks, in which the customers at The Cramalot, all of them except Walt Snell, had been more than generous in their tipping.

Gemma didn't have to open the cedar box to count her money. Before he had died, her daddy had told her once, "A smart woman knows every morning how much money she has in the bank." She already knew how much she'd saved, to the exact penny.

Fifty dollars and seventy-four cents was all she needed. Fifty dollars, and she'd make half that in wages and tips tomorrow.

She'd make the other half the day after that.

"I'll be over to pick it up on Thursday," Gemma told him. And then she hung up the phone.

Thursday. So soon.

Sooner than she'd ever imagined.

"Who was that, Mama?" Paisley asked, her mouth full of Cap'n Crunch cereal they'd both been eating straight from the box.

"The car mechanic. Our car's fixed."

The little girl reared to her knees, cardboard pieces of puzzle scattering to the floor around her. "Mama, I don't want to leave."

"I can't help it, honey bananas. It's time."

The little girl's woebegone voice crescendoed into a wail. "I wanted to be here longer. I wanted to see the roses grow."

"We came here to get to know her, honey bananas. We didn't come here to live."

"Oh, yes, we did. We came because we don't have the trailer anymore. We came because another little girl is sleeping in my bed."

"Listen to me. You have to try hard to understand what I'm telling you." Gemma cupped Paisley's face in her hands and scrunched the child's wet cheeks in earnestness. "It's a grownup thought and you're only a little girl."

"What?"

"Every time Mrs. Bartling looks at us, it makes her look back at herself and think bad things. She thinks of things she should have done differently. She thinks how she lost time with her son because she made him go away."

"Couldn't she look at us, Mama, and just see *us?*"

Tears came to Gemma's own eyes at last. She shook her head, grief-stricken. "No. I don't think so."

"But, Mama. I love her. I've even told her."

"Sometimes when you love somebody the most, you want to do what is best for them, even though it hurts you the worst inside."

"I wanted to make her happy."

"I did, too, sweets. But sometimes there's things that go too deep for happiness."

Gemma's decision had already been made. She would find a baby-sitter for Paisley and work another two weeks perhaps—enough to make gas money to get along to another town.

She'd save enough for a few groceries and a security deposit on another trailer.

She'd ask Alva to write her a recommendation and she'd apply for a job at another restaurant somewhere.

She and Paisley would survive. They had survived before. Maybe, when they got settled, Gemma would buy stamps. Maybe she'd send Grandma Hardeman a postcard. Maybe she'd send a return address and let her grandmother know where they'd gone. Maybe, maybe, Grandma Hardeman would care.

And maybe she wouldn't.

That afternoon after Paisley went down for a nap, Gemma roved throughout Mrs. Bartling's house like an abandoned waif, feeling more lonely and lost than she'd felt on the day they'd scrounged beneath the car seat for coins for a candy bar and hitched a ride to Sandhill Texaco and found the name *Bartling* in a phone book hanging in a phone booth by the road.

As she roamed, she remembered the details she'd discovered and cherished the day they'd first arrived, the faded patterns in the wallpaper, the roses by the door, the tiny bird's nest with the icicle woven among its twigs.

She'd cherished such things when she came because Nathan had made them familiar.

She treasured them now because she had seen Mrs. Bartling hold them dear.

Gemma had a thought. Maybe she should offer Mrs. Bartling her photograph before they left. The one of Nathan at the courthouse. On their wedding day.

Maybe Mrs. Bartling would offer one of Nathan's little-boy pictures in return. Maybe the one in the hallway with Nathan missing teeth.

But, no, she couldn't part with her wedding picture. It was too dear a price to pay.

We remind you, don't we? You see us and remember what you did to make Nathan go away.

Gemma found herself in the hallway outside of Nathan's old room. With one tentative hand, she pushed open the door.

That's the last thing Mrs. Bartling would want around the house. A picture with me in it.

The hinges creaked as the door opened wider. This was her chance. Guilt swept over her.

We're leaving. It might never happen if I don't do it now. Just this once, and no one need ever know.

Gemma nudged the door open all the way. She glanced over her shoulder as if she expected someone to catch her, but nobody was there.

She stepped inside.

For three long beats she stood in the middle of Nathan's room, uncertain what should happen next. The room smelled stale and musty, redolent with mothballs. Gemma trailed her hand along the topstitching of a comforter spread on one of the single oak beds. "What did you run away from, Nathan?" Gemma whispered. "Why would a boy have a room and a mother like this and not come home?"

On the shelf along one wall stood an entire fleet of rusty Tonka trunks, wheels and gears still embedded with sand from someone's sandbox. Beside those, a pile of three frayed, faded baseball caps, one atop the other, tilted to one side like a sod house. Gemma lifted one ball cap and flipped it over. "Bartling," scribbled in Nathan's familiar bold script. "117 Pattison Drive. 436-8576."

For a long, long while, Gemma savored the familiar shape of the cap in her hands, the seams stretched, the sweat-stained brim curled at Nathan's favorite jaunty angle. She held the ball cap and she saw him, she touched him, stroked his head the way she always had, thinking what a miracle she had, that someone loved her. *Oh, Nathan. Oh, Nathan.*

Gemma plopped it on her own head and examined herself in the mirror. "A. H. All-Stars," the hat said.

A garbage truck stopped down the street, began its slow, mechanical rumbling. Trashcans banged together. Gemma froze and listened.

The truck moved on to the next street. Gemma waited. And listened more. She heard her heartbeat in her ears. No footsteps. No sounds of Paisley. No one coming to find her out.

She set about looking again.

With the cap still on her head, Gemma picked up a

small ceramic fisherman, his pole and fishing line dipped in the water, the hook coming beneath his legs and snagged squarely on the seat of his pants.

"The One That Got Away," the little pedestal read.

On the shelf Gemma found more things: a Rubik's Cube that was nowhere close to solved, a coiled dog collar with a rabies tag from 1988, a black AM-FM radio, a book entitled *Amazing Otters*, an extensive rock collection. On the dresser was a pack of BBs, a pocketknife, something that looked like a goose call, a comb, and some pennies.

Not until she opened the closet did Gemma find the first true evidence of a mother deserted.

The door slid open in silence and she stared into nothingness. Only one pair of dress shoes, shining and Sunday best, sitting heel to heel on the floor. Nothing hung on the hooks. Empty hangers dangled. With the exception of an old John Elway football jersey and a letter jacket with track pins that looked like it had barely been worn, there were no personal items in this closet at all.

Gemma didn't know what to think. She fought the urge to sit on the floor and cry. The emptiness here seemed to swallow her. It negated every dear, intimate detail of Nathan's room.

It had been a long, long time since the man she'd married had lived in this place.

Nathan, why?

She hadn't any way to know how long she stood there, staring in, alone. She hugged her arms around her chest and swayed back and forth, like a rocking toy, understanding for the first time this awful, total barrenness—the enormity of a son who would walk away from his mother.

She had no way to know how long she stood there before something made her lean back and glance at the top shelf, and she saw the ancient tackle box.

She noticed it now. It waited high overhead, partially hidden behind several dusty track trophies, shoved completely toward the back, with only one corner visible. Gemma craned her neck. She stood on tiptoe and tried to see.

I wonder what's up there.

She saw a battered tin supply box, rusted around both of its buckles, dented and dirty from what must have been a hundred fishing trips to Lake McConaughy. She could make out only thin lines of color among the scratches. Once upon a time, it must have been blue.

Gemma hadn't any idea why she felt such a sudden, immediate, compelling *need* to examine this box. Perhaps because Nathan had always told her he'd bring her home one day and take her camping. Perhaps because he'd described his favorite morning to her at least a dozen times, crawling out of his sleeping bag and sinking a line before anybody else woke up, as the mist came rising in curls off the water and dawn reflected soft and radiant from the glassy lake.

Whatever prompted her, Gemma could not turn away from the strange beckoning in her spirit. Even if she'd wanted to, Gemma could not dismiss whatever might be inside this mysterious box.

She stretched as tall as she could possibly manage, stretched clear through the ends of her fingertips, and managed only to topple one of the trophies. She caught it with both hands, thankfully, and, still shaking with the thought of it falling, set it on the shelf beside the ball caps.

In desperation, Gemma surveyed the room. She spied

a wooden chair beside Nathan's old desk in the corner. When she tested the chair, she found the legs a little wobbly. It would have to do. Gemma dragged the chair over and climbed up. She grabbed hold of the tackle box handle, hauled it forward, lugged it down.

Gemma hadn't thought what she'd find when she opened the lid. Fishing tackle, she supposed.

She set it on the bed and, at first, that's exactly what it seemed she'd discovered—fishing supplies, neatly arranged in three levels of accordioned trays and tiny compartments. Red-and-white fishing floats. Split shot and swivels. A spool of invisible leader. Eagle Claw snelled hooks embedded according to size on a strip of cardboard.

Gemma raised the second level of trays and peered beneath. Strange. Here, the collection of fishing paraphernalia played out.

Various sets of white papers lay in each cubicle, torn from a tiny tablet and organized according to size. And, upon first look, every one of the pages appeared blank.

What could this be?

Gemma lifted two pages and held them in her hand. She pored over them, wondering why anyone in his right mind would store away empty pieces of paper. She held them up, peering at them, closer to her nose. Closer.

She'd found something. Faint indentations. Orderly scribbles.

Each page had been carefully marked. Only there wasn't any way to read them. These markings were invisible.

Working faster now, Gemma lifted another tray and thought she'd found another layer of fishing lures. But instead, beside a handful of fake worms that looked like

Gummi candy and a round wheel holding every size of weights, she discovered a very interesting item. A pen the likes of which she hadn't seen in years.

An invisible-ink pen.

Gemma recognized it immediately. She'd owned one just like it, from a cereal box.

She tried to recall how to make messages appear. Did she carry the papers out into the sunlight? Did she run them under water from the faucet?

The worst thing she could do would be to handle these wrong and cause them damage.

Like a gift, at that moment, Gemma remembered the answer. A picture of herself lying in her little room, scarcely larger than the bed that held her. "I wrote you a secret message, Daddy. You want to read it?"

"Of course I do. I love reading anything you've written."

"Hold it up to the lightbulb, Daddy. Then the ink appears."

Gemma turned on the lamp beside Nathan's bed and held the first strip of paper next to it. For long moments, nothing happened. But then, like a stain spreading, as quickly as that, lettering materialized. The entire page. Legible and dark.

Oh, Nathan. What is this? Is it something you would have wanted me to see?

Gemma stared at the papers in their little compartments for a moment more, knowing she ought to close the lid and stash it away, knowing she had no right to be here, no right to handle these little-boy notes.

She'd never asked Nathan about his childhood friends. He'd never volunteered any stories. Another groundswell of sorrow swept over her. Here was one of those off-handed questions she should have asked him while they ambled along in the park, holding hands.

Who did you play with when you were little, Nathan? What did you like to do?

Gemma picked up the box again and held it, still open, with the trays raised. At the bottom of the box an entire jumble of fish stringer slid away to one side. Gemma peered down, and made another discovery. Someone had hidden an array of postcards beneath the stringer. Beautiful picture postcards of Lake McConaughy at sunset. Dramatic sunlight angles on ruts carved into sandstone by wagon wheels along the Oregon Trail. The three-story gingerbread house, Scouts Rest Ranch, where Buffalo Bill had lived and rehearsed his famous Wild West Show.

Each of the postcards had been addressed meticulously in Nathan's bold handwriting. Each of them had been postmarked with the date, with proper postage affixed.

These did not have to be deciphered. They could be read just as they were, all in a heap.

The same postal imprint had been stamped, intractable and unyielding, over the handwritten address on each one. An inked hand with a finger pointed backwards. "Return to Sender. Addressee Unknown."

Chapter Twenty

Feb. 8, 1996
Dear Jacob,

I'm writing this because I dont know where you are. Three mornings ago, Mom came in my room and woke me up for school and told me you would be gone today so I shouldn't be looking for you in the sophomore hall. I asked her where you'd gone and she said she couldn't say. I thought maybe you would have gone to Crawford's because you're late working on your geometry project and you spent the night there but she said no, that your project was something I shouldn't worry about. Mr. Abrams stopped me in the hall and said if you were sick he would give me your homework and I could bring it to you. Mom gave me the address at county social services and said I could write you here and you would get it.

I miss you
Nathan

Feb. 13, 1996
Dear Jacob,

Supper times worse then quiet without you to talk to. The whole time, your chair sits there staring at us, empty, and I keep thinking how you used to sit there leaning back on two legs and Dad would say, "Jacob Gary, if you don't sit straight in that chair youre going to fall over and break open your head." Mom wants to take me on a trip to Potter to see her aunts. She said we needed to get out of town. But I said, "How can we get out of town anywhere without Jacob? What if he tries to come home and we aren't here?" She said she didnt think you would be home anytime soon.

Your brother
Nathan

Feb. 16, 1996
Dear Jacob,

Went driving by the social services over in Oshkosh because that's the address Mom gave me but nobody knew anything and said if I wanted to find you I had to talk to some lady named Mary who wasn't there. I'm coming back to find you when I can . . .

From
Nathan

22 Feb. 1996
Dear Jacob,

Christi Owens came up today at school and asked how you are. She said her dad heard that the police came to our house the night you went away. She said he knew about it because he was driving by that Sunday night late when you left and saw the lights flashing. What happened? They've quit trying to send your homework home with me. I have just one question. Dont you want to live with us anymore? WRITE ME!!!

Your brother
Nathan

Feb. 24, 1996
Dear Jacob,

Frank Lubing wants to move you up and get you to play on the Legion team with me even though youre still young enough to play Babe Ruth. When he called, Mom gripped the phone tighter than a baseball bat herself and told Frank it didn't matter about you being drafted because you weren't here and you weren't coming back.

I miss you
Nathan

March 1, 1996
Dear Jacob,

Im sending this to a new address. I used Mom's car and drove over to see you yesterday afternoon. I went to the county services office, that was the address Mom gave me. They told me you'd been there but not anymore. They said you didn't live at this address, either, but I could write and it would get to you. They said for a long time you hadn't even been in Garden County anymore. I never told you but that day I got so mad because you kept following my friends in the hall, it happened because Sam said you hit the ball better than me at the Wheatland tournament.

From
Nathan

March 13, 1996
Dear Jacob,

I want you to understand and know I'm trying as best I can for a seventeen-year-old senior who lives in Nebraska to find you so keep up your spirits if that's the way youre feeling.

Your brother
Nathan

March 21, 1996
Dear Jacob,

I asked Susan Wickstrom to senior prom yesterday. Josh King started saying how Susan wanted to go with me and before I knew it I was asking her just like that.

Don't know what I'm suppose to wear to this Mom says a tuxedo for the prom but all dressed up I'll feel stupid. Then theres the flower problem. Got to find out what color dress she's wearing then go buy her something to match and pin it on her and that scares me. I know youre younger then me and you don't have experience with a prom but it always helped so much just having somebody to talk to about these things. If the roses were blooming I'd go to the cemetery and put one of Mom's roses on that grave you showed me because it didn't look like you had a chance whereever you are to go over and do it.

From
Nathan

2 April 1996
Dear Jacob,

Its youre birthday today, isn't it? Happy Birthday. If you were willing to come home we could go camping at Lake Mac by ourselves and catch all those fish we were talking about. Another few weeks and it'll be warm enough . . .

I miss you
Nathan

April 10, 1996
Dear Jacob,

Susan said everybody wears tuxedos to prom and I can't believe it but its Susan Wickstrom's fault I'll be wearing a suit.

From
Nathan

April 16, 1996
Dear Mr. Bartling,

We have returned several postcards to you via the U.S. Postal Service, including this last one dated April 10 because of unfortunate circumstances. Jacob stayed for a few weeks here in our home, but we have several young children and we decided because of the episodes in your brother's life that he might be better placed somewhere else. Unfortunately, by the time we started getting your cards, he was already gone. I do not know where he is now but I trust that the child services system has worked well and they have found a place where Jacob can be properly cared for. I'm sorry to not have a forwarding address to send you. Since we are in Lincoln County you might try the social services office there at: 457 So. Main Street, Lincoln NE.

All best,
Richard Lovett

April 19, 1996
Dear Jacob,

I got a letter from that Richard Lovett saying how youd lived with them but that you are somewhere else now. Finally got fed up and discusted and tired of getting these letters getting returned in the mail. I drove to social services today and told them I wanted to drive to see you. YOU ARE MY NEW BROTHER AND I DON'T WANT TO LOSE YOU!!! I told them they had to say where you are or else Id have Mom come there and report them. They said that was fine since Mom had already been there and that she'd signed you over to a foster home. Signed you over? What does this mean?

Nathan

April 20, 1996
Dear Jacob,

I asked Mom last night to tell me what she meant by "signing you over" to a foster home. She said it meant you'd be living with a different family. Somebody who lives somewhere else. I yelled and took the car keys out of her purse and drove around Ash Hollow a long time. Almost got hit because I ran the stop sign on the corner of Avenue O but the other car stopped in time. I asked Mom, "How can you just sign him over?" She said she didn't know how she could do it.

I miss you
Nathan

April 22, 1996
Dear Jacob,

I keep thinking about you in a foster home. Youre fifteen. What do you need a foster home for? I keep thinking whether you wanted to go or whether Mom made you do it because she was tired of you being around. She sure won't say, every time I ask her. Hope you got clothes and a good bed with covers since its warmed up enough to go fishing but not much warmer than that. I was wondering if you got a room by yourself or if you share it with somebody like it was here. I was wondering if maybe you went to a place that had a rat since you got so sad about the rat dying here.

Your brother
Nathan

April 23, 1996
Dear Jacob,

I heard Mr. Abrams whisper to another teacher that they were supposed to take you off the list at school. I walked right up to him in the hall and told him he was wrong. I must've done it in a bad tone of voice because he grabbed my shoulders and said, "Youre coming with me, Mr. Bartling." I had to sit in Dr. Mabry's office for all of third period, and then they let me go. They told me they were going to call Mom but I said it wouldn't matter if they did. Dr. Mabry said I better watch myself if I dont want to get into severe trouble. I told him I was going to find you. I told him I was going to bring you home.

Your brother
Nathan

April 24, 1996
Dear Jacob,

I get madder than anything when I'm waiting for a letter from you in the mail and all that comes is just the postcards I sent you coming back. I got suspended and now they say I cant start the season on the ball team because of it. Worse than that, I cant run track so there goes the chance to make a new record for the 440 Relay my senior year. Somebody at school (Im not going to write who) came up and said you were a loser like your dad and that's why you got sent away. I hit him good and he got seven stitches over his eye. That didn't sit too good with Dr. Mabry.

Love
Nathan

April 25, 1996
Dear Jacob,

How could Mom decide she didn't want you around like that? I wish she was the one that left, instead of you. I've heard about it plenty. Moms desert their families and run away sometimes.

Well, it seems to me she's deserted us, but she's staying right here. When Mom got mad about me being suspended, I just told her, "Whats wrong with that? Why don't you sign me away to a foster home, too? Why don't you give up on me and give me away the same way you gave up Jacob?" And she says "That's different" and I say, "I don't think so." She got so mad at me for saying it, her face turned gray. I said, "you get rid of one son, you might as well get rid of the other son, too." Then I told her it was probably her who made Dad leave, in the first place. I told her I didn't think she wanted any of us.

Nathan

April 26, 1996
Dear Jacob,

Im not going to prom anymore. Susan's dad found out about me getting suspended and he talked to Dr. Mabry and they both decided since I am suspended it isn't right to let me go to prom. Thats best for Susan W. I think because by the time that dance rolls around I don't think I'm going to be here anyway. I've had enough looking at Mom and knowing what she did. Told her last night that she had to get you back or else I was leaving, too. She said, "Oh Nathan, you wouldn't do that, would you? Make me choose like that?" I said I would make her choose.

From
Nathan

April 29, 1996
Dear Jacob,

Ive made a decision and I hope you wont get mad at me for being so hard about this but its how I know to fight everything. Mom either keeps both of us or she doesn't get either one, but no matter what she does, the damage is done and I cant go back to seeing things the same way again. It doesn't make any difference whether I stick around here or not. I got suspended so I cant go to school and I cant play ball or run track or go to prom. I know this will hurt her but its just the same as she's hurt you and me so that's fair. Wanted you to know I haven't seen Dad at all since you left. He hasn't come to see us.

Nathan

May 1, 1996
Dear Jacob,

This may be the last postcard you dont get from me because Im true to my promise and if she wont come through, then I wont be living here long. Might as well be graduated and gone already. There isnt anything good around here for me anymore. I told Mom what I was thinking and she said I couldn't do it and she wouldn't back down. If you ever read these I want you to know I fought for you and I love you and I think what she did was wrong Jacob, thanks for being my brother

Nathan

As Gemma read each postcard, she moved slower and slower. When at last she'd completed them, she stared at the last one.

Disbelieving.

Gemma had the awful feeling that all she had known was left behind, that she had fallen over the edge of the world. For surely the world had an edge to it, and she was toppling off, with nothing to hang on to, nothing to understand. She did not know, at this awful moment, where she was headed. Something larger than life, larger than herself, larger than anything, had goaded her on.

How could Nathan have a brother, and never say anything about it?

Gemma had felt, since the day she'd found out Nathan died, that he might still be with her, watching her from someplace not so distant—that he still called for her from somewhere along the sandstone creek bed where they'd often walked or from the shores of Lake Mac where he'd loved to go. But at this discovery she felt as if she'd left even Nathan's spirit behind her. Nothing she knew was as it seemed. She felt a vague sense of deprivation, as if she was homesick, only she didn't know what she ought to be homesick for. Gemma felt erased, empty, blotted out.

With quavering hands, she gathered the postcards and tamped them together on the night table. She laid them exactly where she'd found them, in a neat stack hidden beneath the fish stringer. Her chin dropped to her chest and she didn't move.

Chapter Twenty-One

"Mama? Mama? Where are you?" Goodness, Gemma had forgotten about Paisley. Here she came, waking up. Frantically, she latched the tackle box shut.

"Just a minute, Paisley Rose," she called in her best singsong voice, trying to make it sound as if nothing important was going on. "I'll be there in a minute."

"Where are you?"

"Just a second. I'll be there in a second."

Gemma pulled the chair closer to the closet. It scraped across the floor with a complaint that made Gemma wince. She climbed up, replaced the fishing box on its shelf.

She had carried the chair halfway back to the desk before she remembered the track trophy she had moved out of the way and set on the shelf.

Gemma sighed and carried the chair back. She retrieved the trophy and climbed up again, reaching to put it back where it belonged.

"Mama?" The door swung open and in walked Paisley. "Mama?"

The trophy wobbled. For the second time, Gemma

caught it. "Whew." She breathed a huge sigh of relief. When she did, she grazed another trophy with her knuckle. It teetered, and another did the same beside it, as if they'd been connected, as if they'd been set up to fall like bowling pins.

Desperately, she tried to catch them. She grabbed and caught only air.

Gemma could do nothing but stand on the chair and watch them go.

In slow motion they tumbled end over end, spinning, the shining gold runners on top, golden legs straining toward a goal, arms lifted high over their head with a wreath of victory. Both gold statuettes identical. Both of them hitting the ground. Both smashing to pieces on the floor.

"Look what you've gone and done, Mama." Paisley backed her way out the door, her eyes wide with terror. "Oh, look what you've gone and done."

Although Bea had left her house in a grim mood this morning, it had been, for all the major purposes in her book, a relatively good day.

She had organized her desk and answered what seemed like a hundred phone calls, helping customers with new hookups and electricity questions and bills. She'd even handled one irate lady with great aplomb, explaining in detail why the conversion to natural gas did not make the woman's charges decline.

To celebrate, she and Geneva and several others had walked across the street to the Cramalot for drippy hamburgers and thick chocolate shakes to celebrate her return. The conversation had not hinged upon Nathan at all, but instead upon Geneva's cataract surgery last month, which she claimed made her see so much better that she now realized she had wrinkles. "And you know what?" she'd grinned as she sucked chocolate milkshake into her straw. "I never knew it before, but you all have wrinkles, too."

Only two times had anyone mentioned Nathan all day and those had only been to find out how much money had been donated in his honor to the Antelope Valley Sunday school fund and if anyone had discussed putting up a memorial plaque in honor of the 440 Relay record beside the high school track.

Perhaps the most fulfilling part of the day, Bea decided, was the surprising anticipation of returning home.

During the past long five years, she had left for work early every morning and returned home each evening to find her house dark and silent and empty. Tonight, she'd return to cartoons on the television and the music of birdsong wafting through open windows, and Paisley might even greet her with one of those hugs.

All those long hours at her desk Bea kept thinking, *I wonder what those two are up to. I wonder if they've gotten outside to enjoy the sun. I wonder if they'll leave the puzzle out so I can see what the picture looks like put together.*

Bea stared into her desk drawer as a dozen No. 2 pencils rolled.

She knows I'll never answer those questions. She knows I haven't been talking since all those things she asked me at Nathan's grave.

Bea picked up a tiny bottle of correction fluid and twisted the lid open, used the brush to dab a white gob on a receipt.

I wonder if I shouldn't stop by the Superette to buy more cereal because I'll bet they ate the whole box. I wonder if I should talk to Geneva about her grandson Cory baby-sitting Paisley because I've heard he does that sort of thing.

In the end Bea stopped by the store not only to buy

more Cap'n Crunch, but also to pick up tea bags and lemons so she could make iced tea. She pictured them sitting on the brick stoop out front, sharing details of their day, smelling the roses. And she picked up something for supper, too—chicken to roast for a salad, crisp Romaine lettuce and ginger dressing, with carrots she would teach Paisley to peel.

"I'm home," she sang out the moment she pushed open the screen, juggling the handle of her pocketbook with one arm and the heavy sack of groceries with the other. "What's going on around this place?"

She had expected them to come running to greet her. That didn't happen. *The Flintstones* weren't blaring on television. The windows weren't open. The whole place felt as stifling and empty as if there wasn't anyone there at all.

Nobody had even turned on any lights.

"Paisley?" she called out. "Gemma?"

"Paisley is outside," Gemma said from the kitchen chair in the corner, the corner so dark in the afternoon light that Bea hadn't even noticed her sitting there. "She's playing with Addy Carpenter down the street."

"That's nice. I'm so glad she's made friends with Addy."

"Are you?"

"Why, of course."

There was something in the girl's voice that Bea didn't understand. She stepped into the kitchen and turned on a light so Gemma wouldn't be in shadow. There she sat with the knobs of her knees aligned side by side, her chin propped in the cup of her hand, with an expression Bea couldn't decipher. She sat with Bea's huge Sneed family Bible open and spread wide in her lap, the thick set of pages balanced across her legs.

"You got some reason to be reading the Bible?"

"No." Gemma responded softly, so softly it was like she didn't want to hear her own words. "No. Not the Bible."

"What then?"

Gemma leafed backwards through an entire section of Old Testament Books before her hand came to rest possessively on the frontispiece where Bea could see names, dates, lives, written in her grandmother's hand. In her mother's hand. And in her own. Gemma raised her eyes to meet Bea's. "This is what I wanted to see. The names you've written yourself in the family tree."

Bea set the grocery sack on the counter and began to empty it. She set the lemons in a sunny pile on the windowsill beside Paisley's one-stalked bean. She tore open the box of tea bags and began to align them inside the canister where she kept them. She did all these things because she was afraid to look up, afraid to interpret the inexplicable, afraid to understand the outrage on Gemma's face.

"What are you looking for?" Bea asked across the room.

"I was looking for somebody's name here, and I couldn't find it."

"Somebody's name?"

"Yes."

Without thinking, Bea touched her throat. "Whose name?"

"I was wondering how you could have a son and not write his name in the family Bible."

"Oh, his name's there. Nathan. Don't you see it?"

"I see Nathan's name all right. That wasn't the name I was looking for."

Bea's blood ran cold. This was it, then. Her lungs constricted. She knew, in one loathsome turning point, the name Gemma searched for and would not find.

No.

In that moment, in her sudden helplessness, all of Bea's resolve was forgotten. She cried out in desperation to the very one she had accused of betraying her, to the very one she had charged with not hearing her, of not answering her, of not being trustworthy.

No. No. Not this, Lord. Please. After everything else you've done, don't do this, too.

She answered Gemma, feigning innocence for a moment, buying herself time. "It wasn't?"

"No." Gemma shut the Sneed family Bible with a loud snap. She held the holy book clutched between two hands, a wall between them.

"What name, then?"

A moment passed. Another. "You know which one I mean, don't you? I see it in your face."

"I don't," Bea lied.

"There was a boy here named Jacob. Two years younger than Nathan. What happened to him? Why isn't his name written here with the others?"

Oh, Lord. Please. Not this. Not now.

Even as Bea spoke the words in her heart to God, she said the same words out loud to Gemma. Hair prickled at the base of her skull. "You don't know what you're talking about. I beg you, Gemma. Not now. Leave this alone."

"This is it, isn't it? This is why Nathan left home."

Bea put the groceries away. She threw the lettuce into the hydrator with a loud thud. She slid the chicken breasts across the top tray in the refrigerator and slammed the door. She scooted the grapefruit juice across the metal rungs, making the same sound as an Autoharp.

Gone was the moment she'd imagined, when she would have set Paisley on a stool beside the kitchen sink, tied on the ancient black-checkered apron that had belonged to Bea's mother, and taught her how to use the peeler to skin the carrots in brilliant orange curls. She dumped the plastic bag of carrots on the counter, dug the peeler out of the utensil drawer, and began going after them herself, holding onto a vegetable with one stiff fist while she skinned it with short, vicious strokes. Carrot peel flew against the side of the sink and stuck there.

"Why are you asking about Jacob? I thought you said Nathan didn't tell you."

"He didn't."

Bea left the carrots. She dug a bag of birdseed from the bottom of the pantry and started to bang out through the door. Only then did Gemma lay the Bible aside on the kitchen table to reveal the awful thing hidden in her lap. Glancing there, Bea came to a standstill. Nathan's trophies laid in heaped parts between Gemma's knees.

"No!" Bea let out a shattered cry. She released the bag of birdseed, dropped to the floor beside Gemma's knees. "No. Oh, no."

"I broke them," Gemma announced without emotion. "I went into Nathan's room and I broke them."

Bea turned her tear-stained face up to Gemma's. "Did you mean to?"

"Of course I did. I'm not good enough to be a part of your family and you never wanted us here. Better to prove it now than later, don't you think?"

Bea grabbed for the pieces and swept them into the hem of her blouse. She rocked back on her heels, weeping, staring at the jumble.

"All this time, we've been trying to prove we're good enough for you. All this time, and I've learned there isn't anybody good enough. You aren't the kind of person who *anybody* can prove that to."

"You touched his things."

"Yes."

"You destroyed these."

"Yes."

"The 440 Relay Trophies. District and State. He was so proud of these. More proud than anything else he owned."

Gemma's question might as well have been a rusty knife-blade in Bea's heart. "If he was so proud, you tell me, why did he leave them behind?"

Bea spoke the words from the deep, wounded place in her spirit. "Nathan wasn't kind to you. He wasn't. You know that, don't you? He wasn't."

"Yes, he was."

"So much like his father. If he had been kind, he would have made sure you had a pretty wedding. He would have brought you *home*."

Bea lifted herself from the floor and gathered up what was left of Nathan's treasures. The pain inside her grew so vast, Nathan might have just died again. Bea laid the fragments on the counter and began to piece them together, the same way Paisley and Gemma had pieced together the jigsaw puzzle earlier in the day.

Her shoulders rose and fell with every word. "Maybe . . . I can . . . glue them . . . together."

"Leave them alone. Let Nathan be *gone*."

Unable to face Gemma, Bea retrieved the bag of birdseed and started for the door a second time. "Don't follow me any more. I don't want you anywhere around."

The bird feeder she went to fill had been empty for weeks; the squirrels in Bea's trees always devoured the grain and corn before the jays and the kinglets ever got a chance. Bea removed the roof from the glass-sided feeder and began to pour in the blend of nuts and seed and thistle. She heard the door open and shut behind her. Gemma had followed her.

Bea fitted the roof to the feeder back over the gambrel of the little hut. With her fingers, she spread a thin layer of seed in the little trays. The feeder swayed from a low branch in the box elder tree. Back and forth. Back and forth. "Gemma, I think it would be best if you and Paisley left me alone."

"It's very easy for you, isn't it, Mrs. Bartling, to ask people to leave your life?"

"You read those cards in Nathan's room, didn't you?"

Gemma clutched her elbows with opposite hands. "What does it matter how I found out? What matters is that I know." Bea started toward the house. Gemma trailed right behind her. "Why isn't Jacob's name written with the rest of the family, Bea? Why did you send him away?"

As Bea slammed back into the house, as she returned the wadded bag of seed to its place and started digging for the small globe bulbs to replace the ones that had burned out in the light fixture over the table, the voice came from some place within herself, from somewhere tarnished and wounded and embattled, the place she had quietly sealed off from herself like a tainted cavern.

So maybe you're there, God. So maybe you're listening. Well, if you are, I have to tell you that I am angry. Angry. Every time I try to help somebody in your name, it causes more pain instead.

Bea climbed on a chair and began to unscrew the lightbulbs, one by one.

I gave you a chance once, didn't I? I gave you chances a hundred times. Why should I ever trust you?

"There are things in my life, Gemma, that I will regret until the day I die. I don't need the two of you around to remind me of them."

The lightbulbs in her hand were hot. Unexpectedly so. Crazy. She'd been crazy. Why set out to change bulbs when the light had been turned on? Hot glass seared her palm. She juggled the hot bulbs and tried to get them to the table below her, but she missed. Glass shattered on the floor.

Gemma stood before her with a sprinkling of glass across her feet. "Look at us, Mrs. Bartling. All we ever wanted was to know you. Me and Paisley, two broken things, when all you think about is broken trophies and dusty things that nobody but you even cares about anymore." Gemma reached up a hand for her.

"I don't want you to touch me."

"You've burned your hands. Let me help you down."

"I said, don't *touch* me."

"Okay. I won't." The hurt in Gemma's voice reverberated between them. "I won't." She turned away and unhooked the dustpan from the nail where it hung beside the stove and began sweeping up glass. Each brush of the broom left rills of broken bulb sparkling dangerously on the linoleum. Each sweep sent a little clank of glass into the dustpan. *Sweep. Sweep. Clatter.* "I went into Nathan's room because they called about my car this morning." Scalding tears ran down the sides of Gemma's nose, dripping onto the dirt, the glass, the floor. "It's ready. And I have the money to pay for it. I just thought . . . it would be my chance to . . ."

Bea stepped down from the chair. "You had no right."

"You had another son, Mrs. Bartling. Why don't you still have him now? What did you do?"

"I thought of the two of you all day," Bea said. "I wanted all day to come home and tell you about my day at Nebraska Power. I wanted to tell you how we went out for hamburgers at lunch and how Geneva behaved herself and how I think her grandson Cory might be willing to baby-sit Paisley."

"I want to know why you had another child and he isn't here *now*."

At Gemma's words, "another child," Bea visibly flinched. "I took you in out of the goodness of my heart. There is no other reason. Do you understand? *The goodness of my heart*. You have no right to pursue this, Gemma."

"I was married to your son. I believe I have a right to know the truth."

"You have your car. You've saved up money. There isn't anything holding you here anymore."

"He was a little boy, too. He shared a room with Nathan. You cared about his grades and he went fishing with his father and he cried when your pets died. They woke up side by side in that room where you won't let anybody touch anything. They raced out of this door and caught the bus and went to school together. How can somebody like that disappear from your life as if he never existed? You never even *talk* about him."

"That's because I cannot bear it, Gemma. Nathan was the one who could forgive me my mistakes. The . . . the *other* one . . . is impossible. You don't know."

"Say his name, why don't you? Jacob. Jacob."

Bea grabbed the girl's arm and almost made the dustpan spill. "Hush. Just hush about his name."

"Did you ever love 'the other one,' Mrs. Bartling? The brother you pretend doesn't exist?"

"Yes," Bea whispered, as tears came to her eyes. "Yes, I loved him."

"I finally understand why Nathan ran. I understand

how he wouldn't want to be with you. Because you got rid of his little brother."

"I want you to go. Do you hear me? I want you to get your car and pack it up and leave."

"Of course we will. We never intended to stay," Gemma lied. "Our car broke down once upon a time. That's the only reason we ever stopped by."

"I loved Jacob," Bea said, forcefully now, biting the edge of each word. "I loved Jacob more than you'll ever know."

"Why didn't you ever try to find him? When you saw how much it hurt Nathan, why didn't you at least try to let them talk, if you couldn't bring him home?"

"Stop it! Can't you see the answer to that just from reading Nathan's cards? Jacob never answered any of those letters, did he? Jacob never *wanted* to be found."

Chapter Twenty-Two

"You sit right here and read a good book." Gemma jostled the little beanbag chair until she'd made a nest the size of Paisley and thumped the little hollow with one hand. "This is perfect. Climb in."

"But I'm only four and a half, Mama," the little girl wailed as she wiggled down inside the chair.

"Sh-hhh. You can't make this much noise in the library. They'll ask us to leave."

"But I can't read."

"We'll find a book that's got pictures, then. You can look at pictures instead."

"Will you read to me, Mama? Please?"

Gemma shook her head. "Not tonight, honey bananas. I've got to spend time on the computer. This is why we came."

Gemma had two days before she picked up the Toyota. She had two days for a miracle. She could not stop thinking about Jacob. Maybe because, what little she knew of him, his story seemed exactly like hers.

It would be easier to walk away, Gemma. It would be easier to cut your losses and stop caring.

One minute, Jacob must have had a family. The next minute, he didn't.

Maybe if I found Jacob, she'd think I was good enough. Maybe she'd think I was good enough to belong.

Every night, after Nathan had finished mopping the kill room at Omaha Corn-Fed Packing Company, after he'd washed off layers of blood and grime and gritted his teeth to let her rub ointment into muscles raw and aching from lugging sides of beef on his shoulders, he would escort her to a study carrel at the Creighton University Library, proudly lining his books along the table and showing her notes for his classes, all of them with splendid titles like *American Education and the Interactive Process*, *Rhetoric and Composition*, and *Methods of Teaching Social Studies*.

More often than not, when Nathan went to work on a computer, he had insisted that Gemma sit right beside him, punching the same buttons in the workstation next to his, following the same steps. "I know this scares you, Gemma," he'd tease her in a voice sounding more like a father's voice than a lover's. "Computers are going to be running everything in a few years. It isn't going to hurt you to learn."

"I don't know what I'd do without you," she'd say too loudly, kissing him hard on the cowlick that whorled endearingly in his blond hair as other Creighton students sent them dirty looks for whispering. "I don't know what I'd do without you around to educate me."

And so, Gemma had Nathan to thank today when she signed her name confidently on the dotted line at the Garden County Library and the librarian assigned her to workstation number three.

She had Nathan to thank when she logged on to the

Internet and used the mouse to point the arrow to the top left-hand corner of the screen—the little box that read "Search the Net"—and double-clicked.

As the screen began to appear on the monitor, Gemma scanned the page, looking for web pages or anything else that might be linked to the name Jacob Bartling.

She found only a listing of third-graders from a school in Minnesota and a long babble of information written in German, complete with umlauts that, even if she'd had the inclination to read it, she wouldn't have known how.

Gemma had much better luck when she typed in the words "People Search." An entire assortment of listings appeared, shouting at her with their huge bold letters, touting their promises and their possibilities: *Find Or Investigate Anyone Anywhere; The Ultimate People Finder; ClassMates.com; Locate Anyone in the USA for $39.00!*

One by one, she pulled the sites up on the screen and followed the list of instructions. "Please fill in one or more of the fields below," they each said, so Gemma typed in the relevant information with great care. Jacob Bartling. Born in Nebraska. Over and over again, the same words, locations, dates, names.

Over and over again, the same disappointing message appeared on-screen.

"Sorry, no matches found."

Gemma sighed, her shoulders lifting and falling with her one deep, disappointed breath. She broadened the search and checked the few sites that would search for *any* Jacob Bartling living *anywhere* in the United States.

After a wait that seemed interminable, the tidings

turned up on the screen again, taunting her, making her want to jostle the mouse and thump the computer in frustration, although she didn't dare because she was in the library.

"Sorry, no matches found."

"Hey, Alva T." Gemma wrung out her rag in the huge industrial sink at the Cramalot Inn and hung it over the faucet to dry. "You got a minute? I've got a question to ask you."

Ever since they'd toured the floral displays at the Garden County Fair, Alva had been determined to redecorate her tables with new, novel arrangements each week. The day after the fair had ended, she'd bought tiny terra-cotta pots and had filled them with clay and Tootsie Roll Pops so her customers could both amuse themselves before their meals were brought out and help themselves to candy after they'd eaten supper.

The next week, Alva employed shish kebob skewers and impaled a collection of huge sunflowers she'd picked by the roadside, the great clusters of rough leaves and blossoms as big around as dinner plates—so enormous that the waitresses had to remove all the condiments from the tables and hand-carry them out whenever somebody complained.

It had taken this many weeks before Alva could round up enough cowboy boots from garage sales to use as containers for petunias on her tables at The Cramalot Inn. Alva roved between the tables now, carrying the assortment of boots in a bus tray, trying each one out to see where it looked the best, adjusting the boot toes so they each pointed perfectly toward the salt and pepper shakers.

"You help me fix these petunias to my liking," Alva

said as she held up one pot with three yellow and purple blossoms inside it, "and I'd be willing to answer just about any question in the world."

Gemma began following after her, fiddling with the flowers, but something about that seemed impossible today. Arranging petunias didn't fit when your heart was heavy laden. "If you were out to find somebody lost and you didn't know where they'd gone, how would you go about it?"

Alva held up two boots—one light, one dark—deciding which would look best on the table next to the jukebox. "Well, that depends," she said.

"On what?"

"On whether or not the person you're looking for lives in Nebraska."

Gemma stopped at a table by the window and began adjusting petunias so their blossoms faced forward. "I wish I knew the answer to that. If I did, it would be a whole lot easier. He started out in Nebraska, but I don't know if he ended up there."

"If you knew what county you were after, you could always use a snoop book."

"A snoop book?"

"The Lion's Club in Garden County sells them every year. Only this'll be the last edition because there are new laws banning public access. Somebody in the government's decided it's a bad idea, all of us running around with a county license-plate directory tucked under our front seats."

"I never heard of such a thing."

"Oh, Gemma, you wouldn't, coming from Omaha. Omaha's a big place. I'm talking about rural Nebraska. You see kids parking on the corner and necking, you look them up in the book, find out who they are, and call their mamas to tell them what's going on. You want to know who's parked outside your neighbor's house? Look it up."

"Alva T!"

"You don't like the way somebody's driving, you find out who he is from the snoop book, call him up about suppertime when you know he'll be sitting at the table, and say, 'Joe Cheney, this is Alva Torrington. I didn't much like the way your green pickup with the blue door cut me off at the intersection of Albees and School Street this morning. Don't let it happen again.'" Alva shrugged. "Nebraska is the easiest place in the world to find somebody, if you've got a mind to do that."

Every table had a boot now, but only half of them sported flowers. Gemma picked up her pace, adjusting leaves and arranging blossoms with only half the effort that she'd given them in the beginning. "Alva, if it's so easy to find somebody in Nebraska, how come Mrs. Bartling never could find her son?"

Alva came up beside Gemma and started arranging petunias herself. "She's told you a little about Nathan, has she?"

Gemma nodded, not certain what she should say.

"Well, Nathan was a sly one. That's why he went to Omaha, don't you think? He stayed close by but he managed to hide himself in a big town, all at the same time."

"Did she try to find him?"

"She tried harder than anybody I'd ever seen. And everywhere she turned she hit a dead end. It's always been hard enough getting authorities to go after runaways of any age. But take one that's left a note telling that he's leaving. Take one that's within three weeks of graduation and a month of his eighteenth birthday. No one's willing to put much effort out for that."

"Nobody helped her at all?"

"Oh, they looked for a few months, trying to satisfy her. Somebody found one of his All-Star baseball caps in the grass by the roadside over by Gothenburg. They figure it blew off his head while he was hitchhiking. That was the closest they ever came."

Gemma recalled the times she'd moved with Nathan during the last three years, the way she'd chastised him for not changing his address on his driver's license, the way he always seemed to be catching up with himself, working his paperwork from months behind. Even when he'd signed up for classes at Creighton, he'd used the address of Omaha Corn-Fed Packing because the trailer where they'd lived had neither mail delivery nor phone.

"It all starts to make sense, doesn't it?" Gemma said, not stopping to think what she'd be giving away when she spoke. "I always got so mad at him when he wouldn't keep his driver's license up to date. I used to say, 'If anybody was trying to find you for something, they'd never be able to do it.' And so, when he died . . ." She trailed off.

Alva looked up from the petunias. She stared at her waitress instead. "You knew Nathan?"

Gemma held up her left hand, fingering the plain gold band she wore. "This is Nathan's ring, Alva. I was married to him."

Alva set the tray full of boots down so hard that half of them fell over. "Oh, my goodness." She let the fallen boots lie and hugged her employee. "Everybody thought you were a stranger come to town. Everybody thought Bea Bartling was a crazy, lonely woman, taking you in the way she did. Now, to find out you're Bea's family instead!"

"Yes," Gemma said with a tinge of gloom in her voice. "We're Bea's family. It's been good to be here for a while. It's been good to get to know her some. But we'll be moving on now that my car's fixed. Just as soon as I earn off eight more hours at the museum."

"So, is this why you were asking about finding somebody? Because you were wondering what it was like for her, trying to find Nathan?"

"No. There was somebody else I wanted to find."

Alva T. strolled to the cash register and pulled out a heap of books. "You gonna do something, I believe in covering the territory," she said, winking as she hefted them over and plopped the entire pile on the table in front of Gemma. "Here you go. Anything you want. Snoop books from Garden County, Howard County, Washington County, Lincoln County, Jefferson County, and Nuckolls County as well."

Gemma sat down hard beside the mountain of little directories. She didn't know where to begin.

"They're cross referenced," Alva said, leafing through the top one in the stack. "License plates here. Names in the back. Alphabetical order." She paused with her thumb stuck inside to mark her place. "What name you looking for, Gemma? I'll show you how."

"Bartling," Gemma said, her voice still sounding overwhelmed. "I'm looking for a Bartling."

Alva glanced up, waiting. "A Bartling? Who? What's the first name? Can't go much further without one of those."

"Mrs. Bartling had another son. I've found Nathan's letters to him," Gemma said. "I'm looking for Jacob Bartling."

"Humph." Alva gave a little snort and her thumb slipped free. "You can look as far and wide as you want, Gemma Franklin. You aren't going to find anybody by that name." The book slapped shut.

Gemma scooted the book across the table and began to rifle through its pages herself. "Well, this is funny, Alva. All this time I've known you, and it's never been like you to discourage a person this way."

"It has nothing to do with discouraging a person." Alva had the most unusual expression on her face; Gemma had never seen her quite so solemn. "I care about you too much to let you go off on some wild-goose chase like this. There's no such person as Jacob Bartling. That's all I'm going to say."

Deputy Jay Triplett was loading his uniform and his black Labrador retriever into his truck when Gemma hurried toward him along the curb, the strap of her purse laced over her shoulder, the rest of it flying side-long beside her. "Deputy Triplett!" she called out, raising one hand. "Deputy Triplett, wait!"

He lifted a hand in salute. "Hello, Miss Franklin. Long time no see. Did you have a good time at the fair?"

"We did." Gemma thought back upon the evening she'd spent with Mrs. Bartling—how they'd laughed together, how they had enjoyed being together and had enjoyed the day. "We had a good time. I wish we could do it again."

This man didn't seem nearly so imposing without his regalia of leather pouches, stiff khaki creases, winking badges, and striking shoulder patches. For the first time, Gemma looked up and noticed the smattering of freckles across his nose. She hadn't noticed those before, and this surprised her. Without the visor of his deputy's cap shadowing his face, Gemma could see the light gray-blue of his eyes, the hash marks of dark indigo radiating from the center.

For the first time she realized that he couldn't be much older than Nathan had been.

"I don't know how you fit inside that roller coaster car, Deputy Triplett. It was the smallest one I've ever seen. Much smaller than the ones in Omaha."

"I don't know how I did it, either." He laughed and tucked the tail of his plaid sports shirt into the waistband of his jeans. "How come you haven't gotten arrested for anything lately? There isn't any excitement around Ash Hollow anymore, now that you've decided to lay low."

Gemma laughed, too, but she kept shifting her weight from one foot to the other, knowing that Jay Triplett—trained officer of the law and expert on body language—must notice that she'd come with some specific intent in mind. She waited, neither moving from where she stood, nor replying.

He had another go at silently tucking in his shirt, but he must have remembered that he'd already done it once because he stopped halfway through.

They both spoke at once.

"I see you're leaving work," she said.

"I heard you're leaving Mrs. Bartling's," he said.

"They fixed my car finally. It's time we went out on our own."

"I heard you're still having fun at the museum," he said. "Stringing guitars for Mabel. Washing windows for Mabel. Dusting exhibits for Mabel. And that group from the senior center that goes over on Wednesday mornings. The ones that play checkers in the country store display. I've heard they enjoy having you around."

"I finally beat Orvin Kornruff," she bragged.

"Yes, but he had one hand bandaged, remember?"

"But a person doesn't need both hands to play checkers. A person just needs his head."

Gemma reached up to pet the huge black lab that surged toward them, tongue lolling sideways, to make friends. "What's your dog's name?"

"Fred. After Fred Flintstone. My favorite cartoon."

Silence loomed between them.

"I'd better come back to see you later," she said after a beat. "I don't feel good about bothering you when you're getting ready to go."

"You can bother me any time, Miss Franklin. What is it you need?"

"I've got a question about records," she said. "Some research I'm doing."

"Records?"

"If something happened and sheriff's deputies were called to the scene for some reason, would that have gotten written down into a report?"

Deputy Jay Triplett scratched Fred the dog behind the ears. The huge dog melted against his arm. "Yes. Most certainly."

"What if that report was written a long time ago? Would it still be around?"

"How long ago?"

"Maybe five years. A little more, actually."

"You have dates?"

"It happened in the winter of 1996. February."

"We keep archives in there that date back twenty years. All of it in manila folders and file cabinets. All of it referenced with names, dates, case numbers."

"Could I see them?"

"Not without the approval of the county attorney. Some of it is public record, Gemma. Some of it isn't."

"What makes the difference between it being public record or not?"

"Did this incident have charges filed? Did it ever go to court?"

Gemma thought about that and slowly shook her head. "No." If anything had ever happened that might have gone to court in their family, Nathan would have certainly found out about it. Gemma wracked her brain to remember the exact wording of Nathan's letter.

"Her dad said the police came to our house the night you went away. She said he knew about it because he was driving past and saw the lights flashing."

"This could be a problem," he told her. "If no charges were filed and the case never went to court, it isn't a matter of public record, I'm afraid. I'd have to speak with the county attorney, but it isn't information I can release to you. No matter how much I'd like to do it."

"I don't need to know any details about that night, Deputy Triplett. I only need to find out someone's name."

"Someone's name?"

She nodded. "There was a brother. Living in Mrs. Bartling's house. He wasn't Nathan. He was somebody else. I want to know how to find him."

"How old was this brother? Do you have any information on that?"

"He would have been—" Gemma figured it in her head. "—fifteen."

Gemma regarded the officer hopefully. But her hope plummeted when he shook his head.

"I can't help you there," he told her. "That would be

releasing information about a minor involved in a civil disturbance. No matter how I'd like to give you that information, Miss Franklin, Nebraska state laws forbid me to do it."

Chapter Twenty-Three

Bea Bartling's yard looked as neat as a new pin.

She had taken to puttering around outside these evenings after work, watering, weeding, pruning the roses, mowing the grass.

As each day passed under her care, the rose blossoms had flourished, petals unfurling in giant curls, as big around as a man's fist, fragrant—a yellow as pure and subtle as watercolor paints, tender, newborn. The grass had darkened to a deep, verdant emerald, thick as velveteen, unmarred by wiry strands of crabgrass or bothersome splotches of dandelion. Jays, kinglets, and cardinals flew in short scallops from fence to limb and back again, chortling and bobbing, vying for positions at the feeder and in the uppermost leaves of the maple.

Bea had brought home a set of red bricks from the masonry shop and, for the past two evenings, she had been edging flowerbeds, following a sketch she had drawn from memory of Thomas Jefferson's Serpentine Wall. Each evening after work she had been hauling bricks around the yard, standing back to see, then working piece by piece on her hands and knees like rickrack, using them to border the hollows and swells of the beds.

Only the car didn't fit. An '83 Toyota Corolla in the driveway that had once been white, with chips of paint gone to rust and a dent in the front grill.

"Thank you for letting me wash this thing before we take off," Gemma said formally. "I paid all that money and I feel like I should have gotten back a new car. But it isn't. It's just the same old dirty junk heap that barely got us here in the first place."

Bea read the truth between the words in Gemma's statement. *They were fighting for every mile to get here. How can I just let her drive away like this?*

The sun was sinking behind the ocean of grass to the west, turning the countryside pink and yellow and lavender with the sunset. Bea asked with careful nonchalance, "You taking off tonight?"

"Yes."

"That's good."

"We are."

Bea stooped down and started aligning bricks, overlapping their lengths, burying their bases along the length of the front walk. "You two won't get far, leaving this late."

"We aren't going far. We're just going to the Sissels tonight. Mabel Perkins would be the first one to notify the sheriff if I tried to leave Ash Hollow before I serve out my time. Four hours more, and then I'm finished."

"Where are you going after you're done serving time?"

"Haven't thought about it much. I thought maybe I'd write my grandmother once I got a permanent address.

Maybe she'll come all the way to visit us from Omaha. Maybe she'll—" Gemma stared up at the sky, as if something there would help her finish her sentence. "I'll write you a letter, too. If anybody comes looking for us, would you tell them where we've gone?"

Bea stared at a tree limb somewhere beyond Gemma's left shoulder. "Maybe you'll hear from your grandmother. I'll make certain she finds you if she looks for you here."

"Thank you."

Bea hoped that none of what she felt or thought showed on her face. Dry-throated, she said, "I'll get some food together for the Sissels. With you two coming, they could use some of these frozen casseroles."

"Thank you."

"Take some to Mabel Perkins, too. Tell her I'm paying her back for all those sticky buns you ate."

For a moment, it seemed to Bea as if maybe Gemma tried to delay. The girl took a breath so deep, her entire body seemed to stand at attention, and then to sag. "Well—" Gemma clapped her hands together.

"Yes?"

"Time to go, I suppose."

When they packed the Toyota Corolla in the driveway, the only addition to their belongings was one gigantic bear and one grocery sack filled with new clothes that Paisley loved but Gemma had never worn. Paisley sat clutching her teddy bear in the front seat, her arms squeezing so tight that its stuffing squished up into its head.

Gemma pitched the suitcase in the backseat. She took the sack of casseroles from Mrs. Bartling and stashed them in the trunk. She slammed it shut and turned to Bea. "I'd like to think we're doing the right thing. I'd like to think all this would be better left alone."

"You should."

"Nathan used to say that. 'Some things are better left well-enough alone, Gemma.' But he was *wrong* saying it, don't you see? If he hadn't left well enough alone, you and I might have stood a chance at trusting each other."

Bea held the door for her and said in a cold, bitter voice, "I don't want to hear what Nathan said anymore. I'm sick to death of hearing the things Nathan did and said."

"You know what? I am, too."

Gemma climbed in, shut the door, and turned the key in the ignition. The old Corolla started up first try.

Bea stood straight as a ramrod, her hands hooked over the door handle, not wanting to let go. "There's a reason I didn't write Jacob's name in the Sneed family Bible. I would have, but I never got the chance."

"It's too late for explaining," Gemma said.

"Jacob was adopted."

"Adopted?"

Bea's heart clubbed. Her eyes stung. How long had it been since she'd spoken the truth about this to anyone? "He only went by Bartling while he lived with us. He lived with us five years. Even though he and Nathan had been best friends since they were little. Sleepovers under the stars. Bike treks. Huge bowls of macaroni-and-cheese or popcorn while they watched movies. Even before he came to live with us, even before, Nathan had me feeling like Jacob was part mine."

Gemma's hand faltered on the gearshift. She sat perfectly still for one long moment before she said,

"Adopted people don't fare very well around you, do they?"

"Why don't you take roses with you to the Sissels? If you'll wait a minute, I'll get scissors. They'll smell nice."

"I don't want roses, Mrs. Bartling. You always send people off with roses." Gemma moved the gear indicator to reverse.

"Ray and I wanted to help. That's all. Everything was so awful, and we thought we could make a difference."

Gemma took her foot off the brake. The car began to roll. "A son ought to remain a son—" she pinned Mrs. Bartling with damning green eyes "—no matter the circumstances. You called him your child, but you didn't let him stay."

"Paisley," Bea cried. "Paisley Rose."

The little girl didn't turn toward her window. She didn't say a word.

Bea ran backwards with the car. "Paisley, I'm so sorry."

Her last view, the little girl's bottom lip trembling as she clutched the gigantic bear.

"I know why Nathan loved you both," Bea called out as she finally let go. "You are so much like him."

Bea waved and waved and waved as the taillights grew smaller and smaller, then disappeared up Pattison Drive. She couldn't be sure, but she thought perhaps she saw a little hand, flickering from Paisley's side, catching light through the glass.

Bea walked back inside her empty house. Nothing had changed. Her life remained as barren as the day Deputy Jay Triplett had knocked on her door in the middle of the night and told her that her son had died.

She walked up the hallway, turning out the lights,

then stopped in the doorway to the guest room. The bed had been made. The pillows had been fluffed. The air conditioner had been turned off and the mint-green towels in the bathroom hung carefully in a row.

No sign remained that anyone had recently occupied this room. No sign at all, except for the peach crayon that had rolled and gotten lost beneath the bed.

That's what she'd do, Bea decided, trying to perk herself up a bit. She'd paint the house peach just the way she'd wanted.

Bea bent to pick up the crayon. When she did, she saw a small photograph laying with purpose on the left-hand pillow.

She picked it up, held it close to her nose so she could see without her glasses.

Oh, my. The picture Gemma had showed her at the fair. The wedding picture. Her son the way she'd never seen him before, standing tall and proud, his shoulders squared in a borrowed sport coat, his jaw raised in pleasure. All that time, and he still wanted to be a teacher! He would have made such a good teacher.

All this time, she'd only had eyes for Nathan. All this time, and now it was the girl who drew Bea's eyes.

Standing at his side, so beautiful and young, in a funny green dress that was fancy but didn't fit her, her hair cropped short at the nape and hanging in long strands beside her ears. She held one cellophane-wrapped rose in her hands. She held a world of hope in her eyes.

"What do I do with this?" Bea asked aloud to no one. "What do I do with this?" as she held it out to nothing with two fingers, as if she expected something to take it from her.

No answer came.

Bea buried her face in her hands and didn't cry.

"I don't have an appointment," Bea told Sheila, the church secretary, when she came in. "Please. I need a few minutes with Pastor George."

"I'll get him," the secretary said. "Wait right here. Mrs. Bartling? Are you okay? Do you need to sit down?"

"I'm fine. Really." But even to her own ears, she sounded like she was trying to convince herself, not Sheila.

Not twenty seconds later here came George himself, in a regular green shirt, his face filled with concern when he saw her. He solemnly led her into his office and waited while she settled herself into one of his counseling chairs. "Dearest. Oh, Beatrice. What's wrong? Can you tell me?"

She clasped her hands in her lap and lifted her eyes to him. "Oh, Pastor George," she said at last. "Where is God in all this? Can you tell me?"

George watched her for a long time with somber eyes. "No, Bea," he said at last. "I don't know. And, if I did, I wouldn't be the one to tell you. You have to ask Him to answer that himself."

Disappointed, she dropped her eyes to her hands and stared at them.

"Does He speak to you, Beatrice? Do you try to hear Him?"

"No. I argue with Him. And then I argue more. I tell Him how angry I am," she murmured to her clasped fingers. "I tell Him how angry I am because I asked Him to do impossible things, and He didn't do them."

"I've been praying for you," he told her. "This is the worst time after somebody dies, isn't it? When all the sympathy ends and you're expected to get back to everyday life with a smile? When your house is empty and there's nothing to—"

She stopped him right there. "My house has been empty a long time, Pastor George."

"Yes, but it's emptier than usual now that the Franklins left," he commented. "Paisley and Gemma."

"They didn't want to stay with me anymore."

"Oh, I see." And he did. He understood more than she ever wanted him to understand.

"My faith in God has diminished, Pastor George. And because of that, I am unfaithful to those around me."

"Bea, you're a faithful person. If you weren't you wouldn't be struggling so. A strong heart for God is one that's not afraid to wrestle with Him."

"Oh, George. You were right when I said I might learn about myself. Things have happened that have made me . . . know myself a little better. And that can be a beginning, don't you think?"

She smiled a little smile, and so did he. "Beginnings." He leaned forward, propped his elbows on his knees, and shook his head at her. "If you can cling to beginnings, you'll get by."

"I'm clinging," she whispered to him. "But no matter how hard I try, I can barely hang on."

"It is easier for us to be angry at God than it is for us to change ourselves. Faith is something different than you think it is, Bea. Faith is not a passive resignation to life. Faith isn't fate. 'God will take care of my needs, but if he doesn't, I can't do a thing about it.' That's not faith. As a matter of fact, that's exactly the *opposite* of faith. Even when things seem their worst, you need to expect *all* of God's goodness and love in your life, Bea."

"How can I expect *all* of it, George, when I haven't seen *any* of it?"

"Watch," he said. "Just watch."

Things were certainly different for Gemma and Paisley staying at the Sissels house than they'd been at Mrs. Bartling's.

For one thing, Gemma knew she ought not to complain, but the parsonage was so small that there wasn't a guest room, only a hide-a-bed in the middle of the living room, which couldn't be folded out for bedtime until after the local late news on KNOP-TV had ended. When it did get pulled out at last, the thing sounded like a pickup tailgate coming down, in dire need of WD-40.

For another thing, ever since the Toyota Corolla had backed out of the driveway at Mrs. Bartling's house, Paisley would not talk. She would not respond. She would not laugh. She wouldn't utter a sound.

"You want to sleep on this side of the bed or the other side?" Gemma asked her.

No answer. Paisley climbed in the middle of the bed and sat there, her eyes huge and sad.

"Do you want to wear your pink shorts today, Paisley, or your purple capris?"

No sign. The child only waited until Gemma handed her something and pulled them on, fastening her buttons herself.

"I promise, Paisley Rose. Another few days and we'll be out of this funny, folding bed. We'll find a new place to start. Some place of our own."

At this, Paisley's little mouth opened as if she might say something. But it closed again. No sound. The only thing Gemma knew to do was to give her daughter a hug.

When the doorbell rang early that next evening, Ellen Sissel was heating up a casserole and Gemma had roosted on the edge of the couch, with work from Mabel Perkins she had brought here from the museum; a length of black velvet draped across her knees like an opera skirt as she aligned Francis Clupney's hundreds of tintacks and stickpins and studs. Ellen was just getting the casserole into the oven. She had hot pads on both hands.

"I'll go." Gemma laid the jewelry and badges aside with care. She folded the velvet away from her lap, and went to answer.

Gemma cracked open the door and saw a head with short, cottony dark hair, a fine forehead with blue-gray eyes and hash marks of indigo shooting out from the center. She opened the door further and saw Deputy Jay Triplett waiting on the landing. Only he didn't look like a deputy at all dressed in his plaid sports shirt and pair of jeans ironed with a light crease. He didn't look like a deputy at all with the bouquet of sunflowers and larkspur clasped in his left fist, held so fast that he might have been choking them, leaves and blossoms lolling sideways from such an ordeal.

"Hi," he said, somewhat sheepishly.

"Hi back," she said.

"I called the museum, but Mabel—"

She laughed. "I know. Mabel told you I couldn't talk because I was too busy stringing guitars."

"That's exactly right. I . . . well, I . . ." He jutted the flowers forward as if he only remembered them this instant. "These are for you."

"Thank you."

She took them and they flopped outward in a circle over her fist. "I'll put them in water or something." She started to turn away.

He put out a hand to stop her. "Wait."

"What is it?"

"I . . . well, I . . ." And then Deputy Triplett started to laugh, his confidence seeming to return in a rush. "I was having coffee at the Cramalot and Alva T. told me. About you being married to Nathan."

"Did she?"

"Yes. I'm sorry, Miss Franklin. I didn't know Nathan well. But I saw him playing baseball a time or two. I just wanted to come by and let you know that I offer my sympathy. Until this week, none of us around here knew that you were going through such a difficult time. We're all glad you came to Ash Hollow."

Gemma's hand with the ring came up against the Sissels doorjamb and she leaned on it, stretching her arm, comfortable. "How is Fred doing?"

"Fred?"

"Your dog."

"Fred. Oh, he's fine. Yes. Very fine. He's out in the truck right now."

"Thank you for offering your sympathy about Nathan, Deputy Triplett. It means a lot to me."

"I . . . was thinking something else, too. I was thinking, since I'm the one who arrested you, I probably ought to take responsibility for you because you're stuck here after your car's finished and you're ready to leave. I thought maybe I could help you escape for a while. Maybe take you to a movie or something. Get a banana split over in Oshkosh."

"I don't know about that," she told him with sudden, great care. "I probably won't be much fun. I don't . . .

Well, I loved Nathan very much. It's going to be a long time before I'm ready to see somebody again."

"I understand that," he said. "I know grieving for someone you love takes a long time. But Fred and I were thinking that maybe you could use a *friend*."

Gemma couldn't help herself. She grinned. "Has anybody ever told you you're different without your guns and your handcuffs?"

"Yeah." His one abrupt laugh came from way deep in his chest. "People say that all the time."

With her hand still on the doorjamb, Gemma turned back to her daughter. "I'd like to go," she said, with her head turned away. "But Paisley isn't doing very well and I'd better not leave her."

"I've got a niece who lives in Oshkosh. My sister's little girl. Madeleine. She's five and she lives with about three hundred Barbies. Maybe we could go there for a visit, and Paisley could come with us."

Gemma thought about it. "Okay. *Okay*. That sounds fine. Let me get our things."

Paisley's Barbie didn't talk. It walked across the stage in the new Barbie fashion-show boutique, wore hot-pink clothes with hot-pink sneakers, and carried a hot-pink cell phone. But it never said a word. Madeleine's Barbies did all the talking.

"Thank you for letting us come over," Gemma told Jay Triplett's sister. "She's having a good time. She's just . . . angry with me right now."

"Yeah, I can see that."

"It's been a tough couple of months."

"If you two want to sneak away for an hour or so, Paisley would be okay here," Jay's lively sister volunteered. "I sure don't mind her staying."

Gemma leaned forward and peered close at her eyes. "If I didn't know better, I'd think you were trying to set your brother up or something."

"Nope. Not this time," she said. "He's told me all about you and everything you've been through. He told me he wanted to be a gentle and careful friend." The woman chuckled, and Gemma couldn't be sure whether she was teasing or not. "He came right at me with that. He knows me too well. He knows I've been trying to set him up ever since the 1994 Lewellen Rural High School Cornhusker Ball."

In the end, when they snuck away, they snuck away to the Ash Hollow Cemetery. It was close to town and quiet, with footpaths for walking, a view of the river for miles, and birds fluttering among the sparse gathering of trees.

Gemma didn't know when she'd get back to this precious place again. She told Jay she probably wouldn't have another chance to visit Nathan's grave before she and Paisley left town.

"You don't have to leave town, you know. There's plenty of folks in this town that'd like to see you stick around. Alva T., for one. She's doubled her business with her meat loaf special, and I don't know where she'll find another waitress after you're gone."

"She'll find somebody." Gemma crossed her arms and held onto opposite elbows as they walked. "Good waitresses are a dime a dozen."

"Not in this town, they aren't."

"They are. You'll see."

They walked along pleasantly, stride to stride, hip to hip. He slipped his jacket off and settled it over her shoulders. "You're getting goose bumps." Then he pointed toward the north edge of the burial ground where the plots seemed to be larger.

"My grandmother's over there. My great-grandmother, too."

"You lived here a long time?"

"All my life."

She pointed in the opposite direction, the direction of the North Platte. "Nathan's over there."

"That's a good spot. Overlooking the river."

"Yes."

"Come see this. More local history."

He gestured toward a marker that read, 'Rachel E. Pattison. Aged 18. June 19 1849.' A panel of glass lay over the native sandstone to protect the weathered lettering.

"This is the oldest grave here. She'd been married two months before her husband brought her out on the trail. She died of cholera, is what people say."

"They were so brave on the Oregon Trail. Just trusting, just coming, the way they did."

Jay took her hand and led her around a stand of crumbling granite spires, covered with lichen. "All of these graves are old. All of them are folks who decided to give up on the trail and homestead here instead. I'll bet you one of those ladies buried there is the one who transplanted Mrs. Bartling's roses."

Beyond the decaying spires, Gemma could see the silhouette of Care Goodsell's wheelbarrow, parked upright and waiting, empty, the rake propped beside it in the middle of a vacant plot.

"Oh, he's left it out. That's odd." As she walked toward the old cart, a butterfly flickered past her shoulder, alighted on the wheelbarrow's metal rim. It settled, furled and unfurled it wings, a mosaic of blues and browns mirrored one against the other, the same ethereal pattern as a stained-glass window. "This is Care Goodsell's wheelbarrow. Look."

"Who?" Jay Triplett furrowed his eyebrows.

"Care Goodsell."

"Never heard of him."

"Well, you must have. He's the gardener here. He goes all over the place toting this wheelbarrow. Last time we were here, he even gave Paisley a ride. Wanted to give *me* one, but I wouldn't let him."

"Gemma?" Jay was still looking at her strangely. "Do you remember Lon Johnson? One of the fellows who plays checkers with Orvin at the museum?"

"Of course I do."

"Well, *he's* the gardener here."

"He is?"

"He's the *only* gardener here. There isn't anybody else."

"No?"

"This wheelbarrow hasn't been moved for years. Nobody uses it anymore." Jay pointed to the ground. Smartweed and grama grass had entangled the lone wheel, the two shafts. He was right. This contraption hadn't gone anywhere last week, last month, last year.

Gemma touched the wheelbarrow, its rusted dents and hollows and for the moment didn't know what to feel. But something loving and powerful, electric and satisfying, touched itself back into her hand.

Before he had died, Gemma's daddy had always told her that, if she heard from God, she wouldn't doubt it. She might feel fear. And she might feel awe, perhaps. But never doubt. Never doubt, when she found Him.

She did not doubt now.

You knew about me being lonely, didn't you?

You sent us an angel, didn't you, because you knew this was the place we would need one the most?

For a long time she stood beside Jay Triplett and knew joy. For a long time she waited, counting the flushed colors in the sky, smelling the strong smell of the earth and the blond, drying grass. She heard the chirp of a grasshopper beside her feet and thought it beautiful.

"We ought to go," he said at last.

Gemma made her way around the wheelbarrow. "I know. I don't want to leave Paisley too—" She stepped on something and twisted her ankle. She stumbled forward. "Ouch."

"Watch out."

"What was that? What did I step on?"

"I don't know."

Gemma knelt and parted the grass. She found it. A headstone hidden among tall weeds and rockfall. "I stepped on this."

"Are you okay?"

"If Lon Johnson is the gardener around this place, I'm going to tell him he's missed a plot. He ought to be taking better care of this one." She dug deeper through the grama grass. "It's double. There are two of them here."

"Hm-mmm."

"Why are you being so quiet, Jay?"

"No reason, I guess. I feel spooky when I get around those graves. Those are two of the saddest graves in Garden County."

"What are you talking about?"

"Just read them," he said.

The light had gotten so dim by now that Gemma had to kneel closer, to squint past her nose to see. She read the names aloud. "Sybil Palmer. Jacob Palmer, Sr. Died January 3, 1991." Crouched in the grass on all fours, she had to turn her chin to her shoulder blade so she could see Jay. "They both died on the same day."

"They did."

"What happened?"

He shook his head. "Everybody's been talking about it down at the sheriff's office for years. I've never been the type to discuss things."

"Me neither."

"Although I sure don't know why Johnson isn't mowing the grass."

"Were they in an accident or something?"

"No."

The single granite marker was broad enough to identify both souls. Flecks of feldspar and mica gilded the width of the stone. One half, Sybil's half, was beautifully ornate, engraved with the face of a hovering angel. The other half, Mr. Palmer's half, was brutally simple. A name. A birthday for each. A matching date of death. January 3, 1991. Nothing more.

"I wish you'd tell me what happened."

"I told you. I'm not the sort of person to talk."

But she knew it suddenly. She didn't have to ask anymore. "He killed her, didn't he? He killed her and then he killed himself. I can tell by the stone."

"If you don't come now, Gemma, they're going to call the sheriff out to look for us."

She didn't budge. "You can't distract me from this. When they call the sheriff out to look for somebody, they call you."

He shrugged.

"Am I right about them? Did it happen the way I said?"

He nodded. "Of course you are. You've got the whole

thing figured, just the way it happened. All except for the eleven-year-old son they both left behind."

"The eleven-year-old—?"

She froze, felt her pulse thudding high in her chest.

She read the man's name again. Jacob Palmer, Sr. And calculated the dates, the years, in her head.

"Jay."

A rush of certainty poured through her. Gemma reached for the wheelbarrow as if she might use it to pull herself up. "Thank you," she whispered to the wheelbarrow, knowing with all certainty that Care Goodsell could hear. "Thank you."

Jay Triplett gave her a hand instead. "This child," she asked, her voice scarcely audible as she rose. "Was he a boy?"

"Yes."

"Jacob, Jr.?"

"I think so."

"We have to go back, Jay. We have to go back *now*."

Chapter Twenty-Four

On the huge glass window at The Cramalot Inn, Alva had taped a large yellow sign that read "Help Wanted. Dependable Waitress Needed. Start immediately. Must be able to pour coffee with a smile."

Gemma's Toyota was already packed. The huge bear lay in the rear seat beside the suitcase, soaking up sun.

"Well," Alva said, clapping her hands in front of her apron, trying to pretend like it was just any other day. She bent down to Paisley. "You be good for your mother, will you? And make her promise to write."

Paisley nodded, but didn't say a word.

"Make her promise to bring you back to see us."

Paisley nodded, but said nothing.

Alva straightened and nodded her chin at Gemma. "You two headed out right now?"

"Almost." Gemma glanced around the Cramalot one last time. "I've only got a couple more things to do. I've got to stop at the museum and work one more hour for Mabel Perkins."

"One more hour? She wouldn't let you off from that? That woman!"

"I'm taking Paisley with me so we can leave from there. I've got to make one phone call from here. I've already told everybody good-bye. Even Orvin Kornruff. You and Charlene and Harvey are the last ones."

"We are?"

"Yes. Thank you for trusting me enough to give me this job, Alva."

"Have you told Mrs. Bartling good-bye, Gemma?"

"Yes, we have. When we left her house. It's too difficult, going back again, for all of us, even Mrs. Bartling. She doesn't want us around, Alva. What's done is done."

"Oh sweetie."

"Don't, Alva. I'll just . . ." Gemma started back toward the grill.

The old black telephone hung on the wall in the Cramalot kitchen beside the cook's vast assortment of Revere Ware pots and pans. Just when Gemma figured it was safe to make her phone call, Harvey decided to sauté vegetables, probably for tomorrow's Soup of the Day. "Harvey," Gemma whispered as he reached for a skillet hanging right over her head, clanging it against a saucepan like a timpani drum. She held her right ear with her finger. "Could you please? I'm making a call. Long-distance."

"Gemma's making a call, long-distance!" he sang out like a naughty little brother and thumped his fry pan a little harder. "You'd better leave your money by the phone."

"I always do that." She swatted at the strings of his chef's apron as he sauntered by. But secretly she was thankful he'd said something about leaving money. She'd never had any reason to learn how to make interstate calls from The Cramalot Inn. Ever since she'd arrived in Ash Hollow, there hadn't been anybody out of town Gemma wanted to talk to.

She peered down at the phone number on the perfect white square of paper, one of the scraps they kept within reaching distance—along with those short yellow pencils—at the Garden County Library. A Wyoming number she'd jotted from the People Finder. Jacob Palmer, Jr. In Jackson Hole.

She'd spent too much time talking to Harvey. She'd waited too long between digits and the line had gone dead. Gemma started over again, punching in the 307 area code and then the rest of the number. The little bell came on the other end of the line, the whirr of distance, the recording that said sweetly, "The time is ten-forty-nine where you are calling."

On the other end, it began to ring. Gemma closed her eyes and prayed. *Please. Please.*

A woman's voice answered. "Hello?"

"Hello," Gemma said back.

Oh, my goodness. She hadn't thought it through any further than this. She had absolutely no idea what she should say.

"Hello?" the woman repeated, this time a question.

Gemma couldn't be sure. Harvey kept banging pots and pans around. She thought she might hear a baby. "Is Jacob there?" She plugged her ear with her finger again.

A pause. "Well, no." Soft, confused, with an inflection on the end that meant southern. "He works during the day."

"Oh. Well, I—" Gemma was stumbling over words just as badly as Jay Triplett. "You probably want to know who this is. I'm . . . I'm family. I think."

Gemma was right. She did hear a baby crying. The

woman must have picked up an infant because Gemma heard magnified sounds of whimpering, close to the ear-piece.

"Your husband's name? Did he ever go by something different? Did he ever go by Jacob *Bartling*?"

"No. I don't . . ." The woman seemed to think for a moment, and Gemma's hopes went up. But the final answer, when it came, dashed them again. "No. Not to my knowledge. What on earth is this?"

"Are his parents living? Can you tell me something about that?"

The baby started crying louder. "Who did you say this is?"

"Are Jacob's blood parents living, or are they gone?"

The voice said, "I'm sorry," and sounded like she meant it. "These are not the sort of questions I feel comfortable answering over the phone."

Gemma gave up. This wasn't working. She sighed, defeated. "Will you tell him something? Just say that Nathan has died and that a family member thought he should know. Will you say that?"

"Well, yes. I can say that."

A long silence passed. Both of them waited. Gemma waited for the disembodied voice to ask, "Is there a number or a name, anything, some way he can get hold of you?" But she didn't. She didn't want to. It was obvious. "I really don't think he'll—"

"If that message means nothing to him, it doesn't matter. It's okay."

The voice grew softer, more diffident. And bouncy. Gemma could tell she was bouncing the baby to keep it soothed. "It's just that Jacob's changed so much." A pause, as the voice searched for words. "Remembering hurts him. He doesn't much like to dredge up the past."

Paisley Franklin, known by her bear and by her mother and by Mrs. Bartling as Paisley Rose, had decided she'd be better off not saying another word to anybody she knew.

Sometimes, when she talked out loud, she forgot and broke The Rule.

She tried hard not to break it, but it got harder and harder, the more she got to know people she liked. The more she got to know people she *loved*.

Paisley had broken the rule on the morning when Nathan went away. "I love you, Nathan!" she'd said, squeezing him tight, tight around his legs.

"We'll see you when we get home tonight, Paisley Rose." He'd planted a kiss on the top of her head. "I might even take you fishing."

Nathan hadn't come back for supper. He hadn't come back when it was time for bed. The next morning when she'd awakened with her blanket, her mother had told her he wasn't coming back at all.

Paisley had also broken the rule with Mrs. Bartling. Mrs. Bartling had been in her bathroom, dressed in a yellow pantsuit that made her look sunny as a lemon. "I'm going to work today, Paisley Rose," she'd said, meeting her eyes in the mirror. "It's a big day, I guess."

"I love you, Mrs. Bartling," Paisley had said, hugging her tight, tight, liking the cushiony way her belly felt beneath Paisley's head and thinking she smelled like lemons, too.

That night, she'd come in from playing at Addy's house and heard Mrs. Bartling saying, "You have your car now. I want you to pack it up. I want you to go."

Paisley couldn't guess who she might be in danger of breaking the rule with next. She thought of Madeleine, who had invited her over to play Barbies. She thought of Mabel Perkins, who worked her mouth like a sourpuss and didn't seem much in danger of playing the game at all. She thought of her mother, and that scared Paisley most of all. What if she accidentally said it to Mama? What if she broke the rule then?

There would be nobody left for her.

If not for Mama, there would be nobody left now.

Paisley decided it would be best, safer by far, not to break the rule, not to talk to anybody at all. Whenever she visited the museum with Mama in the afternoons, she played outside while Mama worked and talked to the people who came to see history and have tours. It was amazing, the things you could see when you weren't kept so busy talking. Outside, there were bubbles scooting across the surface of the water in the bucket, flat on the bottom and tall on the top so they looked like buttons. There were mouse holes where the grass had been nibbled short—not shaggy like the rest, but gray and velvety. There were green garden snakes laying in loose tangles on the ground and when you tried to catch one, it got away fast, in the shape of an *S*, even though it had no legs.

If not for being quiet, Paisley might never have found the old upturned boat back behind the willows. She loved it there. It was like a house that she never had to leave. Every day, she'd carried some new thing out there. A rusty can to make a bowl for pretend supper. A gathering of leaves for a pretend campfire. A log stump chiseled into an *L* on one corner that made a nice seat for her bear.

The boat was set up on bricks so Paisley could just get

beneath it and hide. Enough daylight came through the cracks and knotholes so she could see. Here, she talked aloud to her teddy bear about things. Here, she sang the songs God liked when she could remember the words from vacation Bible school.

She remembered when Pastor Sissel had told her, "The Father delights in your singing. No one can praise Him in exactly the same way that you can."

Here, beneath the boat, she prayed. Here, in her secret new house, she listened.

When it was time to go, she heard her mama calling. She climbed out fast because she didn't want anybody grown up to find her secret place.

Paisley would always go out when they called her.

And then she would be silent for another day.

No matter how lonely Bea was, it felt beautiful and right to be reading scripture again.

She held the Sneed family Bible between both hands and took pleasure from the primeval smell of it, from the oniony, brittle feel of the pages when she turned them.

A word in 1 Thessalonians caught her eye. She read one verse, then another.

May God himself, the God of peace, sanctify you through and through. May your whole spirit, soul and body be kept blameless at the coming of our Lord Jesus Christ. The one who calls you is faithful, and he will do it.

Chills ran the length of Bea's spine. It seemed almost as if God was speaking to her. For weeks she had been running from this, hiding in her pain, closing her ears, fighting not to listen.

Not even thinking what she was doing, she flipped back a few chapters. There it was. The same thing. The same word, this time, in 2 Timothy.

If we are faithless, he will remain faithful, for he cannot disown himself.

Over and over again, the words jumped out at her. From all over the Bible, the same message, the same promise, the same glorious refrain.

God is faithful . . . A faithful God keeps covenant and mercy with those who love him . . . By faith Abraham was enabled to become a father because he considered him faithful who had made the promise . . .

Bea remembered a sermon George Sissel had given on Joshua once. In it, Pastor George had said, "Every single promise God made to His people has been fulfilled."

It had been weeks since Bea had gone to her knees. Months since she had lifted up her heart in grace and yearning to a heavenly Father who waited for her in delight as she came. "Oh, Jesus," she whispered to the ceiling in her family room. "Those things in the Bible. Please, I don't want to believe in fate anymore and think that's faith. I want to believe in you, in your faithfulness."

She waited. And listened. And heard nothing.

"Lord?" she asked the ceiling, the brown spots where she needed to paint, the light fixture as old as the hills. "If you've been listening to my prayers, isn't there some way that I can know?"

Still nothing. Nothing.

If you are a faithful God, *isn't there some way that you can tell me?*

She lifted her face. That's where it all began. A small niggling in her breast, a tiny spark of faith that swelled into a quiet, gentle fire. Expectancy. For the first time in months, she *expected* something.

"Lord?"

You didn't want me to give you only chances, did you? You wanted me to give you my whole heart.

"Lord? All this time, have you been hearing me?"

Outside on a fence post, a meadowlark suddenly burst into song, its bold, happy phrases filling the room. Across the way, an afternoon storm cloud was building, rumbling, its mellow thunder echoing like the low notes of a piano across the pasture. Each sound Bea heard seemed to outdo the one before it. A radio in a passing car. Children's voices laughing, flutelike, as they played hide-and-seek down the street. Maple leaves hissing in the breeze. The cadence of a ticking clock.

All the earth seemed filled with sound and song and rhythm.

Does He who implanted the ear not hear? Does He who formed the eye not see? Does He who teaches man lack knowledge?

Something caught hold in Bea's heart that had not been there a moment before. His answer. A knowledge that, until that moment of expansiveness, Bea could not have understood.

Her Father didn't have to struggle to hear anything. He had been the one who, of course, had created the very act of hearing. He had been the one who, to His own delight, created ears and sound.

And Nathan had his own choice whether to listen or not to listen.

From the depths of her spirit, Bea accepted God's powerful, loving answer. From the depths of her spirit, she accepted the familiar, rekindled Presence that she felt beside her, holding her, lifting her above her sorrow.

Show me, Lord. Show me how I can let Gemma into my life. Show me how I can make her stay.

As soon as she asked the question, Bea knew exactly

what she should do. She reached across the coffee table, picked up the fine-point permanent marker laying there. With great care, she turned to the frontispiece in the Sneed Family Bible. "Gemma Franklin Bartling," she wrote in solid, careful letters across one entire line. "Married to Nathan Roger Bartling February 2001." Beside that, she wrote, "Paisley Franklin, child."

I don't know their birthdays. I didn't ask. How silly.

Well, that would have to come later. Bea found another empty line, an appropriate spot just below Nathan's name. "Jacob Bartling," she wrote, just as carefully, just as neatly. "Adopted son of Ray and Beatrice Bartling. Whereabouts unknown."

She ran her hand over the words. As if she could touch those she loved, all of them, by tracing the curves of their names. In the distance, through all the other sounds, she thought she could hear Alva Torrington from somewhere, calling out her name, rattling on a door. "Bea! Hurry."

"Hey? Alva T. That you? What are you doing here?"

Alva still wore her Cramalot Inn apron as she banged on Bea's front door. "They sent me to come find you," she announced, her voice terse, her constant smile gone. Her New Yorker was chugging out puffs of smoke in the driveway. "We've closed the restaurant. Everybody in town's going to the museum to help."

"To help with what?"

"Gemma went to finish up her work at the museum and now Paisley's missing. It's been hours," Alva said. "Gemma wanted me to get you. If she's hidden away somewhere, or if she's hurt, all those other people might scare her. Gemma thinks you stand the best chance to find her. Better than any of the rest."

In late afternoon, when everyone started to search for Paisley, the mercury in the thermometer outside J's Cedar Vu Hardware topped 89 degrees. When night fell, the mercury dipped to 46 degrees and the searchers brought out their flashlights and refused to go home. Alva Torrington and Charlene Grover worked as a team and combed through the pasture across the street. Orvin Kornruff brought his checker-playing buddies and sent them out in installments along the irrigation ditch out back. "Gemma?" Jay asked in front of them all. "She isn't talking. If she was trapped somewhere and somebody called to her, would she answer?"

"She would answer Mrs. Bartling," Gemma said, her voice gone flat and numb with shock.

Deputy Jay Triplett himself did not pull out his clipboard and take the missing child report. Another deputy brought out the papers. Bea stood behind Gemma, holding her up by the shoulders, trying not to succumb to the awful déjà vu of Nathan, listening while Gemma gave her dazed answers.

No, Paisley didn't say she was leaving. Paisley didn't say anything.

No, Gemma didn't know any place she could have gone.

"What was your daughter wearing the last time you saw her, Miss Franklin?"

Bea watched Gemma struggle to recount what clothes Paisley had worn that morning. As any mother would. As Bea remembered herself doing. "No. No hat. She didn't have on a hat. A white T-shirt, maybe. Sandals. And purple capri pants."

"I've been through this," Bea said. "I ought to know what to do."

"Keep calling," Gemma urged her, as they sat with their backs against the outside wall of the museum, shivering from the cool night. "If she doesn't answer anybody else, she'll answer you."

Bea called for hours. She didn't stop, even after her voice grew hoarse.

"What if she's dead, Mrs. Bartling?" Gemma asked. "What if somebody awful has her? What if she's hurt? Or . . . or worse?"

"You have to trust," Bea told her. "You just have to trust."

"I don't want to trust," Gemma said. "I see where trusting has gotten you."

Bea took Gemma's arm, held her elbow tight to make her listen. "No. Don't measure anything by what I've done. I've been so wrong. God has heard me. He's been trustworthy all the time. It's us who have to think about what we're doing. Building up, not tearing down."

Bea pulled her sweater tighter around her shoulders and went off on her own again, backtracking behind the sandstone building, around the floodlights set to illuminate the rear of the building, lifting up a plywood scrap, searching for clues.

She heard footsteps coming from a copse of willows. "Oh, Care Goodsell," Bea said, the tears finally coming to her eyes. "Did you hear what happened? Paisley's gone. Did you come to search?"

"Nope," he said, laughing and scrubbing his sweater sleeve across the bangs of his spiky hair. "I came to find."

"What?" Bea asked.

"You seek and I find," he said, his eyes merry. "'Seek, and ye shall find.' Get it?" He pointed to the upturned hull of an old rowboat that, all this time, had been hidden in the brambles. "Listen carefully," he told her and, when Bea did, she heard. For, of all the sounds she'd noticed these past hours, of all the sounds the Father had shared so she could learn about *His* ears, this was by far the most beautiful sound of them all.

The sound of a child singing—a soft song, a praise song, coming from beneath the boat.

Oh, Lord. Thank you. Thank you. Care Goodsell has found her. You knew it all along, didn't you? Paisley's there, under the boat hull.

"Paisley? Can you hear me? I'm out here."

I am not calling you to always know the answers, Bea. I am calling you to love. Even as I am loving and longing for you.

"I can hear you," a tiny, muffled voice answered. "The boat fell down. I couldn't get out."

People heard and ran from every direction. Able-bodied men surrounded the hull, tilting it sideways. Bea looked for Mr. Goodsell, but he had disappeared in all the commotion.

"Here we go."

"Steady now."

"Watch out."

When Paisley toppled out, it was Mrs. Bartling who grabbed her first to bill and coo. The woman clung to the child and the child clung to the woman. And the woman vowed to her heavenly Father she would never let this one go again.

"I never told you, did I?" she asked, nuzzling Paisley, their tears mixing. "I love you back." Bea couldn't stop saying it, over and over again. "I love you back. I love you back."

Chapter Twenty-Five

The car with Wyoming license plates drove in and parked in front of the Garden County Museum a few minutes before closing time. "Excuse me?" the young man called out when he couldn't find anyone at the desk. "Is there anybody here?"

"Oh, of course there's somebody here." A woman with a nametag that read "Mabel P., Museum Director" appeared from a corner where she must have been hanging guitars. She had a hammer in one hand and a twelve-string Gibson in the other. "There's always somebody here."

"Well, good." He poked his hands in the pockets of his belted London Fog and fiddled with his keys.

"Admittance is free," Mabel told him. "But you might want to wait until tomorrow if you plan to spend much time. We close in—" She inclined her head toward the wall clock hanging beside the desk. "—seven minutes. You wouldn't want to get locked in after closing time. We've had that happen."

"No, that wouldn't be good." He jostled his coins in

his pockets again. He hesitated a moment. "I'm not wanting a tour, anyway. I came looking for directions."

"Oh. Directions. I can do that. There's maps of Garden County on the wall. Flyers on the table. This area has many historical attractions. Anything in particular you're looking for?"

"I'm looking for a house."

"A house?"

"I am." For a moment his deep voice faltered, as if he felt foolish not knowing what so say. "Used to be able to drive right to it. But it's been a long time. Can't seem to find my way."

Mabel leaned the Gibson against the wall. "Which house would you be looking for?"

"Bea Bartling's house. The lady who grows roses. She must still be there."

"There's a leaflet right there. To your left. The yellow one."

"I see it." He picked up the brochure between one large thumb and one large forefinger. "Don't Miss Ash Hollow's Pioneer Rosebush." He tamped it on the edge of her desk. "Thank you."

"House is over on Pattison," Mabel told him. "There's a map on the back."

The man stood over six feet tall, with a lick of dark hair that kept falling across his brow, with eyes bluer than morning sun on Lake Mac. He looked vaguely familiar to Mabel, but she couldn't figure out why.

"Say, you're not—?"

He turned back eagerly, as if he expected her to say his name. She didn't.

"No. Never mind."

He had his hand on the door handle when Mabel

said, "Bea ought to be charging admittance over there. She'd be a rich woman by now."

The man turned toward Mabel one last time. "She been getting lots of visitors?"

"Well, yes. She has. You heard about her son dying, I suppose."

He nodded, with something unreadable in his eyes. "I heard."

Mabel rummaged in her desk drawer and found her own set of keys. "No matter what happens at that house, those roses are always blooming. Got to lock up now. Hope you don't mind."

Bea peered through the peephole, trying to see who was knocking on her door.

Surely Gemma and Jay wouldn't be back from the movie so soon. According to the paper, this one lasted a long time, over two hours—a great bottom numb-er, Jay had joked when he'd come to suggest hanging out and going to a show.

The great hulking shape Bea had viewed through the glass had stepped away from the porch and into the yard. It was a man. Bea opened the door a bit, feeling wary.

Paisley slept in Nathan's room—no, *her* room—inside. Bea had decided she ought to be more careful, now that she had family to protect. She squinted and reached for the porch light. She couldn't see a thing out there. "Hello?"

The man turned, and light hit him full in the face. He raised a hand to shade his eyes from the harsh bulb. "Hey." It was only a murmur, as if he didn't know if he had a right to speak. "Hey there."

At first Bea thought she'd made a mistake. It could be

so easy to mistake a stranger for someone you know. Just in passing. Just catching a glimpse on the street. But here he stood, so handsome, a grown man, much bigger than she'd ever expected him to get, with his sideburns and jaw shaved, his shoulders overflowing his coat, his neck filled out to accommodate what used to be his Adam's apple.

She acknowledged him with one stark, broken cry of recognition. "Oh, *my*."

That was all the permission he needed.

He swept her off the brick stoop and hugged her for all he was worth. "Oh, Mom," he whispered like he'd done when he was an adolescent boy. "Mom."

"Jacob. Jacob."

How to describe the feeling Bea knew of becoming the little one, the dainty one, the one cared for after so many years of being the caregiver. He was broader than Bea by a mile and stood a good three heads taller and when he wrapped his arms around her to walk her inside she felt protected and loved and hugged by King Kong, all at the same time.

She invited him in. He tossed his coat over the back of Ray's old chair, loosened his tie, unbuttoned his collar. He sat on the floor beside the couch, his pants hiked up, his huge legs folded in half at the knees, his head tilted so he could see his adoptive mom. They talked in hushed undertones about everything they could think of—happy and sad things both.

They talked first about Nathan.

"Did you hear he's gone?" she asked, bittersweet tears welling in her eyes, halfway telling him more than she should, halfway afraid, wondering if he might not even know.

"I did," he answered, the same bittersweet tears

welling in his. "Someone called me. That's why I'm here. I thought it was you."

Bea ran her fingers through his hair, touched his head the same way he'd so desperately needed to be touched when he had been a broken, scared little boy. "Maybe Nathan's wife. Gemma." Bea motioned to the picture of her and Nathan she had placed in a frame on the side table. "If she did it, I'm glad she called you. You know if it was me, I wouldn't have felt free."

"I know that."

"You'll meet her. She does things like that. She's got a way about her, bringing people around."

Jacob said he had a wife named Sonja and a boy six months old and a job on a construction crew over in Wyoming. He told her about the places he'd been, the foster families he'd stayed with, the schools and counselors he'd gone to, the dreams he'd counted on. Like coming here.

"I went crazy that night, you know." Jacob examined the button on his cuff. "That night I had the knife. Ray was another parent leaving me, like my dad and my mom before. I took it out on you. You were the only one there."

Bea bent her head to his, unafraid now, when there had been times he had terrified her before. "Yes. I know that, Jacob. I guess I always did. You were angry and hurt. You struck out the only way you knew how." She lowered her face even more, away from him. "I'm the one who might have changed things. I could have fought harder. I could have been stronger. I might have found another way to raise you without letting the sheriff take you away."

"But you weren't stronger," he said, touching her arm. Reassuring her. "No woman would have been. A child left alone with so much anger. Living in a house where there wasn't a man who could pin him down and talk sense into him. Without Ray, you couldn't do it. I think I knew that even when I pulled out that knife. Maybe that was my way of helping you. Maybe I knew already that it wouldn't work for me to stay."

She buried her face in her hands for a moment, then lifted her gaze to his. "I don't know, Jacob. I've second-guessed it so many times. It was easier to blame myself than it was anybody else."

"We were all responsible. I was responsible." He touched her palm and brought it down. "Hey, let's talk about other things. If I brought Sonja and the baby sometime, would you make your lasagna? I've been describing your lasagna to Sonja for forever."

This, momentarily liberating her, felt like the nicest question Jacob had ever asked. "Oh, yes. I want you to bring her all the time. And, when you don't have time to drive, I'll even give Sonja my recipe."

Poignant quiet claimed them.

He started to ask something, but stopped.

He started and stopped again. Twice.

Bea knew without doubt which question would come. And she was right.

"Did you ever tell Nathan?" he finally asked. "Did he ever find out what I tried to do to you? What an awful brother I was? That you had to call the sheriff to protect yourself?"

For a long moment, she waited. "Jacob."

"Did he know that I even tried to hurt the dog? That you bandaged up my hand after I'd gone after you, and told me how much you loved me? And after that they took me to lock-in school?"

"What does it matter now if Nathan knew?" She

didn't want to tell him. When she did, she realized that Jacob would see all she had done for him, and eventually he would count the cost. "Nathan is gone. You and I owe it to him to go on with our lives."

"I cared so much what Nathan thought about me, you know? He trusted me. He said I was the best brother anybody could have."

"Jacob. You don't need to do this. It's over."

"I wanted him to always remember me as somebody *worthy* of being his brother."

"He did, Jacob. He loved you until his dying day."

"So, did he know? Did you ever tell him the awful thing I'd done?"

She took his man-face, saw the resemblance of the boy she'd known so many years ago, as she held it in her hands. "I made a promise to you that night, Jacob. It was the last time I ever saw you, and you were my son. I kept that promise. For a long time, that promise was the only thing of you I had to hold on to."

He lay his own hands over hers, against his cheeks. "You never said anything to him? Ever?"

She shook her head. "I knew how much it mattered to you, son. I never told Nathan what happened or why you were sent away."

Jacob pondered the ceiling for a long while. "The whole thing changed my life, you know. Having to be accountable for my own actions. When you sent me away, you did a hard thing. But you made me grow into a better man."

"Thank you," she whispered to him. "Thank you." She released his face and smiled through glimmering tears. "I've needed to hear that."

Some of this would be better left handled on another

day. But it would be handled. They would build, not tear down.

"Nathan wrote you postcards for a while. He stopped because they kept coming back. They're in your room in that old tackle box where you boys kept all your secret messages. One of these days, you'll want to read them."

"Yes," he said. "One of these days, I will."

The sun rose on Lake McConaughy the same way every September morning, its light glancing off still water, satin mirror, gun-barrel gray.

Gemma didn't want to miss it. She rolled out of her sleeping bag and yanked on a pair of sweatpants, shivering, trying to keep warm.

She'd been joking all evening beside the campfire that she'd be the first one up. But no matter how Gemma boasted, it never happened that way. Bea always beat her to the sunrise. Gemma found her sitting on a rock with a mug of something hot keeping both hands warm, the campfire crackling and the blue coffee pot on, steam curling from its spout.

"I missed some of it." Gemma went to get her own mug out of the camp box. "I went back to get my shoes and the light changed."

"I know." Bea sipped her coffee and wrapped an arm around Gemma. "You have to be fast. It always does."

"Good morning."

Bea rubbed her shoulders. "Good morning back."

"You think there's any fish in that lake?"

"There's plenty. Believe you me, with two teenage boys around the house for a while, I saw more than my fair share of fish from Lake Mac."

"Paisley finally went to sleep last night." Gemma found a flat place to sit on the rock, too, and Bea scooted over. "She says this is the time she's going to catch more fish than Uncle Jacob."

"Well," Bea laughed. "I'd like to see that."

"Me, too."

They contemplated the universe for a few minutes, the sky, the poor doomed fish, the lapping of water on the shore.

"Nathan used to describe this spot to me." Gemma set down her mug and found a good skipping rock. She side-armed it and counted. One. Two. Three. "He used to say it looked like the mallards were gliding on glass water. He always called them drakes. I think he liked that word. Mallard drakes."

"Hmmm-mmm."

"He said there was nothing better than waking up in a place to make you feel like you owned it. Morning is fragile, he said. Makes you belong to something in a way that someone who hasn't slept over never would."

"Smart thing, what my boy said."

"Yeah."

"Same thing fits with family." Bea looked for her own skipping rock. She found a rock, pitched it, and watched it sink. "Same thing fits with faith."

Gemma didn't say anything to that. She listened, learned.

"Faith is like Lake Mac on a still morning. It reflects. A perfect mirror. Like my roses. Isn't that what Care Goodsell says?"

Gemma crossed her arms. "You know, I've been meaning to talk to you about Care Goodsell."

"You have?"

"Yeah."

"What about?"

"I . . ." She hesitated. "Oh, I don't know. It's okay. Maybe it'll wait until another time."

"Yeah. Maybe it had better wait. Here comes Jacob, and I'll bet his poles are already rigged up."

"If Mr. Goodsell asks me to ride in his wheelbarrow again, I'm going to do it. I've decided that much."

"Are you? Well, maybe I will, too."

The car with the Wyoming plates parked and, sure enough, out piled family, out came a jumble of rods, ready to fish. Jacob wasted no time making a perfect cast, arcing the line and the red-and-white float through the air, catching light. "Paisley. Wake up," he warned outside the tent in a gentle voice, obviously torn between seeing his niece and fishing these familiar waters. "If you want to beat your Uncle Jacob catching fish, you'd better get up and get started."

Bea and Gemma watched together from their rock, arms entangled around each other's shoulders, sipping coffee, remembering . . . hoping . . . trusting.

Along the shore, other campers had awakened and had begun to cast out their lines. Children still in pajamas danced as water rippled between their toes.

Two small boys with close-clipped, bare heads skittered up and down the shore, kicking sand, reminding Bea of two other little boys a long time ago.

Something yanked Jacob's line and the fishing float plunged under. Way under.

"Look, Grandma," Paisley said, scrubbing sleep from her eyes and coming to take Bea's hand. "Uncle Jacob's got something!" And Jacob began to reel in the first gift of the day.

Transplanting Harison's Yellow

Harison's Yellow roses are readily available from nurseries and greenhouses that specialize in growing varieties of antique roses. They are also readily available in brambles along roadsides and beside homes all across Nebraska, Wyoming, Idaho, and Oregon. It is true that, in areas where historians could not determine the exact location of the Oregon Trail, they plotted it out by following the roses. These plants can be cut, carried away, and transplanted in exactly the way Bea transplanted her roses onto Nathan's grave.

If you are lucky enough to find someone who will give you a start of Harison's Yellow, follow these directions. To find an appropriate sucker, dig in the ground near a rosebush until you find a little side shoot of plant that has both wooden stem and green sprout attached. Keep this in water the same way you would keep a cut flower.

When this sucker has begun to root, you can transplant the rose into potting soil or into some other good growing medium, and harden it off. To harden off the rose, do not water often after these rootlings are planted in soil. Give moisture only when absolutely necessary.

When transplanting roses from pots into the ground, dig the hole twice as big as a lazy person would dig it, twice as wide, and twice as deep. Plant in a location where roses will receive six to eight hours of direct sunlight. Prepare the soil by working good humus or compost into the dirt until the soil feels good and smells good. If you want to use a commercial product, try Osmocote Granular. Be careful not to work too much into the soil or the roses will burn.

The roses do not want to be planted deep. Plant them the same depth that they have been growing in the pot, in well-drained soil. Water thoroughly. Their roots will eventually reach deep enough to find the moisture they need.

A general gardener's rule is to plant roses in the spring. Harison's Yellow growers will tell you that these roses catch on spring, summer, or fall, whenever there is enough of a season left for the sprouts to stay warm and grow. Be careful to arrange the plants so they are easy to water and weed. A hoe and a sharp steel rake should be used to keep the soil loose and the weeds out.

Author's Note
In Search of Pioneer Roses

Whenever we made the drive to see my grandparents when I was growing up, we always passed by one old rickety farmhouse, grayed from the weather, windows broken out, the porch sagging on one side. This old house had become almost hidden by its overgrowth of brambles, trees, bushes, and wildflowers.

For some odd reason that we could never quite figure out, the trees and weeds and wild roses grew taller close to the porch than they did in the yard.

My father and I laughed every time we drove by, picturing a woman and a man sitting in rocking chairs on that old porch, having a seed-spitting contest—lofting seeds that would someday bury themselves in the dirt and grow.

Perhaps it is this childhood memory of one old house and those growing things that came to life in my heart when a kind gentleman appeared on our doorstep one morning to install the natural gas fireplace we'd ordered. As he worked, he began to tell me the story of his mother's pioneer rosebush, over 150 years old, which had been brought out on a wagon on the Oregon Trail. He told me how his mother coddled the roses and how visitors from all over stopped by to see them and, if they were lucky, to take home a cutting to start in their own gardens.

My mother-in-law, Mollie Jensen Bedford, grew up in Washington State. When I asked her if she knew anything about pioneer roses, she jumped right in with her own stories of yellow bushy roses—how they grew in profusion along the yards, how they'd moved across the western states as the Oregon Trail settlers had planted them, how the girlfriends she remembered always picked them for bouquets.

Harison's Yellow roses actually originated in New York City. George Harison, an attorney and amateur rose-grower, discovered it in the 1830s growing in his backyard. The roses were fragrant and hardy, they spread vigorously, and they resisted disease—all traits uncommon in yellow roses. Harison gave a slip to Thomas Hogg, a local nurseryman, who assigned it its first and perhaps most accurate name, given how far it would soon range: "Hogg's Yellow American Rose." A second nurseryman, William Prince, better equipped to propagate and distribute it, renamed it "Harison's Yellow." In an 1846 rose catalog, William Prince wrote that this rose was brilliant and beautiful. He also wrote that "a hot sun makes its blooms expand and lose much of their beauty."

Rose bushes, advertised "on their own bottoms," not grafted, were sold for fifty and seventy-five cents. But Harison's Yellow suckered so easily that it was most often given away. Roy Sheperd wrote in his 1954 *History of the Rose* (Coleman, reprinted 1978) that, "No old rose is more generally distributed throughout North America nor better known."

Donna Mileti Benenson writes in *Early American Homes*:

Beloved by pioneers, this rose was carried by brides denied more cumbersome mementos of home. They kept cuttings alive stuck in raw potatoes or damp cloths. Flourishing, colonizing, the rose outlasted those who planted it and survives on abandoned homesites all over America. It haunts ghost towns and cemeteries and tumbles down gaping cellar holes. It is seen running wild the length of the Oregon Trail. Still commercially available, still cherished, and still given away as a keepsake, "Harison's Yellow" travels back and forth across our country even today.

When I began writing *A Rose by the Door*, the story of these tenacious roses came first. Bea Bartling, Gemma, and Paisley came next. As I interviewed experts on Harison's Yellow roses, it became evident that these roses, coupled with the history of the brave pioneer women who planted them, reflect a perfect, beautiful likeness of the resilience that God has created in each of our human spirits. On a deeper level, these roses are a humbling representation of God's faithfulness to us and our faith—which is totally dependent upon Him—blooming back to him, through us.

I hope you enjoyed reading this story as much as I enjoyed writing it.

May the Father's love bring its season of blooming into your heart,

Deborah Bedford
www.deborahbedfordbooks.com
P.O. Box 9175
Jackson Hole, WY 83001